Don Wehrman

CALIFORNIA!

The sixth thrilling book
in the WAGONS WEST series—
original, rough-riding stories of
brave men and women of the frontier
bound for glory in their search for
freedom and a new life.

★★★★★★★★★★★★★★★★★★★★★★

WAGONS WEST

CALIFORNIA!

THE CONTINUING SAGA OF DAUNTLESS MEN AND WOMEN UNITED BY A SINGLE VISION— A DREAM OF A LAND BURSTING WITH THE PROMISE OF GOLD!

RICK MILLER,
the former Texas Ranger, now a sheriff,
brings law and order to the wild West
and is driven by his own personal
desire for vengeance.

MELISSA AUSTIN,
the red-haired beauty whose foolish
infatuation for a no-good gambler drags
her to the depths of despair.

WHIP HOLT,
the wagon master who returns to
the frontier to help a desperate friend
and ends up risking his own life.

DANNY TAYLOR,
the crippled young war veteran
whose lust for gold may cost him
the woman he loves.

★★★★★★★★★★★★★★★★★★★★★★

★★★★★★★★★★★★★★★★★★★

HEATHER,
Danny's strong-willed wife who
won't hesitate to wield an ax against
marauders or fight to save her
man from temptation.

CHET HARRIS
Danny's closest friend
finds the price he must pay for gold may
be his very soul.

WONG KE,
Chet's partner, a wise man who
warns Chet that the greatest evil
always lies within oneself.

RALPH HAMILTON
An Eastern attorney,
haunted by a lost love,
struggles across the jungles of Panama
north to a promised land.

PHYLLIS GREGG,
a woman proud as she is pretty,
must learn humility or perish.

RANDY GREGG,
an old frontiersman who stands
by his principles in a maelstrom
of human emotions.

★★★★★★★★★★★★★★★★★★★

WAGONS WEST ★ SIXTH IN A SERIES

CALIFORNIA!

DANA FULLER ROSS

Created by the producers of
White Indian, Children of the Lion,
Saga of the Southwest, and
The Kent Family Chronicles Series.
Executive Producer: Lyle Kenyon Engel

BANTAM BOOKS
TORONTO · NEW YORK · LONDON · SYDNEY

This is a work of fiction. While the general outlines of history have been faithfully followed, certain details involving setting, characters, and events may have been simplified.

CALIFORNIA!

A Bantam Book / published by arrangement with
Book Creations Inc.

Bantam edition / March 1981
2nd printing .... March 1981
3rd printing .... April 1981

Produced by Book Creations, Inc.
Executive Producer: Lyle Kenyon Engel

ISBN 0-553-14260-7

Published simultaneously in the United States and Canada

PRINTED IN THE UNITED STATES OF AMERICA

12 11 10 9 8 7 6 5

CALIFORNIA!

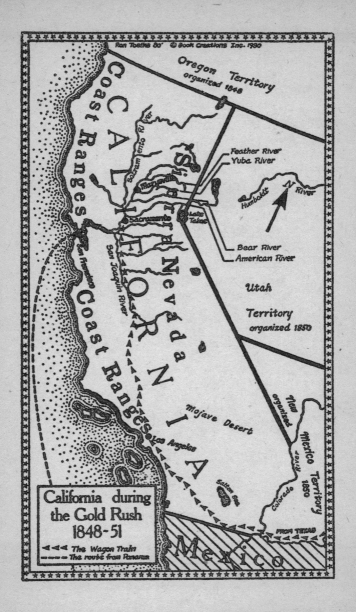

Ron Toelke 80' © Book Creations Inc. 1980

Oregon Territory
organized 1848

Coast Ranges

C O C A L I F O R

Sacramento R.

Rio grande

Sacramento

San Francisco

San Joaquin River

Coast Ranges

Los Angeles

Sierra Nevada

N I A

Feather River
Yuba River

Humboldt River

Lake Tahoe

Bear River
American River

Utah

Territory
organized 1850

New organized

Mojave Desert

Salton Sea

Mexico Territory
1850

Colorado

Jornly

FROM TEXAS

Mexico

California during the Gold Rush 1848-51

◄◄◄ The Wagon Train
‒ ‒ ‒ The route from Panama

I

Rick Miller rode out of the forest and drew his stallion to a halt at the top of a hill, where he looked down on the property his wife, Elisabeta, had inherited. Smoke was rising from the chimney of the single-story ranch house which, like most of the dwelling places in the area, was situated close to the dusty, heavily rutted main road. Cattle were grazing in the fields behind the house, and the view from where he sat filled Rick with the greatest contentment he had ever known. He sniffed, smelled the odors of beef and onions, and grinned, knowing his wife was preparing stew for supper. Shifting the weight of the Colt six-shooter he carried in his belt, he eased his broad-brimmed hat back from his forehead.

Life in California's Sacramento Valley was even more satisfying than it had been in Texas. Not for a moment did he regret having resigned his commission in the Rangers and moving to the territory just acquired at the end of the war with Mexico. His Spanish-born wife had been invited by her elderly relatives to move to the ranch, and when they had died last spring she was fortunate to inherit the property. Rick's luck had been equally extraordinary. On his own since the age of fifteen, he had lived as a hunter and trapper in the Rocky Mountains before migrating to Texas, where he had risen high in the ranks of the Rangers, and now, thanks to the insistence of his neighbors, he had become the sheriff of the Sacramento Valley. The residents here were law-abiding, and his duties were light, so in his spare time he managed the ranch.

John Sutter—the area's largest landowner, who had built the fort bearing his name—had said recently, "Thank God this is a big country. There's plenty of room for the immigrants from the East to establish their farms and orchards and ranches." Rick had to agree. There was something here for everyone. High mountains towered in the distance, there were broad valleys where grain, fruit, and vegetables could be grown in abundance, and fish were plentiful in swift-flowing rivers like the Sacramento and the American.

Elisabeta was happier here than she had ever been. Sheltered as a child by her Spanish parents, the beautiful young woman had been brought to America by a treacherous seducer and had faced ordeals in Texas where she had proved her great strength of mind and perseverence. Then with Rick Miller she had found the love of her life, and they had planned to spend the rest of their days together in blissful peace. Now Elisabeta enjoyed managing their home, spending her days with Rick telling him about the books she loved to read, going for long carriage rides with him, visiting their friends and neighbors. Her pride and joy were her gardens. She planted flowers everywhere, grew giant-sized vegetables, and placed rose bushes on either side of the front door to their house. She was fond of saying, "Darling, this is as close to paradise as we'll ever get."

Suddenly Rick stiffened. An unshaven man in

shapeless old clothes emerged from the woods at one side of the ranch, opened the front gate boldly, and peered in the kitchen window. He had to be one of the scum who had been drifting into the area ever since an employee of Sutter's, a man named Marshall, had found gold in the millrace of a new Sutter mill on the American River, about thirty-five miles from the fort.

Starting down the hill at once, Rick was relieved to think that Elisabeta always followed his strict instructions and kept the doors bolted. A few sharp words would send the man packing. Rick's blood froze when the intruder raised the latch of the kitchen door, opened it, and went inside.

Spurring forward, the sheriff sent his stallion thundering down the hill. He drew his six-shooter, leaped to the ground, and sprinted to the house.

A badly frightened Elisabeta, her coal-black hair tumbling down her back, had been driven into a corner of the kitchen by the intruder who brandished a short, double-edged knife. "You got no reason to be scared, lady," he said. "We'll have us some of that there supper, and after we have a mite o' lovin', I'll be on my way."

Rick burst into the room. "You picked the wrong house, mister," he said.

The intruder grabbed Elisabeta, pulled her in front of him as a shield, and held the knife to her throat. "Maybe I did, and maybe I didn't," he replied insolently.

"I charge you with breaking into my house and threatening my wife." In spite of his anger Rick spoke coolly. "As sheriff of the Valley, I demand your immediate surrender."

"You ain't in charge now—I am," the intruder said. "Make one move, and the woman dies."

Rick had no intention of being bluffed, but at the same time he couldn't place Elisabeta in jeopardy. An icy chill in his eyes, he weighed the situation, and realizing that a kitchen chair was within easy reach, he hooked a foot around one of the legs and toppled it. The chair fell with a crash, and for an instant the intruder's attention was drawn to the chair. That instant was all Rick needed. He squeezed the trigger. His aim was unerring, and he drilled a hole in the man's forehead.

The knife clattered to the floor, and the intruder, an unbelieving expression on his face, sank down slowly, a trickle of blood oozing from the wound.

A white-faced, trembling Elisabeta raced to the safety of her husband's arms. Death was not new to her, and she herself had once been forced to kill the man who had used her in his own murderous schemes, but she was badly shaken by this encounter.

"He can't hurt you now, honey," Rick said soothingly. He held her tight, wishing he could protect her for all time from the unpleasant things in life. She had suffered more than her share.

She clung to him, her violet eyes almost childlike as she looked at her husband. "It was my own fault. I didn't bolt the kitchen door."

"Never mind now." Rick kissed her, then quickly removed the body from the kitchen, wrapping it in an old sheet and tying it to the back of a pack horse. "Hold supper for a spell while I ride into town," he said. "I'll be back as soon as I can. I reckon he was alone, but take no chances. Keep your rifle close at hand."

"Oh, I will," she promised. She looked at the rifle and knew she could use it, but she wished that she would never have to. Why couldn't she and Rick just live in peace in an idyllic world?

Mounting his stallion and leading the pack horse, Rick rode the short distance from the ranch to Sutter's Fort, which some of the newer arrivals were calling Sacramento. His small office and the attached, cramped jail stood on the unnamed main street, and his two deputies, both part-time employees, were playing cards when he entered and unceremoniously dumped the dead man's body on the floor.

"Go through his pockets and see if you can identify him," he said after explaining what had happened. "Round up the people you find at the saloon down the road and see if they know who he was. I doubt if you'll have any luck, though. I suspect he's just another of the rabble who are coming here to search for gold. But we've got to go through the proper motions before we bury him."

Within a short time he was on his way back to the ranch, where Elisabeta had supper waiting. As they ate Rick said quietly, "I've been telling you ever since gold was discovered up at John Sutter's mill that times are changing here. When we first came out here almost a year ago, there was no need to lock a door, ever, day or night. But now the scum of the earth are being drawn to the area. Gold is a powerful magnet, a frightening magnet. Every day new trash are drifting into the Valley. Just today I had to break up two fights. And the situation is going to grow worse."

"I know I was wrong," Elisabeta said. "My only excuse—and it really isn't a good one—is that I've grown so accustomed to the way of life we've enjoyed here that I've found it terribly hard to change."

"I'm well aware of it, honey, and you aren't the only one. The Fosters down the main road lost their clock and most of their furniture the other day when they went to San Francisco without locking their windows. I'm trying to track down the thieves, but I think it unlikely I'll ever find them. There are dozens of idlers in the Valley already, and every time some lucky devil pans more gold, there will be more."

"What will happen when bad people start coming from all over the rest of the United States?" She shuddered.

"The boom may end before then," Rick replied, trying to soothe her. "It may be there isn't all that much more gold in the American River. And there may be none in any of the other rivers in the region. That will discourage the fortune seekers. But even if these hills and rivers are loaded with gold, we'll work out something. If necessary, John Sutter and our other neighbors will authorize me to hire enough deputies to keep order and see to it that the laws are obeyed. When we go to San Francisco next week to see General Blake and his family, I intend to ask Lee if his U.S. Army garrison at the Presidio can provide us with any assistance—assuming we may need it one of these months."

She listened, wide-eyed.

"Just remember this much, honey," he declared. "California is part of the United States now. And those of us who are responsible for the maintenance of order aren't going to let conditions here deteriorate or let society fall apart."

Elisabeta nodded. "Do you know what I can't help wishing, Rick?" she asked wistfully. "I wish gold had never been discovered here!"

"You wish it, I wish it—and so does everybody who has been living here. The Sacramento Valley has been heaven on earth, and we don't want to see a perfect way of life spoiled by greedy fortune hunters!"

President-elect Zachary Taylor, about to become the twelfth President of the United States, looked slightly out of place behind the large desk in his rambling plantation house in Louisiana. And at times the wistful expression on his face indicated that Old Rough and Ready, the hero of the war with Mexico, would have preferred to remain as a major general in the army. But the people had elected him, and he was determined to do his duty. That was why he had summoned the short, mild-mannered man who sat opposite him.

"I know of only three men I can trust enough to tell me the truth about our new California territory," the President-elect said. "Whip Holt's hip is bothering him, and I won't be able to bring him all the way from

Oregon to Washington City. John Frémont has his nose out of joint because of his quarrel with the military. So that leaves you, Colonel Carson, and I hope it explains why I sent you an urgent message when I learned you were in New Orleans."

Kit Carson, perhaps the most renowned of the former mountain men who had achieved fame as guides, explorers, hunters, and trappers in the Rocky Mountains, smiled modestly. "I'm sure Whip would have come if you had sent for him, and John Frémont will come down to earth after a spell. But I'm glad to be of service to you. What do you want to know, General?"

"Anything you can tell me about California!"

"Well, sir, the weather in the southern part of the territory around San Diego is mild, and except for patches of desert, the soil is good. But it is better in the central parts, east of the village of San Francisco. The northern section is very much like the Oregon Territory."

"Let me word my question another way, Carson. Ever since gold was discovered there, a huge migration has been under way. Can California sustain an explosive population growth?"

"Not right off, General. I have no way of guessing how much gold may be there, but most of the thousands who are rushing out to California are certain to be disappointed. In time San Francisco can become a major port because of her great harbor. There are no better farm lands anywhere, except maybe in Oregon and parts of the Middle West. But it takes time to develop farms and orchards, and gold hunters aren't really settlers."

Zachary Taylor made a few notes, then sighed. "How would you suggest I handle the situation out there, Carson, once I'm in the White House?"

Kit Carson grinned, then sobered. "First off, General, I'd double the army garrison at the Presidio. I'd send a frigate or two to maintain order in San Francisco—maybe a gunboat or two as well. And I'd send out as many wagon trains of food as I could. The gold hunters may get nasty when they're hungry."

Taylor frowned. "I very much doubt I can persuade the Congress to provide money to feed men who are leaving their homes and jobs of their own free will to look for gold."

"In that case, General, quadruple the size of the garrison at the Presidio," Kit Carson said. "I tell you plain, sir, there's going to be hell to pay out there!"

Cathy Blake shook back her long, blond hair and, shading her blue eyes from the glare of the sun, stared out at the spectacular view from the lawn of the commandant's house at the Presidio. An old Spanish fort, the Presidio had just been enlarged and modernized by the United States Army. She could see San Francisco Bay, dotted with islands and shielded by low-lying mountains and hills on the far shore. Several sailing ships, including two handsome clippers and a recently arrived schooner, were lying at anchor in what Americans were recognizing as one of the world's finest natural harbors.

Cathy's daughter, Beth, too young to appreciate the scenery, fidgeted and then went to fetch her school books. Her mother had been instrumental in starting the school at the Presidio when the family had arrived.

Brigadier General Leland Blake, en route to his office, emerged from the house and quietly joined his wife. Although gray at the temples since before his exploits in General Zachary Taylor's army during the war with Mexico, he was still a handsome man. Quickly sensing his wife's feeling of pleasure, he said nothing, but merely placed an arm around her shoulders.

She looked up at him, her eyes shining. "Lee," she said, "we saw some scenic wonders when we crossed the continent on the wagon train to Oregon, but the views here are even more beautiful."

Lee grinned at her. "Well," he said, "I just hope it will be quiet here."

"It should be. The war with Mexico is ended, and we've settled our border dispute with Great Britain in Oregon amicably. The Indians in the area are peaceful."

Although he nodded in agreement, his long experience in the army had taught him that tranquillity sometimes was an illusion. He knew that the conditions in California were unstable and that it was likely there would be trouble, but he didn't want to worry his wife unnecessarily. "So far," he said, "I have no complaints."

Certainly his garrison of twelve hundred men, one thousand of them infantrymen and the rest members of small artillery and sapper units, was large enough to handle virtually any unexpected emergency that might arise. He had been fortunate, retaining the friendship of General Winfield Scott, the army Chief of Staff, while at the same time winning the enthusiastic support of General Taylor, who had just been elected President of the United States. They had concurred in his appointment as commandant of the Presidio, and there was no other post he would have preferred.

But his euphoria was jarred when he saw his sergeant major, Hestor Mullins, hurrying toward him, and the expression on the grizzled soldier's face indicated that trouble loomed ahead.

"General," Sergeant Mullins said as he saluted, "there's hell to pay in the town, and Mayor White wants your help. That derelict schooner that just came down the coast from Oregon is filled with gold-hungry men. They're rioting on the docks, and the mayor is afraid they're going to break into a bakery and a butcher shop. He doesn't have enough constables to handle the mob."

Lee wasted no time. "How many are there?"

"The mayor's messenger was kind of vague, sir, but

it appears there may be a hundred. The schooner was loaded to the gunwales."

"Alert Company A, Eighteenth Battalion," Lee said crisply. "They'll carry bayonets and a dozen rounds of ammunition. I'll join them on the parade ground myself." He sent his orderly for his horse, then hurried back into the house for his sword and pistol.

Cathy remained on the lawn, and her smile was rueful when he rejoined her. "It appears I spoke too soon," she said.

"Maybe not. The problem is simple. Some of the newer immigrants in Oregon have heard about the gold strike in the Sacramento Valley and have given up their plans to establish farms and ranches because they're dreaming of getting rich overnight. They're not bad men, Cathy. They've come down here without a penny in their pockets, and they're hungry." Lee patted her on the shoulder. "I don't anticipate any serious difficulties. Expect me home at the usual time for dinner."

"Good. Elisabeta and Rick are due to arrive today, and I'd hate to see San Francisco in an upheaval when they get here."

Lee smiled at her reassuringly, then mounted his gelding and rode rapidly to the parade ground, where one hundred infantrymen were hurrying into formation.

The company commander called them to attention as Lee approached.

After explaining the situation, Lee said, "I want no bloodshed. Hold your lines and if you're given the order to fire, make dead certain you shoot over the heads of the crowd. Unless I'm very much mistaken, one or two volleys will destroy their appetites for loot."

The company commander, also mounted, took his place on Lee's left, and the company started the march to the waterfront. Before they came to the main gate of the Presidio, Lee saw Hector Mullins spurring forward to join them. Lee had to hide a smile; Hector missed no excitement, even though he had not been ordered to accompany the unit.

At the approach of the troops, the few pedestrians who were on the street scattered. San Francisco was changing rapidly, Lee reflected as he looked at the one- and two-story buildings lining the streets. The population had already doubled in the short time he had been here, turning a sleepy village into a town of substance. New hotels, taverns, and lodging houses were going up, and a few wealthy men were talking about building their mansions on the heights of Nob Hill and Russian Hill. At least a score of tiny shops, including bootmakers and food purveyors, had already opened, and it was not accidental that about half were places that sold shovels, pickaxes, and sluicing pans. There was no doubt about it; the gold fever was spreading.

The schooner's unruly passengers had moved inland about a block from the docks by the time the troops arrived, and they were being held at bay by a handful of constables, whose only weapons were long staves. Those in the front ranks of the crowd were taunting the constables, who gradually fell back, trying to form a flimsy barrier with their staves. When the troops marched up behind them, the constables quickly broke ranks.

The company commander called an order, and the soldiers changed their formation. Those in the front rank, ten abreast, dropped to one knee, while another ten, directly behind them, stood shoulder to shoulder. The unit filled the street, making it impossible for the crowd to advance.

Lee sat his mount at the head of the formation and raised a hand for quiet. "Boys," he called, "I can sympathize with your situation. I know that you've just had a nasty voyage coming here from Oregon."

"The flour on board was full of worms, and the bacon was rotten," a bearded man in a thick woolen shirt shouted.

Lee was genuinely sympathetic, but there was little

he could do. San Francisco was too new and raw a town to have put aside funds for the assistance of vagrants. His provisions at the Presidio for his garrison were running low, local produce was uncertain because so many farmers had gone off to the gold fields, and he was awaiting the arrival of a supply ship that would bring his own men the bacon, flour, and beans that furnished the staples of their diet. He had no food to spare.

"I realize that many of you are hungry," Lee replied, "and I'm sorry. But there's ample game in the forests inland, and I urge you to hunt and forage there. You have no right to steal the food that our hardworking shopkeepers have for sale. Just remember, they're trying to make an honest living."

A deep-throated rumble indicated that the mob disliked his appeal.

"This territory has been annexed by the United States," Lee went on, his voice hardening. "San Francisco is a law-abiding town, and I assure you that looting won't be permitted."

The gold seekers stared angrily at this officer with gold epaulets. "Who's going to stop us from taking what we want?" the bearded man demanded in a loud, ugly voice. "You, tin soldier?"

"Let's have no trouble," Lee said reasonably. "In the name of the United States Army, I ask you to disperse. Leave town quietly, and you'll come to no harm."

The mob jeered, and someone threw a rock that knocked Hector Mullins's hat askew. The Sergeant Major reacted slowly but deliberately, drawing his pistol and holding it quietly.

Lee realized he had to act swiftly. He nodded to the company commander, who called an order, and the troops in the front ranks raised their rifles.

The mob stirred uneasily, but those in the front held their ground defiantly, certain that the army would not open fire on them.

Another rock sailed through the air, missing the

head of Lee's gelding by inches. The horse shied, then pawed the ground nervously.

"For the last time," Lee said in a clear voice, "I request you to disperse!" The crowd replied with a shower of rocks, and Lee said to the commander, "You may open fire."

The company commander spoke, and the soldiers in the first two ranks sent a volley over the heads of the milling throng. The sound of the shots echoed across San Francisco Bay, and seagulls resting on the docks rose high into the air, their wings flapping as they circled. To Lee's chagrin the mob held firm, although a few at the rear started to melt away.

Troops in the third and fourth ranks exchanged places with the soldiers in front, executing the maneuver smartly, and again Lee nodded. The company commander shouted, and another volley was fired. This time Hector Mullins took careful aim, and his pistol shot split the heavy wooden club that the bearded leader of the mob was brandishing.

The man's bravado vanished as he looked at the splintered, useless weapon. He dropped it to the ground as though it had suddenly caught fire, then turned and ran. His sudden flight created a panic, and within moments the entire mob was scattering in every direction.

"Break your detail into squads," Lee told the company commander. "Give each a sector to patrol. If they catch anyone breaking into a shop or stealing or trying to intimidate a merchant, place the fellow under arrest. A night in the Presidio prisoner compound will suffice, I think. You'll be relieved at four this afternoon."

Hector Mullins fell in beside him as he started back toward the fort.

"I'm glad you decided all on your own to come back to the fort with me, Sergeant," Lee said. "I was a little afraid that if you caught sight of the man who threw the rock at you, you might feel inclined to part his hair with another bullet."

Hector nodded, chewing tobacco in silence. Then he spat thoughtfully into the dirt road. "The same notion crossed my mind, General," he said. "If there's anything I don't like, it's having people throw dangerous objects at me."

Lee chuckled, then sobered. "I don't want our people alarmed, so don't repeat this," he said. "But I have an uncomfortable hunch we soon may face far worse situations."

The riot was still on his mind late in the day when Elisabeta and Rick Miller arrived. Cathy had given Elisabeta refuge in Texas during the war, while the men had marched together in Zachary Taylor's army, so the two families enjoyed being together, talking about old times. After supper, when Beth went off to bed, the women settled down in the parlor for an evening of gossip while Lee and Rick went out for a stroll.

"You were so good to me back in Texas," Elisabeta said. "I felt so safe and secure at your house, spending those lovely evenings reading in the parlor."

"It was a pleasure having you there," Cathy said, taking Elisabeta's hand. "And you were so wonderful to Beth. She loves you, you know. She talks about you all the time."

As the women reminisced, Lee and Rick made their way across the parade ground. Finally Lee asked, "How are you handling the infiltration of gold hunters in the Sacramento Valley?"

"We aren't," Rick replied. "John Sutter and a few other wealthy men have hired private guards to keep intruders off their property, but everybody else is having the devil's own time. We have some neighbors down the road from us—folks named Foster—who have two young sons and a daughter. They own orchards, their only source of income. Well, sir, half of their crop of apples and peaches has already vanished. Vandals just help themselves at night. I can cite you case after case like that."

"What are you doing about it?"

Rick shrugged. "I've applied to the Valley commissioners for a half-dozen permanent deputies, but I'm afraid that by the time they get around to approving my request, I'll need four times that many."

"I see." Lee told him in detail about the incident that had taken place near the waterfront that morning. "The rioters were bolder than I thought they'd be," he said. "For a minute or so I thought I might be forced to fire into their ranks to cool them off."

Rick was not surprised. "I saw immigrants by the hundreds in Texas, just as you saw them in Oregon, Lee. I'd estimate there weren't more than a couple of rotten apples in a barrel. But the men who are coming here to find gold are a different breed. Most are either bachelors or have left their families behind. They're greedy, they have few scruples, and they're a dangerous breed."

"Dangerous only because they're desperate. Few of them have any clothes other than what they're wearing, and they come with empty purses, pursuing a dream. I've sent a confidential letter to Zachary Taylor, asking him to double the size of my garrison as soon as he becomes President. But even then my hands are tied. It won't be long before California becomes a state, but right now she has no formal standing as a territory and the powers of the federal government are limited. I'll be allowed to intervene legally only in emergencies. Like this morning's riot. My troops aren't here to provide police protection for San Francisco. But I can't feel sorry for myself when I think of your situation, Rick. Good Lord, right now you're the only permanent law enforcement officer in the entire Sacramento Valley!"

"How well I know it." Rick stared in the direction of the bay, which was enveloped in a thick fog. "I was going to ask you if the army garrison here could provide us with some assistance, but I see now that you need every man you've got." Rick sighed. "I know of only one possible solution to my problem. I reckon I'll have to ask for volunteer deputies who are willing to serve part-time. I have the authority right now to swear them in, and I have no doubt that John Foster and some of my other neighbors will be more than willing to serve with me."

"That should be a help."

"It will be, Lee, but only up to a point. As I found out in the years we developed the Rangers, law enforcement is a full-time job for professionals who know their business. Amateurs mean well, and there are situations in which they can be useful, particularly in crime prevention. But it takes someone who has had experience to solve a crime and track down a criminal. What scares me is that the problem in the Valley may get out of hand before I'm given a budget to hire some men."

Lee sighed. "California is the most beautiful place I've ever seen. But if you and I are right—and our estimates of what's to come are too similar for comfort —there's going to be chaos in this area before effective controls can be established."

Chet Harris felt as though his whole world were falling apart. For the first time since he had been a boy, traveling on the wagon train to Oregon, he realized he was not as self-reliant and independent as he had always assumed. Long before moving to Texas, where he had fought with distinction in the war with Mexico, he had been in love with Melissa Austin, and he had rejoiced when she, too, had come to Texas.

He had dreamed about this lovely young woman with deep, green eyes and flaming red hair, and that dream had sustained him through difficult times. After his closest friend and only serious rival for her hand, Danny Taylor, had met and married someone else, he had been convinced that Melissa would become his bride.

Now, suddenly, his hopes were shattered.

Melissa sat across the parlor from him in the Galveston house and repeated calmly her extraordinary statement. "I'm sorry to let you down, Chet," she said. "But I can't marry you, now or ever."

The ruggedly built young man, who had faced enemy fire without flinching, winced and asked painfully, "Why? I—I was taking it for granted that you and I—"

"It was my fault for misleading you for so long, I guess." Melissa's long, tapered hands tugged at a handkerchief, threatening to shred it. "I don't know any other way to tell you this. But I know I don't love you. And it has dawned on me, as I look back, that I never have."

"I see." Chet swallowed hard. "Are you going back to Oregon with Harry and Nancy Canning, now that he's found a new manager for his shipyard here?"

She shrugged, relieved that she could answer truthfully. "I haven't decided what I'm going to do. I may stay in Texas, or I might move elsewhere. My plans aren't definite."

One question filled his mind. "Is there somebody else?"

Melissa hated to lie to him, but she saw no need to compound the hurt she knew he was suffering, and she shook her head so vehemently that her long red hair seemed to dance in the sunlight that slanted in through the open window. "There's nobody," she said, hoping she sounded convincing. "It's just that—well, you and I aren't right for each other. I'm afraid that's the only answer I can give you."

Chet slowly rose, planting his feet apart as though still warding off a blow. As his stepfather, Ernst von Thalman, Oregon territory's delegate to the United States Congress, often observed, nothing was accomplished by beating a dead horse. "I'll think of you often, and I wish you the best of everything in whatever you plan to do in life."

"Thank you. And for your own sake, Chet, please forget me," she said sincerely.

Common sense told him she was right. "I'll try."

"What will you do?" she asked.

"I'm damned if I know. Harry and Nancy are going back to Oregon. I have no idea what Danny and Heather Taylor will do, but I have no place in their lives."

"I've assumed that you'd go back to Oregon, too."

"I think not," he said. "I'm not really needed there, and after the life I've led, I'd find the farm too dull." The thought occurred to him that he had no obligations to anyone now and could do as he pleased. If Melissa had said yes, he would have kept his post at the shipyard and settled in Galveston with her, but now a deep-rooted restlessness ate into him. "Maybe I'll try my luck in California," he said. "Gold has been discovered there."

"So I've heard."

"I've got nothing to lose," Chet said and made a valiant effort to smile.

Melissa stood and held out her hand. "I wish you the best of everything. Try not to hate me."

"I couldn't," Chet replied, then bolted from the house.

He walked a short distance, then halted, trying to adjust to his new, unexpected situation. There had been a measure of bravado in his mention of the possibility that he might go to California, but there was no reason he shouldn't. A hunt for gold would be exciting, taking his mind off Melissa, and there was always a chance he actually might strike it rich. Certainly he knew of no reason to remain in Texas.

Watching from behind the parlor curtains, Melissa felt greatly relieved when she saw Chet walk away, his stride purposeful. Jerome Hadley was due to arrive at any moment, and she had dreaded the possibility that these two men might meet.

Hurrying to her bedroom, she hastily brushed her hair, dusted her nose with rice powder, then added a touch of rouge to her lips and cheekbones. Jerome had told her he liked a bold, forthright look in a woman, and she was eager to please him. Studying her reflection in a mirror, she deliberately opened the top two buttons of her shirtdress. Her better judgment told her not to be foolish or reckless, but she couldn't help herself.

She was wildly infatuated with Jerome Hadley. She knew that the Cannings were right when they warned her that he was ten years older than she was and that they knew almost nothing about his background and weren't even certain how he earned his living. He'd only been in Galveston for three weeks.

But it was obvious from his expensive, handsomely tailored clothes that he was no pauper. He spent money with abandon whenever she dined with him at either of Galveston's two inns, and he was more attentive, more flattering than any other man she had ever known. The fact that the Cannings actively disliked him was irrelevant; Jerome was courting her, not the Cannings, and she found him fascinating, dashing beyond compare.

Now, hearing his tap at the front door, she forced herself to respond sedately to the summons, but her heart pounded when she saw his flashing eyes, and she loved the way he removed his high-crowned beaver hat and bent low over her hand. Never had she known anyone so courtly.

Jerome Hadley's lips parted in a broad smile of approval. "My dear Melissa," he said, his voice ingratiating, "you look even more dazzling than usual today."

"Do you think so?" She was pleased that she had gone to the trouble of primping for him. Most men would have not noticed.

Jerome looked her up and down, and although the Cannings would have called his expression insolent, Melissa was thrilled because he was making it so plain that he wanted her. She had always been circumspect, even prim, in her relations with Chet, Danny, and other admirers, but a feeling of recklessness now filled her. She knew she wanted Jerome as badly as he wanted her.

Soon, perhaps this very evening after they dined

together, she would yield gracefully to his advances. Not that she expected to become his mistress. On the contrary, Melissa had been taught by her late parents to think of marriage, homemaking, and the rearing of a family as legitimate goals, and these basic goals had not changed. She was so certain that Jerome's intentions were honorable, however, that she saw no harm in indulging. Her desires were insistent. Certainly their marriage would follow in a short time.

Jerome held Melissa's cape for her, and it was no accident that his hands caressed her shoulders, gently but firmly. Melissa could not control the shudder of pleasure that shot through her at his touch.

He felt her tremble and knew she was ready to be taken. Never had he encountered a young woman as ravishing or as incredibly naive and innocent. She would blossom under his tutelage and ultimately would be of great value to him. He had long-range plans for her. The first step was to make her believe he loved her. An impassioned affair would bind her to him even more closely.

As a professional gambler he was convinced that one's manipulative skills were of paramount importance, but he didn't deny the role of luck in human relations. Certainly he had been very lucky when he had found a woman as beautiful—and at the same time as ingenuously pliant—as Melissa Austin.

The ranch house that looked out toward the snow-capped mountains that lay to the east of Oregon's growing settlements was quiet through most of the day now that Toby was attending school. But there was more than enough to keep Eulalia Holt busy. Her husband's horse-breeding enterprise had become so successful that at noon she had to prepare a hearty meal for eight hired hands, in addition to her husband, Whip, and his Cherokee foreman, Stalking Horse. Afternoons were spent keeping the books for the ranch.

Today the preparation for the meal was simple because the beef roast cooked itself on the outdoor fire, and all Eulalia had to do, other than slice cucumbers and mix the potato salad, was to turn the meat on the spit from time to time. Whip had gone into town on some errands, so she decided to wait until he returned to eat her own meal.

The hands responded with alacrity when she sounded the dinner gong, leaving their mounts at the hitching posts and washing at the pump outside the kitchen door. It was said that Eulalia Holt was the prettiest woman in Oregon, even if she had a son old enough to be learning to read and write, but the men, as they trooped into the kitchen, took care not to show too great a personal interest in her.

For one thing she was an expert shot and was not reluctant to use her rifle if someone offended her. Even more important, she was Whip Holt's wife, and no one in his right mind wanted a confrontation with a living legend, the one-time mountain man who had led the first wagon train across the continent to Oregon. It didn't matter that he was middle-aged, that his wife's cooking had given him a suggestion of a paunch, or that he sometimes was inconvenienced by arthritis in one hip. His eyesight and reflexes were unimpaired, and he could not only extinguish a candle at thirty feet with a single flick of the long whip that had given him his nickname, but he was still the best marksman in the Oregon territory. It was said his only equal anywhere was his younger friend, Rick Miller.

So the hired hands were discreet, treating Eulalia Holt with the respect that was her due and never cursing in her presence. As was their custom, the men ate rapidly, keeping their conversation to a minimum and never lighting pipes or cigars in her house.

After the men had finished, Eulalia cleaned up, putting away enough food for her and her husband's meal later, then she went to the little room she and Whip used as their office. Business was so brisk she had to devote several hours each day to bookkeeping. Certainly it was no secret that the enterprise was thriving, but only she and her husband knew how great a success they were achieving.

When Eulalia heard the approaching hoofbeats of Whip's stallion, she hastily finished adding a column of figures, then went to the kitchen and put their food on the table. His rapid footsteps told her that his arthritis was causing him no pain, for which she was grateful. Waiting until the last possible moment as he came up behind her, she turned and flung her arms around his neck. As always, even when they had been separated for only a few hours, they embraced and kissed passionately.

"You needn't have waited for me," he said.

"I prefer not to eat with the hands when you aren't here," she replied, "and for reasons I'll never understand, I enjoy eating with you."

Whip's leathery face creased in a grin as he filled two glasses from a jug of cold, home-pressed apple juice, then took their plates and his carving knife from a cupboard. "How did you know I was hankering for the taste of beef for dinner?" he demanded.

Eulalia laughed. "Because you told me at breakfast." She served the cucumbers and potato salad as Whip sliced the meat. "Stalking Horse is picking up Toby at school this afternoon."

"Any special reason?"

"Of course. Toby wants to try out a new colt, and he can have his way more easily with Stalking Horse than with either of us."

Whip chuckled. "The boy's cleverness comes from his mother."

"I'm just glad he hasn't inherited my fears. I worry terribly whenever he rides a new horse."

"There's no need to fret," he assured her. "There isn't a horse on this ranch Toby can't handle."

"What's new in town?" Eulalia asked as they began to eat.

He made a wry face. "I heard at the bank that the price of flour has gone up to fifty cents a barrel."

Eulalia gasped, and Whip continued. "That's just

the beginning. I ran into Tonie, and she made a point of sending you a message. She said to tell you she tried all morning to get some bacon, but there wasn't a slab to be had at any price."

"That makes no sense."

"I'm afraid it makes more sense than you realize," Whip said. "California gold fever."

Eulalia was puzzled.

"The last wagon train from the East arrived here less than two weeks ago. There were three hundred and ten men in the company, including heads of families. At the bank they estimate that almost two hundred of them have gone off to California already."

She shook her head and said, "There's no farm or ranch country better than Oregon."

"The gold bug has a deep bite," Whip said somberly. "I had me a little chat with Paul Thoman, who has being having hell's own time at his shipyard. For the first time he's had to post night guards there so men who have become gold crazy don't steal ships they can sail down to San Francisco."

"Lee and Cathy must be having problems."

"If they haven't yet, they will. And so will Rick Miller. The Sacramento Valley is the heart of the gold country, and Rick is going to need a whole army of deputies to keep the peace there." Whip smiled sourly.

"I'm afraid I don't understand the lure of gold," Eulalia said.

"I do, although I'm too old and too successful and too contented to let it touch me."

She ate in silence for some moments. "If I understand you correctly," she said at last, "you'd want to go off to the gold fields, too. If it weren't for having me—and Toby—and the ranch."

"I'm too old."

"Well, if you also were younger."

"Now you're playing the old game of putting words in my mouth, Mrs. Holt."

"You haven't answered my question, Mr. Holt."

A woman like Eulalia, even though she was the

loveliest and most wonderful of wives, was capable of creating problems where none existed, and Whip ran a hand through his graying hair. "Remember when I started off to Texas because I wanted to help Sam Houston? I had to turn back because I realized I was too old to cross the Rockies alone. And that was years ago. It so happens I have a wife, and I plan to stay married to her. It so happens I have a son. And it so happens I've built up a business that gives us a better living than we ever dreamed we could earn. Why would I be stupid enough to chase rainbows in the hope of finding a pot of gold at the end of one?"

"I knew it," Eulalia said. "You have a secret hankering to search for gold."

Whip laughed helplessly. "If I have such a hankering, it's universal. I don't know anybody—including you—who wouldn't like to come into a fortune in return for little or no effort. You and I happen to be too sensible. We're unwilling to give up a good life when we might gain nothing. But there are thousands upon thousands of people—all over the United States and in Europe, too—who have little or nothing to lose. The growing pains Oregon has suffered are minor. Life in California is going to be a nightmare, no matter what such competent and courageous men as Lee Blake and Rick Miller may do. I thank God we're in Oregon to stay."

"I thank Him, too," Eulalia said, looking at Whip fondly. "This is as good a time as any to break the news to you. Dr. Wizneuski has confirmed that I'm going to have another baby."

Whip gaped at her. "You're joking."

The smile on Eulalia's face told Whip all he needed to know. His meal forgotten, he rose, went to her, and lifted her from her chair. "Woman, this is the greatest news I've ever heard, and I just hope we have a daughter who looks like you!"

Danny Taylor and his bride, the former Heather MacGregor, had delayed their honeymoon for some time, waiting until Danny was fully recovered from the injury he had suffered in the war with Mexico. Now, having spent several weeks in New Orleans, the young couple made their way back to the MacGregor farm in Texas, riding in easy stages. Using the main road that led westward, with their pack horses trailing them, they covered no more than twenty or twenty-five miles each day, stopping at small inns and lodging houses when they could and, when necessary, sleeping in the open, which they also enjoyed.

Danny, who hadn't yet decided whether to establish a homestead or earn a living for himself and his wife in some other way, would have traveled more rapidly, but the Scottish-born, red-haired Heather had her own, private reasons for insisting they move at a slow pace. She had spent a long time nursing Danny back to health and instilling in him the desire to live after he had lost a leg while serving in Zachary Taylor's army. He had grown accustomed to walking with a prosthesis, though he would have a lifelong limp, and he had discarded his crutch permanently only a short time before their wedding. Heather knew he was still regaining his strength.

Realizing he would throw himself into whatever vocation he chose and would work furiously, she wanted him to get his health back before he donned a harness. The military bonus his heroism had earned would support them for another year. Knowing him better than he understood himself, she found endless excuses to dawdle. Some days she paused at length to admire scenery; on other occasions she pretended she was tired, and, when possible, she prolonged their roadside picnic lunches. Gradually Danny's step became firmer, he grew tan again under the Texas sun, and his self-confidence increased.

Occasionally Danny suspected that Heather was dawdling on purpose, but in spite of his eagerness to resume working, he was enjoying the respite, too. If necessary, he knew, a job at the Thoman and Canning shipyard at Galveston awaited him, although he preferred to go into some other line of work. He had spent a number of productive years on the Oregon farm that belonged to Chet Harris's family before coming to Texas, but he wasn't yet certain his disability would permit him to lead a rigorous life on a farm.

One day was like another as the couple headed across the vast Texas prairies. They rode until the heat of midday forced them to look for a small river or lake where they and their horses could rest, and they did not resume their journey until mid-afternoon. Texas was so huge they sometimes rode for several days without seeing any dwellings other than an occasional ranch or farmhouse in the distance. But Heather, whose freckles grew more prominent each day, relished life in the open. She gathered firewood, did most of the cooking, and happily curled up in her husband's embrace beneath their blankets wherever they chose to make camp for the night. She knew Danny's rifle and pistol protected her, and she was as fearless as she was cheerful.

It was late afternoon one day when they found an inviting stand of yellow pines, where they decided to spend the night. Following the only path, they were mildly surprised when they saw a cooking fire ahead. They had to pass the fire but were of one mind: they did not want to stay at a camp made by others.

A gray-haired man in faded buckskins sat near the fire, which he had made in a clearing near a small but swift-running stream, and at their approach he stood, taking the normal precaution of picking up his rifle as he stared at them. His deeply lined face was immobile, except for the working of his jaw as he chewed a wad of tobacco, but all at once he smiled.

"Damned if you ain't Heather MacGregor," he said.

The girl looked at him more closely, then smiled. "I'm Heather Taylor now, and this is my husband," she said, with no trace of her former Scottish burr. "Danny, meet Randy Gregg, the neighbor who lives to the west of Ma and Pa. You met John and Phyllis, his son and daughter, at our wedding."

Danny dismounted, lifted his bride from her saddle, and shook the old man's hand.

Randy Gregg snapped his fingers. "I must be losin' my memory," he said. "I knowed you was married. I was down to Austin, sellin' a lot o' grain, or I would have been at your weddin'." Without further ado he invited them to share his campsite.

It would have been rude to refuse, and besides, Heather's expression told Danny that she liked the old man. So he unsaddled their mounts, removed their belongings from the backs of the pack horses, and turned the animals loose to graze.

Randy Gregg kept up a steady fire of conversation as Heather began to cook their usual supper of beans, bacon, and biscuits. "You look like married life is good for you. That consarned boy o' mine never did have the good sense to ask you to marry him, Heather."

"John and I were never interested in each other, Mr. Gregg," she replied, too polite to tell him that both his son and daughter regarded themselves as far too good for any of the other people in their neighborhood. "What are you doing here, a hundred miles from home, Mr. Gregg?" she asked, anxious to change the subject.

"I had a heap o' thinkin' to do, so I had to get me away from the house to clear my head," the old man said, accurately hitting a small pile of dead leaves with a stream of tobacco juice.

Quietly noting that the meal he had intended to eat consisted of a chunk of cold, greasy venison and a slab of what appeared to be stale bread, Heather added enough food to what she was cooking to provide him with an adequate supper, too.

Randy Gregg looked like an old codger, but he was a successful farmer, and the questions he asked Danny indicated that he was no fool. He nodded approvingly when he learned that Danny had served with distinction in Zachary Taylor's corps.

"My blamed son," he said, "couldn't be bothered to join the army. How'd you happen to come to Texas?"

"It's a long story," Danny said and found himself explaining that he and Chet had joined Harry Canning in founding a shipyard on Galveston Island. Further questioning delved even deeper into his past, and he admitted that he had been a bound boy who had run away from a harsh master and had joined the first wagon train to the Oregon territory.

Randy Gregg let loose another stream of tobacco juice and slapped his leg. "You and me got somethin' in common, boy," he said. "I come out to Texas from Tennessee in one o' the early wagon trains. Back when there wasn't nothin' but wilderness here."

Danny immediately felt closer to the old man and nodded repeatedly when Gregg told story after story about his experiences on the train that had brought him here. In some ways all wagon trains were alike.

Heather interrupted to announce that supper was ready. Randy Gregg promptly got rid of his chewing tobacco, filled a jug with drinking water, and carefully washed his hands and face in the stream, drying his full beard on his sleeves. His appetite was large, but eating did not stem his flow of talk. "I wish my Phyllis could cook like you do, Heather," he said. "She burns bacon, her biscuits are soggy, and I have yet to eat any o' her beans."

Occasionally Randy stared for a few moments into the fire before launching into another story of the old frontier days in Tennessee and his experience in the Texas wilderness. It was difficult to determine which tales were true and which were the product of his imagination, but he was a natural storyteller, and the time flew by.

Not until they had finished eating and were drinking the mugs of steaming tea that Heather brewed did he begin to unburden himself. "You told me you was in New Orleans. I suppose you heard the big news while you was there?"

Danny shook his head, wondering if a new war had broken out.

"Gold has been discovered in California," the old man announced solemnly. "Heaps and heaps o' gold. Only the Almighty in His infinite wisdom knows how much!"

Impressed, Heather and Danny exchanged quick glances.

"The reason I come out here alone was to make up my mind," Randy said, "and now I done it. The wagon that brought me to Texas is still a-settin' in my barn. I aim to fix it up snug and cozy. I aim to sell my property—and I know I'll get a good price for it. I'm a-takin' me out t' the gold country," Randy announced, a ring of triumph in his voice.

"You're going to join in the gold hunt?" Danny could not conceal his surprise.

"Oh, I'm too old to go diggin' with a shovel," Randy said, chuckling. "I'll do some lookin' if it ain't too strenuous. But it ain't the money I'm after. I've had excitement all my life, and California sounds like the place t' be these days for a rip-roarin' time. There's folks from all over America a-headin' there. I saw in the Austin newspaper the other day they're even startin' out from England, France, and the German states. I can still look after myself. My hand is steady, my eye is good, and I can pick a worm off'n a leaf with one shot at a hundred paces. I don't know yet just what it is I'll do when I get there, but I'm goin' to California in my wagon, and I'll have me an adventure!"

"Will Phyllis and John go with you?" Heather asked.

The old man's smile was pained. "Soon as I get back t' home," he said, "I'm a givin' them a choice. I sure as shootin' ain't turnin' the farm over to them because they ain't done a lick o' real work there, and before you knowed it they'd go bankrupt. So they can either come with me or fend for themselves."

Danny felt a sense of mounting excitement. "How do people go about this gold search, Mr. Gregg?"

"Well, it said in the paper that a feller establishes a claim. That piece o' land becomes his property. He sets t' work a-diggin' with a shovel or a pickax, and he sifts the dirt he digs up. If there's water runnin' through the property, he takes a pan that looks like a sieve and holds it in the stream. If his luck is good, he comes up with shiny nuggets that are bein' washed down the river. Maybe all he gets is some gold dust, but enough of it is worth a heap o' money, too. Like it said in the paper, you don't have to be an expert miner t' find gold." The old man took a pinch of tobacco from a small burlap sack and placed it in the side of his mouth.

Danny reached for Heather's hand. Her grasp, as firm as his, told him they were thinking the same thoughts. They were an intelligent, sober couple who knew that people succeeded only through hard work, but they were being tempted by forces that neither quite understood.

Later, before they dropped off to sleep on the far side of the fire from Randy Gregg, they exchanged a few words in low tones. "The way I see it," Danny said, "we wouldn't be taking all that much of a chance. We could get a homestead that isn't too close to the gold fields, and we'd build our house there. We'd make sure it was land where we could grow vegetables or fruit. We'd still have enough cash to establish claims in the gold country. If I find gold, we're in clover. But if I don't, we'll still be in a position to earn a living."

"It sounds right to me," Heather replied. "We'll never have another opportunity like this. Let's do it!"

He grinned at her. "I'll fix up a wagon for us," he said, "and we'll ask Randy Gregg to take us with him."

The old man was delighted, and the matter was settled. But when they returned to Heather's parents' home a few days later, they found that the conservative Innes and Matilda MacGregor were not so pleased with their plans.

"Girl," the stern farmer said, "ye were brought up to have a sensible head on your shoulders. As for ye, Danny lad, I consented to give ye Heather in marriage because I thought ye had brains in your head. Now ye propose to act like a pair of idiots!"

"Suppose ye find no gold," Matilda declared. "Then what will become of ye?"

Danny repeated his basic argument. They had no intention of roaming aimlessly through the gold fields, but would establish a solid homestead where they could plant fruit trees or grow vegetables. He was still not certain that he wanted a life as a farmer, but he was prepared to farm if his search for gold proved fruitless.

Innes shook his head. "Ye've ne'er seen California, either of ye. And with trash from all over the face of the earth going there to look for gold, ye might find life there none too stable."

"At the worst," Heather said earnestly, "we could develop our homestead and sell it for a good profit. The sooner we get there the better choice of land we'll have, and you know that with so many people migrating there the demand for property is going to be great. The way we see it, we have nothing to lose."

Innes MacGregor gave a deep sigh. "It's plain ye've made up your minds, so I'll waste no more words on ye. But mark what I say. The day will come when ye'll regret this insanity and wish ye had stayed in Texas, where ye belong!"

At the age of thirty-two, Ralph Hamilton had achieved a dazzling success in New York, now the largest of American cities, and was the envy of his colleagues. Orphaned in his teens, he had worked his way through Yale Law School, winning his degree with honors. He had served as a clerk for two years in a large Manhattan firm, then struck out on his own, and a combination of hard work, a thorough knowledge of the law, and a consistent refusal to compromise his high principles had won him an ever-increasing number of important clients.

"Ralph," a former classmate remarked, "has everything a man could want. A busy office on Broad Street. A comfortable brownstone home uptown on Fourteenth Street that most attorneys twice his age can't afford. And with every eligible woman in New York chasing him, he's won the hand of the incomparable Prudence Hayes. Some men have all the luck!"

When the comment was repeated to him, Ralph Hamilton merely smiled. Luck had nothing to do with it. He opened his office early, six mornings each week, he rarely returned home until long after dark, and he invariably brought a portfolio with him, reading in his library and writing briefs until late at night.

His housekeeper, the elderly Mrs. Warner, was thoroughly familiar with his ways. His private life was none of her business, but she wondered how the popular, pretty Prudence Hayes was content to be betrothed to a man she saw only on Saturday evenings and Sundays.

The thought sometimes occurred to Ralph that he was fortunate to have found a woman who recognized the importance of his work and was willing to take second place to it until he made his fortune. Walking home from his office one brisk evening because he needed the exercise, he was tempted to put aside the papers he carried in his leather case and go instead to the Hayes's house. Prudence was the one weakness in his armor, and he was madly in love with her.

But self-discipline won the battle with desire. He was meeting a major client early in the morning, and the documents pertaining to an important corporate merger had to be ready for signature at that conference. He would bring Prudence a larger than usual bouquet of roses on Saturday night.

Soon after he arrived home, Mrs. Warner placed his dinner on the table for him, and he leafed through the papers as he ate his broiled fish, vegetables, and salad, confining himself to a single glass of wine imported from France and finishing his meal with a cup of the strong coffee from the Ottoman Empire that was now New York's fashionable brew.

A fire had already been lighted in his library, so the chill had been removed from the room by the time he settled down at his desk for an evening of concentrated labor. He knew precisely what was needed, and his quill pen scratched steadily as he prepared the merger contract. Totally occupied, he was startled when a gentle tap sounded at the door.

"I'm sorry to disturb you, Mr. Hamilton," Mrs. Warner said, "but a messenger just delivered this letter."

Ralph thanked her, and when the door closed behind her, he examined the square of heavy linen parchment curiously. It had a strong, perfumed scent, and his name and address had been printed on the outside in green ink. Slightly bemused, he broke the seal.

The communication was as brief as it was shocking:

Dear Ralph,

Our ways of life are so different that I now know our betrothal was a mistake. I am sure that after due reflection you will agree with me.

Please make no attempt to reach me. That effort would avail you nothing, as I will no longer be at the home of my parents by the time this reaches you.

I have eloped with Ansel Todd.

Yours truly,
Prue

Ralph was so stunned he had to read the letter twice before it made sense to him, and then his whole world fell apart. No longer able to concentrate on his work, he stared into the fire for a long time, his soul in misery, his whole body aching. It was inconceivable that Prue had jilted him and was marrying someone else.

He had no idea how long he sat before he rose stiffly and threw the letter into the fire. He watched it burn, then groped for a decanter of cognac and a bell glass that stood beside it on a silver tray. But he paused before pouring a drink and suddenly changed his mind. Alcohol was the refuge of the weak, and his self-discipline wouldn't permit him to indulge. Instead, gritting his teeth, he forced himself to finish preparing the merger contract. Then, his head bursting, he walked out of the house.

For hours he walked rapidly but aimlessly. Occasionally he absently returned the respectful salutes of constables who wondered why an expensively attired gentleman, obviously sober, should be abroad at this hour. He didn't even hear the tentative greetings from the ladies of the evening.

Gradually he came to realize that his life had lost its meaning. It didn't matter that jealous acquaintances would laugh at him behind his back; the opinions of others had never meant much to him. The one fact that counted was that he would not be sharing his life with Prudence. The house in which he had planned to welcome her as his bride was only a building of stone, wood, and plaster. The thought of his carefully nurtured law practice mocked him. The solid, secure existence he had created for himself had crumbled into dust.

The first streaks of dawn were appearing over the East River by the time Ralph returned home. He bathed, shaved, and changed into clean clothes, then went downstairs to breakfast at his customary hour. He was so pale that Mrs. Warner thought he was ill, but she knew better than to inquire after his health.

Ralph glanced listlessly through the morning newspapers. Suddenly an advertisement printed in bold type in Horace Greeley's *Tribune* leaped out at him:

BE THE FIRST TO FIND
CALIFORNIA GOLD!

For the small fee of one hundred dollars the reader was invited to take passage to the Isthmus of Panama on board "the finest of ships." He would be conducted across Panama, owned by Colombia, and another "splendid vessel" would be waiting to carry the fortunate passengers up the Pacific coast to San Francisco, which was "only a step or two" from the gold fields.

Ralph stared at the advertisement. The prospect of gaining something in return for little effort by making a gold strike had no appeal to him, and under no circumstances could he picture himself armed with a shovel and a sieve. But even in his present state of shock, he was shrewd enough to realize that, with people migrating to California by the tens of thousands, there would be a need for competent lawyers.

Here was his chance to put his miseries behind him. He knew himself well enough to realize he would be in constant torment if he stayed in the same city with Prudence and her new husband. He might see them at any time, perhaps in a restaurant, a theater, or at the home of mutual friends. He would be constantly reminded of his failure. Far better to go to California as soon as possible and start a new life.

The ship that would take him to Panama would sail in a week, so he had to act with precision and dispatch. Proceeding methodically, he sold his house, disposed of his law practice, and made gifts to friends of the personal belongings and furniture he could not sell. Colleagues made halfhearted efforts to dissuade him, but his frosty attitude silenced them.

Leaving no detail unattended, Ralph found new employment for Mrs. Warner and packed his law books in a wooden case, arranging to have them sent to him when he established a permanent address. He obtained a letter of credit from his bank, then went shopping, buying himself work boots, heavy trousers, and several flannel shirts. He purchased a brace of pistols and, as an afterthought, acquired a sword cane with an exceptionally sharp, sturdy blade.

On the day of the sailing he arrived at the dock two hours early, his clothes neatly packed in a leather box light enough for him to carry. A huge crowd had already gathered, and when he discovered he would be expected to share a cabin with a number of strangers, he promptly gave the purser an additional twenty-five dollars, in return for which he was assigned a tiny cubbyhole of his own.

Unlike the other passengers who were everywhere on the overcrowded vessel, he did not go out to the open deck to watch the sails unfurl as the ship moved slowly down the Hudson River past the Battery. New York and Prudence were one, and he intended to put them behind him for all time.

II

The flood of immigrants to California that began late in 1848 became a tidal wave as the great Gold Rush gathered force the following year. Before 1849 ended, more than one hundred thousand newcomers would arrive, most of them men and more than seventy-five percent of them Americans. Among the foreigners who came were the first Chinese ever to move to the Western world.

By the end of the year, more than five hundred sailing ships would ride at anchor in San Francisco Bay, many of them deserted by crews eager to join in the search for gold. Business boomed in Independence, Missouri, and Sam Brentwood, who sold wagon train supplies and was married to Cathy Blake's older sister, Claudia, became one of the wealthiest men in the Middle West.

San Francisco expanded at a dizzy, unprecedented pace and, by the end of 1849, would boast a permanent population of more than twenty thousand, with more transients passing through the community than the overworked city fathers could count. The *New York Evening Post,* founded by William Cullen Bryant, the great poet, noted that the exodus from the Eastern Seaboard was not lacking in blessings. Virtually every bordello on the Atlantic Coast had been forced to close its doors, the *Evening Post* observed dryly, because the prostitutes had joined in the Gold Rush in their own way.

One of Zachary Taylor's first acts after he became President of the United States in March of 1849 was to increase the size of the Presidio garrison. General Lee Blake received even more help than he had requested and was relieved when transports brought him one thousand additional infantrymen and one thousand cavalrymen. His units, which included a far smaller garrison at Fort Vancouver, on the Columbia River in the Oregon territory, comprised the only force west of the Rocky Mountains capable of imposing order on an unruly population.

Rick Miller was less fortunate. The Sacramento Valley, seventy-five miles from San Francisco, was the heart of the Gold Rush country and was inundated. Overnight the sleepy village of Sacramento was transformed into a bustling city. Murder and robbery, mayhem and burglary were common, and the forty deputies Rick was authorized to hire could not handle the ever mounting crime wave. He swore in scores of volunteer and part-time deputies, but as he had predicted, these amateur law enforcement officers found it almost impossible to keep the peace.

Homesteaders like his neighbor John Foster were compelled to keep watch on their properties day and night, and although Foster's sons, Scott and Tracy, were only thirteen and eleven, respectively, he drilled them in the use of firearms, and they stood guard duty, too. "If you were a boy," he told his ten-year-old daughter, Sarah Rose, "I'd have you out there with a rifle in your hands, too."

Rick's work was unending, his administrative duties keeping him in his Sacramento office until a new emergency sent him rushing into the field. He left the once-quiet ranch soon after daybreak and frequently did not return until midnight or later. Concerned for his lovely wife's safety, he insisted on teaching her to use a Colt six-shooter.

"Don't jerk the trigger," he told her as they stood together in the backyard, facing a tree to which he had nailed a target. "Squeeze it steadily."

"I try," the gentle Elisabeta replied. "But I know there will be a loud explosion and that the pistol will come alive in my hand. So I start to flinch even before I shoot."

"That's a common mistake, but practice will overcome it. Try again, and this time empty all six chambers."

She braced herself, then shot repeatedly at the target. Only one of the bullets nicked as much as an outside edge of the sheet of paper, but Rick knew she needed encouragement. "That's much better. Now, let me see you reload and do it again."

Elisabeta nodded her head in agreement, although her heart wasn't in what she was doing.

"You're relatively safe when the hired hands are around in the daytime," Rick told her. "It's the evenings that worry me. When you're alone. Unfortunately, you're not only an unusually attractive woman who is alone here much of the time, but you're also the sheriff's wife. Bums who are seeking revenge against me might try to take out their grudges on you. By the time you try to get help from the Fosters, it might be too late."

He broke off and stared at a nondescript trio in rough work clothes who were walking slowly down the road. The men, aware that both he and the woman with him were armed, took care not to tarry.

Watching the men, Elisabeta knew her husband was right. It was essential in these wild, lawless times that she learn to defend herself. Loathing what she was doing, she nevertheless ejected the empty shells from her pistol, reloaded the weapon, and faced the target again. This time she remembered everything Rick had taught her, and two of the bullets penetrated the target.

"Now you're getting the hang of it," he said proudly.

They were interrupted by one of his deputies, who brought word that a fight at a saloon about ten miles from the ranch had ended in bloodshed. Two men were dead and several others injured.

Rick thrust a box of bullets at his wife. "Keep practicing," he said. "I'm leaving you enough ammunition to keep you busy for the rest of the afternoon."

Elisabeta knew it would be late by the time he returned. Steeling herself, she continued to pump bullets at the target.

An hour passed. Her wrist and trigger finger were sore, and her arm ached, but she did not halt. Now and then a stranger passing down the road caught sight of her. That was all to the good. She would be that much safer when the word spread that the sheriff's wife was well able to defend herself.

Then, unexpectedly, Jane Foster and Sarah Rose arrived at the door. "I was trying to get away from the sound of gunfire," Jane said. "John has the boys practicing with rifles. Are you going to give a half-deaf woman and her child some tea, or must we listen to you, too?"

"You have no idea how glad I am to stop!" Elisabeta said, being careful to empty the pistol before going into the kitchen with her guests.

Sarah Rose happily ate several chocolate cookies that were offered to her and then picked up the pistol. "This is heavy," she said. "I bet it's a good one. Sheriff Miller has better guns than anybody."

"Put that ugly thing down," her mother told her sharply.

Elisabeta shook her head. "It wasn't so long ago that I felt as you do, Jane," she said, checking the steeping tea leaves. "But Rick has taught me better. Be glad that Sarah Rose has no fear of firearms. You have no idea how much repugnance I've had to over-come as I've been learning to shoot."

"I hate guns!" Jane was vehement.

"So do I. But in times like these a woman may be helpless if she doesn't know how to shoot. If I had a daughter, I'd want her to be familiar with rifles and pistols." Even as she spoke the words, Elisabeta was amazed to think that she, who had been so sheltered as a child, could be saying such things now. She smiled at Sarah Rose, who was helping herself to another cookie, and she realized that this little girl was going to have to grow up very quickly in rough and tumble California.

"You sound like my husband," Jane said, sighing. "He's right, of course, and so is Rick. But surely a decent, stable, peaceful world will be established in California by the time Sarah Rose grows up!"

"Only if girls like me know how to defend them-selves, Mama," the child said, obviously parroting a refrain of her father's.

"From what I saw in Texas," Elisabeta said, "and from what I've seen here since gold was discovered, I believe that violence creates more violence. Rick com-plains constantly that he needs more deputies, but even if a force of five hundred men were raised, they still couldn't establish order. Not with more and more men coming into the area every day to look for gold."

"I wish I knew when it would end," Jane said. "Everything else has become so ugly. Tim's store is charging such exorbitant prices that we can't afford to buy staples like flour and sugar from him anymore."

"We're able to buy most of our dry food and bacon through the commissary at the Presidio in San Fran-cisco. The commandant and his wife are old friends."

"You're fortunate, Elisabeta."

"How well I know it. I thought flour was high at fifty cents a barrel. Tim is charging a dollar and a quarter now."

"It's all the other things that are ugly, too," Jane

said. "Sacramento has become one big saloon, and if Rick hadn't stepped in, there would have been a gambling palace only a couple of miles from here!" Jane glanced at her daughter, then adopted the mysterious tone adults sometimes used when they didn't want children to understand. "It's those other places I can't stand."

Sarah Rose grinned at her. "You mean the houses that have red lights burning in the windows, Mama?"

"Sarah Rose!"

"It isn't easy to keep secrets from a girl who has two big brothers," the child replied, still grinning.

"You see what I mean," Jane said, sighing as she sipped the tea Elisabeta poured for her.

"Don't despair," Elisabeta said. "I have great faith in human nature. We're going through an extraordinary experience right now. But eventually life will return to normal here."

"If we could afford to move, I'd pull up stakes and go somewhere else. Almost anywhere."

"Not I," Elisabeta said firmly. "This is the only real home Rick and I have ever known. I love it here, and we're going to stay as long as we live!"

Heather Taylor's father bought Randy Gregg's farm, arranging to take possession as soon as the little wagon train left for California. Danny Taylor arranged to build his wagon near the Gregg barn so Randy could advise him on its construction, and in the days prior to their departure he and Heather spent most of their time there.

As Danny came to know Phyllis and John Gregg, he felt about them as she did. Both were dark-haired and attractive, but they were totally lacking in ambition and were content to drift.

"It appears we'll have to go to California with Pa," Phyllis said, "seeing he's sold the farm out from under us. I've never done any work other than keep house for him, so I wouldn't know what else to do."

From what Danny had seen and heard of her

housekeeping, he knew she couldn't even do that job well.

John Gregg was still more lackadaisical. "I reckon I'll see if I can pick up some loose gold after we get out to California," he said. "Just about anything is better than getting up before daybreak to do farm chores."

Never, Danny thought, would he be placed in a position of having to depend upon John Gregg's aid in a crisis.

Twenty-four hours before the little caravan was due to depart, Danny was tacking the canvas cover to the ribs of his wagon while Heather stretched and held the heavy cotton material for him. They were so absorbed in their work they failed to notice the arrival of another wagon until it loomed up before them on the road that encircled the Gregg farmhouse.

Holding the reins was an exceptionally handsome man with a dark beard and wavy hair. He wore a frock coat and a high-crowned beaver hat. Never had Danny seen such an elegant-looking man driving a covered wagon.

The red-haired young woman who sat beside him was even more striking. Her gown of bright green silk was deeply cut, generously revealing her cleavage. A broad silver belt emphasized her tiny waist, and on her feet were dainty green satin shoes with ridiculously high heels. But her makeup was even more exceptional. Her cheeks were rouged, her mouth was scarlet, and a circle of kohl brought out the deep green of her eyes, as did the matching green salve on her lids. At first glance she reminded Danny of the mistress of a Mexican general who had been captured with her lover during the war.

To his astonishment she waved to him, then called, "Danny Taylor! Of all people! How wonderful."

"My god," he muttered. "It's Melissa Austin." Red-faced, he removed his battered hat and took a reluctant Heather with him to meet her.

Melissa proudly introduced them to Jerome Hadley,

who immediately made it plain that they wanted to join the wagon train. John Gregg came out of the house, his expression quizzical, and Jerome promptly launched into an earnest discussion with him.

Meanwhile, Melissa chatted happily with Danny. Chet Harris had gone off to California several months earlier, according to what she had heard from Harry and Nancy Canning, who had sailed back to Oregon on one of the Thoman and Canning schooners. "What a small world this is," she concluded, laughing. "We came to Texas together, and now we'll be going to California together!"

Heather remained silent throughout the conversation, her back rigid with unspoken disapproval.

"Melissa," Jerome called, "Mr. Gregg will take us with him. On the understanding that he won't be responsible for us."

"That's fair enough," she replied airily. "Our horses are strong, our wagon is sound, and goodness knows we're carrying enough supplies." She had purchased the food with her own money, earned at the Thoman and Canning shipyard, and she had advanced Jerome the cash that had paid for the wagon and team of workhorses, too. His own funds, he had explained to her, rested in a California bank, and he had lost his letter of credit.

Heather did not speak until she and Danny returned to put the last finishing touches on their own wagon. "She isn't wearing a wedding ring," she said, "and she didn't correct you when you called her Melissa Austin. She isn't married to that man!"

"From the looks of it," Danny replied mildly, "I daresay you're right. But it's plain enough they're living together."

Heather's sniff spoke volumes. "I find it inconceivable that you could have been interested in her."

He felt somewhat uncomfortable. "Well, she's changed," he said defensively.

"She looks like a painted hussy." Heather was remote.

"I reckon she does." He had to admit that Melissa bore scant resemblance to the wholesome tomboy who had traveled from Oregon to Texas with such enthusiasm, enjoying reckless adventures.

"I can't help wondering," his bride said, "whether you turned to me because she held you off. Maybe you're just attracted to girls with red hair."

Danny was aghast. Heather was jealous. He wanted to reassure her, to tell her he was supremely happy with her, that he cared for her as he had never cared for Melissa Austin. But she gave him no opportunity to speak. Dropping the length of canvas she was holding, she walked away, her head high.

The journey to California was off to a questionable start, and Danny, wanting domestic peace, vowed to have as little to do with Melissa as possible.

That proved to be no problem. The little caravan set out on the long journey westward the following morning, and it quickly became obvious that Melissa was so infatuated with her lover that she had eyes for no one else. She made it plain that Danny was merely an old acquaintance who meant nothing to her. She fawned on Hadley, always trying to do his bidding and to anticipate his desires, and she was radiant whenever he paid attention to her.

Since there were only four wagons in the company —Phyllis and John Gregg rode separately from their father—they couldn't form the customary protective circle when they halted at the end of a day's march. Instead, they made something of a square, attaching lengths of rope to the wagons and driving stakes into the ground to secure them at the corners. This made it possible for their horses to graze freely inside the enclosure.

Heather took charge of cooking the meals, and Phyllis Gregg was dragooned into helping her. Nothing was said to Melissa, but she volunteered her services, and she did her fair share, even though her new wardrobe was totally inappropriate for physical labor.

"I'll attend to the dishes," she announced one evening, pitching in to work in what soon came to be recognized as a typical gesture.

She put two large kettles of water on the fire to heat, adding soft, yellow soap to one and leaving the other clear. Then, after scraping off the plates and utensils, she cleaned them with almost furious speed and efficiency, plunging her bare arms into the hot water up to her elbows.

"Let me help you," Heather offered.

Melissa shook her head. "One of us can do the job better than two. I can do it faster alone."

Here was no grand lady lording it over others. Her snug-fitting dresses and teetering heels made her look slightly ridiculous when she engaged in manual labor, but that did not deter her, and she did more than her fair share of the less savory chores.

"A little hard work never hurt anyone," she said one evening when Heather offered to take over doing the dishes. "Sometimes I think it's good for the soul."

Gradually Heather got to know Melissa, and one night after supper, when the fire was banked and members of the group had retired to their separate wagons. Heather offered her husband something of an apology.

"I think I may have been mistaken about that woman," she said. No name had been mentioned, but Danny knew whom she meant. "She's rather sweet, actually. She looks so sophisticated and bold, but she really isn't."

"I'm glad to hear it," he said shortly, preferring not to discuss Melissa.

"Actually," his bride went on, "I feel sorry for her. She's hopelessly in love with Hadley. What do you think of him?"

"Not much," Danny said. "He isn't particularly friendly, and he never talks about himself, so it isn't easy to get close to him, but that's fine with me. I don't much like him, although I can't spell out my reasons."

"Well, Melissa shouldn't be having an affair with him. If he wants her to live with him, he should marry her."

"Sure, but their relationship is none of our business," he said.

"It isn't right to keep quiet when you see somebody heading into trouble, so I think we should make it our business," Heather said firmly. "You've known her for years and years. Maybe you should speak to her and try to talk some sense into her."

"Not me!"

Nothing would dissuade Heather. "Then we'll go to her together," she announced.

Their opportunity arose several days later, after the little wagon train had been rolling westward across the Texas plains. As it approached the more rugged, mountainous countryside that distinguished the newly acquired New Mexico territory, Randy Gregg halted the caravan for a day to go hunting. He took his son with him, and when Jerome Hadley also volunteered, he accepted.

Danny remained behind to protect the women, horses, and wagons, and when Phyllis went to a nearby stream, grumbling because she was required to wash her father's and brother's laundry, Heather seized the chance. "We'll have that little chat right now," she said.

A reluctant Danny accompanied her to the wagon that Melissa and Hadley occupied. His sense of embarrassment increased when Melissa appeared in a totally inappropriate, figure-hugging dress made of a flimsy yellow material.

"I just finished making this for myself," she said, preening as she offered herself for their inspection. "What do you think of it?"

"Very pretty," Heather said, forcing a smile. "But won't it get dusty and soiled on the trail?"

"Oh, I'm just wearing it today," Melissa said. "Then I'll put it away until we reach California. I'll need all kinds of nice-looking clothes to wear there."

Heather's long, meaningful glance prodded Danny. He took a deep breath. "In the gold country?"

"Oh, Jerome doesn't intend to hunt for gold," Melissa replied. "His funds are stashed away in banks in San Francisco and Sacramento, and he plans to invest them in some business enterprises that will bring us a good profit. We're going to have a very active social life after we build our house, and that's why I'll need an extensive wardrobe."

Again Danny could feel Heather's eyes fixed on him, so he took a deep breath. "Melissa," he said, "you and Chet Harris and I are very old friends. We went through a lot of dangers together, and we've known each other for a long time. So don't think I'm pushing my nose into something that's none of my concern." He faltered, then forced himself to go on. "I've been wondering—and so has my wife—how it happens that you and Jerome Hadley aren't married."

"Oh," she said, smiling ingenuously, "Jerome has so many friends in California that he wants them to be present at our wedding."

"Isn't it kind of risky to be—well, living the way you are right now?" he asked. He felt himself reddening.

"I don't see why," Melissa said, a note of wonder in her voice. "After all, there's no man anywhere more honorable than Jerome."

Heather stifled a sigh and felt she had to intervene. "I don't for a minute doubt his intentions," she said, hoping she didn't sound too jarring. "But men—like women—have been known to change their minds. Danny has always been fond of you, and I've come to like you, too. It's just that we'd hate to see you badly upset if you should be jilted."

Melissa laughed merrily. "That would never happen," she said with finality. "Jerome and I love each other." Her eyes were as certain as they were innocent.

There was nothing more that could be said, and Heather waited until she and Danny were alone to comment. "For her sake I hope she's right. If Hadley doesn't marry her—and there's no way she can force him to do it—she'll be crushed."

It was Danny's opinion that Melissa was asking for a serious problem, but he said nothing.

The hunters returned in mid-afternoon. John Gregg, an expert shot in spite of his laziness, had brought down a cow buffalo, and Jerome Hadley had shot her calf. Several days would be required to butcher the carcasses and smoke the meat, but no one minded the delay. The successful hunt meant that the company would have ample meat supplies for the better part of the journey to the Sacramento Valley.

Taking three horses with them, John Gregg and Danny went off to begin the task of butchering. They would bring back as much as the three horses could carry. They worked until long after sundown, and by the time they came back to the campsite, the others had eaten and were keeping their supper hot for them.

Randy Gregg, a larger than usual wad of tobacco in his mouth, was playing a game of cards with Jerome Hadley. While Heather fetched his meal, Danny wandered over to watch the two men and saw they were playing poker for what appeared to be only small sums of money.

"I'll call you," the old frontiersman said, a note of satisfaction in his voice. "I've got a pair of kings and a pair of queens." He chuckled, apparently certain he had won.

"Sorry, my friend." Hadley scooped up the money that lay on the ground within easy reach. "I've got a royal flush." He spread his cards, smiling slightly.

"You're doin' great tonight," Randy said. "A royal flush comin' right after a hand with four aces! You're too much for me!"

"My luck has been so good that it's about due to change," Hadley said. He turned to Danny. "Care to play a friendly hand or two?"

"No, thank you," Danny said. "I make it a principle never to gamble."

"Oh, this isn't a serious game," Hadley replied. "We're just passing the time, playing for pennies."

"I've never played poker," Danny said, "and this is no time to start picking up habits I might regret later." He took the steaming bowl that Heather handed him, then sat on a nearby boulder to eat.

Hadley shrugged and wandered off to his own wagon.

Heather sat beside her husband, and Randy made no move to leave. Waiting until Hadley was out of earshot, the old man said in a soft, guarded tone, "I've never seen such luck with cards, and I've played for at least fifty years."

Something in his voice caused Danny and Heather to look at him more closely.

"I don't like t' go accusin' people when I can't rightly prove my accusations," Randy went on, "but I'm willin' t' swear by all that's holy that Jerome Hadley cheats at cards. Man alive, the way he handles them pasteboards is somethin' t' behold. We've been together for quite a spell now, and maybe you've noticed, like I have, that he's never mentioned how he earns his livin'."

"I wondered myself," Danny said, and his eyes narrowed. "Are you suggesting he may be a professional gambler, Randy?"

The old man shrugged. "You know as much as I do. All I can tell you is I seen all kinds."

Heather was horrified. "The way Melissa was talking about him, I'm sure she doesn't know. We've got to warn her."

"What could we say to her?" Danny demanded. "That Randy has suspicions, based on a so-called friendly game? She has already made it plain to us that she believes only what she wants to believe about Hadley. You know blamed well he's not going to admit to her that he's a professional card player who cheats to win. We've already interfered enough, and I say that we leave well enough alone from now on!"

Life on board the Panama-bound clipper ship was chaotic. The available space had been oversold, forcing as many as eight men to sleep in cabins intended for four. The tiny saloon was so cramped that only a few of the passengers could eat there, and the others were forced to form a line on deck every morning and evening for their meals. The food was atrocious. The oatmeal was sour; there were weevils in the biscuits; and when a number of men fell ill after eating pickled fish, the passengers were convinced that most of the fish and meat offered to them was tainted.

The weather became much warmer as the ship approached the tropics, and their discomfort was so great that the passengers began to spend virtually all of their time on the open deck, where the trade winds made the heat bearable. With nothing to occupy them, the men played cards, drank cheap liquor, and, inevitably, engaged in arguments of mounting intensity. The majority of the fortune seekers were a hard lot, a number openly admitting they had served prison terms, and aside from a few who had worked as bookkeepers or clerks, most were tough, brawny men who had worked in the open as carpenters, masons, or loggers.

Ralph Hamilton felt isolated. He had virtually nothing in common with his fellow passengers, and he knew they were suspicious and unfriendly because his clothes, grammar, and manners marked him as a member of the upper class. He was grateful to the purser for his tiny cabin, even though he had paid an exorbitant price for it. He heard others claiming they had been robbed while they slept, but he was secure behind the locked door of his tiny cubbyhole.

But he could not remain in his cabin day and night as the square-rigged ship threaded its way southward through the islands of the West Indies. The heat,

combined with the humidity, forced him to spend
most of his waking hours on deck, and he had to join
the others on deck for meals, although he had thrown
at least a portion of every breakfast and supper over
the aft rail into the Caribbean Sea. The knowledge
that there were thieves in the company made him
cautious, so he carried his wallet with him at all times.
In it were his bank letter of credit and what he
regarded as the relatively small sum of two hundred
dollars in cash. The towering masts and huge sails
provided only a partial, intermittent shield from the
blazing sun, so he packed away his coat in his luggage
box and transferred his wallet to a pocket in his
trousers.

Rolling up the sleeves of his fine linen shirt, he
removed his cravat and went up to the deck, where he
made his way forward to the prow, avoiding the lines
trailing from the maze of sails above him. Only the
clipper ship itself was worthy of the advertisements
that had enticed so many passengers to board it.
Graceful and sleek, it achieved speeds as high as
twenty knots as it sliced through the clear waters of
the Caribbean.

Standing at the prow, Ralph stared out at an island
off to port whose identity he didn't know and didn't
care to learn. He was engaging in the grim inner
struggle of trying to forget Prudence, his law practice,
and his former life. He did not regret his decision, but
with so little to occupy his mind, he was finding it
difficult to shake off his memories. Because of a lack
of space in his luggage, he had brought only two
books with him, and now, after reading both of them
twice, he found time hanging heavily on his hands.

It wouldn't be long before the ship reached the
Isthmus of Panama, he reflected, and perhaps he
could purchase a number of books there before trans-
ferring to the vessel on the Pacific side. That hope
encouraged him.

Someone came up beside him, and Ralph barely
glanced at a fellow passenger with stubble on his

face, a man who displayed yellow teeth when he grinned. "I bet they can fry eggs on the streets of them islands," the man said. "I hope it ain't this hot in California."

"I know very little of the climate there," Ralph replied courteously, "but San Francisco and the Sacramento Valley are located in the temperate zone, so heat shouldn't be a problem."

"Glad to hear it," the man said, beginning to edge away.

Something in his manner alerted Ralph, who clapped a hand to his pants pocket and found that his wallet was gone.

The thief was several years his junior, broad-shouldered and almost as tall, but Ralph was coldly outraged and cast aside caution. "One moment," he said. "I believe something of mine may have—ah—accidently found its way into your possession."

"What do you mean?" The man continued to back away.

"Not so fast, please." Ralph reached out and caught hold of the front of his shirt. "You'll note, if you haven't previously, that this ship flies the American flag. Consequently, the laws of the United States are valid here, and I believe you'll find that every state, county, and city has laws that prohibit stealing."

"What the hell do you mean?" The thief tried to wrench free.

Ralph's grip tightened. "Be good enough to return my wallet, and we'll say no more about the matter. Fate has thrown us together as shipmates, and we may be compelled to spend considerable time together before we reach California, so I prefer not to prosecute you."

"I ain't got no wallet. Leave me go!"

"I regret the need for this," Ralph said, and he punched the man in the eye and sent him staggering backward.

A crowd of idle passengers immediately began to gather.

"My wallet, please," Ralph repeated, then followed with two more blows, a short, vicious left that caught the man in the stomach and a right that caused blood to spurt from his nose.

The man tried to defend himself and flailed wildly. If one of his blows had landed, he could have caused damage, but Ralph moved with ease and agility, avoiding the counterattack as he continued to make every punch count. He was unscathed by the time his battered opponent dropped to one knee, unable to escape because of the tight circle that had formed around the pair.

Groaning, the man reached inside his shirt, then handed Ralph his sweat-soaked wallet. "You didn't have to be so damn rough," he muttered. "I was just playin' a little joke."

Ralph examined the contents of the wallet to assure himself that nothing was missing. Then he smiled coolly. "As much as I regret the use of violence to settle disputes and the need to take justice into one's own hands, it sometimes happens that there's no choice." Holding tightly to his wallet, he pushed through the throng.

A few in the crowd looked relieved and pleased, but the majority regarded him with open hostility.

Very much aware of their emotions he went straight to the quarterdeck, where the first officer had the watch. "Do you have any objection if I engage in a bit of target practice on the aft deck?"

The ship's officer stared at him. "Do you know how to shoot a gun?"

"You'll find I'm quite competent."

"Then help yourself, mister. The captain wouldn't like to make an entry in his log that you wounded or killed somebody by accident. But as long as you know what you're about, you can do as you please."

Ralph thanked him, then went to his cabin for the case containing his pistols and a small sack of ammunition. Returning to the deck, he loaded both weapons and, holding one in each hand, took aim at the crest of a small wave behind the ship's wake. Then he fired the pistols in rapid succession.

The sound of the shots attracted immediate notice, and he saw that in the group that was gathering at a distance was the thief, holding a soiled bandanna to his face. Several of the man's cronies clustered around him.

Only a few feet away Ralph saw a barrel of rubbish that had not yet been thrown overboard by the slovenly crew. He went to it and soon found something that suited his purpose, a cracked drinking mug made of inexpensive china. He held it at arm's length, pretending to examine it, and made certain that his audience saw it clearly. Then he reloaded his pistols, placing one in his belt, and threw the mug into the sea. It bobbed up and down in the clipper's wake.

Ralph drew his second pistol, then waited patiently until the ship had moved about one hundred feet from the mug. Raising one pistol, he shattered the mug with his first shot. The larger remaining section was still visible, so he demolished it with his second shot.

He could hear the crowd muttering behind him. Seemingly unaware of the stir he had caused, Ralph quietly took his pistols below. He had proved not only that he was a first-rate marksman, but that his aim was equally accurate with both hands. Hereafter, it was likely that pickpockets and other sneak thieves in the company would keep their distance from him. These men understood no other language.

It didn't occur to him until that night that he had succeeded in forgetting Prudence for several hours.

Chet Harris was tired, hungry, and in need of a bath when he wearily made his way toward Big George's saloon, the largest establishment of its kind in the Sacramento Valley. Stubborn as well as courageous, he hated to admit defeat now. As an adolescent he had faced many crises without flinching on the long journey across the United States on the first wagon train to Oregon. As an adult he had more than held his own in Rick Miller's cavalry regiment during the war with Mexico. Now, however, his situation was different.

He had exhausted his funds in a fruitless search for gold, losing most of his money on a land claim that had proved worthless. Since then, he had drifted, panning for the yellow metal on the Sacramento and American Rivers where no individual claims were allowed. Most often, others had been panning above and below him, and occasionally one of them had shouted in delight upon finding a nugget in his sieve. But Chet had enjoyed no such luck.

Big George's place consisted of two large rooms on the first floor. Full meals were available in the more expensive of them, where, day and night, provocatively dressed, so-called waitresses brought food to the customers, danced with them to music provided by two fiddlers and a drummer, and, when a man who was so inclined could meet her price, took him to one of the private chambers upstairs. The second room was occupied by men down on their luck. They could buy lesser cuts of beef and ham, loaves of bread, hard-boiled eggs and watery ale for small sums of money, provided they paid in advance, giving their money to the burly, shirt-sleeved man who tended the bar and who kept order with the aid of an iron pipe he kept close at hand.

Chet was so ravenous that he splurged, buying a whole loaf of bread, a half-dozen eggs, and a large chunk of gristly beef, which he carried to one of the long, rough-hewn tables. In spite of his hunger he ate slowly, savoring each mouthful. Shutting out the sounds of talking around him, he tried to analyze his situation.

By tomorrow he would be hungry again, but his money was gone. If he sold his pickax and sieve, he would be unable to continue the hunt for gold. So he faced two choices, both predicated on the knowledge that there were hundreds, perhaps thousands, of desperate men in the Sacramento Valley, each of them willing to work for menial wages while he accumulated another grubstake. He could go to San Francisco in the hope of finding work at a shipbuilding company there, since he knew the business after working for Harry Canning in Texas. Or he could go home to his family's farm in Oregon, which would be an admission that he had shown poor judgment by coming to California in the first place.

Someone sat down at the table on the bench opposite him, and Chet momentarily forgot his own problem because he was fascinated by the man's meal. In one hand the newcomer held a single hard-boiled egg. Chet looked at him, realizing that the short, slender, older man was Chinese. What made him unusual was that he did not in any way resemble the Chinese known as "coolie laborers" who were arriving from the far side of the Pacific in ever-increasing numbers. He wore a heavy flannel shirt and sturdy work pants and boots, like everybody else in the gold fields, but his slender hands were those of a gentleman. The expression of amusement that came into his eyes when he saw that Chet was startled by his unusual "meal" indicated that he was endowed with a quick, acute intelligence. Chet politely averted his gaze.

Condiments were free, so the Chinese salted his egg liberally, then slowly nibbled at it.

A bear of a man with two slabs of bread and a chunk of ham in one dirty hand came to the table, which was fully occupied, and looked in vain for a place to sit. Finally his stare settled on the Chinese. "You, Chink!" he said. "Move your tail! You're sittin' in my seat."

The Chinese looked up at him mildly. "Is mistake," he declared. "I not done eating."

The big man laughed coarsely. "Move before I heave you out of here!" he said, moving closer, his manner threatening.

The slender man sighed, placed his egg carefully on the table, and reached out in what appeared to be a gingerly manner for the other man's wrist.

His tormentor screamed and barely managed to continue holding his food as his knees buckled and he sank to the floor.

"I not done," the Chinese said, calmly picking up his partly consumed egg.

The big man, red faced and still in obvious pain, scrambled to his feet and retreated hastily.

Chet grinned at the man across the table. "That was neatly done," he said.

The Chinese shrugged. "In my country," he said, "one is taught ancient arts. Ways to defend self with bare hands."

"You sure did it." On sudden impulse Chet broke his loaf of bread in half, passed three hard-boiled eggs across the table, and offered him a generous portion of the unappetizing beef. "Help yourself," he said. "It's plain you bought only one egg because that was all you could afford."

The little man drew himself up with great dignity. "You buy, you eat," he said.

Chet shook his head. "There's more here than I can manage."

"Then you save part and eat later." Apparently the man was familiar with the needs of those who worked the gold fields.

"I'll be happier if you'll share it with me," Chet said and meant it.

The Chinese studied him at length, then bowed from the waist and took some of the food offered to him. In spite of his great self-control, it was obvious from the way he relished the food that he, too, was very hungry.

Neither spoke until the last scrap of food had vanished, and then they walked out of Big George's together. Chet extended a hand and introduced himself.

"I Wong Ke," the Chinese said.

"Glad to know you, Mr. Ke."

"Wong is last name, Ke is first name." The Chinese smiled. "In my world many things different from your world. But one thing the same in whole world. Men everywhere love gold. Wong Ke stupid to leave life of scholar in Nanking and come to America for gold. Now have no gold and no money to go back to China on clipper ship."

"We're in the same situation," Chet said. After briefly describing his own background, he added, "I reckon we have about enough food in our bellies to spend the rest of the day and maybe tomorrow morning looking for gold. Let's do it together."

Wong Ke's smile broadened. "We partners," he declared.

Chet's hand enveloped that of the smaller man, but he was not deceived. Wong Ke was well able to take care of himself.

They looked up at the cloudy sky with one accord, both realizing that about six hours of daylight remained. Then Chet asked quietly, "Do you have any special area in mind?"

"If I know where to look, would have gold by now," Wong Ke said.

They continued to move away from Big George's, coming at last to a crossroads where several trails led through the thick woods in various directions. Chet motioned for a halt, and although he could see no one within earshot, he spoke in a low, guarded tone. "I've been searching for a place where the water and land look like they do at the Sutter mill on the American River. Have you seen the mill?"

Wong Ke nodded.

"The general area I have in mind is on the Bear River, about an hour and a half's hike from here."

"We go," Wong Ke said, removing a shovel from his belt and carrying it like a rifle over his shoulder. "We look until hunger make us too weak."

As they made their way toward the northeast through the woods, Chet explained that the area he had chosen was favorable for several reasons. "The Bear is a big river," he said, "so under the mining codes of the California territory, nobody can lay a claim to any section of it. That means we're free to do our prospecting there. For another thing, you'll find men working up and down the Sacramento and the American by the hundreds, but the hills are much steeper and the forest thicker along the Bear, so prospecting isn't as comfortable there."

"Dragons who hide gold keep it in places not easy to reach," the Chinese said complacently.

Chet, who was in the lead, chose to take a round-about route to the site. Leaving the trail after a time, he set out through the thick foliage of the forest. After the Oregon wilderness, the deep woods held no terrors for him, and he was completely at home. His pistol, which he had refused to sell, would kill a wildcat or slow a giant bear if they were attacked, which he regarded as unlikely, and he set a rapid pace.

Wong Ke was unfamiliar with the forest. Brambles tore at his clothes, and sometimes he stumbled over fallen logs and other obstacles, but he made no complaint, doggedly following the tall American who had shown him such generosity.

Late in the afternoon they heard the rushing of water, and a few moments later Chet halted, then pointed. The Bear was a swift-moving river, its flow somewhat accelerated at a spot where it narrowed unexpectedly directly below a small waterfall. The pair could see piles of rocks on either bank, and Wong Ke knew why the spot wasn't popular with other gold seekers. The water was certain to be icy, and a climb over the rocks was hazardous. The ill-matched partners smiled at each other and began to climb over the jagged rocks.

The water was even chillier than Wong Ke had anticipated, but he quietly moved in from the bank until the water swirled only an inch or two below the tops of his boots. Attaching his shovel to his belt again, he rolled up his sleeves, then began to scrape his sieve along the gravel bottom of the river, removing it when it became full and carefully discarding sand, mud, and pebbles.

Chet, being taller, moved a few yards farther toward midstream, where he halted and began to follow the other man's example.

They labored without pause for hours, bending until their backs ached, slowly sorting and ridding themselves of the worthless contents of their sieves until their eyes watered. But neither complained, and Chet smiled wryly. Anyone who thought gold prospecting was easy or romantic work was badly mistaken. His feet felt like lumps of ice, and every muscle in his body cried for relief, but he kept working, as did his companion.

As evening set in, it was becoming increasingly difficult to see the contents of the sieve, and Chet despaired of finding any gold that day. They would have to wait until the morning to continue their search; they would quickly become hungry and tired; and they would probably have to leave the site empty-handed.

Suddenly Wong Ke broke the heavy silence. "I find," he said softly, holding up a chunk of yellow metal the size of a human eye.

Chet's heart pounded wildly as he examined the nugget. As nearly as he could tell, it was pure gold.

Heartened by the strike, the partners returned to their labors with renewed vigor and enthusiasm. In a short time, Wong Ke came up with a second nugget, almost as large as the first, and then it was Chet's turn. He made three strikes in relatively quick succession, and when only a trace of light remained in the sky, the partners looked at each other, then moved wearily ashore.

To keep the location of the site a secret, they trudged almost a mile toward the southwest before they finally halted, exhausted and shivering. They built a fire, and while their clothes and boots dried on their bodies, they discussed their future.

"First off," Chet said, "I reckon we ought to cash in the smallest nugget at Big George's. He doesn't pay near as much as the dealers and brokers in Sacramento, but that one nugget will pay for one tremendous celebration."

"Is fair enough," Wong Ke said. "Other nuggets we sell to dealers in Sacramento. Then we have plenty much money."

"Offhand," Chet said, shaking his head in wonder, "I'd guess our day's work will bring us anywhere from five to ten thousand dollars. Enough to buy a working farm or a business, or even invest in one of the new hotels in San Francisco. So the big question now is whether we keep going together or call it quits and go our separate ways."

Ke grinned, then said quietly, "Chet and Ke partners for long time!"

"That's what I want, too," Chet replied, extending his hand.

They quickly discovered they were of one mind on what to do with their profits. First and foremost, they would buy as many acres of land as they could on both banks of the Bear River adjacent to the place they had found the gold. The river itself would remain public property, but by fencing off the land they would discourage intruders and increase their chances of not being forced to share their bonanza. The exact location they would keep a closely guarded secret. They also planned to purchase ample food supplies and firearms and build a cabin on their property.

"Maybe our luck will run out fast," Chet said as they laid out their sleeping blankets. "But if it holds up, there's a chance we'll become really rich."

"If we find many more pieces of gold, Ke stop thinking he was fool to leave China."

Early the next morning they headed for the saloon. Although breakfast was just being served by the time they reached their destination, the place was already busy. Two cooks were hard at work in the kitchen, the fiddlers who would play during daylight hours were tuning their instruments, and as many as fifteen of the establishment's thirty women were on hand. The majority of the women were white, but several were black, and one was Chinese. All wore dresses with low-cut necklines and deep slits in the sides of their skirts, which showed off their shapely legs. Although the sun was just rising, they had already applied cosmetics.

Supervising the proceedings was the man known as Big George. Six feet, six inches tall and weighing more than two hundred and fifty pounds, he was an amiable host who was eager to promote the happiness and comfort of his guests. He roamed the establishment, missing no detail of anything that might be happening at any given moment. A six-shooter in a holster was strapped to his broad belt, and he also carried a length of lead-filled pipe. When a customer became obstreperous, Big George simply picked him up and threw him out bodily.

As Chet and Ke entered the sanctum, they immediately became aware of the delicious odors of cooking food, and nothing else was important to them. They sought out Big George, and Chet showed him the smallest of the nuggets. "How much will you give us for this?" he asked.

Their host took the chunk of gold and examined it with a care that belied his genial approach. "So you had a strike, boys. How about six hundred dollars?"

"Make it seven hundred, and you have a deal," Chet said, so hungry that he didn't care that they could obtain more from a dealer in Sacramento, a two-hour walk from the saloon.

"Six-fifty," Big George said. He went behind the bar for the money.

Chet and Ke seated themselves at a table in the far corner, and paying scant attention to the semiclad woman who waited on them, they ordered large steaks topped with eggs; fried potatoes; freshly baked bread; and what all men in the gold fields regarded as the greatest of luxuries, a mound of churned butter. Chet wanted a mug of ale, while Ke requested a pot of tea.

The young woman knew from experience that they would pay little or no heed to her until they had eaten, so she kept her conversation to a minimum, then hurried off to the kitchen.

The fiddlers and drummer struck up a lively tune, but the pair at the corner table didn't even hear the music. They sat in a dreamy silence, inhaling the scents from the kitchen.

When their meal was placed before them, Ke cautioned his partner. "Eat much more if eat slow," he said.

They ate steadily but slowly for a long time, enjoying every mouthful. This was the moment they had awaited throughout the endless days they had searched in vain for gold, and no reward could have given them greater satisfaction. Somewhat to Chet's surprise the short, slender Ke ate as much as he himself consumed.

At last they sat back in their chairs, comfortable and content, and Ke ordered another pot of tea.

"What about you, sweetie?" the young blonde asked as she smiled at Chet.

"I reckon I'll switch to whiskey," he said. "The good stuff, not the poison that's guaranteed to eat out your insides."

She fetched their order, then lingered at Chet's side. "Is there anything else you'd like, sweetie?"

His interest was sparked as he inspected her. She was somewhat heavier than any of the young women he had admired in the past, but he had not taken a woman to bed since the army had left Mexico. "What have you got in mind?" he demanded.

Her smile broadened. "We could dance."

"I'm not much for dancing," he said.

Judging him shrewdly, she slid onto his lap and

poured a generous quantity of whiskey into a glass from the jug she had just placed in front of him. "I'm Winnie," she said, "and I got me an idea you and I are going to get along together just fine."

Wong Ke frowned slightly but made no comment. Obviously his partner would spend almost every penny of his share of the money before they left Big George's saloon.

Chet and the woman, snuggling closer, began to talk in low tones, and it wasn't long before they both stood. "Don't leave without me," Chet said to Ke and followed the woman up the stairs.

Ke poured more tea into the chipped mug, enjoying the luxury of adding a heaping spoonful of sugar to it. Out of the corner of an eye he saw the establishment's Chinese trollop approaching him, but he waved her away courteously.

Within the next quarter of an hour a number of the other women also tried their luck with him. Ke smiled, bowed, and shook his head repeatedly, making it plain that he wanted neither their company nor their services. He was eager to go on to Sacramento, sell the other nuggets, and establish the claim to the property on the Bear River. But he waited a long time before his grinning partner reappeared.

"I'm just about broke again, but it was worth it," Chet said.

Wong Ke concentrated on business matters as they started out on the long walk to Sacramento. "If land we want is public property," he said, "we make claim right away at office of California territory. If private property, we find owner and buy right away. All this we do plenty much fast."

Chet nodded, his thoughts already straying to the rewards that awaited them. "I saw a pretty redhead at Big George's, and next time we go there I'm going to have me a session with her," he said. "Man alive, I'm going to enjoy being rich!"

Ke kept his own counsel. His partner was young and impressionable, he realized, and after teetering on the edge of total failure, it was only natural that he would seek the pleasures that awaited the successful. Ke could only hope, however, that ultimately he would achieve the stability that was the goal of a mature man.

III

Rick Miller was late coming home from work, but that wasn't unusual. Elisabeta ate supper alone, declining an offer to eat and spend the evening at the Foster house, and then she read for a time by the light of an oil lamp in the parlor. Eventually she grew drowsy, and having no idea when Rick would return, she decided to go to bed.

Methodically she checked to see that the front and back doors of the ranch house were locked and bolted, then she made certain that all of the windows were closed from the bottom. Often she slept poorly when Rick wasn't home, so she took the precaution of drinking a glass of warm milk before she retired. Finally, before blowing out the candle beside the bed, she checked the loaded Colt six-shooter that she placed on the night table beside her. Thanks to Rick's insistence, she could handle the weapon without fear now, and its proximity comforted her. The long day had been more tiring than she realized, and soon she drifted off into a deep sleep.

Elisabeta had no idea what awakened her. She heard no sound of any kind, but the recognition of an alien presence seeped into her consciousness, and she opened her eyes. A huge, heavy man loomed above her, and directly behind him stood an even taller man. Instinctively she reached for her pistol, but it had vanished from the table.

Now, aware of her helplessness, she was shaken by a deep spasm of terror and opened her mouth to scream. A large hand descended and slapped her so hard across the face that she saw blinding lights.

"Go easy the way you hit her, Slim," the taller man said. "You don't want to break the little lady's neck too soon."

"Yeah, Shorty," the heavyset man replied in a deep voice. "Kind of pretty, ain't she?"

"I seen worse, Slim."

Cringing beneath the bedclothes, Elisabeta knew there was no escape. On the floor beside the men was a burlap sack, and from it protruded one of her silver candlesticks, so she knew the house had been ransacked.

In her quandry she didn't know whether to tell these intruders that her husband was Sheriff Rick Miller. That knowledge might send them fleeing, but it could cause them to react spitefully.

Suddenly the heavyset man jerked down the sheet and blankets, then drew a knife from his belt. "How long since you had some real lovin', little lady?" he demanded.

Fear paralyzed her.

His knife sliced away her nightdress, and she lay naked beneath his covetous, hard-eyed gaze. All at once he hurled himself at her, his weight pinning her to the bed and almost suffocating her. Elisabeta frantically tried to fight him off, but her strength was no match for that of the powerful giant. His foul breath almost choked her, and aware that she could do nothing to halt him, she fell back limply and allowed him to do as he pleased.

No sooner was he finished with her than the taller man took his place. He was equally brutal and vicious. Elisabeta, overcome with pain and humiliation, tried desperately to empty her mind, hoping the torment soon would pass.

The man called Shorty buckled his belt and stared down at the unmoving victim. "You think she could see us clear enough to identify us if she was to run across us again, Slim?" he asked.

Her terror mounting again, Elisabeta tried to shake her head.

"Maybe she could, and maybe she couldn't, Shorty," the heavyset man replied. "Seems to me like we'd be crazy to take the chance."

"That's what I think." The tall man pulled out his knife.

Again Elisabeta opened her mouth to scream, but at that instant the blade plunged deep into her body, and she emitted only a gentle moan as she died.

The pair who stood above her took no risks, however, and both stabbed her repeatedly before they wiped their knives clean on the sheets, then took their booty and walked quietly out of the house through the door, which they had earlier unlocked with a piece of metal wire. They casually vanished into the night.

Morning came, and the sun was rising by the time a bone-weary Rick Miller returned home, hoping to snatch a few hours of badly needed sleep before he returned to duty. As he approached the house, he noted that the front door was ajar, so he leaped to the ground, raced inside, and stopped short in the bedroom entrance. His exhaustion was forgotten when he saw the battered body of his beloved Elisabeta.

The scene would be etched in his mind forever. His happiness had been destroyed, the whole purpose of his being had disappeared.

For a long time he stood, unmoving. Then his experience as a law enforcement officer took command, and he made a professional search, forcing himself to study his wife's lifeless body, then scour the house to find out what was missing. He could conclude from the muddy footprints on the floor that two assailants had entered the house, and he surmised that both had raped Elisabeta and both had participated in her murder.

Rick returned to the bedroom and tenderly covered his wife's body with a sheet. Once again, he stood for a long time, gazing down at Elisabeta's face, now so peaceful looking. He caressed her cheek with his hand, then carefully drew the sheet up over her and left the room.

Rick went to the house of the Fosters, where he sent young Scott hurrying to Sacramento for the undertaker, who doubled as the Valley's coroner. The other members of the Foster family were stunned by his news and almost as badly unsettled by his expressionless face and toneless voice.

"Think hard," he said. "Did you see or hear anything out of the ordinary last night?"

"We were robbed, too," John Foster replied. "The thieves sneaked in and out without waking any of us. The boys and I sleep with our guns, so I reckon they didn't want a fight with the three of us."

Jane sounded almost apologetic as she said, "All they took were the candlesticks on our parlor mantel and a silver carving set from the dining room."

Little Sarah Rose was badly frightened. "I saw the men, and I heard them talking, too."

Everyone stared at her.

Rick's face continued to look as though it had been carved out of granite, but his voice became soothing, almost gentle. "Tell me about it in your own way," he said, "and take your time."

The child's story was simple. She had awakened at some time during the night—she couldn't recall the hour—and had gone down to the kitchen to get some forbidden cookies.

Hearing the rattling of the rear door of the house as

the thieves had tried to unlock it, she had become frightened and had hidden in the storage bin where her mother kept flour, dried beans, and other supplies. The men had actually opened the door of the bin and peered inside, then talked for a time with the door ajar, while the terrified little girl had scarcely dared to breathe.

"One of them was very big around," she said. "He was tall, too, taller than Papa. The other one called him Slim."

The adults nodded, recognizing the primitive humor responsible for the nickname.

"The other one was even taller," Sarah Rose said. "He was just about the tallest man I ever saw. His friend called him Shorty."

"How tall was he?" Rick asked quietly. The little girl didn't know. "Never mind. Tell me how they looked and how they were dressed."

"Well," she said, "they wore shirts and pants and heavy boots, like everybody else hereabouts."

"Were they dark or fair, handsome or ugly?" Rick asked.

"I—I was too scared to notice," Sarah Rose murmured.

Rick questioned her patiently for a long time, but she could add little to what she had already told him. The only information of substance she could supply was that neither appeared to have shaved for several days.

Refusing a cup of coffee, Rick stood. "I'm grateful for what I've learned," he said.

"Have some breakfast with us," Jane urged.

"Thanks, but I want to scour the whole area. I'm going to talk to everybody who lives within a radius of twenty miles."

"Then come back tonight for supper with us," she said.

"And spend the night, too," her husband added.

Rick's expression did not change. "You're good

friends, and I won't forget your kindness," he replied. "But I'll be too busy to waste any time eating or sleeping."

Tireless and grim, he visited every home in the region, his patience remarkable as he sought further information. Only one neighbor could help him. This man had been leaving his house at daybreak, intending to go off to the gold fields, when he had seen two men, one exceptionally tall and the other exceptionally heavy, both dark-haired, driving a wagon filled with all sorts of belongings.

"That figures," Rick said. "Blame near everybody in the area lost something, and the horse and wagon probably belonged to Andy Smith, who says his workhorse and cart were stolen."

Several deputies joined Rick in the search, but no other facts of consequence were uncovered.

Saying nothing to anyone about his own plans for the future, Rick dismissed the hired hands who had worked on his wife's property and then insisted on making a gift of her ten head of cattle to the Fosters. As nearly as anyone could gather, he intended to close the ranch house.

Everyone in the area came to Elisabeta Miller's graveside funeral, at which a clergyman from Sacramento officiated. At Rick's request, she was buried on their property, in a small grove some distance from the house.

Many of the women who were present wept openly, and some of the men had tears in their eyes, too. Rick stood apart from the other mourners, his face as hard and seemingly as empty as that of a grizzled Indian warrior. After the ceremony the minister tried to comfort him with a few words, but Rick appeared not to hear him. The silent widower seemed rooted to the spot as John Foster and his sons filled in the grave.

Then Jane approached him and touched his arm. "Rick," she said softly. When he turned to her, she saw that his eyes were hard and bitter, the haunted eyes of a man who would not and could not rest until he had had revenge.

"We have a spare room," she said. "John and I would like it very much if you would come to live with us for a spell."

He shook his head. "I appreciate the offer, Jane."

"You'd be no bother, and you'd be free to come and go as you please. We always have plenty of food on the table, what with the way my children eat, so there would be more than enough any time you decided to have a meal with us."

"Someday, maybe, I'll take you and John up on that offer," he said. "Meantime, help yourselves to the fruit in Elisabeta's orchard and to the vegetables in her garden. She always thought of you people as her best friends." John Foster had overheard the conversation, and shovel still in hand, he mopped his face with a bandanna as he joined them. "What will you do now, Rick?" he asked.

"For the present," Rick said, "I'm boarding up the house."

"Where will you sleep?"

"I've already had a cot brought into my office in Sacramento."

"But where will you eat?" Jane wanted to know.

He shrugged. "There are enough taverns and inns in Sacramento these days. It doesn't much matter. I don't have all that much interest in food. But never fear," he added, making a totally unsuccessful effort to smile, "I'll be dropping in on you frequently. I'll be riding out this way often to pay my respects to Elisabeta."

Never had either of the Fosters seen anyone so lonely. Only his eyes were alive, and the cold, unyielding determination in them was frightening.

John placed an arm around his wife's shoulders, his pressure indicating it would be wise to leave. "You know where to find us," he said, "and you also know we'll be expecting you to share a meal with us. Regularly."

Rick nodded.

Shepherding their silent children ahead of them, the Fosters took their leave. They looked back as they reached the crest of a hill about fifty yards down the road and saw Rick standing beside his wife's grave, still dry-eyed, his head bowed.

Rick stood motionless for what seemed like an eternity, unaware of the passage of time, the scent of the roses in the garden, or the whispering of the soft breeze that rustled the leaves on the trees. Only as sundown approached did he stir.

"Elisabeta, my dearest love," he said in a caressing tone that no one but his late wife had ever heard, "you were truly my love. I loved you as I never knew I could love anyone, and I'll cherish your memory to the end of my days." For a time he was silent, and when he spoke again his voice was so harsh that his stallion, tethered to a nearby tree, suddenly pricked up his ears.

"I promise you, Elisabeta," he said, "that I'll find the scum who tortured and murdered you. No matter what I must do, no matter how long it takes, I swear to you before Almighty God that I'll bring them to justice. And I won't rest until they're dead."

Tears rolled unheeded down his tanned face as he turned away from the grave.

Cathy Blake held the reins as she sat on the board of her small wagon, then turned toward the dark-haired Ginny Mullins, who sat beside her. "I honestly don't know why we shake our heads when we hear stories about life in the Sacramento Valley these days," she said. "San Francisco isn't what I'd call tame."

Ginny laughed aloud and looked at the armed escort surrounding them. Her husband, Hector, was in the lead, the flap of his holster open, his hand close to his pistol. The eight soldiers of the cavalry troop were equally grim, braced for possible trouble as they rode up the hill after accompanying the two women on a shopping trip. "If anyone had told me I'd need this kind of protection when all I wanted was a length of calico to make some new clothes for my baby and to shop for a few odds and ends, I wouldn't have believed it."

"Nor would I. The problem, of course, is that there are so few decent women in San Francisco now. Every man who sees us instantly jumps to the wrong conclusion. I suggested to Lee that I could go shopping alone if I disguised myself as a very old lady, but he wasn't amused."

"I wouldn't think so," Ginny replied. "The men in this town remind me of the pack of half-starved coyotes we saw in the Wyoming mountains at the end of the winter our wagon train spent there. Remember?"

"I'll never forget them," Cathy said. "Those coyotes were ready to tear us apart, and so are the men who come to California these days."

"I feel sorry for the ladies who aren't protected by the troops and walls of the Presidio," Ginny said, shuddering. "It must be horrible for them, trying to lead normal lives."

"It isn't possible when one lives in a house somewhere in the city, I'm told."

"When do you suppose it will end, Cathy?"

"I have no idea. A delegation of citizens is meeting with Lee this afternoon to discuss the problem. In fact, they were so insistent the meeting be informal that they're getting together at our house instead of in Lee's office." As they drove through the gates, she gestured toward the spacious quarters of the commanding general.

"I hope they find some solution," Ginny said.

"I pray for it, Ginny. After I pick up Beth at the garrison school may I bring her to your house for a visit. She loves to play with the baby and that way we won't be disturbing the men at their meeting."

Ginny readily agreed.

Brigadier General Lee Blake, standing near the parlor windows, was privately relieved when he saw the women and their escort moving down the main road of the Presidio. It was easier for him to concentrate on the business at hand, now that he knew his wife was safe. He looked at his guests one by one; the solemn-faced Mayor White, the hotel owner, the banker, and the newspaper publisher. "As I'm certain you realize, gentlemen," he said, locking his hands behind his back, "I'm in total sympathy with your plight. I regret, as much as you do, the fact that federal law prohibits the use of my troops to police the town in any situation except a grave emergency."

"The trouble is that there are emergencies every day, sometimes every hour," the publisher said, his expression grim.

"I've already exceeded the city budget," Mayor White declared, "but I'd still need to quadruple the constabulary to have an effective police force. And even if the money were available, I couldn't find enough reliable, honest men to hire."

"I know all too well what you mean," the banker said. "My wife hasn't left our house in weeks, and she wants me to sell the bank and go back to the East."

"You can't do that, Bob," the alarmed hotel owner said. "You're badly needed here."

"I'm well aware of it, just as I recognize the opportunities here. But let me go into some detail for you. Normally four constables are on permanent duty at the bank, but the volume of gold passing through our hands these days is so great that I augmented the force with twelve armed guards of our own. So a couple of weeks ago I had a bright idea. I intended to hire some men who would guard Jean whenever she leaves the house. I planned to put them on my private payroll. I conducted interviews for more hours than I could count, and I found precisely two men to hire. For the present they're on the bank's staff, but there's no way a woman as handsome as Jean could leave the house with only two guards to protect her. She'd need a half-dozen."

"I know you're not exaggerating, Bob," Lee said. "But I hope none of you are losing sight of the fact that there are many respectable, solid citizens in San Francisco. There must be twenty physicians in the city, and certainly as many lawyers. There are honest, hardworking shopkeepers, not to mention carpenters, masons, and other artisans who haven't given in to the madness of hunting for gold."

"There are as many honest, decent citizens as there are riffraff," the publisher declared, "but they're intimidated by those who have nothing to lose when they steal and create riots. We're well aware that there's a substantial core of people here who share our disgust with the current situation. That's why we asked for this meeting with you, General."

"I've twice petitioned the territorial legislature to ask President Taylor to issue a decree that will make this entire portion of California an emergency area," Lee said. "Then my troops will be on duty whenever they're needed, day and night. But the legislature is too proud to admit that help is needed. The members won't budge."

"How well I know it," Mayor White said. "I've argued with them until I'm hoarse, but only the representatives from San Francisco, Sacramento, and the Valley are on our side. The others refuse to admit that justice has become a farce here."

"It was just last month," the publisher said, "that a mob burned down the jail after releasing two murderers and about fifteen thieves convicted of grand larceny. I doubt if anything would move them, short of Judge Hilbert's assassination!"

In the silence that followed, the banker looked at each of his colleagues in turn, then faced the army officer again. "Lee, what's your view of vigilante groups?"

"I've always been opposed to the principle of allowing private citizens to take the law into their own hands. There are certain to be abuses when the same people act as accusers and prosecutors, judges and juries and executioners."

"We were afraid you'd feel that way," the publisher said regretfully.

"Hold on, I'm not done yet," Lee said. "Recently my family and I were shocked by the murder of Elisabeta Miller in the Valley. She was the wife of Sheriff Rick Miller and one of my own wife's closest friends. Since her death, I haven't felt the same way about law and order."

The banker looked at the others. "I told you he'd cooperate with us."

"Not so fast, Bob," the hotel owner said. "General, may we rely on your discretion?"

"Certainly," Lee said without hesitation, easily guessing what he was about to hear.

"In recent days," the hotel owner said, "a vigilance committee has been formed in San Francisco. We believe that this is just the first of many such committees that will be formed here. So many people are sick and tired of living in terror and being abused that I—ah—have been told on good authority that the present committee already has two hundred members."

"The membership rolls will be closed when the number reaches three hundred," the publisher declared, then added hastily, "or so we're informed. One of the unique features of the organization is that membership is secret. Each man knows only the other four members of his own unit. If a committee member should be hauled into court and compelled to name names, he could incriminate no more than four others."

"Officially," the banker said, "Mayor White has never heard of the vigilance committee."

"In the immediate future," the mayor said, "our city constables are being informed—verbally, never in writing—about the existence of the vigilance committee. Our poor constabulary is so overworked and weary that I have no doubt that every policeman will find it a simple matter to close his eyes when he sees a vigilance group in action."

"How much action is contemplated?" Lee asked.

"Whatever may be needed," the publisher said harshly. "Murderers will be hanged, and so will anyone who commits armed robbery. Arsonists, women molesters, and ordinary thieves will be tarred, feathered, and escorted out of town. I sincerely hope that no innocents will suffer."

"The executive unit of the vigilance committee has fewer than five members, or so we've been given to understand," the banker said, speaking carefully. "We've been assured that these men are honorable people who intend to keep a tight rein on their subordinates. They think this goal can be achieved by restricting the total membership to three hundred men."

"Will they carry firearms?"

"We're told that at the moment only a few own arms," the hotel owner said, "But that situation is being rectified. The formation of this particular committee has been in the planning stage for some time, and we've—ah—been informed that a shipload of rifles is being sent from New York by clipper. We also hear that pistols and ammunition are coming by wagon train by way of Independence."

"Only the U.S. Army garrison here at the Presidio has the strength to disrupt the committee and force it to disband," the banker said. "Off the record, Lee, do you think that might happen?"

"It wasn't so long ago," Lee said, "that I would have done everything in my not inconsiderable power, gentlemen, to halt you—I mean, to halt the executive unit of the vigilance committee. But when I think of Elisabeta Miller's untimely death—and the need to assign a cavalry escort for my wife on the infrequent occasions she needs to buy goods in town—I'm forced to reconsider the situation."

The tension in the room dissipated rapidly.

"Do we assume correctly, General," the hotel owner asked, "that your troops will continue to be available in situations of major crisis that the vigilance committee won't be able to handle?"

"You may be sure," Lee replied, "that the troops of this garrison will continue to do their duty and will act with dispatch in emergencies."

The others rose, and the newspaper publisher rubbed his hands together. "This has worked out better than any of us dared to hope, General."

"I hope you understand," Lee said, "that if the vigilance committee engages in excesses that violate the spirit of American justice, it will be necessary for me to intervene. For the present I know nothing about the formation of the vigilance committee. In fact, this afternoon's meeting has never taken place. But if you—the committee, that is—go too far, I'll have to consult the three judges of the federal district court who are currently stationed in the territory. Frankly, I'll be influenced by their opinions, and if they should concur in my view that the committee must be disbanded, I'll act accordingly."

"You need have no fears, Lee," the banker said. "The activities of the committee will be under control at all times. Only those who understand the need for discipline and won't engage in personal vendettas are being accepted as members. The screening unit is very conscientious."

Lee shook hands with his guests as he escorted them to the door.

The hotel proprietor grinned for the first time. "I hope that in the very near future," he said, "my wife and I will be able to entertain all of you at dinner and that none of you will need armed escorts to guard the ladies as you travel to and from the hotel. Perhaps it isn't too much to hope that San Francisco soon will become a civilized community."

The clipper's passengers came ashore in small groups by boat after the majestic ship dropped her anchor in a natural harbor on the Caribbean side of the Isthmus of Panama. The jungle foliage was dense —a wild tangle of trees, bushes, vines, and undergrowth. The scene was desolate. There appeared to be only one clearing, in which stood a number of dilapidated fishing huts, nothing more. Not until the following year, 1850, would Americans constructing the trans-Panama railroad initiate the building of what would become the city of Colón.

Ralph Hamilton stood on the sandy beach, beside him his leather box containing his clothes and other possessions, and stared at the graceful palm trees on the fringe of the jungle. Other passengers clustered in groups nearby, none of them certain of what to do next.

The clipper's first officer, supervising the landing, was directing the beaching of two more boats filled with California-bound gold seekers, and Ralph hailed him.

"Where are the guides who are supposed to take us to Panama City, on the Pacific?" he asked.

The ship's officer shrugged. "Damned if I know, mister. It's plain they're not here."

"Are they expected soon?" Ralph tried to hide his feeling of annoyance.

The first officer became belligerent. "Look here. The owners of our company made a deal with some Colombians to provide guides. It isn't our fault if they aren't here; and if they don't show up, there's nothing we can do about it. You folks will have to make your own way to Panama City."

"Your advertisements led me to believe—"

"You can believe anything you want, mister. You don't have a written contract that guarantees you the services of guides. We'll stand by our statement that the schooner sailing from Panama City four days from now will provide you transportation to San Francisco. Transportation you've already paid for. But you'll have to get to Panama City yourself."

Ralph's knowledge of the law told him there was

nothing he could do to change the situation. After he
arrived in California, perhaps, he could institute a
lawsuit against the clipper's owners; but, as the mate
had pointed out, the absence of a written contract
would make it difficult to collect. Besides, a lawsuit
would not solve his immediate problem.

"How far is it to Panama City?"

The ship's officer grinned. "About forty miles, more
or less. You should be able to get there in three or
four days." He walked away abruptly, terminating the
conversation.

The idea of getting to Panama City alone was
ludicrous. It was almost forty miles through some of
the worst jungle known in the world. Ralph decided
he would have to find some natives to act as guides,
though he guessed he would be charged an outrageous fee for their services.

He walked up to a group of natives sitting next to a
shack on the beach. He remembered seeing these men
help unload the small boats that had come to shore,
but they had seemed to do very little work and had
asked for great sums of money. Now they were sitting
around a small, improvised table, playing some kind
of a game with crudely fashioned dice.

Ralph addressed the men repeatedly, speaking in
English and Spanish, until one of them looked up. "I
wonder if you men would be willing to escort me
through this jungle," Ralph said.

The man who had looked up went back to his
game. Ralph, his patience wearing thin, repeated the
question.

"No go, no go," the native said, waving Ralph
away.

"I am willing to pay you well," Ralph said, taking
out a number of bills.

"No want money. Got plenty money." He smiled
as he patted the pocket of his battered trousers. "Only
crazy man go through jungle."

It was clear that, ludicrous or not, Ralph was going

to have to make the trek by himself. Certainly there would be danger, but he believed his mettle would stand him in good stead. He was determined to go on.

Some of the other passengers were already picking up the small sacks containing their only earthly possessions, and small groups were heading uncertainly into the jungle. Ralph watched them, realizing that these people, too, had tried in vain to get someone to assist them and were forced to travel unescorted.

Someone came up beside him and plucked his sleeve. "Take me with you, mister."

The speaker, Ralph saw, was a very young boy, tall and ungainly, who was outgrowing his threadbare clothes. "Who are you?"

"Isaiah Atkins, sir."

"How old are you?"

"Sixteen."

"Tell the truth, Isaiah!"

The boy shuffled his feet in the sand. "I'm thirteen, sir."

"That's more like it. How does it happen I didn't see you on board?"

Staring down at the ground, the boy made up his mind not to lie again. "I—I ran away from the orphanage in Brooklyn. I hated it there. I stowed away on the clipper, and at night I sneaked into the galley for food. Now I'm scared." He spoke bluntly, defiantly.

Ralph's heart went out to a lad who had demonstrated both courage and skill but who now found himself in a situation beyond his depth. "I'm Ralph Hamilton," he said, extending his hand, "and it appears I've just acquired a junior partner."

Isaiah's eyes shone. "You won't regret this, Mr. Hamilton!" he said fervently.

"We'll soon find out. Can you handle firearms?" Perhaps it was wrong to trust the boy, but Ralph was following his instincts.

"You bet, sir!"

"Here." Ralph handed him a pistol. "This is loaded, so be careful. Stand guard over my luggage, if you will, while I attend to an errand that's important to both of us." He turned and walked off in the direction of the fishing village.

Survival was his first consideration, and the prospect of making his way through forty miles of a wild jungle made him uneasy. He and the boy would need food on the journey, so he wanted to buy what he could from the fishermen.

An old man sat in the shade of a mud hut, his back propped against the wall, shielding himself from the blazing sun. From beneath the broad brim of a frayed straw hat, he gazed at the stranger, his face expressionless.

Ralph addressed him courteously, speaking in Spanish. "Good morning, sir. I hope you are well."

The dark, leathery face cracked into a wide, toothless grin.

"I wonder, sir, if I could make a purchase of great importance to me. I am journeying to the Pacific and need food that will enable my companion and me to reach our destination."

"You will need more than food to see you there. You will also need much luck." Saying no more, the old man heaved himself to his feet, then led Ralph to a bin behind the hut, a curious receptacle placed on stilts to prevent ants and other insects from reaching it.

Ralph was in luck. The old man was willing to sell him substantial quantities of dried fish and ground maize suitable for eating, which he placed in a basket woven from plantain leaves. The price, ten dollars, was outrageous, and the old man looked startled when his customer handed him the fee without bargaining.

Ralph hurried back to where he had left the boy, slowing his pace abruptly when he saw Isaiah surrounded by a half-dozen men whose attitude was menacing.

"Keep clear, I warn you," the youth shouted. "This gun is loaded!"

"You wouldn't try to hurt us, would you, sonny?" A bearded man edged closer.

Ralph placed the basket on the ground. Then he removed the cover from his sword cane and drew his other pistol. "Maybe he wouldn't," he called, "but I won't hesitate to put a bullet through the first one of you who lays a hand on the boy or my leather box!"

The men turned to face him and immediately recognized the aloof gentleman who had engaged in accurate target practice on board the clipper. "Let's rush him!" the bearded man said.

"I wouldn't if I were you," Ralph said quietly. "Isaiah, bring the box to me."

The boy picked up the case by its handle and backed toward his new friend, continuing to aim his pistol at the men who were grouped together. Ralph was well aware of the greed in their eyes. "Stand close beside me," he said in a low tone to Isaiah. "When I give the word, switch pistols with me." Ralph took careful aim, then squeezed the trigger and put his bullet through the crown of the bearded man's dilapidated hat.

Isaiah needed no order to change pistols with him.

"If you take a single step closer," Ralph said, his voice conversational, "I'll kill one of you with my next shot. And if that doesn't discourage you, I won't hesitate to decapitate another with my sword. I assure you, gentlemen, that I won't hesitate to protect my property."

The color had drained from the bearded man's face as he examined the neat hole in his hat. "We got us a long way to walk," he said. "We better be on our way."

No one disputed the suggestion, and the entire group headed into the jungle.

Ralph waited until they vanished from sight before sitting on the leather box, motioning the boy to a place beside him, then producing ammunition.

"You've passed the test with flying colors, Isaiah," he said as he methodically reloaded the weapons. "Now we're truly partners."

The boy smiled. "They wanted your leather case, but I wasn't going to give it to them. You trusted me, Mr. Hamilton."

"Would you have shot one of them?"

"Sure, if I'd had to."

Ralph knew he meant it and was satisfied. "I've bought some food that will see us through our journey. Have you had any experience in making your way through jungles?"

"No, sir."

"Neither have I, so we'll be starting as equals. Here, we'll put these supplies in the box. And to be on the safe side, you'd better carry a pistol." Ralph handed the boy a weapon.

Isaiah took it gratefully. "I've always had a good sense of direction. Maybe I can be of some help."

"I'm sure you can." Ralph drew a rough sketch in the sand with the toe of a boot. "This is Panama," he said. "We're here. Our destination is Panama City on the Pacific, which is here, approximately."

The boy studied the sketch, then looked around to orient himself. Obviously taking his responsibility seriously, he was memorizing their present position and their destination.

Ralph noted that all the other passengers were gone. The beach was deserted now, and the clipper was weighing anchor, her captain having decided to go elsewhere for fresh water, putting the Isthmus of Panama behind him as soon as possible.

"We're on our way whenever you're ready," Ralph said. Isaiah grinned at him and hitched up his trousers.

They walked side by side past the fringe of palm trees. Soon after they entered the jungle, they found it nearly impenetrable. Masses of vines, creepers, and prickly bushes formed barriers between mammoth trees, and in places the growth underfoot was waist-high. Ralph took the lead, using his sword to hack a path.

The sun penetrated through the leaves of the towering trees only in isolated patches, but in spite of the gloom the heat was almost unbearable. Sweat ran in rivulets down Ralph's face, blinding him, and he was forced to tie a handkerchief around his forehead so he could see. The boy, although expending less effort, was soaked, too, and after a time he insisted on changing places with his protector. He looked too fragile for such brutally hard labor, but his stamina and strength were surprising, and he persevered doggedly.

There was mold everywhere, and in places the sickly sweet odor of rotting vegetation was overwhelming. Mosquitos whined angrily, incessantly, and occasionally swarms of flies, gnats, and other insects attacked the pair, making them miserable. But they struggled on, parched, their throats burning, and when they came to a pond, Isaiah dropped to one knee beside it, intending to drink. But a weary Ralph quickly tapped him on the shoulder and pointed silently. Two of their fellow passengers were lying dead on the ground, their sightless eyes staring blankly at the treetops. It was obvious they had consumed water from the pond.

Later in the day—neither was certain of the time—they saw an even grislier reminder of the jungle's power. They came across the body of a man whose flesh was being consumed by an army of large red ants, which formed a solid, shimmering mass on his face and body. A dilapidated hat with a hole in the crown lay nearby, and they realized who he was. They had no idea, however, what had killed him.

Isaiah shuddered. "If I'd known what this jungle would be like," he muttered, "I'd have stowed away in a wagon train."

They pushed on, growing tense whenever a rustling sound in the underbrush warned them of the proximity of an animal. But the creatures of the jungle appeared to be timid, and the pair remained un-harmed.

Late in the day Ralph knew they could not continue much longer, but he was encouraged when he found they were climbing toward higher ground, so he called on his reserves of stamina, hoping the boy could do the same. The sound of running water kept them going, and at last they came to a waterfall, the ground around it miraculously clear of trees and brush. Here, for better or worse, Ralph decided they would spend the night.

"Do you guess that water is all right to drink?" Isaiah asked, running his tongue across his parched, cracked lips. "Or do you suppose it has poison in it, like that pond?"

"We'll have to take our chances," Ralph said, know-ing they could not survive without water.

They drank at length from the pool at the base of the waterfall, and to their delight the water was cool, clear, and sweet. Then Isaiah made a remarkable discovery. "Look there, Mr. Hamilton," he said. "With that much water you'd think there'd be a river, but there isn't!"

Beyond the pool, for a distance of at least one hunded yards, Ralph could see nothing but high, thick grass. "The water must go into an underground river," he said. "Otherwise, this whole area would be a swamp."

They opened the leather box, removing a quantity of dried fish and ground maize, which they ate rav-enously.

"I saw two or three different kinds of fruit during the day," Isaiah said. "At least I think it was fruit."

"Our problem," Ralph replied, "is that we don't know what's edible and what's unsafe. We simply can't afford to take risks."

The boy nodded, then stiffened. He had dropped some crumbs, and huge black ants had appeared out of nowhere and were carrying them away.

"My leather box is so heavy and clumsy that I'm

tempted to leave it behind," Ralph said. "But we can't.
It's virtually airtight, no insects can get into it, and
we'll continue to carry it because our food is stored in
it, if for no other reason."

Isaiah was silent for a time. "What do you suppose
is happening to the other people from the clipper?" he
asked at last.

There was nothing to be gained by dwelling on that
question. "I'd rather not think about them," Ralph
said firmly. "We'll take turns keeping guard through
the night, and I suggest you get some sleep right now.
I estimate we covered no more than ten miles today,
at best, and we'll have to move faster tomorrow if we
hope to reach Panama City before our ship sails.
Otherwise, we might be there for a long time."

The boy looked at him in admiration. Here was a
man who was always planning his next move. Isaiah
silently congratulated himself for having selected a
protector well able to help him.

The night passed quietly. No animals appeared, the
insects vanished, and as Ralph kept watch for the
second time, he looked up at a tropical sky brilliant
with stars. He was mildly surprised to discover that
he was thinking of Prudence for the first time since
he had come ashore.

At daybreak they ate a breakfast of fish and maize,
and Ralph, after rummaging in his travel box, shared
with his companion what was left of a bottle of sack
he had brought with him, the better part of it having
been consumed on board the clipper. Then he carefully filled the bottle with fresh water, corking it secure-
ly. "At least we have an emergency supply of water
now," he said, "so we're better off than we were
yesterday."

They descended from the heights, with Isaiah
pointing them in the right direction, and their march
became much like that of the previous day. The
insects reappeared in force at sunrise, the stench of
the jungle was overpowering, and the heat was intense. But Ralph refused to surrender to the forces of

nature and found his companion felt as he did. Isaiah was cheerful, unwilling to pause for rest even when he became groggy on his feet. Twice they came across fair-sized streams, and after satisfying themselves that the water was clear, they drank.

"We're learning," Ralph said. "If water is still, don't touch it. If water is running, it seems safe to drink."

Early in the afternoon they came to a stretch of jungle thick with hanging vines, and Ralph had to slash at them repeatedly in order to clear a path. All at once a particularly thick vine seemed to come alive, and dropping from the overhanging branch of a tall tree, it began to wrap itself around Ralph.

The stunned man realized he was in the grip of a huge snake, its skin shiny and undulating. It was taking a tighter and tighter hold, squeezing the breath from his body. Unable to draw his pistol, he made an effort to remain standing, although he knew that at any moment he would topple to the ground. His arms were pinned to his sides, his useless sword cane fell to the ground, and he realized that his remaining life span could be measured in seconds.

Isaiah's voice rose to a high-pitched scream as he shouted, "I can't shoot the serpent! My aim isn't that good, and I'm afraid I'll hit you!"

Ralph had too little breath in his lungs to reply. He tried frantically to free himself, but the snake's hold became still firmer.

In spite of his terror Isaiah did not give in to the panic that assailed him. Darting forward he picked up the fallen sword cane. Unsheathing the sword, he gripped it by the hilt with both hands and conquered his fear sufficiently to bring the blade down with all his might at the back end of the snake's long, ugly head. The creature was badly wounded, but still did not ease its viselike grip.

Isaiah, sobbing, struck repeatedly, the blade sometimes missing Ralph by inches, and after what seemed like a very long time, he succeeded in severing the snake's head from its body. The heavy coils fell away, setting Ralph free, but the tail thrashed convulsively. Shuddering, Isaiah could not tear his gaze from the tail that still seemed alive.

Ralph needed some moments to regain his breath and composure, and then he took the sword from the boy's grasp, which was still so tight that his knuckles were white. "Thank you, Isaiah," he said. "You've saved my life—and I won't forget it."

By common, unspoken consent, they made a detour around the area of hanging vines before they started forward again. The enemies of man were omnipresent in the tropical jungle, and that knowledge gave the man and the boy only more determination. They pushed on relentlessly until they were ready to drop.

A growing familiarity with the jungle enabled them to find a somewhat smaller clearing on relatively high ground, and they were pleased when they found a small stream flowing through the open area. The water was warm, but a taste convinced them it was pure, and they drank their fill before eating and settling down for the night. After the encounter with the snake they were too exhausted to exchange more than a few remarks.

Before Isaiah dropped off to sleep, however, Ralph said, encouragingly, "We covered far more ground today. With luck we may reach Panama City in another day."

That night he prayed aloud. He had been so busy achieving success as an attorney that he hadn't set foot in a church in more years than he could recall. But here, in this wilderness more primitive than the forests of North America where he had hunted in his youth, he felt close to God again. "Lord," he said softly, "see my young friend and me through our travail, and I'll never fail to honor You again."

In the morning, when they resumed their journey after their usual breakfast, Isaiah started to laugh. "We smell as bad as this jungle," he said.

Ralph had to agree. Certainly Prudence wouldn't know him now, nor would any of his New York colleagues. His hair was matted, bristle covered his face, and his clothes were torn. But he was alive, eager to go on, and with enough of the fish and maize left for one more meal, he felt confident that he and the boy would reach their goal.

Again they plodded for hour after hour, and when they came to open sections, where there was thick shale underfoot and large boulders dotting the area, they were pleased that they had no need to cut a path for themselves. Soon, however, they came to dread such areas. The sun beat down on them mercilessly, and every step was agonizing.

Both were exhausted when they came to a large open space late in the afternoon. The sun, which had moved far to the west, shone directly into their eyes, half-blinding them, and they stumbled as they plodded through the ankle-deep shale.

Neither then nor at any later time did Ralph understand how his instinct for self-preservation prompted him to halt and shield his eyes. So startled that he could not call out a warning to Isaiah, who was in the lead, he saw an animal poised at the top of a boulder, preparing to leap down onto the unsuspecting boy below him.

The animal resembled a very large dog. Muscular and lithe, it had a lionlike head, and its reddish-brown fur blended almost perfectly with the color of the high rock on which it was poised.

Ralph reacted without thinking, snatching his pistol from his belt and simultaneously cocking it with his thumb. The beast opened its mouth in a silent snarl as it gathered to spring, and as it launched into space, Ralph fired.

The animal landed on the shale only inches from Isaiah and collapsed.

Ralph ran forward, prepared to run the beast through with his sword, but it was unnecessary. His bullet had entered the roof of the animal's mouth and had passed through the brain and out the back of its head.

"Now you've evened the score, Mr. Hamilton," Isaiah said in a shaking voice. "You've saved my life."

Ralph studied the dead animal. "That's the first Colombian puma I've ever seen. They're found through Central and South America, or so I've read. Either this specimen was very hungry or the author whose work I read was mistaken when he said they infrequently attack humans."

In spite of the narrowness of his escape, Isaiah had to laugh. Not only was Mr. Hamilton's poise remarkable, but his knowledge was encyclopedic.

Suddenly Ralph raised his head. "Listen!"

The boy strained. "It sounds like thunder."

"It's far better than thunder. Come along!" Ralph took the lead, and after moving through a small patch of jungle that lay on the far side of the shale field, they saw a vast expanse of blue-green water, with waves crashing on a long expanse of yellow sand.

"The Pacific?" Isaiah asked in wonder.

Ralph nodded, and together they moved closer to the water. At least a mile or more to their left they saw a ship riding at anchor, and beyond it they made out some church spires and several buildings of three and four stories. "Panama City," Ralph said. "Your sense of direction is astonishing, Isaiah. Now we've got to make ourselves presentable."

Without further ado he stripped off his clothes and ran into the surf, where he swam with long, purposeful strokes. The boy hesitated, then followed his example. Unable to swim, however, he did not venture into deep water.

"Clean at last!" Ralph shouted, his glee making him sound as young as Isaiah.

They spent a long time in the refreshing sea, and when they came ashore again, Ralph removed his razor, a mug of soft, yellow soap, and a small hand mirror from his leather box. "Saltwater isn't ideal for shaving, but one uses what one must." When he completed his toilet, he looked disgustedly at the crumpled heap of soiled clothing. "Obviously we can't wear those rags again."

"I don't have anything else," the boy said.

"Nonsense. Partners always share, and although my clothes will be a trifle large on you, you'll make do."

A few minutes later both were dressed, with Isaiah wearing one of his protector's shirts and a pair of his trousers. Only his boots were his own.

The transformation in Ralph was astonishing. His frock coat fitted him to perfection, his cravat of black silk was precisely tied beneath his upstanding collar of starched, white linen, and under one arm he carried a tall-crowned beaver hat, with his sheathed sword cane held jauntily under his arm.

"Now," he said, "we'll pay a call on the ship's master."

Isaiah became alarmed. "I can't go with you, Mr. Hamilton," he said. "I'll have to try my luck stowing away."

"Boy," Ralph said severely, "you still fail to grasp the principles of partnerships. We share. I shall attend to the details of your passage." He started off down the beach briskly, seemingly impervious to the heat, and Isaiah had to struggle to keep up with him.

After a short walk they came to the teeming town, where Ralph loftily ignored the stares of passersby, the shouts of merchants who offered wares ranging from tropical fruits to bolts of cloth at open-air stalls, and the solicitations of heavily painted young women. Following the waterfront, he came at last to a dock where a ship's boat was tied. Four sailors who stood on the wharf, chatting, broke off when Ralph approached them.

"What ship is that?" he demanded.

The bo's'n's mate in charge of the gig was struck by his air of authority and raised a hand in a half-salute. "The *Lisolette Thoman,* out of Oregon, sir. The flagship of the Thoman and Canning fleet. With Mr. Thoman himself in command after the regular captain got sick the night before we sailed," he added proudly.

"I assume this is the ship taking the clipper passengers to California?"

"Yes, sir."

"Splendid. Be good enough to take us to your ship's master." Ralph stepped into the boat, placing his leather box beside him, and Isaiah followed. The crew seemingly had no choice and rowed him out to the schooner.

The tall Paul Thoman, standing on deck, could not believe he was actually seeing a resplendent gentleman wearing a beaver hat. Ralph climbed up the ladder, allowing the crew to bring the case containing his belongings. Bowing stiffly, he introduced himself and the boy.

"Paul Thoman, senior partner of Thoman and Canning, who own and operate this ship." Paul had seen many strange sights after leaving Harvard College, spending a year as a mountain man in the Rockies, and then migrating to Oregon on the first wagon train, but he had never encountered anyone like this immaculately attired man in the tropics.

"I was one of the party that booked passage to San Francisco on this vessel," Ralph said.

"I remember your name from the manifest."

"I would like to pay for my young friend's passage and to secure two private cabins, no matter how small they may be." He took his wallet from his pocket, prepared to pay at once.

Paul grinned at him. "Never mind the money," he said. "We'll be sailing half-empty because at least half of the clipper's passengers haven't made the journey through the jungle. I'm delaying our sailing for forty-eight hours, but I'm afraid many of them won't make it." He paused, then asked, "You did sail on the clipper to the Caribbean side of the Isthmus?"

"Indeed, sir."

"And you crossed through the jungle?"

Ralph nodded. "We encountered a few problems," he said. Isaiah Atkins stifled a giggle.

"Come along to the aft deck for a drink, sir," Paul said. "You, too, lad. We'll have some lemonade made for you. I've got to hear about this journey of yours. As Shakespeare asked in *Julius Caesar*, 'Shall we play the wantons with our woes, and make some pretty match in shedding tears?' "

Ralph cleared his throat as they walked toward a table placed in the open to catch whatever slight breeze might be blowing. "Forgive me for correcting you, but I believe that quotation is from *Richard II*."

"Quite so." Paul was unabashed, his wife having corrected his quotations for years. "You're not only a man of learning, sir, but I believe I detect a New England accent."

"Connecticut." Ralph removed his hat as they took chairs. "Yale College and Yale Law School."

"Boston," Paul said. "Harvard." He turned and shouted, "Steward, bring the good whiskey. Let it never be said that a Harvard man entertained a Yale man in a shoddy manner. Now, sir, how in thunderation did you hack your way through one of the world's nastiest jungles and come out looking as though you're about to pay a call on President Taylor at the White House?"

Ralph related the story of their adventures, his account so dry and understated that Isaiah felt compelled to interrupt frequently.

Paul made sure that a glass of lemonade was brought for the boy, then poured two drinks of whiskey, which he mixed with water. "Here's to you, sir." Ralph raised his glass in return.

"You've never visited California, I take it. Well, take my word that San Francisco is a madhouse, and the entire Sacramento Valley is even worse. Are you intending to look for gold?"

"Not necessarily," Ralph said. "I've never believed

in the philosophy that one can attain great wealth in return for little or no labor."

Paul nodded. "Precisely my own sentiments, but there are few in California who see things the way we do. I don't mind telling you I'll pause there just long enough to drop off my passengers, have dinner with General and Mrs. Blake, who are old friends, and sail on to Oregon. Any man who has negotiated the Panama jungle and come out as you have obviously can take care of himself, but I hope you won't mind a word of advice."

"I'll hear it gladly."

"Whatever you plan to do there, however you plan to earn a living," Paul said, "be careful. The vicious creatures in the territory these days are more numerous than the pumas in the jungles of Panama. And the influences there are so insidious that honorable men change their colors frequently. It was John Dryden who expressed it best when he wrote, 'Vice is a monster of so frightful mien, As to be hated, needs but to be seen; Yet seen too oft, familiar with her face, We first endure, then pity, then embrace.' "

Ralph didn't have the heart to correct him, to tell him that the lines that had been famous for more than a century had been written by Alexander Pope. The warning itself was sound, and he knew that what lay ahead for him in California might be dangerous as well as difficult. But having survived the terrors of Panama's tropical jungle, he was looking forward to the challenge.

The little wagon train's journey across the deserts and mountains of the New Mexico territory was arduous but uneventful. Thanks to Randy Gregg's familiarity with the area, overnight halts were made at places where water was available and there was forage for the horses. Patrols of U.S. Cavalry roamed through the region, but their presence wasn't necessary to curb the Indians who made their homes there. The

Apache, Navaho, and other nations still regarded the Americans as their deliverers from the yoke of Mexico, and relations had not yet deteriorated to the point that open hostilities would break out.

The journey was wearying, nevertheless, and the members of the party were relieved when they reached California. They made their way to the Pacific, where they stopped in Los Angeles for supplies, and then began to move up the San Joaquin Valley toward Sacramento. The end was drawing near, and they began to think in terms of what awaited them in the Sacramento Valley. No one was immune from the sense of growing anticipation.

Phyllis Gregg, who had been voluntarily adding to her chores and no longer sulking as frequently as before, best expressed the new spirit one evening when the group was just outside of Los Angeles. They sat at supper around the campfire on a bluff overlooking the Pacific Ocean. "My brother," she announced, "has caught gold fever."

John Gregg smiled but made no comment as he continued to eat his stew of buffalo meat. His sister couldn't resist teasing him. "Don't be shy," she said. "Repeat what you told me earlier today."

"All right, I will." John's handsome face became serious. "Pa has worked for fifty years, and he's still in harness. If I know you, Pa, you'll buy yourself a new farm somewhere in the Sacramento Valley. You'll be at work by dawn every morning, and you won't stop until nightfall. With all due respect to you, that life isn't for me."

Randy watched his son, listening carefully, but continued to spear his food with his knife and chew each mouthful slowly.

"There's a fortune to be made in the gold fields," John went on. "And if others are making it, so can I. It doesn't matter how many hours I've got to put into prospecting every day because the rewards are worth it."

Danny Taylor responded, "I'm aiming to look for

gold, too, but I'm not counting on miracles. The way I understand it, not everyone makes a strike."

"I will." John was jaunty with self-confidence.

Jerome Hadley looked around the circle, his expression smug. "Looking for gold is too much of a gamble for me," he said. "I prefer to invest in ventures that will bring me certain returns."

An adoring Melissa Austin nodded emphatically, approving the stand he was taking, and he stroked her hand.

Heather Taylor had to avert her gaze. It seemed to her that Jerome's gesture was calculated, that he was deliberately rewarding Melissa for her loyalty in the way that a pet dog was given a tidbit in return for its fidelity.

Randy looked around the circle. "You young'uns have your ways, but I'll keep mine," he said. "Johnny is right about me. Sure, I'll probably get me a new farm. On a land claim, if it's available, or with cash if it ain't. Hellfire, farmin' is the only thing I've knowed all my life. You work the soil, and it gives you food. There's no better way for a man t' get along."

Heather was forced to admit to herself that he was right. The lure of gold had faded within her on the long journey, the basic values she had been taught by her hard-working Scottish parents having reasserted themselves. At the same time, however, she realized she had to be fair to Danny, who still hoped to find gold. Their overall plan was sound: they would acquire land and work it while he searched for the yellow metal that, if found, would make them wealthy. But even if he failed, their future would be secure, and so she had no intention of telling him that her own ardor for the project had cooled.

Right now she had more important things to discuss with him. With Phyllis and Melissa helping her, she washed the supper dishes and pots, then joined her husband on the back stoop of their wagon, where he was looking up at the star-filled sky.

"What have you been thinking?" she asked.

Danny shrugged. "Not much of anything. No, that isn't really true. I guess I've been daydreaming. There are so many things I want for you. After I make my strike, we'll get us a house full of the best furniture that's made back East. I'll buy one of those new carriages with metal springs, and then we'll get a team of lively, matched bays to pull it. If they have the silks for fine dresses in San Francisco, we'll get the material there. Otherwise, we'll send to New York for whole bolts of it—"

"I don't need or want all those things," Heather said. "I've never craved luxuries. We were poor in Scotland, and Pa didn't start doing well until we migrated to Texas. So I have no need of fancy clothes and furniture to be happy."

Danny took her hand and held it. "Maybe not, but I want all those things for you."

"That isn't what's important in life."

"What is, then?" he demanded.

"Oh, bringing up the young to be honest and decent and good. Loving each other and loving our children." Heather gazed out at the Pacific, its waters almost black under the night sky.

Danny released her hand, gently took hold of her chin, and turned her face toward him. "Are you saying what I think you're trying to tell me?"

She nodded, her eyes glowing. "You've guessed right. I'm going to have a baby. I've suspected it, but I didn't want to mention it to you until I was sure."

He chuckled, then broke off abruptly and embraced her tenderly.

"Not out in the open where others can see us, Danny Taylor," she protested.

"I'm so happy and proud that I'll kiss you in front of the whole world!"

She yielded, raising her face to his. After a time they moved apart, although their shoulders still touched as they continued to sit side by side. Danny reached down, plucked a long blade of grass, and chewed on one end as he became lost in thought.

"Now," he said at last, "it's more important than ever that I find gold. I know how it feels to be hungry and cold and miserable, never able to call anything your own."

Vividly aware of his unhappy childhood, she could well understand why he felt as he did.

Setting his jaw, he spoke fervently. "I want our sons and daughters to have everything that money can buy!"

Heather felt a sudden stab of apprehension. The knowledge that he would be a father was already changing his attitude toward his coming hunt for gold. What had been exciting but peripheral was being transformed into what he regarded as a necessity.

IV

The change in the fortunes of Chet Harris and Wong Ke was as drastic as it was sudden. With the help of hired men, they built a substantial cabin on their new Bear River property and filled the place with furniture they acquired in Sacramento. They bought horses, too, which made it easier for them to travel to and from town. But they took precautions to insure that their good fortune did not become public knowledge.

The Bear River site where they had first found nuggets continued to yield gold steadily. Some days they had to pan for fairly long periods before finding any, but on occasion they picked up gold very quickly.

Their new wealth increased steadily, but the only outsider aware of their financial situation was the Sacramento gold dealer-banker who bought the nuggets and placed their proceeds in an ever-fattening account. Their profits already were substantial, but Ke, at least, had no intention of stopping.

"We keep taking gold from water as long as gold is

there," he said one night when they returned to their cabin.

"I reckon you're right," Chet replied, grinning. "We have enough money in the bank right now to go on a spree for months. But we could go hungry again after running out of funds."

"Ke never be hungry again. Keep taking gold from river until no more there. I work every day for next month, next year, next two years—however long we keep finding more gold. Someday we be very, very rich."

"The way our bank accounts are piling up," Chet said, lighting a fire in the hearth so they could dry themselves in front of it, "it won't take anywhere near a year to become filthy rich." He rubbed his hands together and chuckled. "That's when I'm going to start living high on the hog."

Wong Ke shook his head. "Not me. I going to invest money. I going to buy ranch and orchard. Maybe I invest in hotel or shipping company. So many people coming to California now that territory has all kinds of opportunities. Factories that make clothes could earn money. Or maybe make bricks for houses. All kinds of ways to put fortune to work."

"Well," Chet said, "I'm just hoping to pile up enough so I'll never have to do a day's work again."

"What you do instead?" his partner asked incredulously.

Chet waved expansively. "I'm going to make love to the best-looking women in California. I'm going to drink gallons of champagne. I'm going to have fancy suits and shirts and boots and hats made to my order. I'm going to take a whole suite of rooms in a hotel, and I'll have my meals sent to me there. All sorts of rare and wonderful dishes. Don't even ask what they'll be, because I don't know. Dishes I've never known existed."

Wong Ke was openly disappointed in him. "Maybe is not right for man always work, never rest," he said, "but is not right to throw away money, either."

Chet's expression became bleak, almost savage. "I never told you about my father, did I, Ke? Poor old Chester Harris. He and Ma had sons, one after another, and the more mouths he had to feed, the harder Pa worked. Even on holidays like Christmas and Independence Day, he worked. When I was little, I'd beg him to take me fishing or hunting, but he never had time. Then, all of a sudden, one day he up and died. Just like that. All those hours and weeks and months and years of nothing but hard labor caught up with him. Ma had a big brood to feed, so she sold our farm, and that's how we happened to join the first wagon train to Oregon."

Ke began to understand why Chet wanted to pursue pleasure so relentlessly. "In China is old saying," he said. "Gods give man eyes so he read and make mind smarter. If read enough, maybe he join gods in celestial sphere after he die."

"I'm more concerned with what happens in this world," Chet said emphatically. "And that reminds me. It isn't all that late, Ke. What do you say to a ride down to Big George's? That new batch of good Pennsylvania whiskey must have arrived by now. You can get salmon or trout or crabmeat fit for a king, and I've never found better beefsteak anywhere. While you're eating," he added, grinning slyly, "I'll renew my acquaintance with that little brunette from Chicago who calls herself the Eel. When she starts wriggling, you know for sure how she got that name."

Ke walked to a table and picked up a thick, leatherbound book. "This is history of America," he said. "I stay in United States and become citizen, so I want to learn about this country."

"Well, I'll leave you to your reading. The night is still young, and I can squeeze in a heap of pleasure between now and daybreak tomorrow."

The Chinese knew admonitions would be a waste of breath, but he could not remain silent. "Too much drink and too many women not good for any man," he said.

Chet laughed loudly. "There isn't any such thing as too much liquor and too many women!" he exclaimed.

The wagon train headed directly for Sacramento, although Melissa Austin and Phyllis Gregg had been eager to make a detour and see San Francisco. The young women were outvoted, however, by those who wanted to find new homes and settle in the Valley.

The travelers were in luck. When they reached the western portion of the Sacramento Valley, they found two adjoining farms whose owners had gone off to the gold fields. Both properties were already under cultivation, each boasted a sturdy ranch house, and because they were shunned by those hungry for gold, they were selling for absurdly low prices.

Randy Gregg saw that the soil was rich and promptly bought one of the properties. After a thorough inspection, Danny Taylor took the neighboring place. Now that Heather's pregnancy was becoming more advanced, he wanted her to have a home of her own in which to settle.

Still another property was for sale, adjoining a farm and orchard owned by a neighbor named Foster, but Jerome Hadley was not interested in it. "You'll never see me behind a plow or pruning a tree," he said. "We'll go on to Sacramento for a spell, and if you come into town, you'll find us in the biggest suite at the best hotel."

Melissa bade Heather and Danny a brief but affectionate farewell. "I'm sure Jerome and I will be married while we're in these parts," she said. "I'll let you know as soon as our plans are set, and I hope you'll come to our wedding."

Heather lacked the heart to say she thought it unlikely there would be a wedding.

John and Jane Foster helped their new neighbors to settle in, and a few days later they invited the Greggs and the Taylors to Sunday dinner after church services. The host and hostess were dressed in their Sunday best, as were their three children, and Heather was glad she was wearing the best of the woolen maternity dresses she had made for herself.

The variety of dishes startled the newcomers to the Valley. The fish came from a local river, and the beef had been bought from the owner of a nearby ranch. There were two kinds of melons and pears, and Jane served new potatoes, creamed spinach, squash, beans, and lettuce, as well as asparagus, which none of the guests had ever eaten.

"We grew all the fruits and vegetables right here on our own property," young Scott Foster said proudly.

His father smiled and nodded. "That's true. I've heard folks from Oregon boast about their crops, but we grow an even larger variety here."

Randy, who was eating with his customary enthusiasm, paused long enough to observe, "Seems t' me the soil and climate hereabouts produce California's real gold. Veg'tables and fruits bigger and juicier than are grown anywhere else."

Foster had known from the outset that he would like the old man. "You talk my language," he said. "I wish the gold prospectors good hunting. Nobody who tills the soil here ever goes hungry."

John Gregg looked up from his plate. "Some of us don't much care for farming. Me, I'm leaving for the gold fields at dawn tomorrow."

"While I stay behind to help Pa with the chores," Phyllis said sourly.

Danny was troubled and glanced at Heather before he said, "Our new property is a gem, all right. I wouldn't say the soil is richer than what I knew up in Oregon, but it's as fertile. I'm tempted to work the land, but I'm even more tempted to try my luck in the gold country. The land will be waiting for me if I don't find gold."

Before anyone could reply, they heard approaching hoofbeats, and Sarah Rose Foster ran to the dining room windows. "Uncle Rick is here," she said, obviously pleased.

Jane Foster filled a plate for the new arrival, and her husband went to the door.

"I know you have company," Rick Miller said, "so I'll be moving on if I'm in the way."

"You're never in the way," his host told him, escorting him into the dining room, where all three of the children immediately surrounded him.

Danny stared at him, then leaped to his feet. "Colonel Miller!" He was astonished and delighted to see the officer in whose cavalry regiment he had served during the war with Mexico.

Rick was equally surprised and held out his hand. "Well, Lieutenant Taylor. So the gold magnet caught hold of you."

Danny noted that, although his former superior smiled, his eyes remained hard and expressionless. Wanting to inquire after Mrs. Miller, the younger man refrained, a sixth sense warning him not to mention her.

The others who had come to California in the little wagon train were introduced to Rick, and he looked hard at Heather, then at Phyllis. "Do you young ladies know how to handle firearms?"

Phyllis shook her head, and Heather said, "Well, I can shoot, Sheriff Miller, but I'm not an expert."

Rick was blunt. "I urge you to learn," he said. "In a hurry. And once you know how to shoot, don't be bashful. Any time you're in doubt, open fire!"

His grim vehemence put a damper on the others' holiday spirits. He ate rapidly, then took his departure, and after he had gone, the Fosters told the story of the tragic fate his wife had suffered.

"I'm glad I didn't inquire about her," Danny said. "Something caused me to hold back."

"He never mentions her," Jane said, "but no matter how busy he is—and with the population still growing like crazy he has almost no time to himself—he visits her grave at least twice a week."

"If the men who killed Mrs. Miller are still in the

area, he'll nail them," Danny said. "He was my commanding officer during the war, and before that he led a group of us from Oregon to Texas, and I came to know him well. There's no man who is fairer or more honorable. And there's no one more ruthless when he's been wronged. If those killers know what's good for them, they'll put the continent between them and Rick Miller—and even then they won't be safe."

Phyllis shuddered. "I'm beginning to appreciate the quiet life we led in Texas."

"Don't let our ways frighten you," Jane said. "Life here can be pleasant enough, provided you're always alert to danger."

Heather guessed she felt vulnerable because of her pregnancy. She couldn't help wishing that Danny would stay home and raise crops on the property they had just bought, but she felt she would be restricting him unfairly if she raised the subject. Their principal reason for migrating to California had been the gold, and he had to have his opportunity to seek it.

Melissa Austin was badly upset and making no attempt to hide her feelings. She had spent the entire night alone in the covered wagon on the outskirts of Sacramento, a pistol beside her in case of need, and the hours had dragged.

It was mid-morning before Jerome Hadley returned. He was freshly shaved after availing himself of the facilities of one of the town's larger saloons, he had eaten a large breakfast there, and he was in exceptionally high spirits. But he took care to conceal the real reasons for his self-satisfaction from his mistress. He had won a very large sum at cards from a trio of miners, and for the first time in a year, he was financially independent.

"The least you could have done," Melissa said, "was to let me know you'd be gone all night. I stayed up for hours, waiting for you, and even when I realized it was likely you'd be away until morning, I still couldn't sleep."

Women were all alike, Hadley reflected. After a man had become intimate with one of them, she thought she owned him. He shrugged, then said indifferently, "I told you I didn't know for sure how long I'd be gone."

"Well, you certainly weren't very considerate." Melissa was sufficiently irritated to feel that the time had come for a showdown. "We've been together a long time, Jerome, and I've been patient. I don't intend to wait forever."

He pretended ignorance. "For what?"

She stared at him, her kohl-rimmed eyes wide. "You persuaded me to live with you by promising to marry me. It was my money that bought this wagon and our horses. You've been telling me for months that once we arrived here you'd retrieve your funds, invest in a substantial business, and marry me. How much longer do you expect me to wait?"

The time had come to take the action he had long known would be inevitable. "Sweetheart," he said soothingly, "I don't blame you for feeling the way you do. You've been patient. More than patient. So we're going to do something about our situation right now. Put on that yellow silk dress I like so much, and we'll go find a preacher I know."

The clinging gown he had mentioned really wasn't suitable for a wedding, but he was being amenable, so Melissa did not argue. She disappeared into the wagon, changed into the provocative attire, complete with high-heeled shoes, and then put on more makeup because she knew he would be pleased.

Hadley grinned approvingly. "You look very special," he said as he hitched up the team of horses.

"Where are we going?" Melissa asked as she sat beside him on the wagon seat and they put Sacramento behind them.

"A friend of mine owns a tavern and inn on the fringes of the gold country. The preacher lives nearby, so we'll go to my friend's place for our wedding celebration, and he'll send off for the minister."

She looped her hand through his arm, sitting close beside him, and was glad she had been courageous enough to speak her mind. Jerome had been taking her for granted lately and had needed a reminding nudge. She thought for a moment about the big wedding celebration they were supposed to have, with all of Jerome's friends in attendance, but she decided to say nothing about it. For now, it was enough to be getting married to him.

After a long drive on increasingly rutted dirt roads, they came to a huge, rambling two-story building. Fiddlers and a drummer were playing a lively tune in what appeared to be the main room on the ground floor, and Hadley escorted Melissa there after telling one of the hired hands to take her clothing box to one of the upstairs chambers.

"If you like it," he told Melissa as he escorted her into the establishment and guided her to a corner table, "we can spend our honeymoon here."

The prospect delighted her. She had grown weary of living in the covered wagon.

Most of the guests in the crowded tavern were men in rough work clothes, Melissa noted, and she was surprised to see they were attended by waitresses, heavily made-up, who were wearing attire that made her feel less conspicuous. Most were young and attractive, but a number stared at her, seemingly puzzled, and a few actually glared at her. Well, she didn't care what they thought.

A huge, grinning man with a pistol on one hip bore down on the couple, and Hadley, rising to his feet, presented Big George to Melissa. "We've come here to be married," Jerome said, one eyelid lowering for an instant. "Maybe you could bring us some of your special drinks, George."

"You bet," the proprietor replied. "They're on the house." He went off to the bar, returning with two glasses.

"I don't care much for liquor," Melissa said hesitantly.

"Oh, this won't hurt you," Big George assured her.

She saw that Jerome was raising his glass, expecting her to do the same, so she took a large swallow, making a wry face at the bitter taste.

"You'll send off for the preacher, won't you?" Hadley asked.

"Right off," Big George replied, but made no move.

The room began to swim, and even Jerome looked hazy to Melissa. Suddenly she felt an overpowering desire to sleep and lurched forward, her head dropping to the table.

Big George immediately summoned an attendant from the bar. "Take her up to the back room and lock her in for the present," he said. "Her clothes are already there. I'll have a little chat with her later, when the effects of the knockout medicine wear off."

The man gathered the unconscious young woman in his arms and carried her to the back stairs. Not more than a half-dozen patrons were aware of what was happening.

The proprietor grinned at Hadley. "She's a real beauty."

"I thought you'd like her," Hadley said complacently.

"I've got to hand it to you, you know how to pick 'em." Big George eyed him. "What's your price?"

"One game of poker, which will go on until I've had the chance to empty a lot of wallets without raising any suspicions."

"Fair enough."

"And one thousand in cash for Melissa."

Big George's smile faded. "That's a mighty high price."

"Your share of what she makes will earn it back in no time," Hadley said.

"Sure, if she goes along. If she doesn't, I'm stuck," Big George said.

"I've been priming her for months," Hadley declared. "She already has a wardrobe and can go to work without delay. As to the risk you're taking, it isn't all that great. I brought her from Texas, and she doesn't know anybody hereabouts."

The proprietor pondered for a time, then shrugged. "I reckon I'll take the gamble," he said. "But I'll want you out of here in a couple of hours. That was a light dose I gave her."

"I won't need that long," Hadley said. "And while I'm at it, I'll go fifty-fifty with you on the profits of my wagon and team if you can find me a customer for them. I'm going to travel light now that I'm alone again." He chuckled, took a deck of playing cards from an inner pocket of his handsome suit coat, and began to shuffle.

Big George went off to arrange a deal for the covered wagon and team of horses, making certain the receipt listed a smaller price than the customer actually paid, so he was able to recoup at least a portion of the thousand dollars he was paying for the girl.

Drifting back to Hadley's table, Big George saw that a poker game was already in progress. A number of men joined the gambler, and the proprietor of the establishment had to admire Jerome Hadley's artistry. He allowed his victims to win just enough to encourage them to play for higher stakes, and he was so deft that none even guessed he might be cheating. Less than two hours later he had won a considerable sum, and as was his custom, he prepared to move on. Most members of his dubious profession lingered too long in an area, and trouble developed when fellow players discovered they had been fleeced.

Big George sold Hadley a gelding, saddle, and saddlebag, further reducing the sum he had agreed to pay under the terms of their bargain. He was relieved when Hadley went on his way before any of the customers could complain about him. Big George believed in avoiding fights and other problems whenever possible.

Going to the kitchen, the proprietor filled a mug with scalding black coffee, then carried it up the back stairs to the chamber at the rear of the second floor,

where he unlocked the door and entered. Melissa
Austin was stretched out on the bed and was just
beginning to stir.

Able to inspect her at leisure, Big George realized
he had obtained a bargain. She was beautiful, with a
slender, supple figure, and far more attractive than
any of the young women already in his employ. Prop-
erly motivated, she could earn a fortune for herself—
and for him.

Melissa moaned quietly and opened her eyes. Big
George went to her, helped her to a sitting position,
and handed her the mug of coffee. She sipped it but
found it too strong.

"Drink it," he told her. "Your head will rejoin your
body by the time you finish it."

She forced herself to take several small swallows,
then moved to the side of the bed and placed her feet
on the floor. "I feel so ashamed," she said, "and
goodness only knows what Jerome must think of me.
That drink must have made me ill."

Big George decided a brutal approach would be the
most effective. "You fell asleep," he told her, "because
you were given knockout drops."

The girl gaped at him, unable to comprehend what
he was saying.

"Jerome Hadley is gone," he told her. "He sold his
wagon and workhorses, and he's moved on alone."

Melissa felt as if her world had fallen apart.
"You—you must be joking. We were going to be
married today."

"He had no intention of marrying you, today or any
other time. Drink your coffee, and your head will feel
better."

She drank without thinking, her mind whirling so
wildly that she didn't know what to say or do.

"If you look back," Big George told her, "this is
what he had in mind all along for you. Look at that
dress you're wearing. There ain't any being worn by
the girls downstairs that will cause the customers to
get any more excited. And from what Hadley told me,

you've got plenty of others just as fancy in that
clothing box yonder."

Melissa quickly began to piece together all that had
happened since Jerome had met her and started to
woo her in Texas, and she felt ill. "You're telling me,"
she said in a small voice, "that he planned all along to
have me become a—a prostitute."

"You don't need to be mean to yourself," Big
George said heartily. "Hereabouts they're called party
girls."

"I—I don't suppose Jerome had any farewell message for me?"

"Well, now, he said he hopes you'll work real hard
so you can pay off what I had to give him for you."

She was aghast. "He—he sold me to you?"

"That's one way to look at it." Big George was
pleased. This one had a balanced head on her shoulders and was neither hysterical nor angry.

"How much?" She didn't know whether to weep or
laugh.

"Fifteen hundred," he said. "But I'll do you a favor
and cut the sum in half. And I'll make it easy for you.
I'll turn over the suite up front to you. I won't make
you wait on tables, like the other girls have to do. Just
wander around where you please, and pick your own
customers. Any time you're annoyed by somebody you
don't like, just signal me. I guarantee he won't pester
you again. And after you pay off the seven hundred
and fifty, me and you will be partners. Just don't try to
cheat me. I don't take kindly to that."

She nodded, then sat in silence for a long time,
trying to order her thoughts.

Big George took the empty mug from her. "More
coffee? Or a drink, maybe?"

Melissa shook her head, flipping back a thick lock
of her long red hair. "I don't like liquor."

"Good. The bartenders will get orders. Whenever a
customer buys a drink for you, you're to be served
colored water."

There was no humor in Melissa's abrupt laugh. "You're assuming that I'm going to accept your offer."

"You bet I am." Big George stood and towered above her. "Me and you both understand that the California territory is part of the United States, of course. You're a free woman, not a slave, so you can't be bought or sold, right?"

Again she nodded.

"On the other hand, you'd be making a big mistake if you walked out of here. I give my girls one hundred percent protection at all times. None of the men from the gold fields violate my girls. Or maim them. Or kill them."

Melissa began to realize her position was even more precarious than she had thought.

"I'm as friendly a fellow as you'll find anyplace," he went on. "The only time I lose my temper is when I've been cheated. I just might lose my temper if I thought I was fifteen hundred dollars out of pocket."

Her heart was pounding, but she managed to keep her tone light. "What would you do?"

He smashed his huge right fist into the open palm of his left hand. "Later on, I'd be mighty sorry I spoiled your good looks. Right this minute you're the prettiest girl in the whole Sacramento Valley. Not only can you become the overnight queen of Big George's, but you'll be rich. If you turn me down, though, and I get mad—well, I might mash your good looks forever. That wouldn't stop you from complaining to the sheriff or one of his deputies. Not that it would do you any good, because there would be no witnesses to the beating. And that wouldn't bring back your good looks, either."

An icy chill raced up and down Melissa's spine. Her stupid, blind trust in Jerome Hadley had placed her in a predicament from which there was no escape. She could blame no one but herself; that, however, did not make the situation any easier to bear.

Big George was allowing her all the time she needed to analyze her position. "I have a hunch," he said at last, grinning at her, "that you're going to be sensible."

Melissa could not control a shiver. In spite of his broad smile, Big George's eyes were cold as he studied her, and she knew enough about men to realize he was not making idle threats. If he wished, this giant could tear her apart with his bare hands, and she knew he would suffer no regrets.

Her pride would not permit her to seek help from her companions on the wagon train journey from Texas, even if she managed in some miraculous way to escape from this saloon-brothel. Danny and Heather were in no position to assist her financially or in any other way, nor were the Greggs. She had many old friends in Oregon, but she knew Big George hadn't exaggerated the fate in store for her if she tried to travel alone through country where men outnumbered women by twenty or thirty to one.

"Still thinking?" Big George asked quietly.

Catching her breath, Melissa nodded.

Suddenly he reached down, caught hold of her shoulders, and lifted her to her feet as easily as he could have picked up a doll. His strength was awesome.

"I'm going to help you make up your mind," he said and began to paw her heavily.

The last doubts vanished from Melissa's mind. She was trapped, no matter how much she might loathe the existence into which she was being forced. Her survival was more important to her than her self-respect, which Jerome Hadley already had shredded.

"Don't tear this dress," she said. "I'm going to need it in my work."

Big George chuckled and released her. He put his hands on his hips, and gazing intently at Melissa, he said. "Well, let's see what you can do."

Melissa realized that the way she performed now for Big George was crucial to her future well-being. Feeling cheap and despising herself, she nevertheless practiced on him, deliberately removing her clothes slowly and striking a series of provocative poses.

He watched her in admiration until his own desire overwhelmed him, and then he picked her up, dropped her onto the bed, and, without futher ado, took her swiftly.

Somehow Melissa was able to anesthetize her body and her mind. A strange young woman, totally unrelated to her, was engaging in sexual intercourse with this uncouth giant. She herself was removed, feeling and thinking nothing.

She was somewhat surprised to discover how quickly the unsavory ordeal came to an end.

Big George climbed off the bed and looked down at her. "Now we're partners, for real," he told her. "As soon as you come downstairs, I'll have your belongings moved to the front suite. If anybody don't treat you right—the customers, the other girls, the hired help—you just let me know. You're under Big George's personal protection now." He swaggered out of the room, closing the door behind him.

Melissa pulled herself to her feet, and as she bolted the door she felt sick. Finding a slop jar beneath the bed, she vomited into it, then dropped back onto the bed.

In spite of her bad judgment and her occasional recklessness, Melissa was endowed with a streak of common sense. Ever since the time, back in her midteens, she had lost both of her parents while crossing the continent in a wagon train, she had been able to make the best of any situation. Now, although she was heartsick, she knew she would be wasting her time on self-pity, just as she would be outsmarting herself if she tried to find some clever way to escape from Big George. Too many unknown perils would threaten her. Somehow she had to make the best of her disgusting situation. She had already learned how to disassociate herself from unwanted lovemaking, and she would refine that art.

When she grew calmer, she dressed again in her

snug-fitting yellow silk gown, then took her cosmetics case from her leather box and repaired her makeup. Staring at her reflection in the cracked mirror above the small dressing table, she added more rouge to her lips, then for good measure painted a black beauty mark on one cheekbone.

The lovely young woman who returned her gaze was somber, unsmiling. "It's my fate to be a whore," she said aloud, "so I may as well be a successful whore."

She left the bedchamber, searched until she found the front staircase, and then descended slowly to the large room filled with miners waiting to be parted from their gold. A steady, tantalizing half-smile was on her lips, her hips swayed, and conversation died away as she entered the room. Big George, she reflected, had been telling the truth when he had said she would reign here as queen.

Heather Taylor's labor pains began about an hour before dawn. Having spent a few months working with Heather to establish their home, Danny had gone off to the gold fields. Heather had been alone in the house for the past month, and she did not now give in to panic. Careful plans had been made for this time of emergency, and she knew what needed to be done.

Dragging herself out of bed and putting on her old flannel bathrobe, Heather picked up a tinderbox and flint, then went out to the unlighted bonfire that stood about one hundred and fifty feet from the back door. Her hands trembled, but she managed to light the fire, and when the flames began to leap toward the sky, she returned to her bed, hoping the plan would be effective.

Twelve-year-old Tracy Foster disliked most chores and hated the days when it was his turn to fetch the wood for the breakfast fire. He dragged himself to the woodshed behind the family's house, then stood for a moment and stared at the bright fire burning on the property beyond his father's orchards. His own duties forgotten, he raced to his parents' bedchamber.

Jane Foster dressed swiftly while Tracy was sent up the road to alert the Greggs, and although only a short time passed, Jane was becoming nervous when Phyllis finally appeared at her front door. Wasting no time on greetings, the older woman and the younger made their way through the orchard, where the grass was heavy with dew, to the Taylor property. Jane had thought of every contingency and had her own key to the back door.

Heather smiled in relief when the pair came into her bedroom. "You have no idea how glad I am to see you," she said.

"We can guess," Jane replied. "How frequent are your pains?"

Heather gestured toward the pocket watch that Danny had left behind for her. "As nearly as I can tell," she said, "it's less than every two minutes."

"Then we may not have too long to wait." Having brought three children into the world, Jane was calm, but she realized that Phyllis needed to be kept occupied. "Find a pot in the kitchen," she said, "and put some water on the stove to boil."

Phyllis hesitated before she obeyed. "Maybe there's time," she said, "for somebody to ride into Sacramento and fetch a doctor."

These newcomers didn't understand the basic principles of life in primitive California. "There aren't more than three medical doctors in the whole Valley," Jane said, "and they're kept so busy patching up men who try to kill each other in the gold country that none of them would take the time for something as simple as delivering a baby. And there's no reason they should. You and I can manage, Phyllis."

Later in the morning Heather's contractions halted, but Jane Foster remained unflustered as she made tea for herself and Phyllis. "I'd give you a cup, too," she told the expectant young mother, "but you might regret it. From the looks of things, I'll wager you'll start again with a rush, and then the baby will be here before you know it."

Heather nodded, hoping she was right. Her pregnancy seemingly had lasted forever, and she was tired of it. At the same time, however, she wished Danny would get home in time for the arrival of the baby. Not that she could blame him for being away. He hadn't expected her to give birth for another two or three weeks, and he had sworn he would return by the deadline, or earlier if he found appreciative quantities of gold.

As much as she hated to admit it, even to herself, Heather was beginning to resent her husband's preoccupation with gold. Her own lifelong sense of values had been reasserted, and she found it difficult to understand why Danny didn't feel as she did. "I really don't care if you ever find gold," she had told him. "This property can give us a good living."

"But think how much more we'll have if I can pick up just a few nuggets," he had replied, his resolve unshaken.

Now a sudden, piercing pain shot through Heather and she gasped, everything but the present driven from her mind. Jane glanced at the pocket watch, looked at Phyllis, and nodded.

The pains came more rapidly, blending into an incessant stretch of searing agony. All at once Heather screamed, "Danny!"

Seconds later, her infant son came into the world. Jane worked feverishly, with Phyllis helping as best she could, and soon the drowsy young mother was cradling her baby in her arms.

"What will you call him?" Phyllis asked.

"Ted Woods Taylor," Heather said, her voice weak. "Ted is a blacksmith up in Oregon. When Danny was a bound boy and ran away to join the first wagon train to Oregon, Ted was the first to become his friend and help him. Danny doesn't forget such things."

Later, while Heather dozed and the baby slept in

his cradle beside her bed, the two neighbors went to the kitchen for something to eat. Jane quickly prepared a meal of cold meat, bread, and fruit as Phyllis watched her in silence. "I wonder—" Phyllis broke off abruptly.

Not one to press, Jane Foster merely looked at her, waiting.

"My brother has been off the gold fields even longer than Danny. And Pa's back is bothering him so bad these days that he's in no condition to go anywhere. So I was wondering what you'd think of sending one of your sons to find Danny and tell him he's a father."

"Conditions in the gold country are too dangerous," Jane replied. "My boys are self-reliant, and they aren't lacking in courage, but there are thousands of desperate men up yonder in the fields. Many of them are hungry, and they wouldn't hesitate to kill a boy for the weapons he carried."

"Then you couldn't take the risk, naturally." Phyllis was firm. "It was just a thought."

"I know what inspired it," Jane said, and a faint smile touched her lips.

Phyllis Gregg didn't realize how much she had matured since leaving Texas. Perhaps it was because keeping house for her father and helping him break up soil and plant crops kept her so busy that she no longer had time to sulk or become bored. "I like Danny," she said, "and I'm sure he loves Heather. I know he's loyal, too. It takes a special kind of loyalty to insist that his son be named for somebody who befriended him years and years ago. So I don't mean to be critical of him. But I know I'd be pretty upset if I were having a baby and my husband were gallivanting around in the gold fields, not even knowing he'd become a father."

Jane spoke quietly. "From what Heather hasn't said, even more than from what she's let on, I'm sure she's hurt. And she has a right to be. Danny's place today is right here beside her."

"I don't think he even knows he's being—well, negligent," Phyllis said.

"That's the tragedy of so many people in these parts. The worst thing that could have happened to law-abiding, loving families was the discovery of gold. My youngsters haven't been bitten by the bug. At least I hope they haven't. But, if they're safe, it's only because they've seen tragedies like the murder of Sheriff Miller's wife. And because my husband and I lecture them until we're hoarse. These days I'm afraid California is full of men like Danny Taylor."

"What you're saying is that he means well," Phyllis replied thoughtfully, "but he gives in to temptation instead of doing his duty."

"That's right." Jane shook her head. "He'll feel awful and will apologize again and again to Heather when he finds out she's had the baby while he was away. But that won't stop him from going off again."

Her brother, Phyllis reflected, was even worse. "Perhaps they're satisfied when they make a strike," she said.

"Very seldom, from what I've seen and heard," Jane said. "The gold addict is like the drinker who craves more and more liquor until it kills him. The gold addict is insatiable."

The clipper ship bound for San Francisco from Panama had been delayed because of an outbreak of dysentery among the crew and bad weather in the Pacific, but when they finally arrived in San Francisco, Paul Thoman made it his business to introduce Ralph Hamilton to General Lee Blake. Through Lee, Ralph came to know a number of San Francisco's leading citizens. He took a room for himself and Isaiah Atkins at one of the better hotels, and for several weeks he investigated the possibilities of settling in the city.

Ralph weighed matters carefully, and one night, as he and Isaiah were finishing dinner in the hotel's dining room, he surprised the boy by saying, "We're leaving tomorrow morning. We're going to Sacramento."

The youngster blinked at him. "But you've been telling me how great the opportunities are here in San Francisco."

"Indeed. With a permanent population of almost twenty-five thousand, as near as Mayor White can tell, and a transient population of several times that number, it doesn't take a great deal of imagination to realize that this is going to be a great city, a very large city. California is well on the way to statehood, and San Francisco is certain to dominate the economic and financial life of the entire West Coast for many decades to come."

Isaiah was bewildered. He had learned to imitate his mentor, using the right forks and knives, improving his grammar, and trying in every other way to emulate him, but he could not fathom Ralph's thinking. "Then how come you want to leave, Mr. Hamilton?"

"It isn't easy to explain, partner," Ralph said, smiling. "You lived in Brooklyn, Isaiah. Did you ever take the ferry to Manhattan?"

"Sure. Everybody at the orphanage did. The superintendent made us work at jobs there."

"I see. And what's your opinion of New York?"

"Well, it's big. And it's tough. And if you can make enough money there, I guess you can live awful good."

"I made a great deal of money," Ralph said. "I owned a comfortable house, and I had a splendid law practice. But I gave up my life there—deliberately." It was strange, he thought, but it was becoming increasingly difficult for him to draw a sharp mental picture of Prudence. Perhaps she had simply been the catalyst for his drastic withdrawal; perhaps he had been less satisfied with other aspects of his life than he had known.

Isaiah continued to look at him blankly.

"Eat your ice cream before it melts." Ralph took a

small sip of brandy and lighted a cigar. "I've decided I don't want to exchange life in one big city for a similar life in another. The challenges in Sacramento will be different. There's a strong move afoot to make it the capital when California becomes a state, and I'm thinking that some day I may become active in politics. In any event, there's more to law than sitting at a desk. So this very day I was able to buy a house in Sacramento through the bank here. For a fairly reasonable sum because it's located between the territorial courthouse and the sheriff's headquarters."

The boy was alarmed. "Will you—take me with you, Mr. Hamilton?"

"Anyone who asks that stupid a question deserves to be left behind," Ralph said. "However, since I've made myself responsible for your education, I know no one in San Francisco who would make certain you spend your days studying. So I'll have to take you with me."

The boy grinned at him, then attacked his dish of ice cream with gusto.

They left the city the following morning, riding two new geldings. A workhorse carried their belongings, which included law books Ralph had bought for himself in San Francisco, as well as a number of textbooks for Isaiah.

Their first day on the road was uneventful. Traffic moving in both directions was fairly heavy, and Ralph, carrying a new six-shooter that he regarded as more practical than his dueling pistols, encountered no problems. At Lee Blake's suggestion, he and Isaiah spent the night at a roadside inn where a strong guard was maintained and sentinels kept watch on the horses in the corral.

The following afternoon, after they reached the Sacramento Valley, trouble unexpectedly erupted. Isaiah was leading the workhorse and paid scant attention when he and Ralph were overtaken by three men riding in the same direction. All at once, however, the boy felt the rope being ripped from his hand,

and the trio, spurring to a gallop, took the workhorse with them.

Isaiah's shout of outrage and dismay alerted Ralph, who drew his six-shooter as he spurred forward, leaving the boy to follow as best he could. In his meetings with various men of consequence in San Francisco, Ralph had been warned repeatedly that he was traveling into an area where lawlessness often prevailed, but he was startled to find himself a victim.

The workhorse could not keep pace with the trio's mounts, so they were forced to reduce their speed somewhat. This made it possible for Ralph to draw closer, with Isaiah doggedly following him. The theft was so blatant that Ralph felt a sense of deep anger; not even realizing he had lost his objectivity, he drew his six-shooter and sent a warning shot over the heads of the fleeing thieves.

The three men were not lacking in courage, but nevertheless they deemed it wise to leave the road. As they started across a rock-strewn field, Ralph took careful aim, then put his second bullet into the shoulder of the man leading the workhorse. As the thief slumped in the saddle, he released the rope, freeing the horse.

The trio had failed in their robbery attempt, and with one of their number injured, they fled from the scene.

Isaiah galloped forward, caught hold of the rope, and led the horse back to the road. "That was mighty fancy shooting, Mr. Hamilton," he said admiringly.

Ralph was still so upset he replied curtly. "My grandfather was a gunsmith. By the time I learned to walk, he was teaching me to use firearms. Isaiah, did you get a good look at those men?"

"Sure."

"Could you describe them, in detail?"

"You bet, sir!"

"Good. We'll do something about this as soon as we reach Sacramento!" Ralph was determined not to let the would-be thieves go unpunished. The fact that he had wounded one gave him only a slight feeling of satisfaction and was irrelevant. What mattered was that the trio would strike others.

The house that awaited them in Sacramento was larger than either had anticipated. It was surrounded by a high fence, which resembled a miniature palisade, and consequently was secure. They took their horses to the barn, but Ralph postponed his room-by-room inspection of the dwelling.

"Isaiah," he said, handing the boy some money, "after you've unsaddled the horses, go to a feed store for some grain. And find a shop where you can buy us some staples—tea, bacon, flour, and the like. We'll go out for most of our meals, but we'll still need some food in the house."

"Where are you going, Mr. Hamilton?"

"The sheriff's office. I'm determined to find those criminals and bring them to justice. The sheriff's quarters are next door, so join me there as soon as you've finished your chores. Your description will be valuable."

Ralph hurried to the two-story wooden building located a short distance down the street. Deputies armed with six-shooters bustled in and out, and it appeared that several cells were located at the rear of the ground floor.

No one paid any heed to the visitor, and Ralph had to halt one of the deputies. "I want to see Sheriff Miller."

"Front office. Second floor."

Ralph climbed the stairs, then peered in through an open door. A gaunt man, with a pair of six-shooters hanging from his belt, the bottoms of the holsters tied around his legs with rawhide thongs, was standing at a desk, looking at a logbook.

Introducing himself, Ralph said that General Lee Blake had asked him to get in touch with the sheriff. Rick Miller smiled as he shook hands, but the hard expression in his eyes did not change. "Any friend of Lee's is welcome here. You say you're a lawyer, Mr.

Hamilton?" Sitting down, Rick waved Ralph to a straight-backed chair.

"Yes. I practiced in New York, and I daresay I'll hang out my shingle here."

"Well, there's a need for attorneys in this jungle, I can tell you." Rick wearily ran a hand through his graying hair.

"I hate to make this an official call, but it can't be helped." Ralph told him about the attempt to steal his workhorse. "If you'll direct me to the prosecutor's office, Sheriff, I'll swear out a warrant. And my young ward and I will provide a full description of the thieves."

Rick's grin was sour. "You're not in New York now. This is the Sacramento Valley. The incident you've just described is so minor that nobody here has time to handle it." He laughed unhappily. "What's more, there is no prosecutor in the Valley."

Ralph stared at him. "You're joking!"

"Unfortunately, I'm not. The Valley commissioners have offered a small salary to anyone qualified for the job, but nobody has come forward. I guess it doesn't pay enough."

"To hell with the pay." Ralph was seething. "What are the qualifications?"

Rick guessed what he had in mind, but it was premature to hope that a volunteer had been found. "First off, the prosecutor needs to be a member of the bar in good standing in one of the states. And he's required to have five years of active practice."

"I've had almost ten. Go on."

"He needs to be a glutton for work because there's so much that needs to be done. And he needs to be either courageous or foolhardy, depending on how you look at it. My deputies and I are fairly safe here in town, but when we go out into the countryside, the boys usually travel in pairs."

"But you don't?"

Rick shrugged. "I'm fairly handy with a pistol, and the riffraff know it."

"I'm not too bad a shot myself," Ralph said. "And I don't scare easily, either."

The former Ranger studied him carefully and liked what he saw. "You're serious about this, I take it."

"I certainly am. No town, no area can survive without obedience to the law and the establishment of order. I heard talk in San Francisco about California applying for statehood in the immediate future, but there's no chance the U.S. Congress will approve unless the criminal element is tamed."

"The pay is the same as mine," Rick said. "Fifty dollars a month."

' "That'll pay my food bills. There will be plenty of time to make money once the area becomes civilized. Where do I apply?"

"I'll take you to the commissioners myself. Right now. Are you prepared to be sworn in at once?"

"The sooner the better." Ralph took his measure and decided General Blake's description had been accurate. Having heard the story of Sheriff Miller's tragedy, Ralph knew the reason for his dedication to his work.

Rick stood and extended his hand. "The office next door has been vacant for months. I have a hunch you and I will make a good team."

It was strange, Ralph thought, but he already felt at home here. His long journey from New York to California had started as a flight, a retreat, but all at once his life was gaining a meaning and a purpose. "I'd like to find my young ward and take him with us," he said. "I don't want him wandering around a town like this on his own.'

"That's smart. And if he isn't a marksman, have him start target practice right off. You're joining an exclusive club of dubious distinction, Mr. Prosecutor. You'll never know from one minute to the next when somebody may put a bullet into you!"

Chet Harris and Danny Taylor had formed their close friendship on the long wagon train journey

across North America. Since that time they had been
inseparable. They went to Texas together and fought
side by side in the war with Mexico. For more than a
year, they had not seen each other, and now, thanks to
an irony of fate, they were separated by only a few
miles. But neither knew it.

Chet and his partner, Wong Ke, worked the Bear
River adjoining their property, gradually accumulat-
ing more and more gold nuggets. The day was not far
distant when, if they continued to save the better part
of their findings, they would achieve lifelong financial
security.

No more than a half hour's brisk walk down the
river from their cabin, Danny was trying his luck.
Standing in the icy water, he dipped his pan and sieve
into the water repeatedly, almost automatically, as he
continued the search for gold, which, so far, had not
succeeded. He was cold, miserable, and hungry, having eaten the last of the food he had brought with
him, and an inner voice told him to give up the hunt.
He had spent six weeks in the gold fields, and with
Heather's baby—his baby—due at any time, he would
be wise to return home.

But he continued to scoop up sand from the river
bottom, then sift it. He was being foolishly stubborn,
perhaps, but he hated to admit failure in any endeav-
or.

Suddenly Danny straightened, his heart pumping so
wildly that he heard a singing noise in his ears. There
were four dull, gold-colored objects in his sieve, each
of them the size of a pea. He walked ashore slowly,
carefully, and stowed the little nuggets in his wallet.
His strike had been modest, but in this short period of
time, six weeks in all, he had earned as much as he
could have made in a year on his new farm.

The sun stood almost directly overhead, and all at
once Danny made another discovery: there were
quantities of gold dust in his pan, too. Carefully he
removed the tiny particles, placing them in a small
glass vial he had brought with him for that purpose.

He was surprised to find that he had acquired the equivalent of a teaspoon and a half of the precious dust.

Now he could go home to Heather with his head held high, and he lost no time mounting his horse and starting on the journey across the Sacramento Valley. He vowed to take the gold into Sacramento, where it would bring him higher prices than were available elsewhere. Certainly he had no intention of spending any of the gold, even though he was hungry. Saloons and taverns were notorious for the way they cheated those who were shortsighted enough to bring gold to them.

This turned out to be Danny's lucky day. In a hip pocket he had two twenty-five cent coins, more than enough to buy himself a beef-steak dinner, along with a glass of ale. So, late in the afternoon, when he saw Big George's looming ahead, he decided to stop there for a celebratory meal.

The place was crowded, but Danny limped to a small, quiet table in the corner. There he ordered beefsteak, roasted potatoes, salad greens, and bread, as well as a pint of ale. The scantily clad brunette waitress flirted with him but desisted when he made it plain that he had no interest in her.

Paying scant attenion to his surroundings, Danny enjoyed the first hot meal he had eaten in days. He paid his bill, then sat back to finish his ale before leaving. The fiddlers and drummer were playing a lively tune, but he was able to shut out the sound. His hunger had been appeased, and he was looking forward to his reunion with Heather.

Someone was descending the main staircase very slowly, a step at a time, and Danny glanced idly in the young woman's direction, then froze. She appeared to be bursting out of her gown of pale ivory silk—what there was of it. Never had he seen such a shocking costume: the woman's breasts were almost totally exposed, and the high slits on either side of her skirt revealed a dazzling expanse of her legs, which were encased in black net tights. Her red hair cascaded down her back.

In that startling instant, Danny recognized Melissa Austin.

The brunette, who was standing near his table, misinterpreted his interest. "If you want her, mister, you'll have to pay through the nose. I won't charge you a quarter of her price."

Danny fled, feeling ill, walking as rapidly as his wooden leg permitted. If he hadn't seen Melissa himself, he wouldn't have believed that she was working as a prostitute in a saloon. Apparently she and Jerome Hadley had parted, but it was difficult to believe she was in such dire circumstances that she was forced to sell her body. She had looked, he had to admit, as though she were enjoying herself thoroughly, relishing the stir she caused and basking in the admiration of the customers. He thanked God that his own interest in Melissa had faded after he had met Heather.

The house was dark when he finally arrived home late that night, and when he found the door was bolted, he had to tap hard on it.

"I'm back!" he called when a sleepy Heather answered his summons, a candle in one hand and a loaded pistol in the other.

They kissed and clung to each other hungrily for a long time, and all at once Danny realized that his wife's slender figure had been restored.

She smiled at him. "Come and meet your son," she said.

He stood above the crib for a long time, staring down at his tiny son.

"His name is Ted Woods Taylor, just as you wanted," Heather said.

Danny was grateful to her, and then a wave of guilt overwhelmed him. "I should have been here," he muttered. "I'm sorry."

"Jane and Phyllis helped me. So I managed." Her tone made it clear, however, that she resented his absence.

Danny moved away from the crib, led her into their own, adjoining bedchamber, and used the candle to light an oil lamp, Then, after making certain the blinds were closed, he emptied the contents of his purse onto the unpainted dresser top. "Four nuggets," he said, "and about the same amount in gold dust."

She nodded but seemed unimpressed.

"I'd have to work this property for over a year to earn what a Sacramento gold dealer will pay me for this haul," he explained.

"Good," Heather said. "With that money added to your war bonus, we'll have a tidy sum. Enough so we can buy the fruit trees we want and have an orchard that will rival that of the Fosters."

He stared at her in stunned silence, making no comment. Apparently she failed to realize that his one gold strike was only the beginning. Often during his absence he had felt guilty, it was true, and it was unfortunate he had been absent from home when the baby had been born. But the gold was more than adequate compensation, and after another strike or two, he could hire people to operate the orchard for him.

He knew Heather well enough to realize she would protest angrily, particularly right now. He would await a more opportune moment to tell her he fully intended to return to the gold fields.

It struck Heather as odd that he hadn't picked up the baby, but she guessed they would need to become better acquainted first. Fathers sometimes found it difficult to express their feelings. "Are you hungry?" she asked, concealing her inner thoughts.

Danny shook his head. "I ate a big meal at a saloon on the way home," he said, suddenly remembering about Melissa, and he told Heather what he had seen.

Heather looked sad. "The poor dear. I wonder if we can't help her in some way."

Obviously a good woman couldn't understand the nature of a prostitute. "Melissa would laugh if we offered her help," he said. "She loved showing off her body to all those men. She knew that if she snapped her fingers they would have crawled around the room after her on their hands and knees. I could tell by her expression that she was just lapping up her feeling of power over them."

Heather had no intention of becoming involved in an argument with him so soon after his return, but she was convinced he was mistaken. She had come to know Melissa well on the wagon train journey from Texas to California, and she felt certain that, behind her customary air of bravado, Melissa was miserable. It was best to change the subject.

"You must be tired," she said.

"Well, this has been one mighty long day, I must admit." He began to undress.

After a kiss and an embrace, he turned over in the bed and within moments was sound asleep. Heather remained awake for a long time, haunted by the feeling that this man, her husband and the father of her child, had become a stranger to her.

V

Eulalia Holt named her daughter Cindy, after her brother's wife, her closest friend since their wagon train days together. When the baby was four months old, Cindy and Claiborne Woodling gave a party in honor of the Holts, and scores of people came to their farm for the barbecue. Whip Holt had retired from his post as head of the Oregon militia, but he was still regarded as a natural leader of the thriving territory, and everyone from the early settlers to the most recent arrivals wanted to pay their respects to him and his wife.

Sides of beef and buffalo, elk and antelope turned on spits cranked by teenage boys, and tables in the Woodling backyard were laden with the bounty of the country. There were melons, apples, pears, and peaches, more than a dozen kinds of vegetables, as well as more different relishes and preserves than anyone cared to count. Many of the ladies had baked breads, and one whole table was filled with cakes and cookies.

The unexpected presence of Ernst and Emily von Thalman added to the festivities. They had just arrived home from Washington City, where Ernie was the official delegate of the Oregon territory to the United States Congress, and they were immediately surrounded by friends.

Only Eulalia and Whip, who had seen the von Thalmans the previous evening, knew how difficult it was for them to maintain a happy façade. They had heard nothing from Emily's eldest son, Chet Harris, since he had written them a short note the previous year, announcing that he was leaving Texas for California. Not only had he failed to write again, but Whip and Eulalia had been pained to tell them that no one else in Oregon had heard from him or about him.

Toby Holt was marvelously protective of his baby sister, insisting on "standing guard" over her while the guests looked at and admired her. But he tired of the sport when little Cindy drifted off to sleep, and he could not resist the urge to take part in the pony races that his uncle had organized for the boys.

Among the last of the guests to arrive were Harry and Nancy Canning, and something in their manner told Eulalia that their tardiness had not been accidental. The Cannings ate sparingly, drinking only token quantities of Claiborne's cider, and they stayed behind deliberately when the other guests left.

"I'm taking Toby and the baby home," Eulalia said to Nancy, "but I'll be back. I know you have something on your minds, and I'll appreciate it if you'll wait for me before you talk about it."

She returned from the adjoining Holt ranch in less than a half-hour, after leaving the children with the new housekeeper, who was a symbol of the family's growing affluence. Whip, the Woodlings, and the Cannings were sitting in front of the blazing parlor hearth, drinking coffee. "The rain is just starting," Eulalia said. "I'm so glad it held off until the party ended."

The others nodded, and it was plain they had been waiting for her before opening a discussion.

"The reason we were late," Harry Canning said, "is because we received a letter just before we left the house."

"And we agonized over it, trying to decide what to do," Nancy added. "The one thing we knew was that we wouldn't mention it to Ernie and Emily."

Harry produced the folded letter from an inner coat pocket. "This was sent by Heather Taylor, Danny's wife," he said. "They've bought property in the Sacramento Valley."

None of the others had met Heather, but all were deeply interested in Danny.

"They've had a baby son they've named for Ted Woods," Harry said. "We'll tell Ted about it in the next day or so, and I'm sure he and his family will be pleased."

"Reading between the lines, I don't think Heather and Danny are too happy these days, even though they've become parents." Nancy took the letter from her husband and glanced through it. "Danny has caught gold fever and is spending most of his time in the gold fields, where he's had one modest strike. Heather seems incapable of persuading him to buckle down at their fruit farm."

"That doesn't sound like Danny," Cindy said. "He was always so conscientious."

"Gold does odd things to people," Whip said, frowning. "Way back, at the annual rendezvous of mountain men, some of the pelt buyers purposely paid the trappers gold for their pelts. I never saw anything like it. The mere sight of the gold caused sensible men to lose their balance, and before you knew it they were spending everything they had just been paid on liquor and women."

There was a moment's silence, and then Cindy asked, "Is there any news of Chet Harris?"

"Not a word, according to Heather," Harry replied.

"She and Danny had hoped to see him, but they haven't run across him."

"How strange, when he was going off to the gold fields, too," Eulalia said.

"It isn't all that strange," Whip declared. "Folks are pouring into the gold country by the tens of thousands. It's easy to miss seeing friends when there are so many people there."

"They've asked Rick Miller, who is the sheriff in the Valley, to keep watch for Chet. That's all Heather and Danny can do."

Everyone had heard of the ugly murder of Rick's wife, and the mention of his name made them even more concerned.

"The worst is yet to come," Nancy said, then read a paragraph in which Heather said that Danny had seen Melissa Austin working in a saloon as a prostitute.

Cindy, who had worked in a Louisville brothel before changing her way of life when she had joined the first wagon train to Oregon, came to Melissa's defense. "We don't know what may have forced her into that situation," she said. "I refuse to condemn her."

"So do I," Eulalia said firmly.

Nancy was badly upset. "Melissa was my dearest friend," she said, "and it makes me ill to think of what she's doing these days. I tried to convince her that that horrid Jerome Hadley was no good for her, but she wouldn't listen to me!"

"There's no point in dwelling on what's past," Harry said. "The problem now is what can be done to help Melissa."

Cindy shrugged. "We'd be wasting our time."

Whip challenged her. "What makes you so positive?"

"Because I know how she feels. No matter what her reasons for becoming a prostitute, no matter how much she may hate herself and the men in her life, she feels the need to justify her existence to herself. I

can promise you she'd become very defensive if anyone tried to reason with her." Cindy spoke flatly,
displaying no emotion.

Eulalia realized how much the effort to remain calm
had cost her sister-in-law. "I'll take your word for it,
Cindy," she said. "I guess all we can do is hope that
Melissa's circumstances change."

"I feel like screaming," Nancy Canning said, "but I
guess I agree with you."

"I don't," Whip Holt said quietly.

The others looked at him.

"Melissa is an adult, not a child," Cindy said.

"She's in her early twenties or thereabouts," Whip
replied. "So, to my way of thinking, she isn't much
more than a child."

Knowing her husband as she did, Eulalia guessed
that a specific plan of some sort was forming in his
mind. She wished, fervently, that he wouldn't continue to feel responsible for the welfare of other people.
But she couldn't change his nature, and she had to
admit that his selfless generosity was one of the traits
that caused her to love him.

"Harry," Whip said, "when is the next Thoman and
Canning schooner sailing down to San Francisco?"

"I believe the next to leave will be at the end of the
month."

Whip nodded. "Reserve a private cabin for me. It
isn't a very long voyage, but at my age I prefer to
travel in comfort."

His sister-in-law shook her head. "I've known you
to do extraordinary things in the past, Whip," she
said, "but this time you're making a mistake. You'll be
dealing with someone who won't listen to a word you
say to her. So what will you do? Pick her up by the
scruff of the neck, bind and gag her—and then bring
her back to Oregon?"

"If I had to," he said, "I reckon I could."

The others were acutely conscious of the fact that
Eulalia remained silent. Whip was aware of it, too,

and grew increasingly uncomfortable. Thanking his host and hostess, he announced that the time had come to return home.

Eulalia remained silent on the short carriage ride, wrapping herself in her coat to ward off the rain that slanted into the open coach. Her husband knew better than to force a conversation on the subject, and he braced himself for the inevitable storm.

After checking to see that the children were asleep, Eulalia entered the master bedroom of the ranch house, where her husband was removing his boots. "Don't be in too much of a hurry to get to sleep, Michael Holt," she said.

He sighed quietly. Whenever she called him Michael Holt he knew he was in trouble.

"I need hardly remind you that you are no longer a conquering hero, or even a mountain man. It wasn't so many years ago, you may recall, that you had to come back home forty-eight hours after you went off to help Sam Houston fight the Mexicans. You had a frightful attack of arthritis, you'll recall. I'm reminding you of all this only because your memory—obviously—is faulty."

"I know I'm middle-aged," he replied. "The lines in my face and the gray in my hair keep me from forgetting. So does the paunch that all your good cooking has made me grow." He grinned at her.

Her green eyes remained stony, and Whip's smile faded. "My hand is still steady. I'm a better shot than anyone else in Oregon. And I can still snuff out a candle the size of your little finger with a whip at thirty feet."

"Are you intending to shoot your way into the saloon where Melissa is working? That would create quite a furor."

Her sarcasm made him wince. "Don't be sarcastic, honey," he said. "I've got to do what I believe is right, and my conscience would bother me something awful if I didn't try, at least, to bring Melissa back here."

Eulalia softened. "I know the way you think, and I understand your feelings. Other wives might be jealous of a husband who went off to rescue a much younger, exceptionally attractive woman." He tried to interrupt. "Let me finish," she said. "I'm very sure of your love for me and for the children. I'm opposed to your scheme for your own sake, not for mine."

"Sometimes," he said, chuckling, "I remind myself of that character you were reading about the other night—Don Quixote, fighting windmills."

"No, you're the finest fighting man of our time, Michael Holt," Eulalia said. "That doesn't concern me. What does worry me are the intangibles. Suppose the pain in your hip flares up again and cripples you?"

"I haven't had an attack in four or five months. All I can do is hope I don't have a flare-up."

It was her turn to sigh. "I don't suppose it bothers you that the California gold country is said to be the most dangerous place on earth these days."

His laughter was genuine. "Have you ever known me to be intimidated by anyone? Or to run away from a good fight?"

"Hardly. But that won't stop me from worrying about you," she said.

He stood, went to her, and gripped her shoulder. "Mrs. Holt, you and I have a lot of living and a lot of loving to do before I go six feet underground in a pine box. I have a son who'll need my advice and help more and more, year by year, as he grows older. And I want the joy of watching you rear our daughter. I've never broken a promise to you, Lalie, and I give you my word that I'm coming back to you. In as good shape as I am right now."

She knew she had lost the battle, so she curled her arms around his neck and kissed him soundly.

"The one thing I mind," he said as they drew apart, "is that you'll have that much more responsibility here while I'm gone."

Having accepted the fact of his journey to California, she felt compelled to be supportive. "The ranch will run itself," she lied. "I'll continue to keep the books, as I always do. Stalking Horse is the best foreman in the territory, and Claiborne will pitch in if any serious problems develop."

Whip knew the effort she was making. "There's nobody like you, Mrs. Holt."

"Or you, Mr. Holt. See to it that you're intact when you come back to the children and me."

Sacramento Valley Prosecutor Ralph Hamilton realized he could not reform the judicial system overnight, but he did his best. "I thought Sheriff Miller was a glutton for work," one of the deputies said, "but this Hamilton is just as active."

Even the judges of the three California territory courts, whose caseloads doubled, were deeply impressed by the newcomer's drive, energy, and dedication. "There are times," one of them remarked to a colleague, "when I almost feel sorry for the criminals who come before me. There are no loose ends in Prosecutor Hamilton's cases. When he issues a warrant, you know Sheriff Miller will bring in the lawbreaker."

The rate of convictions soared so dramatically that one of the San Francisco newspapers took note of the situation: *The Valley may not be a jungle much longer,* the editorial writer observed. *Prosecutor Hamilton and Sheriff Miller are making it fit for civilized habitation.*

Ralph's schedule was as brutal as it was unvarying. He appeared at his office soon after sunrise every morning, remaining there until noon. Then, no matter how busy his day, he always took time to go with Isaiah Atkins to eat in one of the quieter cafés in the area. His afternoon was spent in court, usually followed by a long conference with the sheriff. Soon Rick found it convenient to join Ralph and Isaiah frequently for supper.

The boy was kept busy, too. He spent long mornings pouring over schoolbooks and writing essays, knowing he would be quizzed each night. After dinner, during which he loved to question Ralph about fine points of the law, he practiced his marksmanship for at least two hours in the yard in back of the house. Then, if Ralph was satisfied with his academic progress, he sometimes was permitted to sit in the back of a courtroom and watch the prosecutor at work. These were the occasions he liked best.

He also enjoyed himself thoroughly when he was allowed to accompany Sheriff Miller on a case. "It isn't right for the lad to spend all his days in town," Rick said.

Rick taught the boy to handle firearms, and Isaiah was as quick to learn from him as he was adept at his studies.

"Never fight the kick of a pistol when you fire it," Rick told him. "The discharge tugs your arm up, so let it rise, but make sure you bring it into the right position again before your next shot. Even the experts miss their targets sometimes, so never worry about a shot that goes astray. Learn from your mistakes, remember to squeeze the trigger instead of pulling at it, and it won't take you long to learn."

Isaiah was strongly aware of the differences between Ralph and Rick. The former relied on his intellect, while the latter was a man of action. But what really mattered was that both were devoted to the same cause, that of establishing and keeping the law, and the boy privately was determined to emulate both of his mentors.

Rigid rules were applied to Isaiah when he went with Rick to make an arrest. He always carried his own six-shooter, a gift from Rick, but he was forbidden to use it except in self-defense. He remained unobtrusively in the background when Rick made an actual arrest, and at no time was he allowed to guard a prisoner during the ride back to Sacramento.

"We'd make the law a laughingstock," Ralph said, "if we deputized someone your age, Isaiah. Just keep your eyes and ears open, and you'll learn as much as you will in your reading."

Little by little the boy was permitted to join in the discussions at the supper table when the new prosecutor and the sheriff were plotting a future course of action, and gradually it dawned on Ralph that Isaiah was becoming a sharp, accurate judge of character.

One evening Ralph and Rick were discussing a man they had picked up that afternoon and his plea of innocence. "You'll release the suspect in the morning, I assume?"

"I don't have any choice, Ralph. I swear he's guilty, but I can't hold him without evidence."

"That fellow is guilty as sin," Isaiah said.

"What makes you so sure?" Ralph demanded.

"Well, sir, the man claimed he never stole any gold nuggets. And even though Sheriff Miller and two of the deputies nearly turned his room at that country inn upside down and inside out, they didn't find any gold."

Isaiah stopped and grinned at the two somber men. Neither of them approved of his showing off, but he was so pleased with himself that for once he didn't care. "He's guilty, all right. The heel of his left boot is hollow," the boy said, still grinning. "I saw him stuffing things into it when he thought nobody was looking. I'll bet the nuggets he stole are in his heel this very minute."

Rick hastily excused himself from the supper table and hurried off to the cells on the ground floor of his headquarters.

When he returned a short time later, there was an animated look on his face for the first time since Ralph and Isaiah had known him. "Boy," he said, "it looks like we'll have to swear you in as a deputy sooner than we figured. We found the nuggets precisely where you said they'd be."

Isaiah was satisfied with a reward of a double dessert—a slab of apple and raisin pie topped with ice cream—a confection little known in many parts of the United States that was becoming increasingly popular in the gold country.

Ralph was delighted with his protégé's progress. "Here's a real puzzle, Isaiah. Tell him about the masked bandits, Rick, and let's see what he thinks."

"We've had dozens of complaints that are similar, all of them from men who have made strikes in the gold fields," Rick Miller said. "Every one of them has had the same unhappy experience. Masked riders— some say there are four, and others insist there are about six—cut off the victim, take his gold, and then make off in a hurry. The robberies always take place on a lonely road in the woods."

"The attacks are identical, which is what we find fascinating," Ralph added. "The robbers take great care not to harm or kill their victims. Apparently they realize we'll try even harder to find them if there are killings. When a victim tries to fight them off, they overwhelm him and take his weapons away from him, but they're not bloodthirsty. Even when they tie someone up, he's always able to free himself after they've taken off with his gold."

Isaiah pondered, carefully sifting and weighing what they had told him. They were testing him, and he wanted to make no errors. "There's one thing I don't understand at all. I'm guessing the same criminals are involved in each of these robberies. Well, how do they know that the men they hold up are carrying nuggets or gold dust—or whatever they've found in their strike?"

"Damned if he hasn't dug right to the core of the problem," Rick said.

Ralph Hamilton shook his head. "You've asked the key question, boy. Thousands of men make their way out of the gold country every day of every week, most of them with empty pockets. What we want to know is how the band of masked robbers invariably selects victims who are carrying significant quantities of gold."

"Once we've found the answer to that question," Rick declared, "I'll be well on my way to making some arrests and breaking the case wide open."

"There must be some special trick to it," Isaiah said.

"That's our guess." Ralph smiled at the youth. "Don't trouble yourself overmuch, boy," he said. "I don't want you to take time away from your studies. I just wanted you to know there are times we beat our heads against the wall."

"Some day, sooner or later," Rick Miller said grimly, "we'll find a clue. I never let myself become too discouraged about the business of law enforcement because I've yet to know a criminal who doesn't make mistakes." There was no need to say that he had not given up his private search for the pair called Slim and Shorty, who had murdered his beloved Elisabeta. The day would come when he would find and corner them and would have his opportunity to avenge his wife's death. And a day never went by that he didn't think of Elizabeta and vow anew to get revenge.

Randy Gregg suffered a severe attack of gout, which immobilized him. The affliction was not new, and knowing that no medication would improve his condition, he refused to allow Phyllis to seek help from one of the Valley's few physicians. Instead, he sat in a parlor chair, propping his throbbing foot on a stool, and took an occasional sip from a jug of whiskey.

With John Gregg still off in the gold fields, an absence that was becoming increasingly protracted, his deeply concerned sister discussed the crisis with her friend and neighbor, Heather Taylor. Danny had gone back to the fields, too, much to Heather's dismay, so she and her baby were alone again.

"You and I are in the same boat, more or less,"

Phyllis said. "We're being forced to cope with a life without men." She accepted the cup of steaming tea that Heather offered her as they sat together in the Taylor kitchen. "But there's one important difference. Danny sold the gold from his strike, so you know you won't starve, even if he stays away for months. Pa has been working our farm, which is our only support, and it looks as though I'll have to get out into the fields myself."

Aware of how much Phyllis had matured since they left Texas, Heather couldn't help thinking she was taking on too much responsibility. "You don't have the physical strength to farm your property alone."

"I'll have to try," Phyllis said, shrugging. "It's better than starving. I know I can't count on my brother coming back here with his pockets filled with gold."

Heather sipped her tea in silence for a time. "As you already pointed out, my situation is somewhat different. We haven't even started to develop the orchards here. What fruit trees are left from the days of the previous owners are growing wild. Anyway, I've had a crazy thought, Phyllis, and believe me, I'm being selfish, not generous." She paused. "I've been terribly nervous, sleeping here with just the baby for company every night. I guess I'm competent to handle the pistol and rifle Danny left with me, but I honestly don't know how I'd react in an emergency. And that's the truth."

"I know what you mean. I feel the same way."

"In one respect you're better off than I am. Your father may be crippled, but he can still shoot. So I'd like to make you an offer. Suppose I close up this place, and the baby and I move in with you. Naturally I'll pay my share for food and other expenses. What's more, I grew up working on farms. If your father will keep an eye on little Ted for me, I can work in the fields with you. Maybe, between us, we can do the equivalent of an able-bodied man's work."

Phyllis was overwhelmed. "This is wonderful of you!"

"Not at all. I'll sleep better at night, knowing that the baby and I are under the same roof as you and your father. And I've never been afraid of hard work."

Far more sensitive to others' feelings than she had been once, Phyllis hesitated. "Won't Danny object if you close this place?"

"Let him!" Heather was bitter. "I begged him not to go prospecting again. He was lucky enough to acquire a substantial nest egg, and by investing it in the orchard, we'd have an assured future. But he wouldn't listen to me."

Phyllis had never seen her speak with such intensity and anger.

"I have no intention of spending months and even years of waiting idly for Danny to recover from his infatuation with gold and settle down to work. Regardless of whether he makes another strike, he's gone off to the gold fields for the last time. If he does this to me once more, I'm taking the baby and going back to my parents in Texas. There are limits to the risks I'm willing to take—and the loneliness—and the half-life." Not wanting to discuss the problem any longer, she stood abruptly. "Let's go to your place and see what your father thinks of my idea."

They went directly to the Gregg house and presented the plan to Randy, who was sitting immobile in the parlor's only overstuffed chair. Then he unleashed a stream of tobacco juice at the cuspidor he insisted on keeping at arm's length. "For a couple o' females, you make good sense," he said. "I know you're a worker, Heather, and it 'pears that maybe Phyllis is growin' up."

"Then you agree?" his daughter asked.

"I'd be plumb insane if I didn't. There's no tellin' how long this gout is goin' to keep me sittin' like a frog on a lily pad. But I can still put a load o' lead into any strangers who come moseyin' around." A network of creases spread across his leathery face as he grinned. "And I aim t' be the best nursemaid t' little Ted here that you ever saw. Too bad he ain't a mite older. I'd learn him t' chaw tobacco, and I'd tell him some of the damnedest yarns you ever heard!"

Melissa Austin's success was even greater than Big George had predicted. The other women were forced to obey the proprietor's regulations, but the demand for her services was so great and the fees she charged were so exorbitant that Melissa made and followed her own rules.

She slept until noon every day, then went down the back stairs for breakfast. A handyman brought buckets of hot water to her suite, where she bathed at leisure. She could well afford to have the other women make her flashy, provocative clothes, so she took her time with her fittings, then made meticulous preparations for her day's appearance. Deciding which of her spectacular outfits she would wear took time, and she applied makeup with great care, paying attention to every detail. Perfect grooming was an essential ingredient of the profession she secretly loathed.

The real trick of her success, however, was that of firmly closing her mind and heart to all she was obliged to do. Occasionally she suffered torments of shame and degradation when a coarse stranger made love to her, but in most of her relations she was successful in her refusal to think, her ability to feel nothing.

Infrequently she called on her undiminished sense of humor to restore her sense of balance, but most of the time it was her innate pride that came to her rescue. She had been condemned to the existence of a prostitute, so she was determined to be the best in the business. To the extent that she felt anything, she enjoyed the stir she created every afternoon when she slowly walked down the main staircase at Big George's, with the waves of male admiration and lust breaking over her.

Recalling how flirtatious she had been when still in her teens, she sometimes wondered whether she had been destined to become a harlot. Certainly she enjoyed being admired by men, and she relished the knowledge that she had the power to arouse them. Perhaps her present situation had been more or less inevitable because of her own inner needs; perhaps she was in trouble because of the demands of her own nature.

These thoughts always brought on a strong counter-feeling. She disliked being pawed, and in lovemaking she protected herself by willing her body to become anesthetized. Her clients were buying her considerable physical charms, but they left her spirit and soul untouched. She accepted her way of life because she had no choice. If she fought her fate, she would be severely beaten, and ultimately she would be forced to yield.

Survival, she realized, was far more important than her pride, and she fully intended to survive. And, rather than wallow in self-pity, she had the good sense to make the best of her predicament. So there was no harm done when she enjoyed the stir she created, and it was good to know that none of the other women were in her class.

Big George kept his word to her, and at no time was Melissa compelled to accept the advances of a man who, for whatever reason, repelled her. By being particular in her selection, she had discovered soon after going to work, she made herself even more desirable.

Ordinarily she took one client to her suite each afternoon; at night, after changing her costume, she accepted a second customer. Not only was she not required to be a waitress, but often she sat alone at a table reserved for her. Those who sought her favors were forced to come to her and bargain. Only rarely did she deign to dance with a patron, remaining aloof, cool, and unapproachable. She went upstairs only with men who she knew would pay the outrageous sums she demanded.

However, her manner changed in private, behind the closed door of her suite. Then she appeared to become warm and playful. She soon acquired the knack of simulating great passion. Customers who could afford intimacies with her became regulars—while their money lasted.

At first the other women resented Melissa, but she took care to cultivate their friendship. When a patron didn't appeal to her or lacked the funds to pay her fee, she always took care to turn him over to a less fortunate colleague, who appreciated her generosity. She paid liberally for the clothes made for her, and she never put on airs, joining in off-hours gossip and treating the women with a breezy informality that was lacking in the public front she maintained for the benefit of the customers.

At no time did she really lower her guard, however, and she kept silent when the women criticized Big George, who never paid for the favors he demanded. He was a hulking brute, and Melissa realized that behind his amiable façade there lurked a dangerous, violent man. It was unfortunate that he sometimes confided in her, as she was learning more about his operations than she wanted to know. Strictly for her own sake, she revealed his secrets to no one. Big George was the kind of man who, if she betrayed him, would smile steadily as he choked her to death. Melissa tolerated him, put up with his occasional crude lovemaking, and listened to his confidences because she had no choice.

One day was like another. She had no desire to leave the saloon, often refusing to accompany the other women when they went shopping in Sacramento. She made a point of emphasizing that she was content to stay behind, but her real reason was a dread of encountering the Taylors, the Greggs, or others whom she had known before her life had changed so drastically.

One afternoon Melissa donned a sleek dress of black satin, its neckline slashed to the waist, then amused herself by painting her lips a darker shade than usual, arranging her hair high on her head instead of allowing it to fall freely, and pasting a black satin beauty patch on one cheekbone. It was too bad, she thought, that there was no black lacquer available so she could paint her long nails the color of her dress. She guessed she was bored.

She put her feelings aside as she posed at the top of the staircase, haughty but provocative, remote but desirable. The men below gaped at her, and a new patron called out a vulgar observation, earning a warning frown from Big George. Melissa's glance slid from man to man, and seeing no one she recognized as wealthy, she made her way slowly to her own table, where one of the bartenders brought her a glass of colored water. She sipped the drink as she awaited the inevitable developments.

"H'lo, redhead." The speaker slurred his words as he lurched forward and pulled up a chair. Without looking at him, Melissa knew he was very drunk.

Then she glanced at him, and she went cold. Sitting opposite her was Chet Harris.

Only when she realized that Chet was too drunk to recognize her did her breathing become normal again. She studied him, her confidence slowly returning when he looked at her with glazed eyes, and she saw he had changed since their last meeting. His face had hardened, and although he was her senior by only a few years, he looked much older.

She also noticed in detail his tailor-made shirt of heavy wool, his strong trousers, and his handsome boots of new leather. His belt was expensive and so was the purse hanging from it. The holster in which he carried his six-shooter bore his initials, and on the little finger of his left hand he wore a ring of heavy gold. Here was a man who had acquired considerable wealth.

There was an easy way to confirm her guess. "How is your luck these days, miner?" she asked.

Chet grinned as he tried in vain to concentrate on

the face of the young woman who sat across the table. He knew she was very pretty, but his vision was fuzzy. "My luck is always good, redhead," he said. "I've got money to burn."

Melissa was pleased for his sake that he was doing well. However, the prospect of going to bed with this man who had been the most ardent and persistent of her swains distressed her; perhaps she could delay until he dropped off to sleep. The chance had to be taken. "I'm willing to burn it with you," she said. "How much will you pay?"

"You name it," he said, his eyes unable to focus.

"My usual fee is one hundred dollars," she said.

He felt a need to show off, as he often did when dealing with harlots. "I'll double it."

Smiling at him, she stood, helped him to his feet, and took his arm, afraid he might stumble and fall. Guiding him, she led him to the stairs, pretending to ignore the men who were staring at her. She needed all her strength to help Chet climb the stairs, and she was gasping for breath by the time they entered the parlor of her suite, where he collapsed in a chair.

She sat opposite him, habit causing her to allow her slit skirt to fall away and reveal her firm thighs, clad in black net stockings. "Would you care for a drink?" she asked, following her usual routine.

Chet had the sense to refuse. "One more might put me under," he said. Grinning stupidly, he fumbled in his purse, pulled out a thick roll of one-hundred-dollar bills, and peeled off two of them, which he handed to her.

The money vanished under her skirt, firmly secured beneath her decorative garter of scarlet satin. It was strange, the bad joke of a lifetime, that this customer should be the man who had been so eager to marry her, the man she had rejected because of her infatuation with Jerome Hadley. Perhaps she should have married Chet, even though she had never loved him.

But she couldn't think in such terms now. Steeling

herself, she smiled steadily at him, knowing she would be required to go to bed with him if he began to grope. But Chet leaned back in his chair, closed his eyes, and began to snore, gently at first, then with greater authority.

Melissa was so relieved she wanted to weep but she held back, knowing she would ruin her eye makeup. If she followed the usual procedure utilized when customers became unconscious, she would summon a couple of handymen, who would take him to the backyard and duck his head in cold water until he recovered sufficiently to take himself elsewhere.

For the sake of their long friendship, she refrained. She had known Chet since she had been an impetuous innocent in her teens and he had been a hard-working Oregon farm boy. But she could not allow sentiment for the past to destroy the present, either. She rose, bolted the door, and decided to let him sleep for an hour or two before she had him evicted.

Resuming her seat and lighting a thin, long cigar, Melissa sat quietly and stared at Chet. Temptation was nudging her, nibbling at her, and in spite of her attempts to make her mind totally blank, she found she could not resist the voice that whispered softly in her ear.

Chet's open purse contained hundreds of dollars. How easy it would be to take the rest of his money. As she well knew from the talk of her colleagues, no customer ever complained when he discovered that his wallet had been emptied. Apparently no customer was willing to admit he had been fleeced.

Melissa's dilemma was sharpened by her realization that, if she took the money, she would be acting contrary to her very private agreement with Big George. Under its terms he forced her to tell him when a client had large sums of money or gold in his purse. Subsequently, after the man had departed and traveled sufficiently far from the saloon to remove suspicion from the place, he was robbed, quietly and efficiently, by a party of masked men. Big George always made certain that Melissa received a share of the money.

She despised this aspect of her work. It was bad enough to sell her body, but it was far worse to be an active partner in a vicious, criminal scheme. Again, she had no choice. If she went to the authorities in Sacramento, she knew Big George would not hesitate to kill her. Also, she herself was outside the pale of the law now.

Loathing herself, Melissa stood in front of Chet Harris. She could empty his purse, and no one—including Chet or Big George—would be any the wiser. For a long time she felt rooted to the spot as she stared at the man whose wife she might have become. He was vain, just like any other man, she reflected, and he obviously thought money would buy him whatever he wanted. Well, he had enjoyed good fortune in the gold fields, but he was as big a fool as every other man. She had no respect for any of them.

If she didn't take the money, Chet would squander it elsewhere. If she didn't tell Big George about him, he would still be a prime candidate for the robbery squad, for he looked affluent. She reached into the purse, removed the money, and then, in a sudden impulsive gesture, returned a single one-hundred-dollar bill.

Not including the two hundred he had given her, she counted one thousand dollars. Kicking off her shoes, Melissa went to her bedchamber, where she took a key from a hiding place, then opened the strongbox chained to two bedposts and placed the money in it.

Her stomach felt queasy, and for a moment she thought she would be ill. She opened the window, then breathed cool air until she felt calmer.

Returning to the parlor, she stepped into her shoes, took care to snap Chet's purse closed, and relighted her cigar. Abruptly she tugged at a bell rope, which brought a pair of handymen to the suite. Unlocking and opening the door for them, she gestured in the direction of the still-sleeping Chet, and all at once she felt an unexpected tug of compassion for him.

"Don't be too rough with him," she said. "He's nicer than most."

She averted her gaze as they removed the unconscious Chet, and then she put him out of her mind. Her afternoon's earnings made it possible for her to take the night off, but she didn't dare. Big George might become suspicious. In fact, she had spent so little time with Chet that she could work in an extra client before nightfall.

Checking her makeup in her mirror, Melissa returned to the front stairs and again began her slow, dramatic descent, smiling as she made her subtle search for another man of means.

Whip Holt had taken his stallion, along with an old, comfortable saddle, with him on board the Thoman and Canning schooner that carried him to San Francisco. Dressed in nondescript buckskins and a broadbrimmed hat, he did not look like one of Oregon's most prosperous ranchers. But the sharp-eyed strangers in San Francisco—and he passed many as he rode through the crowded streets to the Presidio—took note of his six-shooter, the knife that protruded from the top of one boot, his somewhat old-fashioned long rifle, and, wound around his middle, the rawhide whip that had given him his nickname. He might appear less than distinguished, but those who preyed on new arrivals decided to give him a wide berth. Anyone that heavily armed had to be dangerous.

At General Blake's residence his newly appointed orderly was astonished by the stir this middle-aged visitor created. Mrs. Blake obviously was delighted to see him, and General Blake broke precedent by announcing he intended to take the day off.

Whip and Lee decided to take a walk, but they didn't get very far. Mist started to swirl in the harbor, concealing the ships at anchor there, and a strong wind, with enough of a bite to cause discomfort, drove Whip and his old friend back into the Blake house.

"Congratulations on the birth of Cindy," Cathy said. "I wrote to Eulalia just the other day, when we heard the news." She found it difficult to remember the time, on the long wagon train journey across the Great Plains and the Rocky Mountains, when she had imagined herself in love with Whip, who had led the train.

Whip thanked her, then looked at both of them. "I need the help of the Blakes," he said, grinning. "I've come down here on an errand I'll tell you about shortly. My wife is annoyed with me, but she'll forgive me if I bring the Blakes back with me for a visit."

"You've made a deal!" Lee said heartily. "I've been wanting to take a leave for a long time, and we've talked and talked about making a trip up to Oregon to see all our old friends there."

"We've postponed the trip again and again because conditions here have been so unstable," Cathy said.

"I begin to doubt if they'll ever improve," Lee added. "So just let us know when you're ready, Whip, and we'll sail with you."

"Will Toby take me for pony rides?" Beth asked. She didn't really remember Toby, but her mother had told her about him.

"No, ma'am," Whip said, smiling broadly. "Toby is big enough to be riding real horses these days, and so are you, young lady. Never fear. Toby will have you cantering and using a lasso in no time."

"When can we go?" the child demanded.

"Not until Uncle Whip attends to some business in California," Cathy said, then sent the child off to her room to do her homework.

"Conditions are still bad here?" Whip asked.

"San Francisco is nasty, but improving, what with statehood pending before 1850 comes to an end," Lee said. "And the Sacramento Valley is just impossible, with chaos spreading north, south, and east as the Gold Rush brings more adventurers to California."

"I reckon Rick Miller can impose order," Whip said. "If anyone can."

"He's doing his best, from all I hear, and so is a splendid young prosecutor from New York named Hamilton." Lee frowned. "But it takes more than a handful of dedicated citizens to turn the tide. You have no idea of the magnitude of the problems until you see how many people have no respect for the law."

"Your troops are kept busy in the city," Whip said.

"They're not as active as they were last year, thank the Lord," Lee said. "I had serious reservations when some of San Francisco's leading citizens formed a vigilance committee. But, as I've told the War Department in my reports, my doubts have vanished. I suspect the decent people in the Valley will need to form some sort of a similar organization before they can clamp the lid on tightly there."

"I reckon something is needed in the Valley," Whip said, then told them the purpose of his trip to California.

Lee was startled, and Cathy was shocked. "We saw Melissa shortly before we left Texas," she said. "She was always a little flighty, and I never approved of the way she flirted with Danny Taylor and Chet Harris. But she was an honorable, decent person—and a lady."

"She isn't any of those things now," Whip said grimly.

"How do you plan to persuade her to return to Oregon?" Lee asked.

"Blamed if I know," Whip had to admit. "I was like an old fire horse when I heard the alarm bell clanging, and I couldn't sleep on board the schooner from

Oregon. I'll have a talk with her, of course, and I aim to find out what Rick thinks. But I'll tell you one thing sure." His jaw jutted forward in a way both of the Blakes remembered vividly. "I'm not leaving Melissa Austin in a Valley saloon. One way or another, she's going back to Oregon!"

Danny Taylor was bone weary, and he was finding it as painful to walk as it had been after his operation. He had worked his way for miles up and down the Bear River, avoiding only an area near a newly built, large cabin, where a middle-aged Chinese armed with a rifle had driven him off after informing him he was trespassing. Uncertain about his rights, Danny had taken himself elsewhere.

His search for gold was painstakingly thorough. Sometimes, when he joined other fortune hunters at campfires in the open at night, he heard stories of men who had found rich veins of ore in the high hills and mountains. But he knew nothing about that kind of mining and doggedly continued to work bodies of moving water, even though most of the others were convinced that no more gold was to be found in rivers and streams.

At last his patience was rewarded on an unnamed tributary of the Bear that flowed down from the snow-covered peaks of the mighty Sierra Nevada that lay to the east. One morning two nuggets were lodged in his sieve, and the following afternoon he gathered in another, along with a teaspoon's worth of gold dust.

Knowing better than to push his luck too far, he decided the time to rejoin Heather and the baby was past due. He had spent more than eight weeks in the gold country, longer than he had anticipated, and he was so tired that, for the present at least, he was no longer lured by the possibility of finding more gold.

Aware that thieves were attracted to the campfires, where large numbers gathered, Danny wisely made up his mind to avoid such groups on his homeward journey. The rewards of his hard search were gratifying, and he didn't want to go back to Heather empty-handed. By exercising care, he had just enough bacon, beans, and flour to stave off hunger.

It was winter in the Sacramento Valley, and a cold driving rain fell from leaden skies day and night. Never had Danny seen such rain, and he was uncertain whether he or his gelding was chillier. He confined himself to one meal a day, retreating as far as he could into the deep woods every night in search of partial shelter and dry firewood.

One night, as he was finishing his skimpy supper and huddling beneath his blanket in a vain attempt to remain dry and warm, he heard someone coming toward him through the woods, apparently attracted by his fire. Reaching for his rifle beneath the blanket, Danny took the precaution of cocking it.

A shaggy-haired, ragged skeleton stumbled closer, then stopped and blinked in the glare of the fire.

"My God!" Danny exclaimed. "John Gregg!"

His neighbor and companion on the long journey from Texas to California stared at him. "Is that really you, Danny? I never know any more what's real or when I'm dreaming."

Danny's heart went out to him, and he became reckless with his remaining supplies, cooking biscuits, bacon, and beans, which John wolfed down greedily.

His story was typical of what happened to the unsuccessful in the gold fields. He had made no strikes in the months he had been searching for gold. After his limited funds had been exhausted, he had sold his horse, his pistol, his spare boots, and his ammunition in order to continue. His craze for gold had been insatiable, forcing him to go on until he had been reduced to his present state.

"I'm just on my way home," Danny said quietly. "Maybe you'd be smart to come with me."

"I reckon so." John nodded vaguely. "How did you make out, Danny?"

Something in his tone, or perhaps the wild gleam in

his eyes that the light of the fire exaggerated, made Danny somewhat apprehensive. The Greggs were decent, law-abiding people, and old Randy was the salt of the earth, but months spent in the gold fields made a man cautious. Frequently, prospectors lost their sense of perspective, and sometimes a man was known to lose his wits completely.

"I did a bit better than you, but not much," Danny said. "I found a little gold dust, that's all."

"Let me see it!" John Gregg's gaunt face came alive.

"I'm afraid this rain would wash it away." Danny's excuse was lame but was the best he could offer, and John seemed to accept it.

In the morning Danny cooked more of his dwindling food supplies, and because it seemed unfair to ride his gelding while the other man walked, he went on foot, too, leading the horse. This slowed the pace considerably, so he knew several more days would be required for the journey.

That night they consumed the last of the food. The next day they came to a cabin on a narrow, rutted road, a battered sign identifying it as a general store, and hunger caused Danny to decide he might part with a small quantity of his gold dust for supplies. A rude shock awaited him.

"I'm charging a dollar per pound for flour," the proprietor said, one hand on the butt of the six-shooter at his belt. "Bacon is five dollars a pound, and so is coffee. But beans are cheap. A dollar will buy you a pound and a half."

Danny was stunned. Even in these times, when merchants in the gold country were becoming wealthy by charging outrageously exorbitant prices for their wares, it should have been possible to spend no more than a dollar to feed two men for several days. He had no intention of squandering the gold dust he had acquired, and under no circumstances did he intend to reveal to the storekeeper just how much gold he was carrying.

"Your prices are too rich for my pocketbook," he said.

The man's shrug was indifferent. He did not suffer from lack of customers.

Danny stalked out, followed by a somewhat bewildered and disappointed John Gregg. "I don't mind paying double what something is worth," Danny said, "but I don't intend to waste all of my gold dust on provisions that will just furnish us with a few meals. We'll go hungry."

John moistened his lips, swallowed hard, and made no reply as they resumed their hike, with Danny again leading the gelding.

Whenever they made their way through patches of woods, the wilderness-wise Danny searched for edible berries, nuts, and roots. But at this season of cold rains, there was little growth in the forests, and other men, also hungry, had already found any food that remained. That night, when they huddled at a fire, Danny remarked briefly, "We'll tighten our belts a notch or two. I reckon it won't kill us to go without food for a few days until we get home." He was determined to keep his gold intact.

John nodded, his expression glum, but he made no comment.

Even more tired than he was hungry, Danny rolled up in his blanket and dropped off to sleep, the fire providing him with some warmth. He had no idea how long he slept, but all of a sudden he was wide awake. His blanket had been pulled aside, and someone was fumbling with the buckle on the purse attached to his belt.

Opening his eyes, he was startled to discover that John Gregg was trying to rob him. Danny caught hold of the younger man's wrist. "I wouldn't do that if I were you," he said quietly.

John started to flail at him with both fists. "I want the gold!" he screamed. "All I need is enough to buy a decent supply of food! Then I can go back to prospecting!"

As Danny absorbed the blows, he realized that John's long stay in the gold fields had robbed him of his reason, at least for the time being. Never one to shrink from a flight, the hero of the war with Mexico took his companion's measure, then sent him sprawling with a single blow to the face.

John began to sob.

Danny knew he would need to expend his own reserves of energy in order to see the two of them home safely.

VI

Heather Taylor cut down two dead trees in the side yard of the Gregg property facing the road, then methodically began to chop them into firewood. Later she would move the wood to the pile at the back of the house.

A heavy rain had fallen all morning, making it impossible to work outside, but she and Phyllis had gone out as soon as it had stopped. Phyllis was off in the fields, and Heather intended to join her as soon as she finished this chore. Meanwhile, her baby was sleeping peacefully in the house, and so was Randy, whose gout-ridden foot still immobilized him.

Reminded of the days when she had chopped wood as one of her chores on her father's farm, Heather thought about her past and her future. Danny's continuing absence preyed on her, and she realized she would have to make a decision soon for the sake of her own peace of mind. She hated to abandon him without saying good-bye or, to be fair, without warning him. She still loved him, so there was at least a chance they could salvage their marriage if he changed his ways.

But she could do nothing while he remained in the gold fields. She would wait a few more weeks, and then, if he still hadn't come home, she would make plans to return to Texas with the baby. How she would love to see her family again, but the very thought of admitting to them and to herself that her marriage might have failed was depressing.

Preoccupied with her thoughts, she was unaware of the approach of two burly men down the road. One was massively built, the other was very tall. Shorty and Slim had spent a considerable time in the Marysville gold country that lay to the north, then had traveled eastward, following the Yuba River to its source in the high Sierra Nevada, finally going as far as Lake Tahoe, on the California border, before doubling back to the Sacramento region.

Nowhere had they found gold, but they hadn't made any great efforts to find it, either. As they had discovered early in their partnership, it was far easier to rob others, and by now they had become so accustomed to crime that they were not in the least bothered when they found it necessary or desirable to kill or maim one of their victims.

Heather first became conscious of the pair when they halted outside the split-rail fence, about fifty feet from her.

"We ain't seen a girl that pretty in a long time, Slim," one man remarked in a deliberately loud voice.

"She's right friendly, too, Shorty," his companion said.

Slim and Shorty! Heather had heard the Fosters discussing the men who had murdered Elisabeta Miller, the men the sheriff sought so desperately. Her heart pounding, she stopped chopping wood and took a fresh grip on the handle of her ax.

"You invitin' us to join you, little lady?" The heavyset man raised the latch, and the front gate creaked open.

Heather was badly frightened, but she did not panic. Life on the Texas frontier had prepared her for this moment of crisis. "If you set foot on this property," she said, hoping they couldn't hear the tremor in her voice, "you'll have cause to regret it."

The tall man roared with laughter. "You wouldn't try to hurt us with that there ax, would you?" He strolled through the open gate.

"If I had to, I would," Heather said firmly. "But there's a better way." She bent down and picked up the six-shooter that lay on the ground beside her.

The pair halted and looked at her in surprise. Women almost invariably were so terror-stricken that they succumbed without a struggle, but this red-haired young woman actually dared to challenge them. Her bravado failed to impress them, to be sure. They would overpower her, as they had so many of their victims, and before they were through with her, they would make her pay for her temerity.

Taking careful aim at the taller man, Heather held her breath as she squeezed the trigger.

The bullet whined past Shorty's head, missing him by inches, and the smoking pistol was still pointed at him. There were other, more amenable women in the world, he decided, bolting and starting off down the road at a run.

The heavyset Slim thought of drawing his knife and intimidating the woman, but suddenly he was looking into the barrel of the pistol.

"You get out of here, too," Heather said, gaining courage. "And don't come back! I missed your friend, but I won't miss you. You're so fat you make a perfect target."

The expression in her eyes told Slim she meant what she was saying. He turned and fled.

Heather did not lower the pistol and continued to watch the pair as they raced off down the muddy road.

Phyllis approached at a run, holding up her skirts with one hand while she clutched her rifle in the other. Heather, weak-kneed now that the emergency had ended, lost no time telling her what had happened.

"Good Lord! Slim and Shorty! We've got to get word to Sheriff Miller right off!"

Heather's mind refused to function.

"Come on." Phyllis led her into the house, where Randy was snoring in his chair. She awakened her father. "You'll have to keep watch with Heather while I go into town to fetch the sheriff," she said.

Wide awake now, Randy reached for his rifle. "There's nothin' would make my foot feel better than puttin' a bullet b'tween the eyes o' one o' them filthy pigs," he said.

Phyllis raced out to the stable, saddled her horse, and cantered off, riding sidesaddle. She turned to wave encouragingly at Heather, who was sitting on the front porch in a rocker, her pistol in one hand.

Phyllis remembered few of the details of the ride into Sacramento. Other riders quickly realized that here was a woman in a hurry, and they moved out of her path, as did alarmed pedestrians. Her appearance forgotten, she reached the headquarters of the Valley authorities, looped her reins over a hitching post, and raced into the building. Learning that Sheriff Miller's office was on the upper floor, she cast aside her dignity as she mounted the steps two at a time, her skirts flying.

A few moments later Ralph Hamilton looked up from a law book and saw a breathless, disheveled woman standing on his threshold.

"Where is Sheriff Miller?" Phyllis demanded without preamble.

Ordinarily Ralph would have turned her over to one of the deputies. But he went out of his way to be helpful, perhaps because he was aware of her anxiety or possibly because he found her exceptionally pretty. "He's out on a case, I believe," he said, standing and offering her a chair. "I'm Prosecutor Hamilton, so I may be able to help you."

Struggling for breath, Phyllis introduced herself and told him what had happened. Her story was disjointed, moving forward in fits and starts.

"Did you see the men yourself?" he asked.

She shook her head, and conscious of her messy hair for the first time, she made an effort to improve her appearance. In spite of the emergency she couldn't help thinking that the prosecutor was very attractive.

Ralph went to the door and called to a deputy. "Tell Isaiah to join me, please, and ask him to bring his gun." He returned to his chair. "We'll leave word for Sheriff Miller, and I'm sure he'll come out to your father's house as soon as he returns. Meantime, I'm anxious to question Mrs. Taylor myself. I'd like to get an accurate description—in full detail—of those two men from her while the incident is still fresh in her mind."

Phyllis was relieved that he was taking charge.

"I hope you're not planning to stay in town for any purpose," he said, "because my ward and I will escort you home."

"That won't be necessary," she said politely.

"In my opinion," Ralph said, "it is very necessary. When killers are known to be in a neighborhood, it doesn't pay to take risks."

Phyllis knew he was right and was flattered by his interest.

When Isaiah arrived a few minutes later, pleased by the prospect of a break in his routine, he was surprised to find Ralph deep in conversation with an attractive young woman. They started out at once, and the boy noted that Ralph gallantly allowed the woman to set the pace.

The talk that swirled around Isaiah on the ride bored him. Phyllis was worried by her brother's prolonged absence and was concerned over her father's health. Apparently she didn't find it in the least remarkable that she and Heather Taylor were doing men's work. Ralph talked at length, too, telling this stranger many things that the boy hadn't known about his life in New York. Both the man and the woman appeared to forget that the boy was accompanying them.

Ralph repeatedly warned himself to move cautiously, and just as repeatedly he ignored his own warnings. He had been so busy and preoccupied for the last months that he rarely thought of Prudence, and even his fading memories of her now seemed unreal. But he could not even recall when he had last been attracted to any other woman. Perhaps Phyllis Gregg was all she appeared to be, but he reflected that he could not allow himself to pay active court to her until he knew her better and had an opportunity to judge her character. One woman had wounded him badly, and he would be stupid if he made himself vulnerable to another.

When they reached the Gregg house, they found the entire Foster family on guard.

Ralph promptly withdrew privately with Heather, who was able to describe Shorty and Slim in detail. He made notes as she talked and was pleased when rounded portraits of the killers began to emerge, including the color of their hair, their complexions, the mole on one's chin, even the qualities of their voices. One walked with a somewhat rolling gait, while the other plodded. Here was valuable data that would be disseminated to every law enforcement agency and officer in California, and Ralph well realized that Heather's powers of observation at last were making it possible to apprehend the killers of Elisabeta Miller.

The youngsters were told to go out into the yard. Isaiah felt somewhat ill at ease with the young Fosters, although he took an instinctive liking to Scott, who was approximately his own age. Tracy, who was even taller and huskier than his older brother, felt compelled to challenge the stranger. "How come somebody as skinny as you carries a six-shooter?" he demanded. "The kickback must bowl you over."

"I can shoot well enough," Isaiah replied quietly.

"I'm better," Tracy said.

Scott frowned at him. "Pa has told you not to brag," he said.

Tracy ignored him and looked Isaiah up and down. "I'll bet my pistol against your pistol that I'm better'n you."

Sarah Rose was outraged. "Tracy Foster, you'll be whaled if Pa and Ma find out you're betting!"

"They won't know unless you tell them," he said, continuing to stare at Isaiah.

"I don't bet," Isaiah said.

"You mean you're a yellow-livered coward," Tracy replied.

Ordinarily those words would have caused Isaiah to punch Tracy. But this was Isaiah's first visit to the Gregg property, and he had come here with Ralph on official business. He shouldn't be getting into a fist fight.

"I accept your wager—and the terms." Isaiah said, then turned to Scott. "Put up a target for us, will you? As close or as far as you like. We'll each fire six shots, and you'll be the judge."

Much against his will and shaking his head, Scott nailed a board to a tree about fifty paces away, then used his knife to scratch a circle the size of a man's fist in the center of the thick board.

"Tell Pa we're going to do some target practice," Tracy said to his sister.

"Tell him yourself!" she retorted, and after he went off to the house, she spoke to Isaiah in a low tone. "He thinks he's so smart. I hope you beat him good and proper."

Isaiah thanked her, then curbed his nervousness. His pistol had been a gift from Sheriff Miller, so it was important that he not lose it.

"You can go first," Tracy said when he returned. "It don't matter to me."

Obviously he was self-confident, but Isaiah tried to forget him. Stepping up to the line that Scott had marked in the dirt, he concentrated on the target, telling himself that this occasion was identical to the countless hours he spent in target practice in his own yard. Raising his pistol and firing in rapid succession, he emptied all six chambers.

Scott went forward to study the target, with Sarah Rose trailing behind him. They studied it, and both were grinning when they returned. "Four shots inside the circle, two shots outside the circle but still on the board," Scott announced.

His brother was shaken. Not even Pa, who was a fine marksman, could achieve better results. He raised his own pistol slowly, took aim, and fired. Then he paused at length before shooting again, and it took a long time before his pistol was empty.

This time Sarah Rose ran ahead of Scott to the target, and when she looked at it, she laughed gleefully.

Scott remained grave. "You won," he told Isaiah. "Easy. Tracy landed only one shot in the inner circle and two outside it."

There was a silence, and Tracy offered his pistol to the stranger from Sacramento. "Here," he said. "I guess you won it fair enough."

Isaiah surprised himself by shaking his head. "No, thanks," he said. "Keep it. I already have my own pistol, and I don't need another."

Scott shook his hand warmly, and Sarah Rose beamed at him. Tracy was disconcerted but was saved the embarrassment of replying when Rick Miller rode up to the house at a wild gallop, flung himself from the saddle, and, not acknowledging the presence of the children, hurried into the house. His expression was so savage that even Isaiah was startled.

Rick immediately joined Heather and Ralph and asked the young woman to repeat her story again. He listened without comment, and his jaw tightened when Ralph read him the descriptions of Shorty and Slim.

"I'll have a thousand *Wanted* notices printed as fast

as we get back to Sacramento," Ralph said, "and I'll borrow a half-dozen of your deputies to take them to every courthouse, post office, and government building in the territory."

"I'll distribute some myself." Rick took a six-shooter from its holster and absently made sure it was loaded. Then, wrenching himself back to the present, he turned solemnly to Heather. "I'm grateful to you," he said, "as sheriff of the Sacramento Valley. And personally. Until Danny and John returned from the gold fields, I'm assigning two deputies to keep permanent watch over you and Phyllis."

When she tried to protest, Rick silenced her with a wave. "We'll handle this as I see fit," he said curtly.

Ralph was relieved, realizing he would have been fearful for Phyllis's sake.

"Now," Rick said grimly, "I can really get to work."

Under the terms of a tacit, scrupulously observed agreement, no law enforcement officer ever entered a saloon, brothel, or gambling house in the gold country. Miners had a need to relax after the rigors of the field, and it was the view of the Sacramento Valley commissioners that the miners could blame no one but themselves if they were cheated and robbed.

This opinion was based on necessity rather than on philosophical grounds. There were far too many sporting establishments in the Valley and far too few law enforcement officers to police them. So it was understood that such places were out of bounds and that anyone who went to one of them could not complain if something went amiss during a visit.

Occasionally, to be sure, fights with guns and knives broke out, especially in some of the smaller saloons, and it was understood that when human life was at stake, the deputies were free to enter the establishment and end the disturbance.

Never had any law enforcement officer set foot in Big George's saloon. The giant proprietor, armed with his six-shooter and a lead-filled iron pipe, maintained order in his own way, and on the infrequent occasions when a number of customers became unruly at the same time, Big George's burly assistants literally threw them out into the road or the fields.

So the appearance of Sheriff Rick Miller, chief law enforcement officer of the entire Sacramento Valley, was totally unexpected. As he made his way across the main room, more and more customers recognized him and gaped at him, as did a number of the women. The fiddlers and drummer stopped playing, stranding several couples on the dance floor; a card game in progress halted abruptly; and a deepening silence spread through the place. Soon there was no sound but the click of Rick's heels and the jangle of his spurs as he slowly walked the length of the room.

Big George materialized from a private room behind the bar and, smiling broadly, advanced to meet the unexpected guest. "This is a pleasure, Sheriff," he said.

"I'm sure it is," Rick replied dryly, ignoring the proprietor's outstreched hand.

Big George was equal to the occasion. "Join me." he said, leading the grim-faced officer to a corner table. "Which will you have—a glass of first-rate Kentucky whiskey or some fine Spanish brandywine?"

"A cup of black coffee will do me just fine," Rick said.

Big George signaled, indicating that he wanted one of the bartenders rather than a flimsily clad waitress to bring the drink.

Rick took a paper from his pocket and unfolded it. "Ever see these two men?" he asked.

Big George studied the *Wanted—Dead or Alive* notice and was telling the truth when he shook his head. If Sheriff Miller was conducting a personal search for these criminals, it would be stupid to harbor them. "If they show up here, Sheriff, I'll send word to you right off."

"Thanks." Rick sipped the coffee that was placed before him.

Eager to win his favor at little cost to himself, Big George expanded on the offer. "If you can spare a copy of this notice, I'll post it in back of the bar."

"I intended to ask you to do exactly that," an unsmiling Rick said, handing him the poster.

The proprietor immediately summoned the bartender, and a few moments later the notice was nailed behind the bar.

"I've been told that some pretty rough types come here from time to time." Rick's gaze seemed casual, but he was taking advantage of this unexpected visit to study every detail of the place. "However that may be, Shorty and Slim are tougher than most. They're murderers, they're rapists, and they're ruthless bastards. Take no chances if they show up here."

Big George stroked the lead-filled iron pipe that he was carrying in his belt. "We can take care of all kinds," he said.

Rick didn't hear him. He was staring up at the top of the staircase.

Big George cursed silently. Melissa, the queen, was making her afternoon appearance, clad in a gown of glittering silver cloth that showed off far more than it concealed of her body. There had been no opportunity to warn her not to put on her show until the law enforcement officer had departed, and now it was too late.

Rick continued to gape at her.

The realization dawned on Big George, who saw him following her movements closely as Melissa slowly descended the stairs, that Sheriff Miller was fascinated by her. Well! Here was an opportunity that had to be pursued. If she could insinuate herself into his good graces and promote an affair with him, Big George would be able to expand his illegal operations in the Valley without fear of apprehension. Already valuable, Melissa could become a priceless asset.

"That's Melissa," he said.

"I know." Rick's voice was harsh.

Big George summoned her with a sharp wave as

she reached the bottom stair. Then, muttering a few apologetic words, he left the table.

Melissa made her way to the table of the man who appeared to be an important customer, her hips undulating seductively, a provocative smile fixed on her heavily painted lips.

At Big George's order the musicians struck up a tune, and the silence in which the saloon had been enveloped was broken. Many people started talking simultaneously, and a woman's shrill laugh rose above the noise. Big George stood behind the bar, grinning quietly. His luck was almost too good to be true.

Suddenly Melissa's blood turned to ice. Rick Miller was watching her approach, his hard eyes boring into her! Rick Miller, for whom she had formed a deep, enduring respect when he had conducted a group of settlers, of which she had been a member, from Oregon to Texas. Rick Miller, whose admiration she had long craved.

Somehow her feet continued to propel her forward, and she did not falter, even though Rick studied her with such critical, detached care that his eyes seemed to penetrate her mind and heart. Flushing as she reached his side, Melissa was so suffused with shame that her only defense was that of losing her temper. "What's the matter?" she demanded. "Haven't you ever seen a pretty woman?"

"I never expected that the world would see quite so much of you," he replied mildly. Then his manner changed, and he rasped an order: "Sit down!"

It would have been impossible for Melissa to deny that voice of command, and she sat, tugging in vain at her dress as she tried to cover her thighs and legs.

A bartender brought two drinks, the best whiskey in the house for Rick and colored water for Melissa, but Rick waved him away.

"I first knew you," he said, speaking slowly, "as an impulsive, sweet youngster in her teens, who enjoyed the greatest thrill of her life when she stowed away in a party bound for Texas."

"That girl doesn't exist anymore." She lacked the courage to clamp her hands over her ears and flee from him.

"Then you performed needed work at the shipyard Harry Canning established at Galveston. Texas had to build a navy, and you pitched in."

"Why do you mention all this?" Melissa demanded, and summoning the bartender, she ordered two glasses of whiskey. "Real ones," she said.

"I saw what you did to some of the boys in my regiment during the war with Mexico. You played Danny and Chet off against each other, which may not have been fair, but it was harmless fun. And the last I heard, you came to California with a professional gambler, Jerome Hadley."

"So that brings us up to date." She seized her glass from the bartender and took a deep swallow.

"Not quite," Rick said, his manner unyielding. "There are some gaps."

"What in hell do you want to know?" she cried.

He shrugged. "Whatever you care to tell me that will explain this extraordinary transformation. It may not be any of my business, but I'm making it my business."

Big George was concerned as he watched them. Melissa and the sheriff appeared to know each other, and both looked upset. Perhaps his luck wasn't as good as he had thought.

Melissa's shrug was as indifferent as her voice was cold. "There isn't much to tell. Jerome deserted me. No, he did more than that, actually. He sold me to Big George. And here I am."

"There are laws against enforced prostitution," Rick said, "and as the chief law enforcement officer in the Valley it's my duty to—"

"Relax, honey," Melissa said, interrupting and raising her glass to him. "I paid George off shortly after I came here. Now I'm here because I like it. I'm the most successful, highest-priced whore in California, maybe in all of the United States, and I love it."

In spite of her bravado, Melissa felt a crushing sense of embarrassment. She had looked up to Rick Miller since the moment she had met him, and her outrageous conduct on the trail to Texas had been a series of deliberate attempts to attract his attention. Even in those days, however, she had known in her heart that her approach to winning his respect and admiration had been all wrong.

Well, he certainly wouldn't respect her now. By acting brazen and bold, she had just gone out of her way to drive nails into her own coffin. And that couldn't be helped. She was damned, she knew it, and the only thing she could do was to force herself to take a totally unrepentant stand. She lifted her glass and started to drain the contents.

Rick took the drink from her and emptied it onto the sawdust floor. His movement was so swift that he completed the act before Melissa quite realized what had happened. "It may be you're the highest-priced prostitute in the whole world," he said thoughtfully. "I'm not familiar with current rates. But when you tell me you love it, you're a liar."

Hostility to him almost overwhelmed her. Or perhaps it was burning sense of shame. Whatever it was that was consuming her, she was unable to reply.

What Melissa failed to recognize, however, was Rick's ability to see through her façade. How well he still recalled his late wife's playacting and dissembling when she had imagined herself in trouble with the law because of her inadvertent involvement with a murderer.

His experience had taught him that some women were natural prostitutes. But, unless he totally misjudged Melissa's character, she could not be placed in that category. Her toughness and bravado were just a front she was putting on for his benefit. He was certain she hated her work and hated herself even more. But he also realized that she saw no real escape from her dilemma—she needed more time to find her way out of the maze in which she was trapped.

Very well. He would grant her as much time as she required, but he knew, deep down, that sooner or later she would free herself from her present existence.

"My late wife," Rick said, "was the most compassionate of women. I try to keep her in mind at moments like this."

She hadn't known his wife had died, but he gave her no opportunity to comment. "If she were still alive, she'd insist that I take you away from Big George's, force you to scrub your face, and put on some decent clothes—and then she'd tell me to find you an honorable job. Well, Elisabeta wasn't very practical, and she didn't know the world all that well. I can't throw you over my shoulder, Melissa, and carry you out of here against your will, kicking and screaming. If you truly want to live the life of a slut, I know of no law that will compel you to change, no law that makes it possible for me to force you to change. On the other hand, if you really want to change, all you need to do is call on me."

His gesture was so thoughtful, so sweet that she had to fight back the tears that threatened to destroy her makeup. "Why are you being so nice to me?" she asked in a choked voice.

"As a Ranger in Texas," he said, "and more recently in my present work, I've seen all kinds of bums and criminals. Yes, and prostitutes. Some of them are just naturally no good. Some of them have the ability to reform if they're given the chance. Maybe I'm just remembering the wholesome youngster with a mop of wild red hair and spirits to match—who had such a craving for adventure. Maybe, after what you've gone through—and that's something only you know—that girl isn't as dead as you've tried to lead me to believe."

"The reason I always liked and respected you so much," Melissa said, "is because you were always honest with me. With everybody. Well, I guess I owe you honesty in return." She picked up his untouched drink, challenging him, and took a large swallow.

Rick made no attempt to take the glass from her and instead waited patiently.

"I'm unfit for any other kind of life now," she said. "Where could the former queen of Big George's find respectable work? What decent man in his right mind would marry the most brazen, notorious whore in the gold country? I'm stuck, Rick, and you know it as well as I do. Admit that I'm right."

"Only if you demand to be stuck," he said.

Melissa shook her head fiercely. "I'm more of a realist than you are, honey. Believe me, I've learned the hard way. Ten years from now—as long as I keep my figure and the lines don't show too much in my face—I'll be doing exactly what I'm doing today. And if I'm ever lucky enough to retire, my one hope is that I can go to some place, far away, where my reputation won't follow me. So—thanks for the offer, honey. And drop in again when you want a good long laugh!"

The ragged, unkempt John Gregg wept when he walked into his family's house, saw his invalid father, and greeted his sister. Danny Taylor, who had escorted him home, was succinct in his advice. "John," he said, "will be all right after he gets a few square meals under his belt."

Danny himself was astonished when he found his wife and baby living at the Gregg house, and questions crowded his mind as he took Heather into his arms. She allowed herself to be embraced, thankful that he had returned to her unharmed, but even as she felt comforted by his touch, she steeled herself for the showdown she was determined to precipitate at the first possible moment.

Her reasons for moving in with the Greggs made sense to Danny, and he listened as she and Phyllis explained how they had been sharing the work on the farm. Heather had behaved sensibly, he said, but he became white faced and silent when he learned she had been forced to drive off Slim and Shorty.

Conscious of John's failure to find any gold after a long search, Danny saved the news of his own strike until he and Heather were alone. Then he beamed proudly as he showed her the nuggets and gold dust. "It's no great fortune," he said, "but it's like the last time—more than I could have made by working the orchard for at least a year."

The moment of crisis had come, and Heather clenched her fists. "Then you're satisfied with what you've done in the gold fields."

"Well," he said, "I've heard stories about men who have done a heap better, although I haven't actually met or run across anybody who has made a real fortune. But most of the poor devils who have been prospecting are like John Gregg, dead broke and starving. So I can't complain."

"I can," Heather said quietly. "I hope you aren't thinking of going off again."

"Not right away, maybe," Danny said. "But these infernal rains will end when spring comes, and then I guess I'll try my luck again."

She looked at him, and although her words were defiant, her attitude was surprisingly matter-of-fact. "If you leave me for one more trip to the gold fields," she said, "the baby and I won't be here when you come back. In fact, unless we reach a firm and final understanding right here and now, I'm taking Ted off to my folks' place back in Texas, no matter how difficult it may be to get there."

Danny was so stunned he could only gape at her.

"We had an agreement that you'd look for gold when we came to California," she said. "I knew it was a mistake the first time, but I didn't say anything, and I kept my mouth shut when you went prospecting again. You've been fortunate, but your luck could change for the worse—"

"Or for the better," he interjected.

"Maybe so, but I can't stand not knowing whether

you're dead or alive. I'm glad I've been able to help Phyllis, but you and I have done nothing to build our own future. The gold you've found will come in handy, and I'd be the last to deny it. We can put some aside for times of trouble. We can invest in apricot trees and grape vines, which will bring us a better yield than other fruits, although we may need longer to get started. If you want me here, you'll go to work."

He bridled. "You're wrong if you think I've been having a grand old time in the gold fields. Matter of fact, I haven't had a bite to eat for days."

"I'm sure it hasn't been easy," Heather said, "just seeing how gaunt and tired you are makes me realize it. And makes me know, too, that I'm not going through this experience again. I love you, Danny. I want to spend the rest of my life with you. I want us to bring up Ted together—according to the standards you and I believed were right when we first got married. And eventually, when life in the Valley becomes less hectic, I'd like more children. But if I'm going to devote my life to you and our family, you've got to give me stability in return. This is no sudden decision. I've thought about little else all this time you've been away, and my mind is made up."

"If there's anything I don't like, it's an ultimatum," Danny said frowning. "How soon must I give you my answer?"

"If you need time to work it out in your mind," she said, "you and I don't have much of a future together." Perhaps she was wrong to be holding a figurative gun to his head, but she had to be honest with him.

He was torn, but after a moment's pause he capitulated with a lack of grace. "I think you're being shortsighted," he said, "but you give me no choice. If I'm forced to choose between my family and gold, I'll take you and the baby. Naturally. But we're making a bad mistake. We have a chance to become filthy rich, and we may be sorry for the rest of our days."

Heather had won but realized her victory was hollow. She lacked the experience and finesse to have achieved the same goal without arousing her husband's hostility. Now she had erected a barrier between herself and Danny, and she not only had no idea how to tear it down, but she also was afraid there might be no way it could be removed as long as they lived.

Whip Holt sat with Rick Miller and Ralph Hamilton in front of an open fire in the parlor of the prosecutor's house after supper. Rick was delighted once again to be in the company of the legendary mountain man, and Ralph was greatly impressed as he listened to Whip speak.

"The first time I saw California," Whip said, "I came out here with a brother mountain man, name of Kit Carson. San Francisco was called Yerba Buena, and it was just a little port and a few buildings. And there were only a few ranches in the Valley. This was great country in those days, and what amazes me is that it wasn't even fifteen years ago. I've had my fill of the new San Francisco, and just seeing Sacramento since this morning, all I can say is that the territory is choked with carrion."

"I felt pretty much as you do when I first came here," Ralph said. "Greed isn't a healthy magnet, and easy money breeds corruption. But California will be admitted to the Union as a state before the year ends, and I'm convinced that ultimately a great future lies ahead for the whole Pacific area."

"There's no need to convince me of that. I've been living in Oregon for a long time." Whip smiled, then sobered. "What bothers me is the question of how long it will take to clean out the scum."

Rick stared into the fire. "As I see it, that depends on how hard a few of us like Ralph and me work and how much help we get. The vigilance committee in San Francisco is doing a great job, from all I hear, but there isn't enough of a nucleus of prominent people here to do the same thing. For the next year or two, anyway, we'll have to depend on paid deputies and on the volunteers we can persuade to join us. But people are becoming discouraged. The deputy sheriff in Sacramento was recently killed trying to evict poachers off John Sutter's land, and my other deputies complain about being underpaid and overworked."

"If anyone can bring law and order into the Valley, you can, Rick," Whip Holt said.

"I appreciate that, Whip. There's no other man around whose opinion I value so highly."

Ralph looked at the famous man. "May I ask why you've come to California, Mr. Holt?"

Whip unhesitatingly explained his mission. Melissa Austin had been close to his family and to a number of others in Oregon, and he had heard disturbing news about her. So he had come to the Valley in the hope of finding her and, if possible, persuading her to return home.

"I'm afraid you're wasting your time, Whip," Rick said, relating in detail his own frustrating meeting with the girl.

Whip listened in silence, his lips compressed.

"I'm afraid nothing will persuade her to change her ways," Rick concluded.

"I first knew her as a youngster," Whip said slowly. "She was a mite flighty, and she liked to flirt. But she was decent and good. You can't tell me she's all that different now."

Rick shrugged. "Any customer at Big George's who can afford her fee has the right to go upstairs with her."

"That's what I assume," Whip said, "but I'm talking about something else. You've known prostitutes, and so have I, who enjoy their way of life. They wouldn't change if they could. They've led their kind of existence since they were youngsters. And the whole point I'm making is that Melissa Austin never seemed to me to be that sort."

"Nor to me," Rick said. "But she wouldn't listen to a

word when I tried to persuade her to leave Big George's place."

"You won't mind if I have a chat with her?"

"Help yourself, Whip. I've spent enough time on her when I should be using every minute to hunt down the men who murdered my Elisabeta."

"Tell me," Whip said, "do you have any leads on those killers?"

"None that amount to a hill of beans, Whip." Rick's clenched fists were a symbol of the frustrations that overwhelmed him. "When we're living in a part of the country where there are criminals everywhere—and it seems only a minority of the folks who have come out here have any respect for the law—it's like hunting for an acorn in a pile of snow. The acorn stands out fast enough once you locate it, but you have to shovel snow for day after day after day."

Whip looked at him sympathetically. "Don't let your failure interfere with your resolution."

"I'll get those devils if it's the last thing I ever do. I'll stick to my guns, never fear."

Accepting Ralph's invitation to stay at the house as a guest for as long as he wished, Whip indicated that he would ride to Big George's saloon the following day. Alone with his host at breakfast for a time, he took advantage of the opportunity for a private conversation to inquire in detail about the death of Elisabeta Miller, a subject he had refrained from discussing with Rick.

Later, as he rode toward the gold fields from Sacramento, Whip reflected that the need for order in California was even greater than he had thought. He had known lawlessness in many forms throughout his own turbulent life, but the quiet of Oregon in recent years had spoiled him.

Aware from what Rick had told him that Melissa made no appearance until afternoon, he took his time on the road and was even more dumbfounded than he had been in town by the appearance of the men he saw. Most were unshaven, their clothes were filthy, and their hollow-eyed, gaunt expressions told him they were hungry. It was axiomatic that men who went without food were dangerous, and he told himself it was fortunate that life in the gold country and its environs wasn't even more chaotic. Rick Miller and the equally earnest Ralph Hamilton had their hands full, and he was sorry he wasn't a few years younger so he could pitch in and work with them.

A cold rain began to fall, so Whip pulled his old poncho of buffalo hide over his head, and the heavily oiled garment warded off the worst of the rain. When he reached Big George's place, he was glad to warm himself at the hearth that stood near the long hardwood bar. This was the sort of weather that caused the ache in his hip to act up, and he was lucky that, so far, he hadn't been incapacitated.

The saloon was as busy as any Whip had ever seen. At least thirty or forty men were lined up at the bar, and an even larger number filled the tables, where flimsily clad waitresses brought them drinks. Several of the women eyed him speculatively, but he used an old trick to avoid them, seemingly looking through them without seeing them, and they did not annoy him.

Still chilled after his ride, Whip finally moved from the hearth to a table and ordered a small glass of brandywine.

The woman who brought it to him lingered beside him after he had paid her. "Want some company?"

"As a matter of fact," he said, "I'm here to see Melissa."

The woman looked him up and down, her expression indicating that his clothes didn't look as though he could afford Melissa. "Are you sure I won't do instead?"

Whip wanted to discourage her, but at the same time he was too honest to give her the wrong impression. "Sure," he said, "you'd be just fine if I wanted what you think I want. But I just want to have a little chat with Melissa."

"Do you want a message delivered to her?"

Afraid she might remain in her quarters rather than face him once she learned he was here, he shook his head. "I'll see her whenever she shows up."

Somewhat bewildered, the woman gave the proprietor a verbatim account of the conversation.

Big George was upset. Melissa had been disturbed since Sheriff Miller's recent visit, and it appeared that more of the same might be in store. Certainly this heavily armed, quiet-eyed man who exuded an air of self-controlled power was no typical miner. His stallion, which he had left with one of the grooms, was a splendid, expensive mount, and the saddle was expertly crafted; and although the visitor's clothes were somewhat worn, his arsenal—including a rifle, pistol, double-edged knife, and the rawhide whip—had cost a pretty penny.

Big George felt certain the gray-haired man was not one of Melissa's ardent customers.

She had remained in her suite, refusing to appear for twenty-four hours after Sheriff Miller had spoken with her. If she withdrew again after this stranger had words with her, she would be costing Big George a substantial revenue loss. That prospect pained him.

It was simple enough to take care of the situation before Melissa came downstairs. Big George moved to the center of the bar, then halted beneath the huge red, white, and blue candle that burned overhead, directly behind him, whenever the saloon was open for business. From that vantage point he would orchestrate his assault.

A small sip of brandywine was enough to convince Whip that the liquor served in this saloon was barely potable, and he pushed his glass to one side. Suddenly it occurred to him that at least a half-dozen men, some at the bar and several sitting at nearby tables, were observing him, watching every move he made. Their steady scrutiny made him uncomfortable.

It pleased Big George that the middle-aged stranger was rising to the bait by becoming annoyed. It should be easy enough to get rid of him before Melissa made her dramatic entrance.

At the proprietor's surreptitious signal, a number of additional men showed an interest in the outsider.

Whip had known the West before many of the people in the establishment had been born, and he was well aware of the trick being played on him. For some reason—perhaps because the management wanted him to keep his distance from Melissa—he was being subjected to what, in the old days, mountain men had called "the treatment." If he objected to the stares, the group would rush him and throw him out. Even if he said and did nothing, he well might be in for trouble.

Pretending to pay no attention, Whip slowly came to the conclusion that the activities around him were being directed by the tall, heavyset man who stood behind the center of the bar. Guessing that he was Big George, Whip waited patiently for developments.

He did not have long to wait. A bearded man at an adjoining table called to him. "You're a deputy sheriff, ain't you?" He made the question sound like an accusation.

Whip smiled inoffensively and shook his head. "No, sir," he said. "I'm strictly a private citizen."

Another man took up the charge. "Then how does it happen you carry so many weapons?"

"I've done it for so long that my ways have become a habit, I reckon." Anyone who knew Whip would have been warned by his deceptive calm, almost meek tone.

Big George gave the open signal that the time had come to act. Drawing his lead-filled length of iron pipe from his belt, he called in a loud, clear voice, "I say the old man is a police spy."

The group at the bar faced Whip, and those at

nearby tables stood, forming a semicircle around him.

He had hoped that even a threat of violence could be avoided, and he had wanted to remain inconspicuous, but neither of those goals could be obtained. Sighing gently, he uncoiled the whip from around his middle and, as he stood, simultaneously reached for his six-shooter.

The whip cracked with the authority of a pistol shot, and the rawhide end wrapped itself like a serpent around Big George's thick wrist, then jerked the lead-filled pipe from his grasp.

As it clattered to the floor, Whip's pistol sounded, the single shot extinguishing the candle that burned only inches above Big George's head.

He, his subordinates, and his friends stood frozen.

The whip released the proprietor's wrist, then flicked ominously at Whip's side while the muzzle of his pistol traveled in a semicircle. Whip's would-be attackers understood his gesture: he had them covered.

"If any of you boys are looking for a fight," he said, "I'll be glad to oblige you."

No one moved or spoke.

He smiled lazily at the proprietor. "You're Big George, I take it."

The proprietor nodded.

"I don't think much of your hospitality," Whip said. "I'm a peace-loving man, but if you're otherwise inclined, we can make the arrangements."

So total was this lone, gray-haired man's domination of the situation that no one present thought it odd that he should be able to intimidate fifty to seventy-five potential enemies.

Suddenly a young woman's voice rose behind him. "George! All of you! Have you lost your senses? This is Whip Holt!"

Along with a handful of other mountain men, among them Jim Bridger and Kit Carson, Whip had acquired an awesome reputation as a ferocious fighter, no matter what the odds against him. Big George had to make the best of a sticky situation. "My apologies, Mr. Holt," he said. "Sorry I didn't know you." He reached beneath the bar for a bottle of his best brandywine, which he held up as a peace offering.

Melissa Austin, dazzling in white, took the bottle and carried it to the table, along with two glasses.

"Thanks, Melissa," Whip said. "I didn't want anyone to be hurt."

She seated herself opposite him, her face masklike. "I knew the second I saw you that you came here because of me. Apparently George knew it, too, and was trying to protect me."

"He went about it the wrong way." Whip studied the heavily made-up girl, but there was no hint of censure in his voice as he said, "Eulalia sends you her love. So do the Cannings. And the Thomans. And a great many other good friends."

"When you go back to Oregon," she said, speaking evenly, "tell them to forget me. The girl they knew no longer exists."

Whip caught hold of her wrist. "Look at me, Melissa," he said, a quiet urgency in his voice.

Melissa forced herself to lift her gaze to his for an instant before she flinched and turned away.

"Rick Miller has told me about his talk with you," he said. "I don't believe in going over the same ground again, just as I don't believe that beating a dead mule will persuade him to haul a cart. All I ask of you, Melissa, is that you give some thought to the possibility of coming home. Don't reject it automatically by telling yourself that nobody gives a damn about you. A whale of a lot of people give a very big damn."

"I'll never forgive you if you make me cry," she said in a choked voice.

He rose to his feet, his movements surprisingly swift and agile for someone with his arthritic condition. "We'll just make good and sure the door is left open," he said and started toward the bar.

The men who were crowded there moved aside

hastily to make room for him. Whip faced Big George, and although his tone was conversational, it was suddenly so quiet in the saloon that his words carried to the far corners. "George," he said, "you may not have known that Melissa has friends. Old friends who are interested in her welfare. I'd hate to hear that anyone abused or scared her, you know." His knife appeared in his hand. "Because I'd scalp any man who didn't treat her right. Yes, sir, I'd scalp him alive, and that's a promise."

Big George found it difficult to return the steady scrutiny of the older man's pale eyes.

"In the last few minutes," Whip said, "I've decided to stay in Sacramento for a spell. I'm sure it's understood that anytime Melissa wants to come to see me, she's free to do it. Or anytime she wants me to pay her a visit here, she's free to send for me."

Never before had Big George met anyone he couldn't frighten, and under the circumstances he nodded.

"Maybe she will," Whip said, "and maybe she won't. What's important is that she'll make up her own mind." He turned, grinned at Melissa, and then started toward the door.

One of the men at the bar, hoping to impress the proprietor, reached for his pistol. Whip whirled around, convincing many of the spectators that he had eyes in the back of his head. His rawhide whip leaped across the intervening space, and the pistol flew high into the air, then fell to the bar.

Not looking back again, Whip left the place, retrieved his stallion, and started back toward town. He didn't like to indulge in theatrical gestures, but on occasion it was necessary in order to make a point.

His mind seethed on the ride to Sacramento. Night had fallen by the time he reached town, and after a short search he found Rick Miller at supper in a small, quiet restaurant with Ralph Hamilton and Isaiah Atkins. All three watched him as he came toward them.

"I wouldn't have been much good as a clergyman,"

he said, drawing up a chair and joining them. "I'm not one for delivering sermons, and I believe folks have to make up their own minds about doing good or doing evil."

There was no need for Rick to ask whether he had seen Melissa.

Whip turned to Ralph. "How soon are you going to need that guest room in your house?"

"Keep it as long as you please, Mr. Holt!"

Whip grinned at Isaiah, then sobered as he looked first at the prosecutor, then at the sheriff. "I've got a real problem," he said. "If I don't show up in Oregon pretty soon, my wife is going to be mad as a hornet. But if I show up without Melissa in tow, she's going to be badly disappointed, and so are a lot of other people. What's more, if I leave now, with the law here in as bad a mess as it is, my conscience will bother me something awful. I'd rather have my wife upset with me than face my own conscience."

Rick, guessing what Whip had in mind, extended his hand. Whip gripped it firmly. "Just in case Melissa changes her plans, I'll stick around for a while," he said. "Meantime, I can help you look for your wife's killers and clean up enough odds and ends to keep Prosecutor Hamilton busy. I reckon you'd better swear me in, Rick—at no pay—as a temporary deputy."

The newly expanded King's Castle Hotel was San Francisco's finest, and not even in New York, Boston, Philadelphia, or Chicago was there a more luxurious hostelry. The furniture, thick rugs, and crystal chandeliers had come from the Eastern Seaboard, and no expense had been spared in creating a haven for those who could afford the establishment's amenities. Not only were the living quarters handsome, with views of the city and bay from its site at the summit of one of the highest hills in town, but also the meals in all three dining rooms were prepared by chefs as expert as Europe's best.

Far from the least of the hotel's attractions was the

iron-clad security it offered those who were fortunate enough to stay there. Overall conditions in San Francisco had improved drastically since the vigilance committee had inaugurated its operations, but in most hotels burglaries were commonplace, and it was not unusual for guests to be accosted by robbers in the corridors. Such crimes were unknown at the King's Castle. The management maintained a force of trained, armed guards, most of them men who were hired as they retired from duty at the army garrison. They patrolled the lobbies, corridors, and gardens in pairs, armed with six-shooters and heavy clubs, so crime was unknown there. And guests were charged accordingly.

Thanks to its growing reputation, the King's Castle was used for local functions. On September 9, 1850, California was admitted to the Union as the thirty-first state, and the official banquet in honor of the occasion was held at the hotel. In attendance were the new state's highest-ranking officials, as well as many of San Francisco's more prominent citizens and their wives. Also on hand were representatives of the federal judiciary and the commandant of the Presidio and his wife, Brigadier General and Mrs. Leland Blake.

The nine-course dinner was sumptuous, as befitted the occasion, and the speeches that followed were mercifully short, the publisher of the city's leading newspaper having remarked that people would fall asleep after eating so much if the addresses were long-winded. The affair was held in the grand ballroom at the rear of the second floor, and for the first time since the United States had acquired possession of California, the ladies wore evening gowns.

Cathy Blake was the most attractive woman present, at least in her husband's opinion, and many of the guests agreed with Lee. Radiant in a peach-colored silk gown, she looked like a young girl rather than a mature woman. Lee, who was resplendent in his gold-trimmed dress uniform, had never been more proud of her.

Even though some of the guests had consumed considerable quantities of alcohol, common sense rules prevailed. Those who were staying at the King's Castle as guests retired to the bar on the ground floor for a nightcap after the festivities, but they were not joined by those who had to return to their own homes. Midnight was approaching, and soon the streets everywhere in the community would be unsafe.

Not that the Blakes were worried, to be sure. As Lee's aide-de-camp brought him his dress cape and hat, along with Cathy's cloak, the young officer murmured, "The cavalry escort is waiting with your carriage at the side entrance, General."

Lee nodded his thanks, and after he and Cathy said good night to the other guests, she took his arm, and they started down the broad staircase to the ground floor.

Suddenly Lee frowned. Mounting the stairs slowly and coming toward them were a young man in evening clothes and two blonde young women whose tight-fitting, revealing dresses promptly identified their calling. They were clinging to their male companion's arms, and all three were laughing raucously as they wove from one side of the staircase to the other.

Cathy took a firmer grip on her husband's arm, and he automatically shielded her from the trio. All at once she clutched his elbow hard, and at the same instant he knew why: the man was Chet Harris, who was too intoxicated to recognize them. They continued to stand, staring, as he and the blondes disappeared from view on the landing.

Obviously disturbed, Cathy looked after the trio.

Lee quietly urged his wife forward, and when they reached the ground floor, he summoned his aide. "Lieutenant," he said, "go to the hotel management and find out all you can about a guest named Chet Harris. Then come straight to my house with the information."

On the carriage ride back to the Presidio, Cathy

finally said, "I was so startled I'm not even certain it was Chet we saw."

"It was," her husband assured her. "At the risk of jumping to conclusions, I'd say he's suffering no financial strain and is enjoying the city's high life."

Soon after they reached the house on the grounds of the garrison, they were joined by the young aide. "Mr. Harris," he said, "has made a fortune in gold. He's taken a suite for a couple of weeks at the King's Castle. The management also told me he has a partner, a Chinese named Wong Ke, who is registered in a small, single room." Because of Cathy's presence the officer was embarrassed. "Apparently Mr. Wong leads a far more quiet social life."

"Go back to the hotel first thing in the morning," Lee said. "See Mr. Wong, and ask him if he'll be good enough to call on me at his earliest convenience."

As they went to bed, Cathy asked, "What are you planning to do about Chet?"

"I'm making no plans as yet," Lee replied. "Let's move one step at a time."

They were surprised, the following morning, when Wong Ke arrived with the aide as they sat at breakfast. Conservatively dressed in a dark, well-tailored suit, the Chinese accepted a cup of coffee, then came to the point. "You know my partner?"

"We've known him since he was a boy," Lee said.

"His mother and stepfather are old, dear friends," Cathy added.

Ke smiled faintly. "Good," he said. "Maybe they help."

Lee Blake asked him about Chet's overall situation, and Ke was succinct. They had made a number of substantial gold strikes, and in the immediate past they had stumbled into a real bonanza when they had found a surface vein on their property. For months they had been comfortable, but now they had acquired great wealth.

"That's grand for Chet," Lee said.

"Not good, General," the Chinese replied. "Now

Chet drink too much whiskey, spend too much time with bad women. Money is wasted if man does not invest wisely. I try to tell Chet now is time to use money well before he spend his share on foolishness, but he no listen to Ke. The more I talk the more he spend on girls and whiskey and gambling."

"It may be that we can be of some assistance, Mr. Wong," Lee said. "How long do you plan to stay in San Francisco?"

"A few more days. Then we go back to property on Bear River and sell it." Ke shrugged. "After that we come to San Francisco again, and maybe Chet kill self with liquor and women."

"You and I will keep in touch," Lee said. He insisted on sending Ke back to the hotel in an official army carriage.

"Now what?" Cathy demanded when her husband came back into the house.

"Infantry skirmishes will accomplish little or nothing," he said. "By the time we could persuade Chet to listen to us, he could squander a fortune. This situation calls for the employment of heavy artillery."

Over the years of their marriage, she had grown accustomed to his use of military imagery. "You mean his family, of course."

"Right," Lee said. "I'm sending a courier up to Fort Vancouver today, so if you'll write a letter to Emily and Ernie, it will be delivered without delay. It isn't easy, particularly for a young man, to keep his balance when he finds himself rolling in wealth for the first time in his life, so don't judge Chet too harshly."

"I'll try, although he's behaving stupidly."

"Gold does different things to different people," Lee said. "Chet's mother and stepfather can straighten him out—if anyone can."

VII

Danny Taylor awakened before dawn every morning, and by daybreak he was at work, planting new fruit trees or cultivating the ones he had planted earlier that year. After spending two hours or more in the orchard, he returned to the house, at Heather's insistence, for a substantial breakfast of pancakes, eggs, bacon, and toast. That was the only meal he consumed during daylight hours. Returning to the orchard, he remained there until the coming of night made it impossible for him to keep working. He took no holidays, and on Sundays Heather, taking the baby with her, went off to church with Phyllis Gregg and the Fosters.

There could be no doubt that Heather's ultimatum had changed her husband. The prospect of losing her had transformed him, and no one in the Sacramento Valley was more diligent. No matter what the weather, he labored in the open, his rifle beside him.

Danny was fulfilling his responsibilities in earnest, but Phyllis realized, as did the Fosters, that he and

Heather were far from happy together. Their conversation was strained, and they discussed only what was necessary. At nightfall, when Danny came in from the orchard, he played with his son for a time, but he appeared to be doing a duty in which he found no pleasure.

He and Heather continued to sleep in the same bed, but he refrained from making love to her, and she didn't know how to handle the delicate situation. At no time did he mention the subject of gold to her, and she knew that her threat to leave him if he returned to the gold fields was directly responsible for their estrangement. She had forced him to remain at home and live up to his obligations, but her victory was hollow.

Too proud to discuss the problem with Phyllis, who had become her closest friend, Heather suffered in silence. But she knew something had to be done to break the impasse. One night, after she had put the baby to sleep and placed a late supper of beef stew and a loaf of hot bread on the kitchen table, she looked at her silent husband, then took the plunge.

"What are you thinking, Danny?" she demanded.

He ladled a generous quantity of stew into his bowl. "Not much of anything. At the end of a long day I find it easier not to think."

"Well," she said, "I spend most of my waking hours thinking and analyzing these days, and the results don't make me very happy." He glanced at her, then concentrated on the food before him and made no reply. "I don't believe you're very happy, either," she said.

"I do what's expected of me," Danny said curtly. "I don't know of any law that makes me laugh while I work."

"I'm not complaining," she replied, speaking very quietly and calmly. "You've done all I've asked of you. But I've taken all the joy out of life for both of us."

"There isn't much joy in getting an orchard into shape," he said. "It'll be a spell before we can enjoy the benefits, as both of us have known from the day we bought this place." He broke off a chunk of bread and soaked it in the rich gravy.

"I'm not sure which would have been better," Heather said. "To have taken the baby and gone back to Texas or to have kept quiet and let you go off to the gold fields again."

"If you and Ted had vanished," he said, "I'd have followed you to the ends of the earth."

His flat statement was so unexpected that she didn't know what to say next. Danny studied her. "You think I want to go back to the gold fields?"

She could only nod.

"Then you don't understand. I hated prospecting even while I was doing it, but I couldn't stop. Do you see what I mean?"

"No." She was bewildered, and only his willingness to talk about the touchy matter was encouraging.

"The lure of the gold fields," Danny said slowly, thinking aloud, "was like the lure of whiskey to alcoholics. From what I've seen, although I've never felt that way myself, a fellow continues to crave whiskey —all the while knowing it will kill him."

"That's the way you feel about hunting for gold?"

"I don't rightly know. I'm still working it out in my head. I hated the search, and even when I found the nuggets I brought back with me, I felt no real satisfaction." He paused. "But all that has nothing to do with you. Or the way I feel about you. It was your help and encouragement that made it possible for me to walk again after the operation. I didn't fall in love with you lightly, and I don't take my marriage vows lightly. You were right to call me to task. My proper place is right here, looking after you and little Ted."

Heather's relief was infinite. "Just so I know you love me," she said "nothing else matters."

Danny stared at her. "You've thought I stopped loving you?"

She inclined her head.

As he recovered from his surprise, he tried to examine their situation from her viewpoint, and at last he nodded. "I reckon I can't blame you for drawing certain conclusions. Just be patient with me for a spell longer."

"For as long as you want and need."

"I feel the pressures of getting the orchard into shape so it will begin to earn an income for us. And all the while I'm trying to get over the craving to go back to the gold fields just once more and try my luck."

Now that she knew he needed her, her confidence in their joint future began to be restored.

"Every day that craving grows a little less," Danny said, "so be patient with me."

Heather had shown unlimited patience during the long months when he had learned to walk again. "Don't think you're the only one who is tempted," she said. "I was as eager as you, remember, to get rich and lead an easy life. The reason I pushed so hard at you is because I knew one of us had to take a firm stand. And you can do it better than I can."

Danny stared at her. "Why didn't you tell me?"

"You've had enough problems." Her strategy was proving effective.

He shook his head. "I've been feeling sorry for myself, when all this time I should have been thinking and worrying about you."

The tears that came to her eyes were real. Her instinct had guided her, and the crisis that had threatened to destroy her marriage could be overcome.

Danny stood. "When I was a bound boy," he said, "there was nobody I could ask for help, and I had to rely on myself. So I guess I just formed the habit of looking inside myself and working out my problems alone. I guess I'm just beginning to learn that in a marriage a man has a partner in his wife."

She watched him as he approached her, and she smiled as he raised her to her feet, embraced her, and kissed her.

For the first time since their marriage, the supper

dishes weren't washed and dried until the following day.

John Gregg did his best to pitch in, do the work on the farm that his father's illness prevented the older man from doing, and help his sister with some of her more difficult chores. As Phyllis remarked to Ralph Hamilton when the prosecutor came for a Sunday visit, John appeared to be accepting adult responsibilities for the first time.

But appearances were deceptive. John was doing what was required of him because he had no choice. He had a roof over his head and was eating regularly, but he hated the drudgery and dreamed of returning to the gold fields. Others were striking it rich, and he believed his luck would turn. He put the hardships he had suffered out of his mind, and he daydreamed about the rewards he would reap.

One problem was that he could confide in no one. He avoided Danny Taylor, whom he had tried to rob, and who seemed to have overcome his lust for gold. Randy continued to swear that only hard labor brought permanent benefits, and it was no longer possible to communicate with Phyllis, who not only admired the hard-working Ralph but held him up to her brother as an example.

So John bided his time, concealing his overwhelming urge to return to his search for gold. Only his father's precarious physical condition prevented John from sneaking off at dawn, and he promised himself he would leave as soon as the old man's health was restored. Thanks to the unabated influx of gold-seeking immigrants, prices were still soaring, and the young man had the sense to realize that food growers were in a position to earn substantial sums as long as the boom lasted.

What irritated John more than anything else was the lack of change. Today was like yesterday, and tomorrow promised to be no different. Phyllis awakened him at daybreak, coming into his room and shaking him when he failed to respond to her call. She gave him a large breakfast, then sent him out into the fields, and there he was expected to remain until sundown, planting and weeding.

Occasionally, when Phyllis went into Sacramento to attend to some errand or when she stopped at the Taylor house for a cup of tea with Heather, John found it convenient to relax in the shade of a tree. But his sister always knew when he shirked, and as her sermons were intolerable, he found it easier to work steadily even when no one kept an eye on him.

His father paid no attention to anything John did. The old man was suffering from chest pains as well as gout these days, and when he lost interest in food, too, Ralph insisted on bringing a physician from town to see him. Nothing could be done to improve his condition, the doctor said, but he left the patient a prescription to ease his pain. A half-teaspoon of laudanum, a powerful opiate, was mixed with water, and Randy enjoyed quick relief. The laudanum made him drowsy, however, so he spent the better part of each day sleeping.

Phyllis wanted a vegetable garden near the house, and John, after ignoring her request for days, finally consented to break up the soil in what had been an unproductive patch of side yard facing the road. He was working with a shovel there when his sister went off for a cup of tea with Heather.

Continuing to dig, the young man brooded. Phyllis was free to come and go as she pleased, and if she chose to spend an hour gossiping with a neighbor, no one criticized her for it. But he was called lazy anytime he elected to rest. Increasingly upset, he finally rebelled, dropping his shovel and sitting under a tree. He was doing his sister a favor, he told himself, and he would return to work when she came home and resumed her own chores.

Two large man approached slowly down the road, and John watched them idly. He vaguely recalled having heard something about a pair of strangers who had come into the neighborhood during his absence, but his thinking had been so fuzzy when he had come home from the gold fields that he couldn't recall any details.

When the pair drew closer, he raised a hand and waved.

Shorty and Slim returned the gesture, then paused and leaned on the split rail fence. "What happened to the redhead who used to live here?" the taller of the pair asked casually.

John had to think for a moment before he realized the stranger was referring to Heather. "Oh, she's joined her husband at their own place down the road," he said. "She was just staying here when he was off in the gold country. I wish I was back there myself," he added.

The pair looked at each other, then at John. "Did you have any luck?"

Like most prospectors, John Gregg hated to admit he had suffered complete failure. "I guess I didn't make out too bad," he said. "Others have done worse."

Shorty grinned at him. "What did you find—nuggets or dust?"

"Nuggets," John replied, trying to make his alleged find sound important.

"You brought 'em home with you?" the husky Slim wanted to know.

"Sure."

"And you live here, huh?"

John nodded casually.

Suddenly the pair climbed over the fence, and Slim's sharp, double-edged knife hovered a half-inch from John's throat. "If you know what's good for you, little fellow," Slim said in an ugly voice, "you'll hand over them nuggets right now."

The alarmed John tried to sit upright, but there was no escape from the knife. "I—I didn't mean it," he gasped. "I spent months looking for gold, but I never found any. Honest!"

"You wouldn't try to fool us, would you?" Slim caught hold of his shirt front and began to twist it.

"I'm telling you the truth, I swear it!" The expression in the heavyset man's eyes sent chills racing up and down John's spine.

"Go have a look, Shorty."

The giant headed toward the house while his companion continued to menace the young man with his knife. John wanted to urge him not to disturb his sick father but was too terrified to speak.

Slim continued to hold the blade close to his throat. "I hope you wasn't lyin' to us, little fellow," he said. "Me and Shorty, we hate liars about as much as we like gold."

After what seemed like a very long time, Shorty emerged from the house. At that moment Phyllis, walking home from the Taylor house, reached the top of the hill. She stopped short, aware that her brother was being threatened, and all at once she knew the two intruders from Heather's detailed, graphic description. They hadn't seen her, so she fled back in the direction from which she had come, hoping she could get Danny to help her brother in time.

"There ain't a single nugget in the house," a disgusted Shorty said. "And there's nothin' else worth takin', either. There's an old man in one of the bedrooms. Either dead or sleepin'. I tried to wake him up, but I couldn't."

Slim lost patience. "Where's the gold you brung back with you?" he asked in a rasping voice.

"I've told you the truth! I found no gold!" the terror-stricken John shrieked.

Slim caught hold of his hair and in a single, swift motion slashed his throat. "No good, lyin' bastard," he said, cleaning his knife on the shirt onto which John's blood was already pouring.

"You shouldn't have done that, Slim," Shorty said, sounding regretful.

"Serves him right!"

"Sure, but why waste your knife on him when there

was nothin' to gain? The old junk in the house ain't worth takin'." Shorty shook his head, returned to the road, and resumed his stroll.

His companion quickly joined him. "I guess we better make ourselves scarce in these parts again," he said. "I just wish we had a few nuggets to show for what I did."

A short time later, when Danny Taylor and John Foster arrived on the scene, both carrying rifles, they found John Gregg lying in a pool of blood, his sightless eyes staring up at the clear sky.

"Thank God we made Phyllis stay behind with Heather," Danny said as they raced into the house where Randy Gregg continued to sleep peacefully, unaware of his son's murder.

Scott Foster was sent into town, returning with Sheriff Miller, Prosecutor Hamilton, and several deputies. After examining the scene of the killing and arranging for John's burial, they went to the Taylor house and questioned Phyllis gently.

There was little she could tell them other than to confirm that her brother's murderers had been Shorty and Slim. Aware that she herself had narrowly escaped death, she shuddered violently.

Ralph poured her a small glass of the brandywine that Danny and Heather kept on hand for emergencies. "Drink this," he said. He felt powerless to comfort her.

When Whip Holt arrived, he and Rick pieced together what had happened. "From the way every bureau drawer and wardrobe in the house was ransacked," Rick said, "it's plain that Slim and Shorty were searching for valuables."

"Apparently they killed young Gregg out of spite when they found nothing worth taking," Whip said. "And they spared the old man because he slept through all the commotion."

That night Rick and his special deputy stayed at the Gregg house. Randy never woke up. The Taylors insisted that Phyllis remain with them. By morning she was sufficiently in control of her emotions to break the news to her father.

Randy sat propped up in bed on several pillows, nodding reflectively. "It don't surprise me none," he said. "I always knowed that boy would come to a bad end."

The funeral services, held the next morning, were mercifully brief. Rick Miller stood alone at the back of the small assemblage, overcome with a sense of cold, impotent frustration. His wife's killers had committed another murder, but they were still at large. He had been tempted to resign so he could devote his full time to a search for them, but Whip had persuaded him to retain his post, saying, "In the long run you'll be doing everybody in the Valley a greater service."

Randy did not attend the funeral, instead sleeping through the morning while two deputies guarded him. For his sake everyone adjourned to the Taylor house for something to eat.

Ralph had been awaiting an opportune moment to speak with Phyllis in private, but he realized he would have to create his own moment, so he asked her to walk in the garden with him.

"I've been wondering what plans you've been making for the future," he said.

"I've been too numb to think," she confessed.

"Well, I've taken the liberty of reviewing your situation in my own mind. It's clear enough that you can't operate the farm, look after your sick father, and attend to your own chores, too. The only way you can work the farm would be to hire someone reliable—if there is such a person."

"Even if I knew where to find someone, I couldn't afford to hire him," Phyllis said. "I've had a vague idea of moving Pa and me in with Heather and Danny—and trying to sell the property."

"You'll get a far better price for it if you take your time," Ralph said. "As the gold fever subsides, people are going to recognize the value of land that can be used for agriculture. Hold off, and you'll get several times as much."

When she started to protest, Ralph said, "Hear me out. Obviously you can't stay on in the house with your father—not with those killers still roaming free. I'm sure the Taylors will be pleased to have you and your father with them, but that's only a temporary solution because their house is too small."

Phyllis bristled. "If you're suggesting that I ask for public charity—"

"Hardly," Ralph said, interrupting. "I have a solution. Isaiah and I rattle around in that big house of ours in town, even with Whip Holt staying with us. So I'd like to offer you a post as my housekeeper. You'd have a suite of your own, and your father would have his own quarters. What's more, the doctor lives a few doors away and could look in on him every day. I'll be more than happy to pay you any wages you think equitable."

Aware of his growing personal interest in her, she smiled faintly and shook her head. "You're being too kind to me, Ralph. You're inventing a job for me."

"No such thing! If you won't take the post, I'll have to find someone else. You'd be doing me a favor, you know. Isaiah is growing up to be a barbarian in an all-male household. He needs a lady to guide and advise and help him."

Phyllis suspected he was exaggerating but couldn't be certain. "I can't be beholden to you—"

"It won't be easy work, I promise you that. I never know what time I'm able to eat supper. More often than not, Sheriff Miller joins me, and at least once or twice every week some of the deputies gather with us, too. What has struck me rather forcibly is that your needs and my needs coincide."

"Pa wouldn't be a burden on you?"

"Certainly not! He and Isaiah would be good company for each other, and think of how much the boy could learn from him."

Phyllis was too weary and heartsick to think clearly,

but she had the sense to realize that Ralph was flattering her and might even be creating the post for her. She and her father would be safe in Sacramento, however, and the increased medical care available to him was a major factor. If Ralph's motives were other than honorable, he would not ask her to bring her father with her.

"I'll accept," she said, "on the condition that either of us can back out at any time."

"Agreed." He immediately made arrangements to have Randy transferred to the house in town that same day.

For the first time in weeks he thought fleetingly of Prudence. She had done him a favor by jilting him, he reflected. The life he was developing in California was far different from what he had known in New York, but he was here to stay. The challenges, personal as well as professional, were far more intriguing.

Ernst and Emily von Thalman sailed to San Francisco from Oregon a scant twenty-four hours after receiving Cathy Blake's letter. Taking a room at the King's Castle Hotel, they sent word to the Presidio that they had arrived, and a short time later General Blake's aide-de-camp appeared to escort them to the garrison.

The old friends who had shared so many trials on the wagon train had a joyful reunion, but it was tempered by thoughts of Chet and the mission that had brought his mother and stepfather to the city.

Ernie, a wealthy Austrian baron and a colonel in the cavalry before he had become an American citizen, brought up the subject with characteristic bluntness. "Cathy's letter was so delicate we learned nothing from it," he said. "Tell us straight out about Chet."

Lee briefly described having passed Chet on the staircase at the hotel. Ernie's smile was wry. "You should have been a diplomat instead of a soldier, Lee.

If I read correctly between the lines, he was too drunk to know you."

"Well, yes," Lee said in embarrassment.

"I suppose it would be best if I don't inquire too closely about the ladies who were with him," Emily said.

Cathy had been her friend long enough to be frank. "They weren't ladies," she replied.

"As we understand the situation from Chet's partner, a Chinese gentleman of great dignity," Lee said, "they've had a succession of gold strikes, bringing them large sums of money. Mr. Wong wants to invest in various enterprises. He's told us none of the details, but my impression of him is that he's a prudent, shrewd man. So far Chet is enjoying himself too much to think in terms of the future."

"He was brought up to know better," Emily said.

Ernie came to his stepson's defense. "In Vienna, when I was Chet's age, I was something of a hellion myself," he said. "Obviously, there are many temptations in San Francisco today. Probably more than there were in Vienna when I was young."

Lee agreed. "Chet is being foolish, but he isn't malicious, and there's no real harm done if he can be straightened out."

"That's why we've come here," Ernie said. "What's the first step?"

"I suggest you get in touch with his partner," Lee said. "I'll give you his address."

Ernie wrote a brief note to Wong Ke, and a special courier was hired to take it to the cabin on the Bear River. Emily curbed her impatience and seemed to understand her husband's warning that their direct intervention could do more harm than good.

In the meantime there were unexpected developments that no one could have predicted. Chet became bored with the final negotiations for the sale of the Bear River property, and leaving the transaction in Wong Ke's capable hands, he rode off in search of amusement. Fate led him to Big George's saloon, where he arrived in mid-afternoon.

Melissa, who looked outrageously spectacular in a red gown that matched her hair, had just made her customary dramatic entrance, and seeing no one who appeared worthy of her attention, she went to her regular table. She saw Chet come into the room, realized he was sober, and knew there was no way she could escape.

A direct confrontation being unavoidable, she made the best of the situation by catching his eye and smiling. Chet was dumbfounded. He halted abruptly, as though struck across the face, and after staring hard at her, he walked slowly to her table.

Melissa knew he had no memory of their other meeting. "You're surprised to see me, honey," she said. "Sit down."

He took the chair opposite her, still gaping at her and too astonished to speak.

"You're looking well," she said and knew she lied. His face was puffy, and there were dissipated hollows beneath his eyes. It was clear that his wealth had done nothing to make him happy. Suddenly she regretted having robbed him, even though she knew Big George's cutthroats would have taken his money anyway.

Chet shook his head, then reached for the glass of whiskey that a bartender placed before him. "How in blazes are you—"

"My story isn't all that unusual." Melissa gently took the glass from him and placed it back on the table. It would be far easier to deal with him if he remained sober. "I misjudged Jerome Hadley, and here I am."

She looked more beautiful than ever, in a blatantly obvious way, and Chet's mind continued to whirl. Certainly he was no longer in love with her and never thought of her from one day to the next. For the sake of what they had meant to each other, however—or what he thought they had meant—he wanted to make a gesture on her behalf. "What can I do to help you?" he asked simply.

The quiet question, with no strings attached, unnerved her. Every man who came here wanted her, and Chet's willingness to come to her aid touched her deeply. In spite of his weaknesses, he was a decent, kind person, and remembering their last meeting, she felt guiltier than ever. "I'm doing fine," she said. "There's nothing I need." As far as she was concerned, her vocation had settled her future, regardless of her wishes in the matter.

Melissa placed the emphasis on him. "I wasn't at all surprised to see you," she said, "because we met here some weeks ago."

"We did?"

"You were too full of whiskey to know me. Or to remember the occasion."

He grinned at her a trifle foolishly. "I reckon I've been drinking more than is good for me," he said, "but I've been celebrating. My partner and I really struck it rich in the gold fields."

"I'm glad for you, Chet," she said. "You always worked hard for every penny you made. What are you going to do with your wealth?"

"Blamed if I know. I'm having too much fun spending it right now to worry about what lies ahead."

The thought occurred to Melissa, forcibly, that although there was literally nothing he could do for her, she was in a position to help him. She owed him something for the money she had stolen from him and because of their friendship, which went back to their teenage years. She wanted to do what she could to set him on the right path. "I suppose you've come here to drink, play cards, and go upstairs with a woman."

"That was the general idea," he said, her candor making him uneasy.

"Well, I'm available. But not for a fee. After what we once meant to each other, I couldn't charge you, honey."

Chet shook his head emphatically. "I couldn't do it with you, Melissa. I haven't forgotten the past, either."

There were far more important things she could give him. "Suppose you carry out your plans for the day. What then?"

"Well, my partner and I are going on to San Francisco tomorrow. We're leaving these parts for good."

She made a shrewd guess. "I suppose there are women you know in the city." He could only nod. "And all the whiskey and champagne you can drink."

"There's nothing wrong with that," he said defensively.

"I'm the last to deliver a sermon, and I wouldn't urge anyone to avoid an occasional spree. If I did, I'd soon be out of business myself." Her smile was ironic. "But it's so easy for a man to take the wrong fork when the road ahead of him splits, and when he does, that can be the end of him."

Chet nodded but was only half-listening.

She knew she had to capture his complete attention. "See the gray-haired man over in the corner?" She nodded in the direction of a ragged, haggard figure who was emptying and cleaning brass cuspidors.

"That old bum?" Chet asked.

Melissa nodded. "It wasn't so long ago when that old bum, as you call him, came out here. He was one of the first to arrive. Back in Ohio or Pennsylvania—I can't recall which, and it doesn't matter—he was the owner of a large sawmill. He had a wife, a family, and he owned a large home. He sold everything and came out here, determined to find gold. He never got any closer to the gold fields than Big George's. It was so easy to spend his money on liquor and women, and when his funds started to run low, he turned to gambling."

Chet stared hard at the man, whose eyes had a tragic, haunted look.

"He cadges drinks from customers who feel sorry for him. His life is finished, Chet. He doesn't care how cheap and vile the liquor is that he drinks, and one of these days he'll drop dead. I'm sure his family back East will neither know nor give a damn."

He shuddered slightly. "That could never happen to me," he said.

"Never?" she asked sharply, then stood. "You come with me." Gripping his arm firmly, she pulled him to his feet.

Unwilling to create a scene, Chet allowed her to lead him up the stairs to her suite. "Melissa, I've already told you I wouldn't feel right making love to you—"

"Sit down and listen to me!" she commanded, pointing to a chair in her sitting room. "There won't be any lovemaking today. I'm not in the mood for it, either. I've learned more about the world than you know, maybe more than you'll ever know. And what impresses me most is that no one is really strong. Every man has a weakness. Every woman has a weakness. Indulge and pamper yourself too much, and that weakness will come to the surface. Right now you wouldn't touch the liquor that the old bum downstairs has to drink. But if your funds ran low—and they could—and if you had his craving, his need to forget, you'd drink poison, too."

"Why are you telling me all this?" he demanded.

"Because it wasn't so many years ago, when we were youngsters back in Oregon, that I thought I was in love with you. That was before I discovered I'm not capable of loving anyone," she added bitterly, speaking more to herself than to him. "In my line of work I've come to know a great deal about human temptations."

It was difficult for him to realize that this glittering, worldly creature was the Melissa Austin with whom he had been in love for years. She was more flamboyantly attractive now, to be sure, but she was also very hard.

"You mentioned that you're leaving this area. What are your long-range plans, Chet?"

"My partner and I are looking into various kinds of business. California is growing so fast there's no end of opportunities here. But I'm not ready to settle down yet."

"Why not?" she demanded. "I'll tell you why. Because you'd rather indulge yourself. So you're putting the cart before the horse. Invest your money. Organize your business and lead a productive, useful life. Then you'll be earning the right to spend a night drinking champagne with some woman. Or finding your pleasure in countless ways."

Chet knew she was right but hated to admit it.

"How much money are you carrying right this minute?" Melissa's long, painted fingernails tapped on the top of the table that stood beside her.

He opened his purse and began to count. "I have nearly a thousand in paper money," he said at last, "and maybe another thousand in this vial of gold dust."

"If you don't squander it here," she told him scornfully, "and that would be very easy to do, you'll still lose it before the day ends."

"How so?"

"Because a band of thieves will attack you before you've ridden very far from here." Her tone became crisper. "Put the paper money in the sole of your left boot. Spread it out so you won't limp." She rose, vanished into the bedchamber, and returned with a flimsy stocking of black silk, which she handed him. "Now pour your gold dust into this. Spread it out, too, so there are no lumps, and hide it in your right boot. When the thieves assault you, they'll assume you spent all your money on me."

"How do you know so much?"

"Do as I tell you," she said, sounding annoyed. "It wasn't so long ago that you worked for the better part of a year to earn a thousand dollars. I hate to see you throwing sums like that to the winds."

Chet did as she directed and felt grateful to her.

He tried to express his appreciation, but she cut him off and seemed to be working herself into a fury. "I want no thanks! Now get out—and stay away! I hope I never see you again!"

Unable to understand the burst of temper, Chet nevertheless obeyed her and took his leave. Not pausing for as much as a single drink in the saloon, he decided to go directly to San Francisco, where he would arrive ahead of Wong Ke.

The encounter with Melissa had been unsettling, but at the same time he felt as though a weight had been lifted from his shoulders. She hadn't told him anything he didn't already know, but because of the feelings he had once felt for her, he had listened and understood the truth for the first time. It was ironic, he thought, that Melissa, at the low point of her own life, had shown the insight and understanding to reach out to him just at the moment when he had come so close to floundering.

Chet's ruminations were interrupted when a group of masked men emerged on horseback from a wooded area, their guns drawn. Several seemed amused when his purse proved to be empty, and he heard one of them mutter, "Trust the queen to take every last penny."

Resuming his journey after the would-be thieves released him, Chet knew he was doubly indebted to Melissa, and he decided to visit a jewelry store as soon as he reached San Francisco. There he would spend the entire two thousand dollars she had saved him on a diamond bracelet or a pair of earrings for her.

That night he stayed at a small, secure inn below Sacramento, and late the next afternoon he reached the King's Castle Hotel, where his customary suite awaited him.

"We have some other guests who have inquired about you, Mr. Harris," the manager said. "A Mr. and Mrs. von Thalman from Oregon."

Chet went straight to their room. "What a wonderful surprise," he said as he embraced his mother and shook his stepfather's hand.

He did not realize that his own total sobriety was the best surprise. At dinner that evening, Emily and Ernie knew he was cured when he told them in detail about various business enterprises in which he and Wong Ke were thinking of investing. They did not know what had caused this change in him, but they were delighted. They would be spared the pain of confronting him. Toward the end of the meal his mother asked him, "Have you thought seriously of marrying and settling down?"

His loud laugh, which was his only response, startled her. He could not explain there had been a time when marriage to Melissa Austin had been his greatest ambition Now, when he could afford marriage, he could no longer even contemplate union with Melissa. They lived in different worlds, and it was ironic that she, now a prostitute, had turned his footsteps in the right direction.

President Zachary Taylor had died suddenly and unexpectedly in midsummer, 1850, and his place as the Chief Executive of the United States was taken by Vice President Millard Fillmore, a politician of no particular stature, and the last member of the Whig party ever to hold that high office. Never one to take risks that could be avoided, the new President was cautious in all things.

In the private opinion of the outspoken Major General Winfield Scott, Chief of Staff of the army, President Fillmore was far worse than careful. *In my view,* Scott wrote to Brigadier General Leland Blake, *our new Commander in Chief is a coward.*

The reason for the Chief of Staff's anger was easy enough for a fellow officer to understand. In August, a month after Fillmore became President, he directed General Scott to issue a new order to the commanders of all army garrisons, forts, and posts. Henceforth, troops would be used to quell civil disturbances and uprisings only when no other means of maintaining order was available and the safety of citizens was in jeopardy. What was so infuriating about the order, which was announced in the nation's newspapers, was its very vagueness. It sounded as if the new President were suddenly putting severe restraints on United States troops.

Lee Blake fumed, too, when he received the new order in October. Ernie and Emily von Thalman were dinner guests at his house, as were Chet Harris and Wong Ke, and Lee discussed the problem with them candidly. "I'm none too sure of the new President's intent," he said. "How is it determined—and by whom —that no other means of keeping order is available? And who decides when citizens are in jeopardy? The governor of a state? The legislature? The law courts? Or the commandant of a garrison, whose hide will be roasted by some segment of the press, regardless of what he does or fails to do?"

"As someone active in politics," Ernie said, "I believe President Fillmore's order is shortsighted."

"The worst of it is that he's issued it publicly," Lee said. "I received official notification from the War Department just yesterday, and because the subject is so sensitive, I assumed it was to be treated confidentially. But today all the San Francisco newspapers printed the story, which will be picked up by scores of smaller newspapers all over California."

"Obviously," Ernie said, "someone at the White House is making mighty good and certain that President Fillmore's orders aren't being kept secret."

Cathy Blake saw that Wong Ke was puzzled, and she felt as he did. "Why should it be a mistake to let the public know the President's stand?" she asked.

"Our situation right here in San Francisco offers a perfect example," her husband replied. "By now the city must have a permanent population of close to thirty thousand, with at least that many transients in town, too. Yet the vigilance committee, with a total force of no more than three hundred men, has helped keep order here. There's a valid reason for that."

Wong Ke shrugged, making it plain that the ways of Americans were beyond his comprehension.

"The reason is simple," Lee said. "Every criminal in town, everyone who has had anything to gain by a disruption of the peace, has known that the army has stood behind the vigilance committee. They've known my troops were prepared to intervene any time the vigilance people couldn't handle a situation. I haven't had to send the garrison out on riot control duty in months. The threat has been enough."

"Now," Ernie explained further, "thanks to the President's muddle-worded order, that threat has been removed."

"Oh, dear," Emily murmured.

"Criminals can read newspapers, just as you and I can read them. They believe President Fillmore has handcuffed me, and they know for certain that without the support of the garrison there's no way on earth three hundred vigilantes are going to keep the lid on this town. Ernie," Lee continued as he looked down the dining table at his old friend, "how much longer are you and Emily planning to stay on here?"

"We have no definite plans," Ernie said. "Chet and Ke have asked me to join them when they inspect a large cattle ranch that's for sale. They've been offered one of the newspapers, too, so I want to go over the ledgers with them."

"Ordinarily I don't advocate running away," Lee said, "but I urge you to go back to Oregon and give whatever financial advice you care to offer from there."

"It's going to be that bad here, Lee?" Emily asked.

"Call it an educated guess. My intelligence section keeps a finger on the pulse of the underworld, and we're anticipating a rather violent explosion at any time."

Chet, who had been listening carefully, spoke up

for the first time. "Do the vigilance people know it?"

"Of course," Lee said. "They're prepared to react quickly. And in full force. But the odds against them are enormous, especially if the unruly element gains the upper hand."

Wong Ke asked the question that was in the mind of every person at the dinner table. "What you do if trouble comes now, General?"

"There's nothing in the new orders that requires me to obtain the approval of state, local, or federal officials before I intervene. President Fillmore is urging me to stand aside and take no action, but he isn't forcing me to do it. At least that is the way I interpret the new War Department directive, the way I choose to interpret it. If I'm mistaken," Lee concluded, giving Ke a pained smile, "the worst that can happen is that I'll be discharged from the army in disgrace."

For the next twenty-four hours, rumors of impending disturbances swept through San Francisco, with each story feeding on those that preceded it and contributing to a sense of public apprehension. The justices of the California Supreme Court were asked for an informal opinion of the President's orders, as were the members of the federal judiciary in the new state. No two jurists held the same opinion, and the dissenting views added to the confusion.

All members of the vigilance committee were summoned to duty. Now wearing distinctive red, white, and blue armbands, they patrolled the streets in pairs, their small numbers making it plain to law-abiding citizens and criminals alike that the committee was woefully lacking in personnel.

Lee Blake asked his judge advocate, his legal advisor, for a formal opinion. Hoping to protect himself, the officer prepared a document of many pages that formed no conclusions. Lee reacted by quietly canceling all leaves and placing his entire garrison on alert. These moves were not publicized, however, because he didn't want to contribute to the already soaring tensions.

The trouble started late in the afternoon when a bakery that stood adjacent to one of the new hotels near the crest of Nob Hill closed its doors. Instead of selling loaves of bread hot from the oven to customers who waited in line outside the establishment, the nervous baker locked his doors and lowered his shutters. Before the latter operation was completed, however, an irate patron threw a rock that broke a front window.

The sound of that single pane of glass shattering echoed from the heights to the bay, from residential areas to business districts, and was louder and more insistent in the neighborhood of saloons, dance halls, and gambling palaces known as the Barbary Coast. The violence that broke out simultaneously in all parts of the city seemed like an act of spontaneous combustion.

The crews of several merchant ships tied at the docks came ashore en masse, armed with spars, which they were prepared to use. Men hurried from saloons and brothels into the streets, armed with weapons ranging from six-shooters and rifles to clubs and pitchforks. Volunteer firemen reported to their duty stations, even though no alarms had yet been sounded.

Offices and shops that had been anticipating an emergency closed at once and were either shuttered or barricaded. The doors of private homes were closed and bolted, and horsemen, carriages, and pedestrians vanished from the streets.

Banks, jewelry stores, and the better hotels, all of them employing private guards, sent their sentries to combat posts. At the King's Castle, Ernie von Thalman, Chet Harris, and Wong Ke were among the many guests who volunteered their services and provided their own firearms. The patrons of other hotels did the same.

Virtually every restaurant, inn, tavern, and saloon in the city closed without delay, and supplies of food and liquor were made secure in heavily guarded cellars.

The women of San Francisco, still badly outnumbered by the men, literally vanished from sight. The brothels turned away customers, windows were closed, and doors were bolted.

At nightfall the storm broke. Vandals broke into the mansions of a number of well-to-do citizens, attempts were made to scale the walls that surrounded hotel gardens, and an organized assault on the main entrance of the First Bank of San Francisco was repulsed, the guards there firing rifles and six-shooters steadily. Fires, apparently set by arsonists, broke out in various parts of town. Residents braced themselves for a long night of looting.

The vigilance committee demonstrated that, in spite of its small size, it was a cohesive, disciplined force. Every team had been given a specific area to patrol, and nothing deterred the members from making their rounds continually. They could not cope with every emergency, to be sure, but in little more than an hour after the disturbances began, the city's principal jails, one near the waterfront and the other at the edge of the downtown business district, were filled with prisoners.

At the Presidio a deceptive air of calm prevailed. Sentries stood duty on the bastions of the fort and at the gates, and ten cannon were massed near the arsenal, ready to repel any invaders foolish enough to make an attempt to steal the arms and munitions stored there. Infantry battalions had already moved into battle formation, live ammunition had been issued, and every soldier had affixed his bayonet to his rifle. Cavalrymen carrying sabers as well as rifles stood beside their mounts on the parade ground.

Wives and children had been requested to retire to their homes and stay there.

General Blake established his command post in the Presidio's highest turret, and by the light of spreading fires, he watched the growing turmoil through his field glasses. Occasionally a member of the intelligence section, attired in civilian clothes, entered the fort and hurried to the commandant to report. Operations officers had spread maps of the city on tables, and by the light of oil lamps, they marked the districts where the turmoil was spreading.

The first indication of panic came from Mayor White, who sent Lee Blake a short note. *Constabulary too small to cope*, he had scribbled.

A short time later one of the leaders of the vigilance committee sent word that his hard-pressed men were finding it increasingly difficult to stem the tide. Then one of the intelligence agents, bleeding from knife wounds on his arms and chest, reached the Presidio with word that looting was under way in the Barbary Coast district, where the worst trouble was expected.

Lee Blake decided he had waited long enough, and his bugler, playing a short, crisp call, summoned all senior unit commanders to a council of war. Most were already nearby, and they gathered quickly.

"Gentlemen," Lee said, "I cannot in good conscience stand aside any longer. I have tried to observe what I regard as the spirit as well as the precise directive of President Fillmore's order. I hate to see American troops fire on American civilians. The night will be bloody no matter what happens, but it will be worse if we fail to intervene decisively. If any of you sincerely believes I am disobeying the order of the President, speak up now. I'll relieve you of your command without prejudice."

Not one officer raised his voice.

"Thank you for your confidence, gentlemen. Our tactics must be simple. Each unit has been assigned to a different district, with the cavalry initially going to the farthest points. Use whatever means you find necessary to halt the demonstrations. Hold your fire until you're attacked, as many will be. Order your opponents to cease operations and surrender. When they refuse to obey, use every means at your disposal to insure their immediate compliance. Don't fire indiscriminately, but keep in mind that some of you will be facing criminals and disreputable hoodlums. Any questions?"

"Yes, sir." A lieutenant colonel commanding a battalion raised his voice. "If I understand you correctly, General, you're instructing us to shoot if necessary. Shoot to kill. This is to be no mere exercise where we try to scatter mobs."

"Make your own judgments, gentlemen, and you shall have my unqualified support," Lee said firmly. "Even as we talk here, the problems become worse; the situation throughout the city becomes wilder and more unmanageable. Order cannot be restored by pacific means. Hot lead and cold steel, applied forcefully and with dispatch, are needed to prevent total anarchy and much higher death tolls. Maintain contact with the units on your flanks, and as you achieve order, draw your noose tighter, moving toward the center of what is a rough circle. I'll make a mobile command post with Cavalry Troop K, so I can use the horsemen as messengers."

He nodded to his brigade adjutant, who dismissed the officers, and they promptly dispersed, joining their units and hurrying to their assigned posts.

The movement was accomplished smoothly. Members of the garrison were professional soldiers, volunteers all, and many had seen combat in the war with Mexico and in fights with various Indian nations. They knew what was expected of them and accepted their responsibilities calmly.

From a technical standpoint Lee was pleased that the garrison dispersed so rapidly and efficiently. He alone had set the men in motion, and it was possible that President Fillmore would demand his resignation from the service. That was a risk he took knowingly. The alternative was that of seeing San Francisco in chaos.

One of the first infantry units was sent to the foot of Telegraph Hill on the inner curve of the crescent-shaped harbor. The city's principal warehouses were located there, housing food and tools, newsprint and medical supplies, as well as thousands of other items brought in from other parts of the United States. If deprived of them, the city could not function.

Lee, following the battalion with his cavalry escort, was relieved to see that the troops had reached the area in time to make it secure. No attempt had yet been made to loot the warehouses, and now it was too late, with the soldiers throwing a cordon around the district and allowing no civilians to enter.

The principal thoroughfares leading inland from the waterfront were Washington and Clay Streets, both potentially explosive. Flimsy wooden shacks lined both streets, and between them stood canvas tents, fragile dwellings of light wood erected by Chinese newcomers, and even mud huts, which were used by destitute miners. Garbage littered both streets, and those who lived in the district, having little or nothing to lose, were far more reckless than were the residents whose houses were made of brick and stone.

Crowds were already gathering on both Washington and Clay Streets, and they grew larger on the heights that rose from the harbor as the soldiers occupied the area below them. Lee moved closer with his escort and quickly recognized the defiant attitude of the throng. Men cursed, shouted, and shook their fists, and stones were thrown at the jittery horses.

Then someone set fire to a shack, which burst into flames, and the conflagration spread rapidly through the area. In many places the fires soared skyward, then quickly died away, and within moments looters poured into the district, searching the ruins for anything of value. Some were so eager for spoils that they turned over still-smoking rubble with the shovels they had carried with them to the gold fields.

There was little of real worth in these slums, and the destruction of the huts would be no loss to the city. But the fires served as rallying points for men who were searching for excitement, and the danger that the flames might spread to other parts of San

Francisco was very real. Lee realized that the mobs had to be dispersed.

He assigned the task to two battalions of infantry, sending one up Clay Street and the other up Washington, with the troops marching six abreast. The civilians occupied higher ground, looking down on the advancing soldiers, so they held a natural advantage. Volunteers promptly erected barricades, a nearby brickyard was raided for ammunition, and those who possessed firearms were persuaded to move into the front lines.

Studying the faces of the men in the mob, Lee Blake feared that violence could not be averted. These civilians were the paupers, those who had failed in the gold fields and had been unable to find employment either in San Francisco or in the Sacramento Valley. It made no sense that the United States Army should become the object of their rage, but it was the symbol of authority, and, consequently, they found the troops a perfect outlet for their frustrations.

As the two battalions moved up toward the heights slowly and cautiously, burning firebrands were hurled down at them, followed by a hail of bricks. At Lee's command both units halted, and he rode up Washington Street, with several members of his cavalry escort clustered behind him.

"Fellow citizens," he called, "in the name of common sense, stop this nonsense while there's time. Your enemies have been failure and hunger and idleness. Soldiers who come from your home towns and once were your neighbors have no quarrel with you now. Help them keep the peace. An effort is being made to provide jobs in construction for all who want to work, so no one needs to starve. In the name of the United States Government—I request you to disperse and go about your own business peacefully!"

A man with a deep voice shouted an obscenity, and a shower of bricks and stones descended on Lee and the members of the staff. Sergeant Major Hector Mullins sucked in his breath audibly; everyone in the group felt as he did.

Then someone in the crowd discharged a rifle, and the bullet whined over Lee's head. He tried to ignore the provocation, but others in the mob were encouraged, and within moments a barrage of fire, some of it from ancient muskets, forced General Blake and his entourage to retreat hastily.

Lee promptly summoned the commanders of the two infantry battalions that still held their positions near the bases of Clay and Washington Streets. "I'm sorry to say we can hold off no longer," he told them. "The mob has taken our passive response as a sign of weakness. Look up there. Men are already heading toward other parts of town with torches and firearms. Unless we act quickly and decisively, the entire city will be burned and looted."

His subordinates knew he was correct, and they braced themselves for his order.

"Both battalions will advance, capture the heights, and make prisoners of any men who resist," Lee said. "Wait until the civilians open fire before you reply. I still pray they'll be sensible. But, if they won't, try to restrict the number of casualties."

Within moments the two battalions were in motion up the heights, the infantrymen advancing with fixed bayonets.

Lee watched grimly in the glare of burning hovels and tents. Circumstances had forced him to be the commander of troops who were being compelled to open fire on fellow Americans, but he had no alternative.

Civilians hiding behind mounds of garbage and rubble above the troops fired raggedly, and two infantrymen in the front rank moving up Clay Street were struck, one suffering a shoulder wound and the other losing an earlobe. As they fell out of line, others stepped forward and took their places.

"You may sound the 'Open Fire,'" Lee told his bugler.

The crisp notes rose above the shouts from the hill and the steady, rhythmic pounding of the soldiers' boots on the hard-packed dirt of the road.

The two battalions reacted simultaneously, and sharp volleys rang out. The challenge had been accepted because there was no real choice, and the battle was joined.

The mob was stunned, and then, suddenly, its rage increased. Apparently these men had not believed that the troops would accept their dare, and now they replied with a heavy fire of their own. Only their poor marksmanship, which was made worse by the bottles of cheap whiskey being passed from hand to hand, prevented the battalions from suffering severe casualties.

The troops neither halted nor hesitated as they marched stolidly up the heights.

Liquor gave the civilians a sense of false courage, but they faced a steady fire, and the sight of the steel bayonets further unnerved them. Here and there men began to run from the barricades.

The battalion commanders replied by sending their men charging on the double. The panic became contagious, and the ranks of the defenders broke. Every man was on his own now, and even the most reckless and shortsighted realized the battle had been lost. A relieved Lee gave the order to cease fire.

The troops spread out, climbing through debris and making their way across backyards as they rounded up rioters. At General Blake's direction the prisoners were taken to the waterfront. There the ringleaders were identified by chastised rebels anxious to save their own skins. Those who had been responsible for the insurrection were taken by boat to one of the small, uninhabited islands in the bay, where they would remain isolated for the rest of the night. In the morning they would be taken to the law courts, where they would face a long list of charges.

As word of the insurrection's failure spread quickly through the city, the troubles in other districts subsided. Would-be looters and those who had hoped to break into banks, hotels, and shops changed their minds. Within a very short time the garrison was able to restore order everywhere.

Lee and his staff went to the King's Castle Hotel, where the governor, the mayor, and other officials had gathered to await the outcome. As they entered the establishment, they saw that a number of the guests were still stationed at hastily erected barricades.

Ernie von Thalman and Chet Harris stood side by side, each armed with a rifle, and Lee paused for a word with them. "How did you fare?" he asked.

Ernie's grin was rueful. "The hospitals will be busy tonight."

"This was like the old days on the wagon train," Chet said.

The casualty reports, submitted by every unit, were lower than Lee had feared. Eleven members of the garrison had been wounded, but all were expected to recover. The rioters had suffered more severely, with three men killed and thirty-seven hurt.

The governor, mayor, and two U.S. Congressmen thanked Lee for preventing a massacre of innocent people. Without his knowledge they wrote a joint letter to President Fillmore, praising the commandant for his firm resolution and devotion to duty. A number of prominent citizens added their signatures to the document, which was sent to Washington City via the overland route the following morning.

The preparation and dispatch of this document solved Lee's remaining problem. In theory he could still be subjected to censure for violating the spirit of the presidential order directing senior military officers to refrain from using their troops as policemen. But California's highest-ranking civilians were thanking him effusively for saving San Francisco from destruction, so it was safe to assume that the cautious new President would leave well enough alone.

Dawn came before the last reports were tallied and the last ringleaders of the uprising apprehended. Lee and his staff road back to the Presidio through the streets littered with rubble, and occasionally they passed smoldering ruins. But the difference in the atmosphere was striking. The air of menace had vanished, and even though the city was enveloped in its usual early morning fog, the sun already was trying to break through.

Cathy, who had spent a sleepless night, greeted her husband with a warm embrace as he came into the house, and they were soon joined at breakfast by Beth, who promptly bombarded her father with questions about the night's activities.

"Papa is tired," Cathy told her, "so don't pester him now. By the time you come home from school this afternoon, you'll be able to read the whole story in the newspapers. Besides, you'll be late for school if you don't hurry."

Rarely abashed, Beth grinned at her father.

"I'll tell you this much right now," Lee said. "San Francisco is a far safer place to live today than it was last night. Perhaps it won't be long before the whole state becomes civilized."

VIII

If it was true that San Francisco was becoming more tranquil and tame, as Lee Blake predicted, the same could not be said for the rest of the new state. Far to the south, San Diego was suffering from an unprecedented winter drought, but the heaviest snowfall in many years blanketed the peaks and passes of the Sierra Nevada. An unexpected thaw in January, 1851, caused the Sacramento River to overflow its banks, and Sacramento itself was inundated. Even the palisade surrounding John Sutter's old fort was undermined, and when the flood waters receded, they left a thick sediment of sticky, heavy mud in their wake.

"This place is an unholy mess!" Phyllis Gregg declared, and her feelings were echoed by scores of other householders. Isaiah Atkins abandoned his studies for several days to help Phyllis clean the cellar, but they were fortunate that no permanent harm was done. The contents of several warehouses that stood on the riverfront were ruined, and the buildings had to be moved to higher ground.

Man soon demonstrated that he could be as brutal as the forces of nature, although few people were told about an incident that left the authorities shaken. Phyllis suspected that something was amiss when Ralph Hamilton came home late for supper one evening, looking pale. He showed no interest in his food, and only by exerting a great effort could he engage in even token small talk with Randy Gregg and Isaiah.

After supper, when Randy went off to bed and Isaiah retired to his room to study, Ralph surprised his young housekeeper by helping himself to a mild drink of whiskey. "I'm expecting Sheriff Miller to join me soon," he said.

Accompanying him to the parlor, where he built up the fire already burning in the hearth, Phyllis now knew there was trouble somewhere. But she had come to know Ralph well enough to ask no questions. He could be closemouthed about pending cases when he wished, but more often than not he spoke freely in her presence.

Tonight it appeared that he was deeply concerned. "I thank the Lord I brought you and your father into town from the open countryside," he said, sinking into a chair and sipping his drink.

Phyllis set a long straw on fire and handed it to him so he could light his pipe.

"Did you know the people in the house behind the Taylors and next to the Fosters?"

She shook her head. "Not too well, because they moved in just a short time before I came here with you. Their name is Baker, and they had a little farm in central Illinois. What I liked about them was their lack of interest in gold. They came out here all the way from the Middle West because there's an extra growing season in the Sacramento Valley. I know how important that can be."

"Mrs. Baker is dead," Ralph said harshly. "So is her husband."

Shocked, Phyllis looked at him. "Was it—"

"Murder, apparently. Rick rode out there as soon as

the word came in to us. I'm waiting to hear the rest from him."

"There have been so many deaths in that one neighborhood," Phyllis murmured.

He nodded grimly but made no reply. She continued to sit with him, wishing there was something she could say or do to ease his tension.

A short time later a stone-faced Rick Miller arrived.

"Shall I leave the room?" Phyllis asked.

The former Ranger shook his head. "Stay around, if you like. Provided you have a strong enough stomach."

She offered him a drink, which he refused, and decided to remain as long as she could.

"We've pretty well pieced together the whole portrait, thanks to Sarah Rose Foster," Rick said.

"Was it—what we thought?" Ralph asked.

Rick nodded. "Let me begin at the start. At some time this afternoon—we don't know even the approximate hour—Edna Baker was raped and then choked and bludgeoned to death."

Phyllis gasped and covered her face with her hands.

"Mrs. Baker had supper cooking on the stove," Rick went on. "Well, through a stroke of luck, Sarah Rose spent the afternoon doing homework at the house of a friend. She saw lights burning in the Baker kitchen as she cut across their property, and when she looked in the window, she saw two large, rough-looking men eating the meal that Mrs. Baker had been preparing."

"One moment," Ralph said. "By this time Mrs. Baker was already dead?"

"Yes, to the best of our knowledge. Sarah Rose recognized the men because she had seen and heard them the night she was hiding in her parents' kitchen —the night Elisabeta died." Rick's voice became husky, but he continued. "The girl became frightened and ran home. Her father hadn't come in from the fields yet. She found him—and her brothers, and by the time they fetched Danny Taylor, too, more had happened. Tom Baker came in for supper, not suspecting anything out of the ordinary. The men killed him. They had already ransacked the house. The killers must have escaped just minutes before the Fosters and Danny arrived. Scott Foster—a bright boy if ever there was one—checked the food left on the plates and told me it was still warm."

Listening to the details of the cold-blooded murders, Phyllis felt ill.

"Slim and Shorty again?" Ralph asked in a bleak voice.

Rick nodded. "Sarah Rose was pretty upset, but I managed to get descriptions from her." He clenched his fists.

"Why do you suppose they keep coming back to the same neighborhood?" Ralph demanded.

"Maybe they're taunting me with my failure to catch them." Rick was furious with himself.

"It's more likely that they feel they're safe in the area because they haven't been apprehended yet," Ralph said gently.

"Well, it's only a matter of time before they strike again." Rick stood and began to pace. "We can't tolerate any more meaningless slaughter, so I'm stationing several deputies in the area on a permanent basis. I'd consider myself directly to blame if anything happened to Heather Taylor or Jane Foster. Or the children. I'm worried mainly for the women. Like all murderers who kill repeatedly, this pair falls into a pattern. When they ascertain that the husbands are away working in the orchards or fields, they come to rob the house and brutalize the women. Whip is going to stay there for a few days. Not that Shorty and Slim are likely to come back so soon, but his presence will comfort Heather and Jane."

"They should leave the area," Phyllis said.

"They can't just go off and leave their families behind," Ralph said.

"Besides," Rick added, "there's no telling exactly where they may make their next attack. For all we know, they could show up right here in Sacramento."

"Tomorrow," Ralph said, "I'm going to issue an official warning to all women in the Valley and urge them to keep their doors and windows closed and locked at all times."

Phyllis's flesh crawled, and she had to rub her arms briskly.

Rick stood, looking and sounding wearily discouraged. "You may want to join a meeting in my office when Whip comes back to town in a few days, Ralph," he said. "He has some thoughts, long-range rather than immediate, for setting and baiting a trap. Ordinarily I'd reject a scheme like that without giving it a second thought. But I have such great respect for Whip Holt that I've got to give really serious consideration to any suggestion he makes."

"I'll be there," Ralph said.

Rick said good night to Phyllis, then added, "Don't bother to see me to the door, either of you. I'll let myself out."

Ralph smiled without humor. "Under the circumstances," he said, "I intend to make certain the front door is bolted after you've gone."

Phyllis continued to sit, staring vacantly into the fire. An idea was beginning to form in her mind when Ralph returned.

"I don't want you unduly worried," he said. "Rick was just speculating when he said Shorty and Slim might appear in Sacramento. Anything is possible, of course, but they seem to prefer isolated houses. Sacramento is too heavily populated for them."

Phyllis nodded absently. "What did he mean when he said Whip Holt wants to set a trap and bait it?"

Ralph threw another log on the fire, then resumed his seat opposite her. "Offhand," he said, "I can't tell you specifically what Whip may have in mind. What would normally be done in a case like this would be to set up a household in a house or cabin that's isolated—but not too isolated. Then we'd persuade some courageous lady to move there. A woman attractive enough to draw the attention of the killers. We'd surround her with enough belongings to make it appear that she's well off, that her house is worth robbing. We'd hide enough guards to overpower Shorty and Slim when they'd show up. Our sentries would keep watch day and night for as long as it might take. Weeks, most likely."

She nodded but remained silent.

"What I dislike most about that sort of scheme is that it can backfire," Ralph said. "People other than Shorty and Slim might appear to rob her. And that period of waiting can be nerve-destroying, especially for the lady who is the target."

"I'll volunteer," Phyllis said in a small but firm voice.

He gaped at her in utter astonishment.

She thought he hadn't heard. "If it will help to catch those horrible men, who must be insane, I'll volunteer to be the bait in the trap."

Ralph replied loudly and with great force. "Never!" he exclaimed. "I won't permit it! I forbid it!"

Phyllis glanced at him in surprise. "But I'm such a logical candidate," she said. "Heather has a husband and a small baby. Jane has three growing children. Papa is comfortable here, and I'd arrange to have someone do the cooking and housework while I was away."

He drained his glass, then placed it on the table with such force that he almost shattered it. "You'd actually set yourself up as a target for a pair of criminals who have already committed a number of vicious murders!"

"Well, from the way you've described it, I wouldn't have to do much of anything except sit and wait," she said. "So I wouldn't have to be all that courageous. Besides, you, Rick, and Mr. Holt wouldn't allow anything bad to happen to me."

"Mistakes can be made," Ralph said angrily, "angles

can be overlooked, and plans can go awry. You were badly hurt when your brother was killed, and you're not going to be placed in a position that will cause you additional distress."

"Perhaps I want to do this for John's sake," she said. "For a long time I was as listless and lacking in ambition as he was. I changed, and I believed with all my heart that Johnny would change, too. He was murdered before he had the chance to prove himself, and I can never forgive his killers for that. So I have every right to ask that I be allowed to become the decoy."

Ralph exerted great self-control and replied gently. "You have every right to ask," he said, "every right to insist that the sheriff and the prosecutor give you the opportunity to avenge your brother's death. Your request is reasonable, equitable, and appropriate. All the same, I ask you to withdraw it." Ralph paused a moment, then went on. "You force me to hold a premature discussion with you. I would have preferred to have waited for another six months, at the least. I dislike impulsive behavior." Ralph glanced at her briefly, then looked away. "On occasion," he said, "you've attributed high motives—even noble motives —to the offer that brought you and your father into this house. Regardless of the convenience to you, and it can be argued that you've found the situation truly convenient, my fundamental motives were selfish."

Phyllis began to catch the drift of what he was attempting to say, and with difficulty she concealed a smile.

He took a folded hankerchief from the breast pocket of his conservatively tailored suit, wiped perspiration from his forehead and upper lip, then started again. "You've never wondered why I gave up a successful practice of law in New York and came to California," he said. "At least, you've never inquired."

"There was no need to ask," she replied. "Isaiah

told me. You were jilted." Had Isaiah been present he would have been thrashed.

"In my opinion," she went on, "the young lady in question was shortsighted and flighty. Knowing nothing about her, I would nevertheless brand her as stupid."

"Why is that?"

"Because you're extraordinary. I refuse to explain in detail because you'll become impossible if you gain too good an opinion of your virtues."

Ralph was too flustered to realize that she was encouraging him, in a none-too-subtle fashion, to declare himself. Embarrassed by her flattery, he was at a loss for words.

Afraid she had gone too far, Phyllis misinterpreted his silence. "You must love her very much," she said.

"I put her out of my heart, mind, and life a long time ago," he replied firmly.

Relieved, Phyllis waited for him to continue. It would be only natural for him to tell her now of his growing interest in her. Instead he fell silent again, and in her frustration Phyllis became somewhat reckless. "I'm lucky that I never suffered your kind of unhappiness," she said. "I've been very careful not to let myself believe I'm in love until I've come to know the man well enough to understand and appreciate his character."

Ralph was startled and dismayed. "You—you've come to care for someone?"

His concern was so heartening that she couldn't help smiling as she nodded.

Still not aware of her feelings for him, he replied stiffly. "I hope you'll be very happy together."

She knew he needed still another nudge. "I hope so, too, but it may be we'll never get together. He'll have to propose before I'll be able to accept."

Ralph became indignant. "How could any man be stupid enough not to propose to you?" he demanded.

Unable to reply, Phyllis could only return his gaze.

The expression in her eyes finally revealed the truth to him, and he grinned sheepishly. In that instant the world was transformed, and he laughed aloud as he reached for her. "I guess I'm a damn fool, all right!"

Holding each other they kissed for a long time, then Phyllis disengaged herself and took a single, backward step. "I accept your proposal, sir," she said demurely, then added in a rush, "and I promise you that I'll never hurt you."

The next morning, while Phyllis was preparing breakfast, Ralph formally asked her father for her hand. Randy was delighted. "I never would have knowed she had the good sense t' latch onto somebody like you!" he said.

At the breakfast table the happy couple broke the news to Isaiah. In their own joy they failed to note that the boy's eyes looked glazed and that his smile was stiff and his manner strained.

The day was busy, and not until that evening, when Isaiah failed to appear at supper, did they realize anything was amiss. Randy went on to the boy's room to fetch him and returned with a brief note that he had propped on his pillow.

You don't need me, he wrote, *so I don't want to be in your way.*

Phyllis burst into tears. "I had no idea he'd feel we didn't want him!"

Ralph was badly upset, too, and hurried off to obtain help from Rick Miller. The two men spent the better part of the night searching for Isaiah, but they could find no clue to his whereabouts. He had taken only a small bundle of clothing and his six-shooter.

The following day Ralph offered a reward of one hundred dollars for any information that might lead to the boy's return.

"I'll never forgive myself if anything happens to him," Phyllis said.

"It isn't your fault," Ralph said, trying to comfort her. "Isaiah never knew any affection until I came into his life, so it appears he wasn't able to understand that

I could love two people at the same time in different ways."

The sun's rays slanted through the windows of Melissa Austin's bedroom, awakening her shortly before noon. She had never felt worse in her life, and she moaned aloud. Her head felt twice its size and was throbbing. Her left cheekbone was sore to the touch, and so was one thigh.

Gradually her memory of the preceding night came back. The client she had brought upstairs to her suite had been well-mannered and fairly sober, more of a gentleman than most of her customers, and he had agreed to pay such a handsome fee for her services that she had consented to have several drinks with him.

Not until she hauled herself out of bed did the rest of the nightmare come alive again. The client had surprised her by demanding that she engage in a variety of unnatural acts with him and had become violent when she had refused. She moved slowly to the mirror, and realized that she would need a heavy layer of cosmetics to hide the ugly welt on her cheekbone, and her thigh was already black and blue. It was surprising that he could have inflicted so much damage on her in the short time it had taken Big George's strong-arm men to respond to her urgent tugs at the bell rope.

In disgust Melissa averted her face from the mirror. No! She forced herself to study her image again, taking in every detail. Her normally luminous eyes were puffy and bloodshot. Perhaps it was just her imagination, but the muscles of her face seemed to sag, making her resemble an old, weary hag. Certainly the mark the customer's fist had left on her cheekbone was very real, and as she felt the place gingerly, she was relieved that, at least, he had broken no bones.

She loathed herself, and she hated her profession. She couldn't even go down to the kitchen for breakfast until she covered the bruise.

Rick Miller and Whip Holt had been right. She should get out of her profession while she could, take her earnings, and start a new life somewhere where she wasn't known. If that was possible.

Which it wasn't. She had achieved a notoriety that extended the length and breadth of the Pacific Coast. After more evenings like last night—and she knew there would be many—she would truly grow old and coarse before her time. Discouraged and heartsick, she donned a flowing negligee that would not reveal the thigh bruise, then forced herself to go down to the kitchen. In a few hours she would be expected to make her customary, dramatic appearance in the saloon.

Everyone on the staff had heard of her problems. The other women were sympathetic but did not dwell on the subject when they realized she had no desire to discuss the incident. She thanked the guards who had rescued her, then went off to a quiet corner with her mug of black coffee and a thin slice of toasted bread, the only food she could force herself to eat.

Gradually the ache in her head began to subside, but Melissa still felt out of sorts, and she glanced up in annoyance when she heard a commotion nearby. The chief cook, a burly man who prepared food expertly until he consumed too much whiskey, was very angry, and as he brandished a meat cleaver, she realized he had already been drinking more than was good for him.

"Get out!" he shouted. "Now! Before I chop you into pieces!"

Facing him was a tall, almost painfully thin teenage boy, and what impressed Melissa was that he did not flinch even when the meat cleaver grazed him. "Please, mister," the boy said, "I'm not asking for anything free. I'll chop wood, I'll wash dishes, I'll do any jobs you'll give me. All I want in return is a meal or two."

Melissa couldn't guess how someone that young could have found his way to Big George's saloon. But it was plain that the boy was very hungry, and she had to admire his courage. She had no idea what impelled her to call out sharply: "Marty, stop scaring the kid! Go about your business!"

The cook stared at her, as did a half-dozen others in the kitchen.

"Boy, come over here," she commanded.

He walked toward her slowly, a glimmer of hope in his eyes.

"What are you doing alone in this part of California?" she demanded. "Why aren't you with your family?"

"I don't have a family, ma'am. I came to try my luck in the gold fields, but it hasn't been very good."

Melissa looked him up and down, and her heart went out to him. She would have denied vehemently that she was endowed with as much as a trace of maternal instinct, but she sensed that her compassion sprang from some deep-rooted, essential femininity. Beckoning imperiously, she motioned him to a place opposite her at the small kitchen table. Then she went to the serving area, where she filled a heaping platter with baked ham, fried potatoes, bread and butter, and the baked beans that were the staple of every gold prospector's diet. Returning to the table, she placed the platter in front of the boy. "Eat!" she commanded.

He needed no second invitation and began to devour the food ravenously.

His appetite confirmed Melissa's guess. He had gone hungry for days. She waited until he had cleaned his plate before she asked, "Who are you?"

Looking uneasy, he replied, "I'm called Isaiah."

"And you want a job?"

"Yes, ma'am, any job." He had suffered indifference at best and more than his share of cruelty since running away from Ralph Hamilton's house, and he couldn't understand why this beautiful, young red-haired woman with the hard green eyes was showing an interest in him.

Not until much later did it dawn on Melissa that

her kindness was a way of easing the guilt and disgust that her life caused her. She loathed herself for being so proficient and successful in the vocation that had been thrust upon her, and her kindness to the boy who so desperately needed assistance made her feel she was doing some good in the world.

It was possible there was even more to the situation than merely easing her guilt. Isaiah was homeless, drifting without roots, and so was she. It was startling to realize that she was able to identify with the child.

"Tell Big George I want a word with him," she called over her shoulder.

No one else in the establishment had the power to summon the proprietor, but he could not ignore the request from his single largest source of income. He strolled into the kitchen. his lead-filled pipe in one hand, and he looked quizzically at Melissa. "I hear tell you had some trouble last night." he said.

"Yes, and I don't want it to happen again," Melissa said curtly. "Neither of us would be very happy if I had to stop work for a week or two."

His joviality vanished. "The boys moved fast when you finally got around to calling for help," he said. "You've got nobody to blame but yourself if you misjudge a customer."

"I'm taking no more chances," she said and gestured toward the wide-eyed, silent boy. "Hire him."

Big George's laugh was explosive. "You want a child for a bodyguard? You've got to be crazy."

Everyone else in the kitchen laughed, too.

Isaiah felt his face reddening. He hadn't expected the young woman to mock him.

But Melissa did not laugh. "I want him stationed right outside the front door of my suite whenever I take a client there," she said. "He'll keep his ear glued to the door. I'll work out a signal with him, a password. Any time he hears me say it, he'll run for help. Fast. Which will bring the guards to my suite before some insane man can break my bones."

The idea had merit, and Big George's grin faded.

"The rest of the time," she continued, "the boy can do odd jobs around the place, cutting firewood or washing dishes or whatever. Provided everybody concerned remembers that I'm his permanent, number one assignment."

Big George nodded slowly.

Melissa knew what would appeal to him. "He won't cost you a penny, George. Give him his meals and a place to sleep. I'll attend to his tips."

Big George immediately became expansive again. "Well, now, there's nothing to lose, is there?" He turned to Isaiah and demanded, "You heard, boy? You agree?"

Isaiah had no idea what the red-haired young woman expected of him, but the prospect of eating regularly and having a place to sleep was irresistible. "You bet, sir!"

"All right, we'll try it out." Big George turned and stalked out.

Melissa was not only doing a good turn for a waif who obviously needed assistance, but she was also helping herself. The pain in her head was reduced to a dull ache, and for the first time she thought she might be able to drag herself through another interminable day and night with men who wanted her body. "Help yourself to more food," she told the boy. "Take whatever you like, as much as you like. When you're done, come up to the suite at the second floor front, and I'll give you your instructions." She swept out of the room, her peignoir gathered around her.

Isaiah was in a daze as he loaded his plate. Thanks to the beautiful woman's intervention, no one objected, and even the cook who had threatened him with the meat cleaver no longer seemed to resent his presence. He still didn't know what functions he would be performing on the young woman's behalf, but she had befriended him in an hour of great need, and he swore he would give her total loyalty in return.

Not that the relationship would be permanent. His experience with Ralph Hamilton had taught him not to expect too much from anyone. Just thinking about Ralph made him so homesick that he felt an ache in his throat. The worst of it was that he couldn't blame Ralph; he suspected that if he were a grown man, he would fall in love with Phyllis, too, or with someone like her. She and his new red-haired benefactress were different, though, and it didn't matter that he couldn't figure out the reasons. For now, with his immediate future assured, he was prepared to put his memories of home behind him—the only real home he had ever known—and would do his best for his new friend.

Danny Taylor finished his day's work a little earlier than usual, and it was still daylight when he limped through his orchard on his way back to the house. His new trees, scores of them, had taken root, and he was pleased. Some would begin to bear fruit at the end of the new growing season, and the others wouldn't be far behind. He had good cause to be satisfied with his labor.

Tired after his long day, Danny nevertheless smiled quietly. He owed his sense of satisfaction to Heather, and never would he be able to repay his debt to her. By standing firm, forcing him to choose between her and a return to the gold fields, she had made it possible for him to find complete contentment. His own sweat was nourishing his trees, and he no longer questioned his future. He would spend the rest of his life in this orchard, and little Ted, who would learn all his father could teach him, would inherit a flourishing business.

It was strange, Danny mused, but he had lost his craving for gold. He had sold his nuggets and dust, and the cash he had received was safely deposited in a Sacramento bank, where it would shield him and his family if an emergency should arise. Heather had cured him.

His sense of euphoria increasing as he drew nearer to the house, Danny suddenly halted. Dusk was just beginning to fall, and it was still light enough for him to catch a glimpse of two strangers on his property, loitering in the grove of fruit trees behind the house. They might well be Shorty and Slim. In any event they were trespassing.

Taking no chances, Danny lifted his rifle to his shoulder. As he did the pair fled.

The sound of a single rifle shot echoed across the hills, bringing Heather from the house with a six-shooter in her hand.

"I missed them," Danny said, annoyed with himself.

Asking no questions, his wife handed him the pistol, and Danny explained to Heather what he had seen. She realized, by his description, that the men were Shorty and Slim.

"It's uncanny," Danny said, "the way those two suddenly appear out of nowhere. It's as though they have a sixth sense. No sooner has Whip Holt left to go back to Sacramento than Slim and Shorty show up again."

John Foster and his younger son, Tracy, having heard the rifle shot, arrived on the run from their own nearby property, and the boy was sent off to Sacramento with word that Slim and Shorty appeared to be in the neighborhood again.

As a precaution, the entire Foster family gathered at the Taylor house. So did a number of other neighbors. The men brought their arms, and the women brought food for a communal supper. A threat to one family was a threat to all.

It was mid-evening before Rick Miller and Whip Holt arrived, accompanied by a haggard Ralph Hamilton. Danny repeated the story of the incident but was unable to answer most of Rick's sharp questions. "I wouldn't swear the men I saw were Shorty and Slim because I never saw them before. All I can tell you is that both of them were big, and both wore dark clothes. They started to run when they saw me lift my rifle, and I'm sorry to say I'm so badly out of practice that I missed both of them by several feet."

Whip tried to console him. "It happens to everybody who doesn't keep up, Danny. Spend a half-hour every day putting bullets into a target, and you'll soon have your eye again."

"It's good the way folks hereabouts respond when they hear a shot," Rick said, "but that isn't enough. I'm going to increase the patrols of deputies in this area at once."

"I wonder," Whip said, "if it would help to apply to the governor for special funds so we can offer a substantial reward for Slim and Shorty, dead or alive."

"It can't do any harm," Rick replied.

"But I doubt if it will do much good, either," Ralph said. "I've had dozens of responses to my offer of one hundred dollars for information on where to find Isaiah, but every last one who has come to me has been a swindler. I've yet to be given a genuine lead."

Danny was disappointed. Having been an orphan himself, he understood the plight of Isaiah Atkins better than anyone else.

"I'll go with you tomorrow to see the governor, Rick," Ralph said. "Anything that might be instrumental in rounding up those killers shouldn't be overlooked, and we've got to catch them before they find new victims."

Whip now realized it unlikely that his suggestion of a reward would be effective. Criminals tended to protect each other, and mere thieves, swindlers, and card cheats would think twice before going to the authorities with information about murderers, who would not hesitate to strike hard and fast at informers.

His own sense of dissatisfaction rankled, and Whip, unaccustomed to failure, was becoming increasingly restless. He had written letters to Eulalia, explaining his progress—or lack of it—and she had written in return, saying he should do what he had to do. Although he knew that he had absented himself from Oregon for far too long and had no right to neglect his family, he hated to go home empty-handed. He had come to California in the hope of persuading Melissa Austin to return with him, but she had been adamant in her refusal to change her way of life. He had stayed on to help Rick Miller apprehend a pair of vicious killers, but Shorty and Slim were still at large, their elusiveness mocking the authorities.

Something had to be done soon to force a climax. Rather than wait to have their meeting in Sacramento, Whip expressed his thoughts about setting a trap for Slim and Shorty as he, Rick, and Ralph were riding back to the city. "I remember a year I spent in the high Rockies with the Arapaho," he said. "There was a no-good, thieving bobcat that used to hang around the Arapaho town. Most ornery critter you ever saw. He'd wait until a warrior would go out alone. Then he'd attack, just to be mean. He mauled a half-dozen braves pretty bad, but he was so clever we couldn't track him. Finally we set a trap for him."

"What kind of a trap?" Rick asked.

"First off," Whip said, "I kept a chart of the area that the bobcat frequented most often. Then I went out there and concealed myself in a secure spot. I had a solid rock wall behind me, so there was no way he could jump me from behind. Then a warrior who had a lot of courage—young fellow by the name of Long Claw—volunteered to be the victim. Every day and every night for a week he wandered out and puttered around near my hiding place. Well, the bobcat took the bait. I shot him in midair as he was leaping toward Long Claw."

They rode in silence for a time, and finally Rick said, "We've got some pondering ahead. I see two problems. The first is finding the right trap for Shorty and Slim. And even more important is finding someone with the courage of Long Claw to act the part of the victim."

Ralph explained to the others that Phyllis had volunteered to act as a lure to catch the murderers but that he had asked her to withdraw her request. "Phyllis has never dealt with criminals and hardened types. I don't think we can allow her to expose herself to great danger."

The others agreed, and Whip mused aloud, "Any woman who takes part in such a scheme must have a lot of courage but also had better know how to deal with ruthless men."

Phyllis Gregg insisted on postponing her wedding until Isaiah Atkins was found and returned safely, but a full month passed after the boy's disappearance, and she and Ralph Hamilton began to wonder if they would ever be able to marry without the shadow of Isaiah coming between them.

Then, one day, a gold prospector down on his luck wandered into the prosecutor's office. "I saw your notice about that there boy who vanished," he said. "Maybe I can help, and I sure could use that one-hundred-dollar reward."

Ralph listened indifferently at first, then became increasingly anxious as he heard the man's story. The boy—or someone who strongly resembled him—was working in a large saloon called Big George's that was located near the edge of the gold fields.

"I noticed him special," the miner said, "because he not only does odd jobs around the place, but he's kind of a mascot to one of the harlots there, a real beauty. Follows her every time she takes a customer up the stairs. Damned if I know what he does up there, but I heard tell he always follows her."

Ralph questioned him at length, and the man's description of the boy was that of Isaiah.

"Come back in forty-eight hours," Ralph told the miner. "If you're right, you'll get the money. With my thanks."

Rick and Whip offered to accompany him. "You know yourself that Big George's is a mighty rough place," the sheriff said. "The customers who hang out there don't have much use for law enforcement people, and you won't be all that popular if they find out you're the prosecutor."

"I prefer to go alone," Ralph later told Phyllis, after declining the invitation of Rick and Whip. "If Isaiah should be there, I think I can deal more easily with him if I'm by myself. I don't want him to get the idea that a whole posse is coming after him."

She understood his point but was worried. "If the saloon is as unpleasant as Rick says, won't you be taking a big risk?"

"I'll be armed, naturally," he replied confidently. "And I've yet to encounter a situation in which I can't take care of myself. Besides, if Isaiah should be there, our only hope of getting him back here is to persuade him to return voluntarily."

A court case kept Ralph occupied the following morning, so it was noon before he was able to leave town, his six-shooter resting in its holster, the bottom of which was tied to his leg with a rawhide thong. As he rode off into the hills, he was unaware how little he resembled the New York attorney he had been. He wore boots, a broad-brimmed hat, and neatly tailored buckskin trousers, the only concessions to his profession being his black frock coat, high-standing collar, and dark, plain cravat.

It was mid-afternoon when he reached Big George's place and gave his horse to a waiting groom. The blinds in the saloon were drawn, with oil lamps providing the illumination, the rays of light cutting through a haze of pipe and cigar smoke. A score of men were standing along a bar that occupied one wall, while others were eating and drinking at numerous tables. A card game was in progress at one long table, and sharp-eyed men were exchanging piles of metal chips. Two fiddlers and a drummer were playing a lively tune, and several men were dancing with young women attired in a minimum of clothing.

Ralph crossed the huge room, found an unoccupied table, and sat. A blond woman promptly appeared beside him and asked what he wanted, making it clear she included herself as a suggestion. Having eaten nothing since breakfast, he ordered some beef, bread, and ale. The woman flounced away, obviously nettled by his lack of personal interest in her.

Ralph became conscious of someone's steady gaze and saw that a far more attractive young woman, a redhead, was sitting at the adjoining table. The thought flicked his mind that she was far too pretty to be working at Big George's.

She smiled steadily at him. He had to make a beginning, so he did not discourage her. A moment later she rose and approached him, her hips swaying. "May I join you?"

Ralph rose, held her chair for her, and asked what she wanted to drink.

His good manners, as well as his clothes, told Melissa he was a man of means, so her smile became even more dazzling. He startled her by saying, "You must be Melissa. I've heard Rick Miller and Whip Holt speak of you frequently."

She waited until he was served his food and drink before she demanded, "Who are you?"

"My name is Hamilton."

"Prosecutor Hamilton?"

"Yes, that's right."

Melissa was irritated. "If you've been sent here by Rick to save my soul—"

"My presence here has nothing to do with you, Miss Austin," he interrupted icily. "I've come on private business of my own."

"Oh?" She relaxed a little, and her smile reappeared, although it was tentative and wary.

"I'm looking for a tall, thin boy in his early teens named Isaiah," Ralph said, cutting to the heart of his mission. "I've been told I could find him here."

"Do you carry a warrant for his arrest?" she demanded, her voice sharp.

Ralph stared at her for a moment, then grinned

quietly. "He's not in trouble with the law. And for your information, a prosecutor sends deputy sheriffs into the field to serve warrants. That happens to be a legal function he does not perform himself."

A bartender appeared with the glass of colored water that would serve as Melissa's drink.

"Ask George to join us at once," she said.

The bartender hurried away.

Melissa averted her gaze, making it plain she did not want to communicate with Ralph again until the proprietor appeared.

Within moments Big George loomed up beside them. "You having a problem, Melissa?" he asked, his manner threatening as he scowled at the well-dressed stranger.

She smiled sweetly as she shook her head. "This is Sacramento Valley Prosecutor Hamilton," she said.

Big George looked as though he had been slapped across the face and instantly became defensive. "I run an honorable place. I give value received for food and drink, my girls don't cheat their clients, and I defy you or anybody else to prove my card games aren't honest! So why come snooping around here?"

"Sit down, George," Melissa said. He obeyed, pulling out a chair. "Mr. Hamilton is looking for Isaiah," she said.

"I've told you a hundred times I'm not comfortable around that boy. He's just too damn smart for his age!" Big George's face grew red.

Ralph was quietly elated. So Isaiah indeed was here.

Melissa continued to take charge. "I've been assured that Isaiah has broken no laws."

The big man glared at the visitor. "Then what do you want with him?"

"He's my ward," Ralph said. "Due to an unfortunate misunderstanding, he ran away from home."

Big George took a bandanna from his hip pocket and mopped his face. "My God! The prosecutor's ward. Mr. Hamilton, the boy is a minor, so he can't give any testimony against me or my place that will be accepted in any court."

"I have no intention of taking you to court, sir," Ralph said. "I've come here in the hope that I can persuade Isaiah to return home with me."

Melissa understood instantly and put a hand on Big George's arm. "Let me handle this."

"All right," he said grudgingly, "but get that boy to hell and gone out of here in a hurry. I don't want any prosecutor's kin hanging around my place." Big George looked defiantly at Ralph. "Nothing personal, you understand." He heaved himself to his feet and stalked off.

Ralph raised an eyebrow as he turned back to Melissa. "Trust me," she said.

"I don't have much choice in the matter, do I?"

"I've grown fond of Isaiah, and I want what's best for him. He doesn't talk about his past, so perhaps you'll tell me. Why did he run away?"

"Because I'm being married. He thought he wasn't wanted any longer."

"Is that true?"

"Definitely not!" Ralph said.

"I can understand how he feels. But we'll have to be careful. If he sees you right now, he may take off again." She thought for a few moments, then looked pleased with herself. "I have it. Come with me, won't you?" She rose.

Leaving his unfinished meal on the table, he placed money beside his plate to pay for it. "Where are we going?"

"Up to my quarters," Melissa replied, taking his arm, her smile dazzling as she looked up at him. "You're now posing as a client, so try not to look so disapproving."

Ralph realized he had to go along with her scheme, whatever it might be, so he reluctantly returned her smile as she led him toward the staircase. The knowing expressions on the faces of a score of patrons made him uncomfortable.

"Isaiah is being notified right now that I'm taking a customer upstairs," Melissa murmured as they climbed to the upper floor. "He'll be along in a minute or two, so just do exactly as I tell you."

He nodded. "Tell me just one thing. Why are you going out of your way to be so considerate?"

"Isaiah will be better off with you than he is here. Give him a year or two in this place, and he'll grow up like all the rest who work for George. If he goes with you, he'll have at least a chance to lead an honest, productive life."

The woman might be a prostitute, Ralph reflected, but at heart she was a decent person. "I won't forget this kindness, I promise you," he said. "Regardless of how this turns out, I hope I'll have the opportunity to return the favor."

She thought of the abuse and indignities she had suffered at the hands of clients. "I'll remember that," she said. "I don't know what I might do, but one of these days I just might accept your offer."

He wanted to question her, but they had reached her suite, and she waved him inside, then raised a finger to her lips. "Don't speak again. Isaiah might recognize your voice." She waved him toward the bed-chamber, which stood beyond the sitting room.

Ralph hesitated. If she and Big George wanted to discredit him and destroy his standing as prosecutor, all they would need to do would be to send several witnesses bursting into the suite, men who could claim they had found the prosecutor in a compromising situation.

Melissa knew what was going through his mind, and her gaze was steady. He decided to take the risk and went to the inner room, which was dominated by a huge, four-poster bed, piled high with satin pillows. There were no chairs in the room, so he perched uncomfortably on the foot of the bed.

Melissa came as far as the door and pulled it almost closed. Then he heard her walk to the outer door and open it. "Come in for a minute, Isaiah," she said.

"I thought you had somebody with you," the boy replied in obvious bewilderment.

At the sound of his voice, Ralph's pulse beat more rapidly.

Melissa closed the door. "Sit down," she said, then called, "You may come out now."

Ralph stood slowly, braced himself, and opened the door. "Hello, Isaiah," he said, trying to speak calmly.

The boy leaped to his feet and saw that Melissa had stationed herself in front of the entrance, blocking it. Then, like an animal at bay, he looked around wildly as he realized there was no escape.

"Sit down, please," Melissa told him. "No one is going to hurt you."

Isaiah faced Ralph defiantly, an aggressive posture his only defense. "You had no right to come after me!" he shouted. "I'm doing fine, and all I want is to be left alone."

"Phyllis and I very much want you to come home, where you belong," Ralph said.

Tears came to the boy's eyes, but he shook his head savagely. "I don't want anybody feeling sorry for me!" he cried.

Melissa gestured to Ralph that she wanted to take charge. She went to the boy, placed her hands on his shoulders, and forced him to sit again in the easy chair. "Listen to me," she said. "I think you owe me that much."

"I owe you everything."

She dropped to her knees beside his chair. "You and I haven't talked about this before," she said, "but you know, of course, how I earn my living here."

"Well, sure." Color rose in the boy's face.

Suddenly her manner changed, and she became scornful. "How long do you suppose you can earn a living by standing guard outside a whore's door? Do you really think you're building for the future?"

Isaiah clenched his fists. "You need me! You helped me when I was in need, and I won't desert you."

She softened, and Ralph detected a hint of sadness in her voice as she said, "Don't worry about me, Isaiah. I managed for a long time before you came into my life, and I can do it again."

"But who will summon the guards if one of the men you bring up here gets nasty?"

"It shouldn't be too hard to find someone else, you know," Melissa said gently. "The job doesn't require much skill."

The boy had no reply.

She put a hand on his arm. "Mr. Hamilton not only offers you a real future, but he needs you."

He shook his head, clenching his teeth.

"Don't you think it may be possible," Melissa asked him patiently, "for someone to love more than one person?"

"I—I don't know."

Ralph stood silently, making no move and not daring to interrupt for fear he would break the spell that Melissa was weaving so expertly.

"What's your feeling for Mr. Hamilton, Isaiah? Be honest," she continued when he made no reply. "I can see in your face that you love him."

"Sure," Isaiah said defensively. "Why wouldn't I? He was the best friend I ever had."

She nodded, then lowered her voice to a near-whisper. "And what do you think of me?"

"I love you, too. You've been wonderful to me."

Melissa stood abruptly and smiled. "There you are. You love more than one person. So what makes you think Mr. Hamilton loves you any less because he's going to get married?"

"I don't know." Isaiah was miserable as he stared down at his scuffed, worn boots.

Melissa signaled to Ralph to talk.

"Do you hate Phyllis all that much?" he asked.

"I don't hate her at all, except for her taking you away from me and changing everything. She was good to me, much nicer than she had to be."

"I'd like to make you a deal," Ralph said. "Come home with me, and I honestly believe you'll find nothing is changed when Phyllis and I are married. In fact, you should be happier than you ever were, because she loves you, too. If I'm wrong, I give you my pledge that you may come back to work for Melissa."

His eyes enormous, Isaiah turned to Melissa and asked an unspoken question.

"I agree," she said. "Mr. Hamilton is being very fair."

Isaiah turned to Ralph for the first time but still couldn't meet his gaze. "If you really want me to come back," he muttered, "I'll do it."

Trying to hide his relief, Ralph extended his hand. "If we can rent or buy a horse for you, we'll be home in time for supper. Phyllis is making your favorite in the hope you'll be there to celebrate."

The boy's face lighted. "Pot roast and dumplings?"

Melissa laughed. The boy turned to her, suddenly ashamed of his exuberance. "I'm going to miss you."

"I hope you'll be too busy," she replied briskly. Then, unable to maintain an impersonal note, she embraced and kissed him. "That's so you won't forget me." Then, before he could reply, Melissa's voice rose shrilly. "Now get out! Don't hang around here! Just go!"

Ralph realized she would become hysterical if they lingered. So he bowed to her deeply to convey his gratitude, then put an arm around the boy's shoulders and led him toward the stairs. The door closed quietly behind them.

"I'll see what I can do about getting a horse for you while you gather your belongings," Ralph said. "I'll meet you at the stable."

They parted on the ground floor, and Ralph was in

luck when the groom offered him a sound gelding for a fee of five dollars. He knew that animal dealers in Sacramento were asking at least double that sum for comparable horses, so it was plain that the price was low because the gelding had been stolen. Under other circumstances he would have refused, but he was eager to return home with Isaiah as quickly as possible.

Isaiah soon joined him, carrying his Colt revolver in his belt.

"Where are your other things?"

The boy smiled shyly. "I'm wearing everything I own. After I ran away, I sold everything for food. Except my pistol."

In the long run, Ralph thought, the experience might prove beneficial to the boy.

They started off at a slow canter, slightly handicapped because Isaiah was riding bareback. As they rode down the road that grew narrower on the approach to a large patch of woods, Ralph found himself pondering the future of Melissa Austin. Certainly Rick Miller had been right when he had discussed her one evening with Whip Holt in Ralph's presence. "She's different," he had said. "I've had to deal with more prostitutes than I care to recall in my years as a law enforcement officer, and she's the only one who doesn't fit the mold."

Her manners were those of a lady, but the qualities that set her apart were deep below the surface. Others seemed to enjoy their life, but she approached her profession mechanically, displaying a sense of reserve. It was almost as though she were rejecting her vocation, even while engaging in it. In any event, aware that he was in her debt, that she alone was responsible for Isaiah's change of heart, Ralph hoped she had meant her vague remark to the effect that someday she might come to him for assistance.

Tonight—or tomorrow at the latest—Ralph would give a full report to Whip and would do whatever he

could to persuade Melissa to put her present way of
life behind her. If she didn't want to go back to
Oregon with Whip, which was likely, it would not
prove difficult for her to begin anew somewhere else
in the growing United States.

Preoccupied with his thoughts, Ralph paid little
attention to his immediate surroundings as he and
Isaiah rode down the path into the deep woods. He
was astonished when two masked men, both mounted
and carrying single-shot pistols, appeared ahead of
them, blocking the trail. Within moments two others
moved through the underbrush on the left, as did a
pair on the right, and a seventh man, masked like his
comrades and holding an old-fashioned musket,
moved onto the trail from the rear.

Ralph and Isaiah had ridden into a trap.

"Don't get upset," the leader called as the two
travelers were forced to slow their horses to a walk.
"Just do what you're told, and nobody will get hurt.
You look plenty rich, mister, and you're young enough
to enjoy life for a lot of years to come. So just hand
over your purse and that watch at the end of the chain
that's hanging from your waistcoat pocket. Then you
can be on your way again."

It occurred to Ralph that they were unaware of his
official position, and he had no intention of telling
them. They might be less charitably inclined if they
knew he was the prosecutor.

"What makes you think I'm carrying a purse?" he
called, stalling for time.

The leader became impatient. "A man who wears
fancy clothes don't make trips without carrying plenty
of cash. Hand over your money before we get nasty."

Ralph pretended to reach for a nonexistent purse in
his hip pocket and instead drew his revolver, firing it
as he raised it. The shot was difficult, but he nevertheless managed to knock the leader's pistol from his
grasp.

Isaiah was encouraged and drew his own Colt. His

bullet passed through the crown of the second man's hat, thoroughly alarming the robber.

Rarely had the bandits been opposed by their cowed victims, and their dilemma was compounded by the strict orders under which they conducted their operations. Big George had warned them never to kill or seriously injure any man whom they robbed. The authorities were too busy to handle simple cases of robbery but would be certain to pursue murderers.

Of all the group, the leader was in the worst position. His pistol was lying on the ground, and there was no way he could retrieve it.

Continuing to press his horse forward at a rapid walk, Ralph took aim a second time.

The leader fled, disappearing into the woods, and the accomplice who had been at his side a moment earlier had no desire to become a target again. The wild gleam of anticipation he saw in the eyes of the young boy who was pointing his Colt at him cooled the thief's ardor, and he, too, beat a hasty retreat. Isaiah's second shot sped him on his way.

Ralph turned in the saddle to the pair on his left, but they were infected by the leader's panic and disappeared. Within moments the remaining trio also vanished, and the path was cleared of obstacles.

Ralph continued to hold his Colt as he increased his pace. Isaiah, staying close beside him, did the same.

Not until they emerged from the woods and came to a neighborhood of small farms and ranches, with the houses of settlers facing the road, did Ralph drop his pistol back into his holster and speak for the first time. "You did well, Isaiah," he said. "You drew your revolver quickly, and you fired it without hesitation."

"I just did what you did, sir," the boy replied. "I was too scared to think."

"You couldn't have done better. Between us we chased off a band of rascals without losing either my money or my watch." He paused, then added pointedly, "Now you can see how much you and I need each other."

His remark cleared the air, and a slow grin spread across Isaiah's face. "I guess we do make a pretty good team," he said.

They rode steadily, their pace too rapid for conversation, and they came to Sacramento soon after sundown. Lights were burning in the parlor of the old, rambling house, and Phyllis Gregg sat anxiously peering out of a window. When the gate opened and the pair entered the property, leading their mounts, she ran to the front door.

"I thank God you've come home, Isaiah," she said fervently as she held out her arms to the boy.

Isaiah saw the joy in her eyes, felt her tears on his face as she embraced him, and knew he truly belonged here.

IX

Big George's saloon did a thriving business at all hours but almost invariably was filled to overflowing in the early hours of the evening. Crowds two and three deep lined the bar, hungry men ate substantial meals for which they willingly paid steep prices, several card games were in progress, and the harlots moved up and down the stairs with their customers in a constant parade. Only the table where Melissa Austin sat alone, taking her time in making her choice of the evening, was an oasis of tranquillity. Men shouted and laughed, told stories, and quarreled.

The fortunate showed off their gold nuggets, which they sometimes sold to the proprietor so they could play cards or pay for the favors of one of the women. The atmosphere was festive, and most of the patrons were in a holiday mood.

But Melissa was aware of subtle changes that the less observant had not yet noted. Fewer miners were making strikes of consequence in the gold fields. Fences were being erected around more and more gold-producing properties as these plots were purchased by men who had become wealthy, had formed companies, and were now hiring others to do their mining for them. Immigrants were still coming to California by the tens of thousands, but Melissa saw that the peak of the Gold Rush had passed.

Soon newcomers would begin to discover that the land here was marvelously fertile, as it was in Oregon, and then whole families would migrate to the new state. Three years had passed since gold first had been discovered, but the days of opportunity for the man who owned only a pan or a pickax were coming to an end.

That knowledge spurred Melissa's increasingly strong desire to change her way of life. She had accumulated a large sum of money, most of which she had deposited in a Sacramento bank on one of her infrequent visits to the city. Her nest egg was large enough to buy a property of consequence, but she had no intention of establishing a farm or ranch and operating it herself. She had no desire to return to Oregon, where people would whisper about her, and if she moved to San Francisco, her reputation inevitably would follow her there.

So she continued to ply her trade, even though she had come to hate men and loathe their greedy love-making. She cursed herself for stupidity, yet she didn't quite have the courage to break the patterns of the existence she led.

Glancing around the room now, she saw no one who interested her. Perhaps, one of these days very soon, before Whip Holt lost patience and went back to Oregon, she might ride into Sacramento and seek his advice, even though she was afraid he would insist that she accompany him to Oregon. Perhaps she would go instead to Prosecutor Hamilton, who was far more sophisticated and might be able to offer suggestions on how to make a fresh start.

A husky miner interrupted Melissa's reverie by pretending to stagger against her as he passed her table, and he managed to paw her swiftly and expertly before he straightened and grinned at her.

Cooly she crossed one leg over the other, revealing the long slit in her skirt. The miner's grin broadened.

Melissa reached beneath the decorative garter that rode high on a net stocking, her fingers closing around the hilt of the knife she had carried for protection ever since young Isaiah had gone back to Sacramento. She drew the blade, looked at it for a moment, and then glanced up at the miner, her eyes as cold as the steel in her hand.

"Touch me again," she said, her tone quietly conversational, "and I'll slice you to ribbons."

The man's smile faded, and he backed away hastily. He had been told she was tough and independent, and now he was willing to believe every story he had heard about her.

Melissa slid the knife back into her garter and continued to survey the noisy crowd.

Two bulky, heavyset men, both dressed in black and each carrying a revolver, shouldered their way to the bar, shoving aside those who stood in their path. A number of men resented their behavior, but the pair were too big and powerfully built to risk arousing their anger by protesting. The two newcomers ordered glasses of whiskey and pints of ale.

Little by little, almost imperceptibly at first, the crowd became quiet, and those at the bar edged away from the pair. All at once Melissa knew the identity of these newcomers: they were Shorty and Slim, wanted by the authorities for a whole series of gruesome murders, mostly of women. They were displaying incredible nerve, coming here when a *Wanted* notice describing them in detail was posted behind the bar.

Gradually it dawned on Melissa that Shorty and Slim were inspecting her, taking in every detail of her appearance. The taller of the two moistened his lips and said something to his companion. Melissa couldn't hear his words, but she was very much aware of his leer. In all her time at the saloon she had never seen men ogle her in that fashion. She became alarmed as she thought that they might be planning to come over to her table or that they might even be discussing her murder!

The heavier man replied before taking another swallow of whiskey. Then, as he drank his ale, he continued to watch her.

His eyes, she thought, were like those of a snake. A series of chills shot up and down her spine, and after rubbing her bare arms briskly, she gave a surreptitious signal to one of the bartenders.

A few moments later Big George sauntered to her table and sat down opposite her. "What's your problem?"

"There are two big men who came in just a few minutes ago," she said. "I'm sure they're Shorty and Slim."

"They are," he replied curtly. "I've already checked their descriptions on the poster."

"You're going to send for Sheriff Miller?"

"Hell, no!" Big George said, speaking quietly but emphatically. "I'll grant you that scum like that do my place no good. But as long as they behave themselves, they can drink here. Their money is as good as anybody else's. I've never been an informer, and I'm not going to start now." His grin was lopsided. "Maybe I have a few activities of my own that I want to keep hidden, and I don't want to set an example to informers."

"That's your business," she said. "But keep them away from me, George. Far away. They make my flesh crawl."

He chuckled. "You mean you wouldn't take one of them upstairs if he met your price?"

"They're rapists as well as murderers. They're demented, cold-blooded killers. The way they were looking at me when I sent for you made me ill. I warn you, George, if they come near me, I'm going to create a scene."

His smile faded. "Don't you worry, 'Lissa. You're my most valuable property. I don't want a brawl with bruisers the size of those two, but if they start to annoy you, I'll see to it they're thrown out." He stood and patted her bare shoulder. "You know you can depend on me to look after you," he said as he strolled away.

All Melissa knew was that, in this jungle, she had to rely on herself.

A deep, resonant voice sounded close to her ear. "You're more radiantly beautiful than ever, my dear. Your life seems to agree with you."

She looked up in astonishment, saw Jerome Hadley, and promptly forgot Slim and Shorty. Her seducer moved the vacant chair closer to her and did not wait for an invitation before he seated himself.

"You have some gall," Melissa said, her voice seething with the hatred that had been bottled within her ever since he had betrayed her.

"I was hoping that by now you'd be grateful to me for creating new opportunities for you. Allow me to order you a drink." Without waiting for her reply, he signaled to a bartender.

Still too shocked to think clearly, she continued to stare at him.

"It's plain you've done well," he said. "You seem to be operating here apart from the other girls. Your earrings, bracelets, and rings are expensive, and so is your gown—what there is of it." He laughed lightly.

"What do you want, Jerome?" Her voice was metalic.

"My dear girl, how can you question my motives? You're the most renowned of my protégées. They sing your praises from San Diego to San Francisco to the back country of Oregon. A magazine in New York has printed a short story in which you appear, thinly disguised, as the heroine. And I've heard rumors that a naughty song about you has become very popular in Chicago, although I haven't had the good fortune to hear it as yet."

Melissa wanted to cringe, to hide from the world for the rest of her days, but instead she faced him boldly. "You still haven't told me why you've come to see me."

He took their drinks from the bartender, then raised his glass in a toast. "I was in the area, not having passed this way in many months, and I was not only hoping to engage in a friendly game of cards here, but I was most eager to see how you were faring."

"Your concern overwhelms me," she said.

He patted her hand, then gripped it hard so she could not withdraw from him easily. "Don't be bitter, my dear. Surely you realize that you and I weren't meant for each other."

"Yes, that thought has crossed my mind from time to time." She stopped struggling, and he released her. She was taking the wrong approach. She had to match his cleverness, so she studied him closely, looking him up and down, then deliberately moved her chair closer to his. "You're looking quite prosperous yourself."

Mollified by her more amenable attitude, he replied, "Appearances can be very deceptive."

"But not in your case, surely." Melissa stroked his arm. "This suit is new since I've last seen you and so are your boots and shirt. What's more, the diamond stickpin in your cravat is handsome."

"A mere illusion," Hadley said, obviously enjoying her increasing warmth. "I won it in a game of chance from a fellow player who had lost all of his cash. Not until later did I find out the diamond is badly flawed, little better than glass. But it does impress the uninitiated."

Melissa picked up her drink, then looked at him over the rim of her glass. She was increasingly certain he wanted something from her, and he would be far easier to handle, far more malleable if she pretended she was still infatuated with him. "You'll never know how much you hurt me when you went off without me," she said, pouting.

"I didn't abandon you willingly," he said giving a deep sigh. "You'll never know how upset I was or how many sleepless nights I've spent. But it couldn't be helped. When I tell you the whole story, I'm sure you'll understand I had no choice. I was forced to go on alone."

She didn't care to listen to the lies he had undoubtedly invented to soothe her. What really surprised her was that she had been so naive and innocent at the time that she had been unable to see through the pretenses of this shallow man. "Talk of the past can wait," she murmured, leaning a bare shoulder against him. "What's more important is that you're here. How long will you stay?"

"That depends on how I make out at cards. If my winnings are sufficiently substantial I—ah—sometimes deem it wise not to linger too long in the neighborhood."

She looked up at him, her eyes wide and shining. "I was such a child when you and I last saw each other that I wouldn't have known what you meant. But I do understand it now."

"I'd think so," he replied, stroking her arm. "You've had quite an education here."

"I've become a very different person—in some ways. But in others I've remained constant." Melissa snuggled closer to him, confident he believed she still cared for him.

"You don't think too badly of me, then?"

"Not really," she lied. "I tried so hard to hate you, Jerome, but I couldn't."

He continued to caress her as he spoke cautiously. "Perhaps you'd be willing to prove that to me."

"How could I?" Melissa freed herself from his grasp while continuing to lean close to him, her eyes on his.

"I'm a bit down on my luck at the moment," Hadley said. "I'm sure you must be earning a splendid income these days. Aren't you?"

She nodded vaguely. "I don't do too badly."

"Well," he said, "I was hoping you'd stake me for tonight's card game. You could regard it as an investment. Say you let me have three thousand dollars—no, five would be better. I can give you an unconditional guarantee that you'll have twice that amount in return. Before the night ends."

"A guarantee, Jerome?" She hoped she looked sufficiently wide-eyed.

"Of course. You realize by now that I don't lose at cards!"

She thought it likely he would cheat and win, but even more likely that he would vanish again without repaying what he would owe her.

She was unaware that a number of patrons were watching as she supposedly went about the task of seducing a client. And she had forgotten for the moment the continuing, sharp interest of Slim and Shorty, who continued to observe her closely.

Curling an arm around his neck, Melissa murmured, "I think I have enough money on hand to give you what you need."

"Five thousand?"

"If that's what you want, honey. But I hope you know what I want." Her fingers trailed up and down the side of his face lightly in a teasing caress.

"After the card game," Hadley suggested, "we could spend the rest of the night together."

Even now, she knew, he was lying to her. The moment he finished fleecing the gullible poker players he would depart without a moment's hesitation. But her contented sigh lulled him. Meanwhile, as her fingers continued to stroke his face, her other hand crept to the hilt of the knife that her garter held secure.

She drew the blade swiftly, her grip on his face tightened, and she deliberately slashed him with the knife, inflicting a cut that extended from his temple to the base of his jaw. Jerome Hadley's scream of pain brought all activity in the saloon to a halt.

"Now, you bastard," she said, speaking loudly and

clearly, "you're going to be so ugly that no woman will ever look at you again."

He stared at her dully, shock and pain in his eyes, as he clapped a hand to his bleeding face.

Melissa calmly wiped her blade on his new suit to clean it, then thrust it back into her garter.

The room was in an uproar. At the sight of the wounded Hadley and the unflustered Melissa, men began shouting obscenities and threatening to start brawls. Several husky bartenders and guards quickly surrounded the couple.

Big George had never seen such a commotion in his saloon. The thought occurred to him that there might be more than one man in the excited crowd who would see this as an opportunity to settle an old score with him and would run to the authorities to report the incident. It would look a lot better if he called for Sheriff Miller himself and had Melissa soften the sheriff up after he arrived. Big George could take care of Hadley.

Hurrying to Melissa's table, Big George shouted orders to a subordinate. "Ride to Sacramento as fast as you can get there! Get Sheriff Miller out here. Personally." He paused long enough to feign a smile as he raised both hands for quiet. "No fuss, gentlemen! No trouble! Have a free drink on the house!"

Melissa smiled quietly as he approached the table.

"Take Hadley upstairs," the proprietor told two of his guards. "Put some brandywine on his cut, even if you have to hold him down to do it. And make sure he stays around until I get up there and talk to him. I don't care if you have to tie him to a bed, but keep him here." He turned to Melissa, his hands on his hips. "I do my damnedest to keep sheriffs away from here," he said. "But look at what you've done. They've got to investigate an attack like this. They have no choice."

"I had none, either," she replied. "You and I know why I did it to him."

"We'll talk privately," he said.

Melissa walked beside him and, aware of her audience, rolled her hips as she and Big George mounted the stairs.

No one in the establishment noticed in all the excitement that Shorty and Slim slipped away, leaving the instant they heard the sheriff being summoned. They were long gone before anyone realized they had vanished.

Melissa sank into a chair in her sitting room and twirled the gold nugget hanging from a gold chain around her neck. "Spare me your lectures, George," she said.

He glared at her. "I ought to beat some sense into you."

"But you won't," she said sweetly, "because you'd have too hard a time trying to explain the bruises to the sheriff and his deputies."

He shook his head. "Why did you do it, 'Lissa? You know how hard I try to avoid the law. Yes, and you know the reasons, too."

"Just as you know that Hadley started me in my career by selling me to you. And, if that wasn't bad enough, he had the nerve to ask me tonight to stake him to a loan of five thousand dollars so he could start a card game."

Big George nodded thoughtfully. "Well," he admitted, "you had cause. Especially since Hadley didn't offer me a share of his winnings. He knows I always get a percentage." He lowered himself into a chair opposite her. "Now we've got to think about you."

"I'm just fine, thanks."

"The reason I asked for Sheriff Miller himself to come out here is because he knows you. And maybe he's sympathetic to you. If he isn't, you'll have to soften him."

"Why?"

"You don't seem to realize you're in a bad spot. If Hadley brings charges against you, you'll be arrested and tried. Now maybe a couple of my men and I can—ah—persuade Hadley to tell the officers that the carving was an accident. If you soften Miller up a bit and tell him the same story, there's nothing he can do to you."

"But it wasn't an accident," Melissa said. "I wanted him marked for the rest of his life. He'll never be able to fool another woman with his oily charm the way he fooled me."

"If you're put in jail for safekeeping and then tried, you could miss weeks here. That's what I'm trying hard to avoid." Big George scowled. "Think of the money we'll lose in those weeks."

The world, she reflected, was filled with greedy men who tried to take advantage of the weak.

"Of course," he continued, "no judge will send you to prison if you claim you attacked Hadley in self-defense. Come to think of it, that's your best, sure-fire approach. We'll let Hadley tell Miller the carving was an accident, but you claim you did it because he tried to assault you. I'll get a couple of bartenders to substantiate your story, and you won't even be taken into custody."

She smiled blandly but made no comment.

He rose to his feet and towered above her. "You got it straight? Self-defense!"

She nodded, seemingly agreeing, but other ideas were seething in her mind.

Big George walked to the door, then paused. "I'll get Hadley headed in the right direction. You stay here—and don't come downstairs again—until the sheriff and his men get here." Having given specific orders and assuming they would be obeyed, he left the suite.

Melissa sat motionless for some time while she put her thoughts in order. Then she stood, taking care to lock the door, and immediately began to pack her clothes and jewelry in her leather traveling boxes. When she discovered there was insufficient space for all her belongings, which included the cash-filled strongbox she had not yet deposited in her bank account, she removed several of her older dresses from one of the boxes. Even then she had to sit on the lids of the cases to close them.

Patching her makeup, she looked at her reflection in the mirror and smiled. She had made a monumental decision, and for the first time since she had come to this sleazy place, she was at peace within herself. Returning to her chair in the sitting room, she relaxed and waited for the authorities to appear.

Even though she assumed that the sheriff would not delay when he learned she was involved, a long time passed before she heard a sharp tapping at her door.

Rick Miller and Whip Holt stood in the corridor, with three deputies and a grinning Big George behind them. "Stay out here and keep everybody away," Rick told one of his assistants, then turned politely to Melissa. "May we come in?"

An unhappy Whip followed him into the sitting room and closed the door. "It grieves me that you're involved in a mess, Melissa," he said.

"But it doesn't surprise us," Rick added. "You're bound to have serious problems when you lead an unsavory life in a place like this."

He sounded irritated, Melissa thought, as she invited them to sit.

"All right," Rick said gruffly. "What's your story?"

"I have none," Melissa said.

His annoyance increased. "We've just seen this fellow Hadley, whose face is a mess. He'll carry a heavy scar for the rest of his days. He tells us you slashed him by accident, but that's impossible."

"I've never known anyone to use a knife by accident," Whip added, his manner sorrowful because he sympathized with her.

"Big George tells us you used the knife in self-defense," Rick said. "In fact, he insists on it. Is that what you claim?"

"I demand to be placed under arrest and taken into Sacramento," Melissa replied calmly. "All my luggage is packed, and I'd like to take my property with me."

"Hold on," a concerned Whip said. "If it's true you

used a knife to defend yourself, we have no reason to arrest you. And I suspect that's so because Hadley refuses to bring any charges against you."

Ignoring Whip's remarks, Rick stared intently at Melissa. "I wonder if I really heard what I just heard," he said, "and if it means what I think it means."

Melissa nodded. "Can Big George hear us talking?"

"It isn't likely," Whip said. "One of the deputies is standing outside the door."

"All the same, I don't want to take any chances," she said. "If you take me into custody, there's no way he can stop me from leaving with you?"

"None," Rick said, an appreciative light appearing in his hard eyes.

"Then I refuse to make any statement until I'm placed out of harm's way in Sacramento."

Rick stood, hooking his thumbs in his belt. "Make sure you leave nothing behind that you want," he said.

"I've already done that," she said. Now that she had put her plan into motion she was becoming frightened.

Rick smiled at her, a hint of admiration in his voice. "Melissa Austin, you're under arrest. Are you carrying any weapons?"

"My knife."

"Well," he said, "you'd better keep it. Even with an escort, you have a long ride into town."

The situation began to dawn on Whip, and he grinned broadly. "You went pretty far if you knifed Hadley as a way of getting out of here," he said.

She shook her head. "I'll tell you all you want to know—and a great deal more—after we reach Sacramento." She picked up a long silk cloak.

Rick held it for her as she donned it, relieved because it concealed her skimpy gown. Then he opened the door and summoned the deputies. "Take this woman's baggage, which you'll find just inside the door of the other room," he said. "We've taken her into custody."

As two of the deputies went in to fetch the traveling

boxes, Melissa stepped into the corridor, flanked by Rick and Whip.

Big George blocked their path. "Do I get this straight?" he demanded. "You've arrested her?"

"You heard right," Rick replied calmly, his eyes narrowing.

"On what charges?"

"Are you her lawyer?"

"You know damn well I'm not, Sheriff!" Big George roared.

"And I assume you're not her husband or a blood relative." A cold smile lighted Rick's face.

The proprietor knew he could not allow himself to fall into the trap of admitting he operated a bawdy house and that the woman was a prostitute. Under the new, hastily prepared laws of the young state, which were already being revised to close obvious loopholes, he could be prosecuted if he admitted he owned a brothel and identified one or more of his employees. If no such admission were made, however, he was safe. "She's a friend," he said lamely.

"Then the charges against her are none of your business," Rick said as he started forward.

Big George continued to stand in the way, and with no communication between them, Rick and Whip reached for their six-shooters. Aware he had been defeated, the burly proprietor stood aside.

Melissa's entrances into the main room of the saloon were invariably dramatic, but this was her most spectacular appearance. The unencumbered deputy led the procession, his rifle in both hands, ready for use. Melissa descended the stairs slowly, her face devoid of all expression. She was flanked by Sheriff Miller and the buckskin-clad Whip Holt, both with their right hands on the butts of their six-shooters. And bringing up the rear were the two deputies who were carrying the leather boxes, their wariness making it plain they were ready to drop their burdens and use their own firearms if it should become necessary.

The fiddlers and drummer stopped playing, and a deadly hush settled over the assemblage as a grim Big George stood at the top of the staircase, observing the forcible removal of the young woman whose activities had earned him unequaled profits. The bartenders and guards watched him for the signal that would send them hurtling forward in an attempt to overcome the representatives of the law and set Melissa free. The enraged Big George was tempted but knew resistance would be useless. It was common knowledge in the Valley that it didn't pay to tangle with Rick Miller, who would return with fifty deputies and a writ closing the doors of the establishment if he encountered interference in the performance of his duties.

Several of the women began to weep, and Melissa raised a hand in a wave of farewell to them. Some had become her friends, and she would miss them, which was more than she could say for anyone else in the saloon.

Another deputy waited outside with the party's horses, and Rick breathed a sigh of relief when they reached the open. "We've made it so far. Tie those boxes behind you, boys." He turned to Melissa. "I reckon you'll have to ride with me. If I'd known you were coming back with us, I'd have brought a mare and sidesaddle for you."

A ghost of a smile appeared on her lips as she said, "I don't need a sidesaddle."

"I remember," he replied, recalling the high-spirited tomboy, innocent and filled with restless energy, who had challenged the men to races across the desert when he had led a party across New Mexico to Texas.

Melissa's sudden grimace indicated that she, too, had a vivid recollection of the person she once had been and whom she obviously preferred to the woman she had become.

Rick mounted his stallion, then reached down and lifted Melissa into the saddle in front of him. Without hesitation, she pulled up her skirt as she straddled the horse, indifferent to the exposure of large expanses of net-clad legs and thighs. Holding the reins, Rick put an arm around her to steady her, deliberately keeping his other hand free so he could use his six-shooter in an emergency.

The heavily armed group started for Sacramento, their pace deliberate because of the traveling boxes and the awkwardness of Melissa's position on the stallion.

A number of patrons and employees gathered in front of the saloon to watch the departure of the woman who had won such notoriety there.

Rick and Whip remained wary and were prepared for a sudden assault, but no one had the courage to brave their wrath. A fitting farewell was sounded by one man with a deep voice who called, "Good luck, 'Lissa. Come back to us soon!"

They rode in grim silence until they passed through the deep woods and came to the open road beyond it. Then everyone relaxed, and Rick could feel tension draining from the body of the woman who sat so close to him.

"I hope you're ready to go back to Oregon with me now," Whip said to her.

"I can't," Melissa replied. "Not now or ever. I couldn't stand knowing that every decent woman in the territory was whispering behind my back."

Whip, in spite of his long and varied experience, didn't know what to reply.

Rick took no chances and made a gesture behind Melissa's back to silence Whip. She was trembling now, and after what she had undergone tonight, Rick was afraid she would dissolve in tears. "We'll talk later," he said.

Again they were silent, and for the next hour no one spoke. The moon rose over the rugged hills, ascending into a star-filled sky, and even the breeze that blew down from the Sierra Nevada to the east was balmy. Spring had come to the Sacramento Valley.

Even though there was almost no chill in the air, Melissa shivered.

"Do you want to borrow my coat?" Rick asked her.

"No, thank you. I'll be all right. I was just thinking."

He knew better than to question her, that it was far better to let her ramble.

"I did a lot of rotten things in the time I spent at Big George's," she said, as though talking to herself. "Nasty, greedy things. But tonight was the first time I ever drew blood from another human being."

"From what I've heard of Jerome Hadley and what he did to you, he deserved being slashed."

"I-I'm not sorry, I must admit," she said. "But when I saw the blood streaming down his face and knew that I was responsible, I thought I was going to faint."

"Don't think about it," Rick told her. "He'll carry a vicious scar for the rest of his days. And every law enforcement officer in America will be grateful to you."

"Why is that?"

"Because card sharks who prey on honest men are a menace to society. I'll send notices to every sheriff in the country, and all of them will be on the watch for Hadley. It will be much harder for him to cheat the gullible hereafter."

"I wouldn't be so upset if I had just lost my temper and cut him," Melissa admitted. "But I planned it while I was flirting with him. I slashed him deliberately."

Rick couldn't help chuckling.

"Good for you," Whip said.

"I agree," Rick declared. "What you did took real courage."

If their approval soothed her and improved her spirit, she gave no sign of it.

"Where do you suppose we ought to take her?" Rick asked Whip as they drew near Sacramento. "We'll have to get the facts of tonight's incident straight for the record. And we've got to settle her future."

"Since I'm under arrest," Melissa said, "I assume you'll take me to your jail."

There was a hint of exasperation in Rick's voice as he said, "You're not actually under arrest, as you well know. And unless you provide me with facts that change my mind, I have no intention of placing any charges against you. What's more, even if you're guilty of a dozen crimes, I can't lodge you in the jail. We have no cells for women there, and the prisoners would riot if I showed up with you."

"I intend to bargain with you for my safety," Melissa said.

Rick was puzzled by her remark, but he said nothing.

Whip solved the problem. "I suggest we take her to the prosecutor's house. Ralph has a good many spare rooms, and he's grateful to her for Isaiah's return. There's another advantage, too. The house is so close to headquarters that it'll be no problem assigning deputies to stand guard over her."

"Agreed," Rick said.

They made their way down the muddy waterfront road facing the Sacramento River near John Sutter's old fort, and soon they came to the house, where Rick shouted a greeting.

Isaiah Atkins came out to unlock the gate and was overjoyed when he saw the woman. "Melissa!" he shouted.

For the first time that night her smile was real, and when Rick lowered her to the ground, she embraced the boy.

Ralph Hamilton was pleasantly surprised when he came to the door, and he immediately agreed to Melissa's staying with them.

Phyllis Gregg was startled by Melissa's daring appearance. Although she echoed Ralph's hospitality, Phyllis's manner was reserved. She studied the newcomer closely, then went off to prepare one of the guest rooms.

Rick and Whip went to the parlor with Melissa, and at her suggestion the prosecutor joined them.

In response to their questions she told them the whole story of the incident that had been climaxed by the slashing of Jerome Hadley. Holding back nothing, she revealed that he had wooed her in Texas and had persuaded her to use her savings to buy the horses and wagon that had brought them to California in Randy Gregg's train. She went on to explain how Hadley had given her a drink that had caused her to lose consciousness, then had sold her to Big George.

"You could prosecute him," Ralph said. "There are laws that prohibit white slavery."

"It's a little late for that now," she replied dryly.

"Well," he said, "I won't issue a warrant for you based on what you did tonight."

There was a moment's silence, and then Rick said, "Damnation, Melissa, we succeeded in getting you out of Big George's place. Now you'll simply have to decide what you're going to do about your future. You say you won't return to Oregon with Whip—"

"I can't!" she cried.

"Then what in the devil will you do?" Rick demanded. "You'll be in hot water again if you go to some other bordello—"

"Never!" She lowered her voice and spoke with great intensity. "I'd rather die than spend one more day as a whore."

Whip was encouraged. He could understand her reluctance to go home with him, but her new stand, if she meant what she had just said, would make it possible to find peace and security for her somewhere.

"I've been thinking about this meeting with the three of you for some time," Melissa said. "And I'm prepared to strike a bargain with you. I'm in a position to give you some information that you badly want and need to know. I'm willing, if you wish, to testify in court as a witness for the state. In return, I want to be assured of complete physical protection until I can figure out how to rearrange my life. I've had my freedom for only a few hours, remember, so I'll need time to make plans."

Rick exchanged a glance with the prosecutor. "You have a deal," he said.

"First I'll give you a bonus that has no connection with our bargain. I'm sure you won't hear it from anyone else."

They stared at her as she revealed that she had seen Shorty and Slim at the bar earlier in the evening and that she had immediately recognized them from the descriptions in the *Wanted* notice.

Whip Holt hastily changed his own plans. He had been on the verge of announcing that, inasmuch as Melissa was now in good hands and would not go to Oregon with him, he would return home himself without delay. If there was a real chance of capturing Slim and Shorty in the near future, however, he would stay in California a little longer to help out.

"Describe the men you saw," Rick ordered brusquely.

Melissa told him in full detail, her account more graphic than any he had received previously. "I've grown accustomed to men's stares," she concluded, "but no one has ever looked at me the way those two did. I know I wasn't just imagining things. I swear to you that if they could have raped me and then killed me—right then and there—that's what they would have done."

Rick cursed under his breath.

"They weren't in the saloon when we left?" Whip wanted to know.

She shook her head. "I looked for them when we came down the stairs, but they weren't there."

"You can bet they didn't hang around after Big George sent for me," Rick said wearily.

"We're grateful to you," Ralph said to Melissa. "Anything we learn about them is a help. Rick isn't the only one with a personal stake in capturing Slim and Shorty. I want them caught, too. They were responsible for the death of John Gregg, who would have become my brother-in-law."

So Phyllis Gregg was the woman the prosecutor was going to marry, the woman whose romance with him had caused Isaiah to run away. Melissa told herself she should have guessed from the looks Phyllis was giving her earlier that evening. "I'm sorry to hear about John," she said. "I met him when we came west. I liked him."

The knowledge that Slim and Shorty were still in the area upset Rick. So his impatience wasn't directed at Melissa as he demanded, "What's this deal you're offering us?"

She resented his tone and was sharp in return. "No doubt you've heard there have been a number of robberies in those woods we rode through tonight."

Rick concentrated instantly on the immediate problem. "You know something about those robberies?" he asked.

"Everything," she replied. "The operations are directed by Big George. The thieves are in his employ and share with him. One is the bartender at the saloon, and two others are strong-arm men on the staff. The rest spend a lot of time at the saloon but don't work there. I was directly involved in the operation myself."

"You?" Whip was surprised.

"I hate to incriminate myself," Melissa said, "but I've got to have this off my mind and conscience. Another woman—named Bessie—and I were the only ones who took part. George forced us to tell him when we entertained customers whose purses were really filled with money. Most of the time we conveniently forgot his instructions, but when he came to us and got nasty, we had to tell him."

"What do you mean when you say he forced you to tell him?" Ralph Hamilton asked quietly.

"Well, he threatened to beat us up if we didn't cooperate. I liked to think he was bluffing, because I couldn't have worked if I'd been black and blue all over. Bessie wasn't as popular as I was, so I think he was trying to teach me a lesson, too, one time when he really slammed her around after she held information from him. She couldn't work for more than a week."

"Coercion was used to obtain your cooperation," Ralph said. "You will not be charged as an accessory in these crimes."

She was more relieved than she had been for longer than she could remember and thanked him with a genuine smile.

"You're willing to testify against George and the men who actually commit the robberies?" Ralph asked.

"I am." Melissa felt like wilting.

"This is a real break," Rick said. "Those thefts in the woods have been plaguing us."

"Will Bessie cooperate with us, too?" Ralph demanded.

"After George slapped her around so badly, she ran off," Melissa said. "I heard she went to San Francisco, but I'm not sure."

"Just try to find a harlot named Bessie in the brothels of San Francisco," Rick said unhappily. "That job could take years."

"So we're left with only one witness." Ralph pondered for a time. "Is there any one man who leads these raids?"

"Yes, a bartender named Charlie. He's big. And almost as tough as George. And he never missed an angle. He even persuaded some of the women to give him a portion of their earnings. He claimed he sent their clients to them. He just tried that one time with me," she added in an undertone.

"Sheriff Miller," Ralph said crisply, "our approach to this case becomes obvious. Set a trap. Assign enough deputies to catch the band while they're actually engaged in the act of robbing someone. That will not only give us the second witness we require under the law, but you can round up the entire gang."

"Fair enough, Mr. Prosecutor." Rick matched

Ralph's formality. "But that doesn't bring Big George himself into our net."

"There's a way," Ralph said. "We offer a lighter sentence to the bartender, Charlie, and to any of the others also willing to implicate George as the actual head of the operation."

Rick hooked his thumbs in his belt. "We'll start working on the case first thing tomorrow morning. But it will take time. Are you willing to hang around here," he asked Melissa, "until we cast our net and haul in a load of fish?"

She shrugged. "I have no place else to go. Maybe I can make some plans if I have a little time."

"You're welcome to stay here as long as you please," Ralph told her.

"And you'll have complete protection by my deputies, day and night," Rick assured her.

"I'm staying here myself, you know," Whip added.

"That settles it," Ralph said, "and I think we've done enough for one night. Miss Austin, we appreciate your cooperation. It's fortunate for us that you decided to leave Big George's place."

Somewhat to Melissa's own surprise she sniffled. "I guess I'm not accustomed to being called Miss Austin," she said, then took herself to task for being sentimental. "Aw, hell, I'm just tired."

"Of course you are," Ralph said as he went to the door. "I'll ask Phyllis to show you to your room."

Moments later the two young women mounted the stairs together. Phyllis was distant. "Isaiah has carried your leather boxes to your room."

"Thank you, Phyllis." Melissa could not stifle a yawn.

"I'm glad I have the opportunity to add my thanks to those Ralph has expressed to you for the return of Isaiah." Phyllis remained chilly. "Will you be with us for long?"

Melissa shrugged. "For a while, it seems. Mr. Hamilton and Rick can give you a better idea than I can."

Phyllis directed her toward a chamber at the end of

the corridor. "I'm not sure I'd have known you, Melissa."

Having anticipated her disapproval, Melissa was neither surprised nor hurt. She had to expect this from every self-respecting woman she met. "All of us change," she said, trying without success to smile. "You've changed for the better. Let's say that I've just changed." She paused at the door. "I was sorry to hear about your brother."

The door closed before Phyllis could reply. She hesitated, then went down to the parlor, where she found Rick departing and Whip on his way to bed. "Would any of you gentlemen like something to eat, or a nightcap?"

"I'm too old to eat at bedtime," Whip said. "It gives me indigestion." He plodded slowly up the stairs, refusing to admit to himself, much less to anyone else, that the arthritis in his hip was beginning to bother him again.

"I'm starting to work at dawn tomorrow," Rick said, "so I'll be on my way."

When Ralph was alone with Phyllis, he said, "Let's have a glass of wine so I can unwind a bit."

"Of course." She filled two small glasses from a cut-glass decanter, then handed one to him.

Ralph grinned at her. "Your nose is out of joint. Out with it, my dear."

"You've actually offered that woman the hospitality of this house. It's your right, of course, but that doesn't mean I approve."

So that was it. "For one thing," he said gently, "we're indebted to her for Isaiah's return. I'm not forgetting it, and I hope you don't."

"I'm well aware of it." She was unyielding.

"Equally important, Miss Austin is going to work with the prosecution on a very important case. She's helping us bring a gang of criminals to justice. Nobody's forcing her to cooperate with us, mind you. She's doing it voluntarily." He sipped his wine.

Phyllis left her glass untouched. "Very noble of her. Must we postpone our wedding because of her—and this case?"

"Certainly not," he assured her, laughing.

She was not mollified. "Ralph, I know Melissa Austin well. We came all the way from Texas to California in the same wagon train. She was a shameless hussy then, the way she carried on with Jerome Hadley, and she's far worse now!"

"Her morals, or her lack of them, are irrelevant. We need her help, and she needs our protection in return. The arrangement is that simple. When certain elements realize that she is acting against them in ways that will send them to prison, her life will be in jeopardy. Rick and I believe this is the best, safest, and most convenient place for her to stay. And Whip, who knows more than the rest of us put together, feels the same way."

Phyllis knew his argument made good sense, but she was still uneasy. "I just hope the arrangement stays simple," she said stiffly.

Ralph's knowledge of women was still woefully inadequate, but he was learning, and all at once he understood the reason for her behavior. Laughing and shaking his head, he said, "You're afraid that Melissa will exert her charms on me—and that I'll find her irresistible!"

"The possibility has crossed my mind," she conceded.

"You're totally wrong." He knew it would be a mistake to tell her in so many words that her jealousy was absurd. "Let me give you the best reassurances of which I'm capable." He took her in his arms and kissed her fervently.

"That's very convincing," Phyllis gasped as he released her, and afraid she would lose her self-control if he embraced her again, she bade him good night and hurried off to her own room.

As she undressed, however, her feeling of distress

returned. She knew she was attractive, prettier than most, but neither she nor any other woman could compete with Melissa's flamboyant, outrageously advertised beauty, and no decent woman was as experienced in dealing with men. They would be living under the same roof, and Ralph already had shown a high regard for this intruder, his approval of her apparently unaffected by the kind of life she had led. The future promised to be difficult.

In the morning, after spending a troubled night, Phyllis came downstairs a little later than usual to prepare breakfast and was surprised to find that the kitchen was already busy. Her father, Whip, and Isaiah were sitting at the table, and Melissa was standing at the stove. Her appearance was astonishing. Her face was scrubbed clean, and once again she looked young and vulnerable.

She was efficient, Phyllis had to hand her that much. She was cooking oatmeal for Isaiah and had added raisins and cinnamon to the bubbling pot. Potatoes were frying in a large pan, strips of bacon she had already cooked sat at the back of the stove, where they were kept warm, and she was scrambling eggs for Randy and Whip.

All of them were enjoying themselves. Randy, looking more alert and cheerful than he had in many weeks, was telling one of his tall tales, sending Melissa and Isaiah into paroxysms of laughter, while a grinning Whip quietly interrupted from time to time, embellishing the story.

"Let me get your breakfast for you, Phyllis," Melissa said.

"Thanks, but that won't be necessary."

"Maybe not, but I'd like to. I've done no cooking for a long time, and you can't imagine what a pleasure this is."

Phyllis had to consent and settled for her usual toast and coffee.

Ralph appeared, took in the scene, and, casting

aside his customary reserve, joined in the festivities, even consenting to eat some eggs and potatoes in addition to his standard morning fare of toast and coffee.

Not until everyone was seated did Melissa strike a serious note. "Mr. Hamilton," she asked, "am I permitted to go out of the house?"

"I would think so," Ralph replied, "provided you accept an escort of deputy sheriffs and depending on where you want to go."

"I need to visit a general store," she said. "I don't own one respectable dress or one comfortable pair of shoes. I've got to buy some material for a wardrobe."

"That will be fine," Ralph said. "Let me give you something to cover your expenses."

"Oh, I have enough money to last me for a long time," Melissa said. "That's the least of my worries." She turned to Phyllis. "Will you come with me? To be honest with you, I have no idea what to get, other than some kind of calico and some wool. It's been so long since I've worn what—other women wear that I'll need some help and advice."

There was no way the request could be refused, so Phyllis agreed to accompany her.

Ralph went off to work, first kissing his betrothed. Whip, eager to start organizing the pursuit of the bandits, accompanied him, while Isaiah went upstairs to study and Randy retired to the parlor to read the morning newspapers. The two women were alone.

"If you don't want to come with me," Melissa said bluntly, "I won't hold you to it."

"I've already said I'd go," Phyllis replied. "Why would I back out?"

"Because you don't like me." Melissa spoke quietly but firmly.

Phyllis was flustered. "Well, I—I—"

"There's no need to deny it, honey. You've made it plain enough in your attitude. You don't approve of my past, and all I can tell you is that I don't think very highly of it, either. But there's more to it than that. You're afraid I intend to steal Ralph Hamilton from you."

Phyllis turned crimson. "He likes you. And you're so much more attractive than I am that—"

Melissa gave a harsh laugh. "Forget it. He may like me, but he loves you. And I'll tell it to you straight. I'm sick to death of men. There isn't one I want!"

X

Mail was delivered twice weekly to householders in the Sacramento Valley, a sure sign of advancing civilization, as everyone in the area agreed. But there were many residents who rarely received letters. Heather Taylor heard from her parents and sisters in Texas occasionally, but it was a family joke that no one ever wrote to Danny.

So, when a letter came for him in an expensive envelope of heavy linen, bearing a San Francisco postmark, Heather immediately took it to him in the orchard, where he was at work, then stood and waited anxiously.

Danny wiped his hands on the sides of his work pants, then carefully broke the seal and unfolded the letter, his frown turning to a broad grin as he read. "It's from Chet Harris," he said. "He heard from his mother and Ernie that we were living in the Valley, and he got our address from General and Mrs. Blake."

"He's in San Francisco?"

"He is now. He says he and his partner spent a long time prospecting on the Bear River and struck it rich there. He was up in Oregon for a visit, and now he's come to San Francisco. He wants us to meet him there on Thursday of next week. He's reserved a suite for the three of us at the brand new Regal Hotel."

"That's the very fancy place?" she asked.

He nodded, still grinning.

"I don't think we can afford a suite at a hotel that grand, dear."

"Chet is paying all of our expenses. Hotel, meals, everything. He insists on it."

"Well!" Heather said. "I guess he really did strike it rich."

"This isn't just a social get-together," he said. "Chet makes it very plain that he wants to discuss a business matter with me."

"What kind of business would he have with the owner of a little orchard in the Valley?"

"Blamed if I know," Danny said. "But we'll find out soon enough. We'll use our own horses and borrow the Fosters' carriage."

"I have no clothes that would be suitable for a fancy place like the Regal."

Danny chuckled indulgently. "I reckon we stashed away enough from my nuggets and gold dust to buy you a new dress in San Francisco. Just the other day you were telling me there are stores there where a lady can get clothes already made instead of just material."

"But that's so extravagant!" Heather was shocked.

Danny hugged her. "I can begin to see daylight ahead in the development of the orchard," he told her. "So we're going to go, and we'll splurge on a dress. I'll arrange with Scott Foster to keep an eye on the property for us while we're away."

His enthusiasm was so great that she couldn't spoil his pleasure. "All right, dear, we'll go. But we'll talk again about squandering money on a dress."

But he had already made up his mind.

They left home late in the morning the following Wednesday, with the baby propped between them on the seat of the small Foster carriage, and they made the journey on the heavily traveled dirt road in two days, stopping overnight at a small, clean inn that Rick Miller had recommended to them.

A liveried groom stationed at the impressive portico of the Regal Hotel took their horses and carriage to the stables at the rear, another liveried attendant whisked away their modest luggage, and when Danny announced his identity at the front desk, an elegantly attired assistant manager conducted the Taylors to a suite, where they had a commanding view of the bay on one side and of the still-growing business district on the other.

"I hope you'll be comfortable here," the assistant manager said as he bowed and departed.

"Comfortable!" Heather stroked a velvet chair, stared at a damask-covered sofa, and walked through the suite in a daze. Even little Ted had his own small bedchamber. "I've never seen anything this wonderful. I don't think I dare sit down. And just look at the satin coverlet on our bed! I've never owned a dress made of satin that expensive!"

Before Danny could reply, a quiet tap sounded at the front door, and he hurried to answer the summons. A few moments later he called in excitement, "Heather! Come here quick."

She raced into the sitting room from the larger bedchamber. "What's wrong?"

"Nothing in all the world!" He pointed to a huge basket filled with apples, peaches, and pears, then removed a box of chocolate candies, a vial of perfume for Heather, and a large bottle of champagne bearing a French label. "This is a gift from the management," Danny said in wonder. "They hope we'll enjoy our stay here."

"We're out of our element, that's sure," the awed Heather replied.

A heavy pounding sounded at the door before he could reply. "Danny, you rascal, open up!"

Danny threw the door open, and he and a handsomely attired Chet Harris pounded each other's backs like two small boys, both of them talking simultaneously.

Heather stood aside, self-conscious because Chet was followed by a middle-aged Chinese, impeccable in a conservative, Western-style suit.

The old friends disentangled themselves, and Chet, who had been best man at Danny and Heather's wedding, kissed Heather lightly on the cheek, then presented his partner, Wong Ke, to the Taylors. Still chortling, he lifted little Ted high in the air. "A husky, good-looking boy!" he exclaimed. "You don't know how fortunate you are!"

He was the one who was truly fortunate, Danny reflected. Chet radiated the self-confident poise of the wealthy and seemed completely at home in these luxurious surroundings. It was true that he had aged, and with wrinkles at the corners of his eyes and lines across his forehead, he looked far older than his years. Obviously he had known suffering in his quest for riches.

Chet tugged at a bell rope, and a matronly, smiling woman came into the suite. "This is Mrs. Ramey," he said. "She'll look after Ted while we go downstairs to eat."

"I've had six of my own, Mrs. Taylor," the woman said, "so don't you worry for a minute. Your son is in good hands."

"Our table is waiting," Chet announced, "so let's be on our way."

A wave of panic swept over Heather. "I—I haven't had a chance to buy my new dress yet," she murmured. "I can't go anywhere looking this plain and frumpy."

Wong Ke shook his head. "No way to improve on nature," he said. "Lady who has beauty does not need silks and jewels."

"Always listen to my partner," Chet said, taking the reluctant young woman's arm. "He's never wrong."

The main dining room stood off the lobby and was breathtaking in its splendor. Hundreds of smokeless French tapers burned in several huge chandeliers of glittering crystal. The thick carpeting was worth a king's ransom, and the walls were covered with frescoes depicting the development of America from its early colonial beginnings to its present.

Another series of shocks awaited Danny and Heather when they examined the ornate menu. A portion of smoked salmon cost one dollar, and the stunned Danny was reminded of the days in the none too distant past when he and Chet had caught their own salmon in the Columbia River and smoked it themselves, Indian style. A cup of vegetable soup cost twenty-five cents, ox-tail soup was forty cents, and turtle soup—whatever that might be—was priced at a half-dollar. Crabs from San Francisco Bay were priced at seventy-five cents, and the management charged two dollars for an order of roasted beef, which included only roasted potatoes, three vegetables, a portion of salad greens, and a sherbet to clear the palate before the next course. It was amazing that even the rich could afford to pay such exorbitant prices.

"I—I don't think I'm very hungry," Heather said.

"Nonsense!" Chet replied. "I'll order for all of us." He did, naming dish after dish and including three different kinds of wine.

"Do you always eat like this?" Danny asked him.

"Always," his old friend replied. "Although I must admit I don't touch the wine. Alcoholic drinks caused me some problems, so I gave them up."

Heather admired the gleaming, heavy silver flatware, the exquisite china, and marvelously thin glasses. "These table settings must have cost a fortune," she said.

"Is so," Wong Ke confirmed. "Chet and Ke own part-interest in Regal Hotel."

"We invest in just about everything," Chet said,

grinning. "We've put money into one of the local newspapers, a bank, and a new iron foundry that will produce frying pans and pots—and make it unnecessary to bring such goods all the way from New England. We've gone into the China trade, and thanks to Ke's connections there, that business is flourishing, too."

"We start with gold," the Chinese said after a small army of waiters and their assistants served the first course. "Now all we do turn to gold."

Heather glanced at her husband and saw no envy in his face, which relieved her. His pleasure in hearing about his old friend's great success appeared to be genuine. She herself was curious about Chet and couldn't resist asking, "This is none of my business, but how does it happen that you've never married?"

He seemed surprised by the question and thought at length before he replied. "I'm not sure I know all the reasons," he said. "First off, I was brokenhearted —or thought I was—when Melissa Austin turned me down. After Ke and I made our first big strike, there were many women in my life. Too many. And lately I've been too busy building our financial holdings to give much time or thought to women."

"Melissa came to California in our wagon train, you know," Danny said, then spoke at length about her relationship with Jerome Hadley.

Heather tried to warn him with a glance not to say too much, as it was possible that Chet would still find the subject sensitive, but Danny was oblivious. "We heard a great deal more just recently from Rick Miller," he said. "Hadley was a no-good gambler and sold her to a saloonkeeper in the Valley named Big George. She became the—ah—star attraction at his place."

Chet surprised Danny and Heather when he announced, "I know all about Melissa. I ran into her at Big George's, and I don't mind telling you I was dumbfounded. But would you believe, she spent an hour lecturing me about my careless, drunken ways. If it wasn't for Melissa, I wouldn't be where I am today. Now I just wish someone could strike some sense into her head and get her to leave that place."

"Apparently she has left. Rick indicated that she's reformed, and I gather he sees her frequently. Whether socially or in connection with his law enforcement work, I don't know. He doesn't say. In fact, he's very vague about her current whereabouts and activities, and you know Rick. He shuts up tight when there's something he doesn't want to discuss."

"Wherever Melissa may be, I wish her well," Chet said.

He seemed sincere, and Heather couldn't help wondering if he was still in love with Melissa after all this time. There was no way of knowing without further, intimate questioning, and she had no right to probe.

Danny was not as obtuse as his wife had thought. He changed the subject by asking about Chet's mother and Ernie von Thalman. Chet explained how his mother and stepfather had visited him in San Francisco and how pleased they were about his success in the gold fields.

"Before they left to go back to Oregon," Chet said, "Ernie had given Wong Ke and me financial advice about a half-dozen business enterprises."

Danny and Chet then talked at length about Whip Holt, whom both had idolized since boyhood.

"I'm surprised he's still in the Valley," Chet said.

"I know he wants to go back to Oregon as soon as he can," Danny replied.

"Why doesn't he, then?"

Danny shrugged. "I gather he's staying to help Rick on a couple of cases. He doesn't talk about it, and he can be even more tight-lipped than Rick."

Course after course was served, and Heather could only pick at the rich meal. Even Danny, whose appetite was still huge, could eat only a portion of each dish.

Eventually they were offered bell glasses of brandy, which only Danny and Ke accepted, and all of the men lighted cigars. Chet waved the hovering waiters out of hearing range. "Let's talk business," he said. "There's been a new gold field discovered recently. In Oregon!"

Danny stared at him. "Plainly you're not joking."

"Indeed I'm not. In the Rogue River Valley."

Danny remembered the area well. It was located at the southern end of the Oregon territory, directly across the California border, and was a rough, primitive wilderness of forests and mountains, with the turbulent Rogue River churning through narrow ravines and canyons. "Is it a big field?"

"Not as big as California fields," Ke said.

"But big enough to spark a new gold rush, you can be sure of that," Chet said. "Word of the find is just now seeping out and becoming public knowledge, so we expect disappointed California prospectors, new recruits from the East, and the usual rabble from all over the country to pour into Oregon."

"Chet and Ke among first to hear about Oregon gold," the Chinese said.

"That's right," his partner declared. "And we bought a large tract of land right on the Rogue River itself. We've had tests made, and we know there's plenty of gold there."

Danny felt his excitement and tension mounting but tried to look unconcerned as he carefully removed a length of ash from his cigar. "There must be a reason you're telling me all this."

"Plenty good reason," Ke said as he exchanged a swift glance with his partner.

"Our own days in the gold fields are ended," Chet said. "We don't have the time or inclination for that kind of life anymore. But we need someone who can take charge of our mining operation there, and it won't be easy work. We need someone who has the strength to handle a tough crew of miners. Someone ruthless and courageous enough to drive off poachers. Above all, we need a manager who is honest and won't try to cheat us. You came to my mind right off, Danny, and you're at the top of our list."

"Well, now," Danny said, grinning. "I'm flattered."

Heather's heart sank; she was afraid that her husband's yearning for gold was being revived.

"The position we have in mind entails great responsibility, and we're willing to pay accordingly," Chet said. "We're prepared to offer you a substantial guarantee as a base, as well as a solid percentage of the profits."

Danny studied the glowing end of his cigar. "How long do you estimate the field will yield gold?"

The Chinese shrugged. "Maybe one year, maybe longer."

"Naturally you'd expect me to be there the entire time," Danny said.

"Naturally." Chet turned to Heather. "I'm sure you already know this, but it would be at least six months, maybe the better part of the year before you and the baby could join Danny. As you can imagine, conditions in the area will be unsettled for quite some time."

"It will be the Sacramento Valley all over again," Danny said.

Heather's dread threatened to overwhelm her, but she made a desperate attempt to conceal her feelings. Danny had worked hard in the orchard, and she could not deny him this opportunity now, if it was what he really wanted.

"What's your reaction?" Chet asked.

"This offer has come at me out of the blue, so I'd like to think about it."

"Of course. Maybe I can help you put the offer in perspective. This is none of my business, but what kind of an income does your orchard earn?"

"By next year, when most of my trees should be producing, I expect to clear a thousand dollars. If all goes well."

Heather found her voice. "That's double what we'd

have made if we had claimed a homestead in Texas and raised corn and wheat there."

Wong Ke was sympathetic. "Work of farmers plenty hard," he said.

"Too hard and too monotonous for me," Chet said. "I thank the Almighty I'll never have to go back to the family farm in Oregon." He looked at Danny. "Our guarantee will pay you a thousand a month. As much in one month as you can make on your orchard in a whole year. And depending on how much gold you find on the property, well—the sky is the limit. I can't promise, of course, but if the surveyors who made the tests for us are right, you well could become wealthy."

If he survives, Heather thought, in a savage land where the greed of men for gold is so great that they kill without conscience.

Danny retained his balance. "We've been invited to the Presidio tomorrow to have dinner with Lee and Cathy Blake," he said. "Will you give me until the following day for your answer?"

"Certainly," Chet said. "In the meantime we'll put a closed carriage with a driver and bodyguard at your disposal. Most of the city is safe these days, but it would be wise if Heather stays clear of the waterfront. If there's anything Ke and I can do for you between now and the day after tomorrow, just let us know. We maintain permanent quarters at the hotel."

The holiday was spoiled, and the taste in Heather's mouth was bitter. Through the exercise of great willpower, Danny had cured himself of his yearning for gold, but she was afraid he would find Chet's offer irresistible. Her own stand undoubtedly had been responsible for his success in putting his search for gold behind him, but she could not interfere again. The offer he had just received was bona fide, and if she tried to prevent him from accepting it, the strain on their marriage well might become intolerable.

Phyllis Gregg had to admit to herself that she had been mistaken about Melissa Austin, whose relationship with Ralph Hamilton was cordial but impersonal. Not only did she refrain from flirting with him—or with anyone else—but she was making a determined, sustained effort to change her ways. She continued to use no cosmetics, not even rice powder or a little lip rouge, and the new clothes she was busily sewing for herself were unnecessarily severe. Furthermore, she seemed pleased when, accompanied by her usual escort of deputy sheriffs, she relieved Phyllis of the marketing chores. "No more than a handful of men even glanced in my direction," she announced happily.

Phyllis knew nothing about the matter that took her to the law enforcement headquarters each day and didn't want to know.

At Rick's request Melissa prepared detailed descriptions of each member of the band of robbers, and then she wrote a long, formal statement, to be used in court, describing the operation in full. Rick guided and advised her in its preparation, and she made a number of revisions in it.

She put the finishing touches on it by candlelight early one evening in his office, and he read it carefully, then locked it away in his safe. "This will help hang Big George and his accomplices," he said. "We're grateful to you for what you've done. I have no right to ask anything else of you, but I'll ask it anyway, if you're willing to do still more for us on this case."

"I'll gladly do anything I can," she replied strongly. "George is as responsible as Hadley for what happened to me, and I won't be satisfied until I see him in hell."

Her intensity did not surprise him. "Come along, then, and we'll have a little chat at supper. There's a new inn that's just opened recently, and they'll give us a corner table where we can talk privately."

Melissa was flattered by the unexpected offer but shook her head. "Phyllis is expecting me."

One of Rick's rare smiles lighted his face. "Not

tonight she isn't," he said. "I told her this afternoon that you're going out with me."

Apparently he had felt certain she would be willing to go farther in her cooperation with the authorities. In any event, she seemed to have no voice in the matter, but she felt compelled to protest. "I'll have to go back to the house and change." Her unadorned dress of plain wool was unsuitable for dining out.

"You look just fine," he insisted.

Perhaps she was mistaken, but she thought she detected an expression of admiration in his eyes. Never before had he indicated that he approved of anything she did, so she went with him meekly.

The new inn, located in the rapidly growing northern part of the city, overlooked the river, and its irregular-shaped dining room was subdivided into alcoves, which made it possible for Rick to claim a table that would ensure them of privacy.

Melissa was startled when he ordered a bottle of wine. It had not occurred to her that he regarded this dinner as a social occasion.

"First off," he said, "I want to know the mechanics of what makes the thieves decide when to strike. Did they act only when you or the other woman gave them the word?"

"Oh, no. Not necessarily. If they spotted someone well off, preferably traveling alone, they always were quick to move in to rob him."

"Ah, that's what I hoped. What you're telling me is that they keep a watch for travelers."

Melissa nodded.

"At what time of day?"

"Late in the afternoon and early in the evening. I don't know what made them decide those hours are the best, but they never attack earlier or very late at night. Possibly because somebody riding alone may be more alert to danger when it's late. George always wants to make sure there's no bloodshed. A man who is robbed won't have as much attention paid to his problem as one who has also been wounded."

Rick absorbed the information in silence. Then he asked, "Is the victim assaulted only on his way out of the saloon?"

"Indeed not. George is too clever for that. Sometimes, when a traveler looks well-to-do, the band strikes in the woods before he even approaches the saloon."

He liked what he heard. "Let's say the sentinel sees someone he thinks is ripe for plucking. Then what happens?"

"He rides quickly to the saloon and gives a signal to Charlie. In almost no time, enough men are assembled to race off to the woods and catch the victim before he comes out into the open again. They spoke freely in front of me, and they always knew where to find him because there's only one trail that leads through the woods."

"Good. You confirm an aspect I had already figured out for myself. Now I have only one more favor to ask of you, Melissa. Are you willing to confront the leader of the band and some of the others—separately and individually—once we've taken them into custody? Our aim is to break them down so they'll start talking freely and incriminate George."

"I'll do anything you want," she said simply. "But what makes you so sure you'll be able to catch the robbers in the act?"

Even though none of the other patrons could hear their conversation, he lowered his voice. "Between you and me, Whip Holt is going to pose as the rich traveler."

Melissa was shocked. "Aren't you taking terrible chances? I mean, he's so much older, and even though the robbers take precautions, there's always the chance he'll be hurt if he refuses to give them his money."

"No man alive is better able to take care of himself, regardless of his age," Rick said with firm conviction.

She knew better than to argue with him and concentrated on her meal. When he spoke again, his voice was gentle. "Have you given any thought to your long-range plans after we've completed this case?"

His tone surprised her, as did the real concern she saw in his eyes. "I've thought about it every day, but I go round and round in circles. San Francisco is too wild, and Melissa of Big George's is too well known there. I—I'm too much of a coward ever to go back to Oregon. I have no reason to return to Texas, which is a long way from here. The East Coast is even farther, but I might be able to settle there without anyone finding out my past. I don't like the idea, but it's the only solution I know."

"What would you do there?"

"Well," she said uncertainly, "I've saved enough to buy a little house, but that's as far as my thinking goes. I'm not qualified to teach school, and though I'm a good seamstress, I'm not clever enough with a needle to make sewing a profession." She shrugged. "I'll have to be satisfied with just existing, I guess."

"You're young," Rick said, "and you don't need me to tell you that few women anywhere are as attractive as you. You need to settle down with a husband."

"Don't mock me," she said angrily. "No man in this part of the country would marry the whore from Big George's saloon. And if I decide to move to New York or Baltimore or Philadelphia, let's just suppose I found someone I could care for enough to marry. I'd have to tell him the truth about my past. I—I couldn't live under false pretenses with any man. And who would want me once he learned the truth about me?"

"Don't be so quick to run yourself down," he said. "You have many qualities that earn respect, and it isn't very hard to imagine love growing out of that."

Melissa sat immobile, looking down at the table. He stared at her for a moment, then placed his hand over hers. "I'm not handing you a line of sweet talk just to make you feel better, Melissa. I've known you for a long time, and I mean what I say. You'll have a great deal to offer the man who wants to marry you."

She did not withdraw her hand, but her voice

trembled as she said, "If you don't stop being kind to me, Rick Miller, I'm going to disgrace both of us by crying my eyes out. I don't want anyone's charity. I've proved I can take care of myself!"

In his opinion, the life into which she had been tricked proved the contrary, but he forced his voice to sound casual as he refilled their wineglasses. "We won't worry about what happens that far ahead. For the present we'll bear down on putting Big George and his confederates behind bars."

"I don't think anyone can advise you," Lee Blake said after Danny Taylor had told him and Cathy about Chet Harris's offer. "Your decision will have to depend on what you want in life."

"You make his decision sound easy, dear, but it isn't, I'm sure." Cathy looked at her husband, then at the young couple who sat side by side on the parlor sofa in their house. "Even leaving aside the possibility that Danny might rake in a large sum through his percentage of a mining operation's profits, the salary that Chet and his partner have offered is a powerful temptation."

Danny nodded gravely. "It sure is. If I give up a year of my life to supervise the gold mining in the Rogue River Valley, there's so much I can buy for my wife and my son."

Heather wanted to scream that money couldn't buy happiness for her, and she realized it would be unfair to mention her fear that Danny, like Chet, might become accustomed to affluence. Chet had been coarsened by his wealth, and the same might happen to Danny.

"There are many aspects to consider," Lee said. "One of them is the personal danger."

Danny waved aside that possibility. "I spent enough time in the Sacramento Valley gold fields to know the problems. There's always the chance that a stray bullet might kill me, but with the disappointed gold prospectors who are still wandering around, that could happen to me while I'm at work in my own orchard. I can look after myself, Lee."

Cathy turned to Heather, intending to ask what she wanted, but she bit back the question. The expression she read in the younger woman's face, although veiled, made her uncomfortable. Heather desperately wanted Danny to reject the offer and remain at home but was doing her utmost not to influence the decision she thought he alone should make.

"You haven't seen the post," she said instead. "Some of the views are spectacular, so let me show you around before the sun goes down."

Lee knew his wife well enough to realize she had some reason for terminating the discussion so abruptly. He was further confused when he saw that Danny, who had asked for the advice, was relieved that the subject was being dropped.

The rest of the visit was pleasant. Cathy conducted the guests on a tour of the grounds, and later, at supper, they chatted at length about mutual friends in Texas and Oregon. No further mention was made of the job offer.

After the Taylors returned to their sumptuous hotel suite, Ted awakened and was irritable, so it took Heather some time to soothe him before he dropped off again. Then she went into the parlor to join Danny. Unaware of her presence, Danny stood at one of the windows, looking with unseeing eyes in the direction of the lights on the ships in the harbor.

He was so lost in thought that Heather crept off to their own bedchamber, where she took her time undressing. The contrast between her flannel nightgown and her elegant surroundings amused her, but as she slipped on her old bathrobe, she decided not to mention the subject to Danny. Perhaps she was afraid to give him the opportunity to reply that by going off to the Rogue River Valley he would be able to buy her nightwear of the finest silk imported from China. It would be far too difficult to explain to him that she felt at home in her plain nightgown and robe, that she would be uncomfortable wearing silk.

Heather's glance fell on a Bible, the property of the hotel, that rested on a bedside table. Sitting on the edge of the bed, she leafed through it, not looking for anything in particular. Danny was wrestling with his problem, she knew, and it was her duty not to interfere.

Something caught Heather's eye, and she turned back the pages, searching until she found the place, in one of the Psalms of David:

Lord, who shall abide in thy tabernacle? Who
    shall dwell in thy holy hill?
He that walketh upright, and worketh righ-
    teousness, and speaketh the truth in his heart.
He that backbiteth not with his tongue, nor doeth
    evil to his neighbor, nor taketh up a reproach
    against his neighbor.
In whose eyes a vile person is contemned; but he
    honoreth them that fear the Lord. He that
    sweareth to his own hurt, and changeth not.
He that putteth not out his money to usury, nor
    taketh reward against the innocent. He that
    doeth these things shall never be moved.

Heather read the Psalm several times, wishing she had studied her own Bible more frequently, as she had done when she had been a child. Marriage, the long journey from Texas, and the problems she had encountered in California had distracted her, and she vowed to return to the ways she had known throughout her earlier life.

Pondering the Psalm, she knew that Danny was a good man, righteous and law-abiding. Even the lure of gold had not tempted him for its own sake, and he had sought it because of the security and luxuries it could provide for his family. Her own desire to spend the rest of their lives in their own snug house while he tended his orchard was irrelevant to the dilemma he was facing. It was right that she stand aside, allowing him to make his own decision on the basis of what he deemed best for her and their son.

She prayed to the Almighty to empty her heart of resentment if Danny decided to go to the new gold fields of Oregon. She would submit to that decision with good grace and would wait patiently for his return.

Sitting for a long time with the Bible clasped in her hands, she returned to the present only when she realized that she could not hear her husband pacing in the next room. Bracing herself, she went to the door.

Danny was still standing. He had returned to the window and was peering out into the night. A heavy San Francisco fog had descended, and mist swirled on the far side of the pane of glass.

"Are you coming to bed?" Heather called softly.

He turned slowly, the ordeal he had been undergoing etched in his weary face. "I thought you'd gone to sleep," he said. "Are you awake enough to talk?"

Heather nodded, knowing he had made up his mind.

He motioned her to the sofa, then sat opposite her in a chair. "It's after midnight, and in a few hours we'll be meeting again with Chet and Wong Ke. Ever since they made me their offer, I've thought about little else, as I guess you know."

Again she nodded, but didn't speak.

"I know you must have an opinion," Danny said, "but I thank you for letting me work this out for myself. It hasn't been easy for me, and I hope you won't be angry or disappointed if you don't happen to agree with what I think is best."

She dug her fingernails into the palms of her hands. He intended to go off to the Oregon gold fields.

"Chet's offer was so generous and fair it bowled me over," he said, "and I doubt if I'll ever in my life have another opportunity like this."

"I know." She prayed for the strength to conceal her heartbreak.

"There's so much I could buy for you and Ted," Danny said, "that just thinking about it has made me dizzy. And what makes this decision so difficult is that the situation isn't what it was when I went off alone to the gold fields in the Valley. We know gold has been found on the Rogue River. What's more, I'd be working for others as well as for myself, and I'd have an ample guaranteed income. A heap of money."

She wished he would say the fatal words instead of spelling out his reasons in such detail.

"Even so," he said, "the principle is the same. The last time I came home you stopped me from going prospecting again, and you were right. Chet and his partner are asking me to gamble with them, and I've sworn off gambling."

Heather couldn't believe she had heard him correctly. "You're not going off to the Rogue River?"

"If I leave now, all the work I've done in the orchard will have been wasted. I'd come back next year with a fatter purse, but the work would have to be done all over again. I reckon you'll think I'm crazy to be turning down such good pay, but I've staked my future on my fruit trees, not on finding gold in Oregon or in California or any other place. Maybe I'll never be rich, but I'll always have my pride, knowing I did what was right."

Heather could not speak, and the tears streamed down her face. She could make only a feeble attempt to brush them away.

Danny misinterpreted her reaction. "I'll always do my best for you and the baby. In the long run—"

A wild laugh, mingled with her sobs, interrupted him, and Heather leaped to her feet, throwing her arms around him. "My prayers have been answered!" she cried.

For a moment he looked at her in bewilderment. Then, as understanding dawned, he embraced her in a bear hug and kissed her.

"I'm glad we're going home tomorrow," she said at last as they moved from the sitting room to the bedchamber.

"So am I," Danny said. "A fancy place like this isn't for the likes of us."

Whip Holt crossed the street from Ralph Hamilton's house, where he had changed into his new finery, and presented himself for Rick Miller's inspection. Sheriff Miller eyed him carefully and grunted his approval, but made no comment.

"Very impressive," Ralph said.

Melissa Austin, who had been invited to be present for the occasion, had serious doubts. Whip's suit of dark worsted was indeed impressive, as were his high-crowned beaver hat and the loose, silk-lined cape that covered him from his shoulders to his knees. But one thought nagged at her. "You're a perfect target now, I'll admit," she said. "But with all those expensive clothes, it may take you too long to draw a weapon when the robbers surround you."

As she spoke, Whip put one hand inside his cape, and the moment she finished speaking he produced his long rawhide whip. "Don't you worry about me," he said. "After spending all this time in California, I don't aim to bungle the one job I know I can perform."

Early in the afternoon a dozen deputies, leaving their headquarters unobtrusively in pairs, took the road that led toward the gold fields. After a short interval Rick followed them, traveling alone, and then eight more deputies took their departure.

Ralph and Melissa remained behind at headquarters with Whip, who gave the sheriff and his men a long head start. Then he looked out of the window, squinted at the sun, and announced, "I'll be on my way."

Ralph shook his hand. "Good luck," he said.

Still troubled, Melissa said, "I feel responsible for

this whole operation. Please be careful. I could never forgive myself if something happened to you."

Whip grinned at her. "I've been in more tight places in my lifetime than I can remember. It will take more than a band of cheap crooks to bring me down."

She reached up impulsively and kissed him. "For your family's sake, don't take needless risks," she said.

Still grinning, he left the building, mounted his stallion, and started off, riding at a steady pace. It was essential that he reach the rendezvous shortly before sundown, so he paced himself carefully, riding at a full gallop after he left Sacramento behind him, then slowing to a canter. When he saw the wooded area ahead from the top of a hill, he reduced his pace to a sedate walk as he opened the flap of his holster and loosened the whip at his waist that his cape so artfully concealed.

Studying the terrain that lay ahead, Whip saw no sign that Rick and his deputies were in the vicinity, but he knew they had already taken up their places of concealment in the woods. Rick was reliable and would be on hand when he was needed.

Suddenly a lone rider appeared, seemingly out of nowhere, and rode at a gallop down the trail that led through the woods.

So far so good. That man was the lookout for the robbers, and Whip wanted to give him enough time to summon the band. So he halted, dismounted, and wasted time by pretending to adjust his saddle. He and Rick only had this one opportunity to catch the thieves. If anything happened to spoil the operation, Big George and his men would become wary and might wait for weeks or even months before attempting another robbery.

Whip had already made up his mind that, after this operation ended, he would return home to Eulalia, even though it appeared that Melissa would not come with him. At least he would be able to report that her reformation appeared to be sincere, so perhaps his own stay in California had not been wasted.

He mounted his horse again, then rode very slowly through the woods.

Someone unaccustomed to the wilderness would have heard nothing, but faint, distant sounds told Whip that several of Rick's deputies had fallen in far behind him.

The sun sank lower, making the woods darker. Conditions were perfect, Whip reflected. If Rick and his subordinates adhered to their tight schedule, he would face the band alone for no more than two and a half minutes. A great deal could happen in that time, to be sure, but he was not overly concerned about his ability to defend himself.

Ah! Sounds in the underbrush to his left, behind him, and to his right told him that members of the band were moving into position before "surprising" him. He drew his six-shooter, holding it in his left hand beneath his cape, and his right hand closed around the handle of his whip. Now he was ready for his foes.

He did not have long to wait. Two masked men appeared on the trail directly ahead of him, both armed with pistols, which they pointed at him.

Whip deliberately drew closer to them before he halted and called loudly, "What's the meaning of this?" His voice echoed through the silent woods, and he felt certain that Rick and his men heard his shout.

Other armed men, all of them masked, showed up on all sides, surrounding the supposedly wealthy traveler.

The burly leader called, "Do as you're told, and you won't be hurt. Throw your purse to the ground in front of your horse. And come to think of it, I'll take that hat, too. I've always had a hankering for a beaver hat."

Stalling for time, Whip replied easily. "The hat

wouldn't fit you," he said, his voice still unnaturally loud.

"Why the hell wouldn't it?" the tall bandit demanded.

"Because anyone who tries to rob me has no brains. The hat would slide down over your ears." The rawhide whip sang out, hissing ominously.

Before the masked leader realized what was happening, the whip coiled around him, pinning his arms to his sides and making it impossible for him to use his pistol. At the same time he found himself staring into the muzzle of his supposed victim's six-shooter.

"If any one of you raises firearms," Whip said in a conversational tone, "I'll put a bullet between the eyes of your friend yonder."

The leader tried to free himself from the whip's coils, but the rawhide was jerked tighter.

"Tell your men not to try any tricks on me, or you're dead," Whip said, moving forward until no more than ten feet separated his horse from that of the leader. The tall bandit saw the icy calm in the eyes of the middle-aged man, looked again at the muzzle of the cocked six-shooter, and gave the order.

By now Rick and his deputies should have arrived on the scene, but as yet there was no sign of them. Very well, Whip reflected, he would be obliged to proceed on his own. "One by one," he said, "you'll drop your pistols and rifles to the ground. Nice and easy."

Several of the bandits did as they were told, but one, who sat his mount on Whip's left, started to edge away.

"No, you don't!" Whip said sharply. "Do as I tell you, or your friends will hold a joint funeral for you and Charlie."

The man on the left halted, then hurled his rifle onto the ground.

"Do I know you, mister?" the leader asked in a shaken voice.

"That depends," Whip replied, still holding him immobile with the rawhide while menacing him with his six-shooter, "The name is Holt. I had something of a name in the Rockies a spell ago, but I doubt if any of you are old enough to remember those days."

"My God. Whip Holt." The man behind Whip, who had been debating whether to make an attempt to disarm him, let his pistol fall to the ground.

A moment later Rick and his deputies burst into the open, ready for action but quickly discovering that none was necessary.

"Sheriff," Whip said, "you're just in time for me to hand these prisoners over to you."

The deputies took charge, and Whip let the length of rawhide fall away from the leader. Within a short time the hands of all six bandits were tied behind them, a long rope was attached to each in turn, and their weapons were collected.

Rick reviewed his subordinates' handiwork. "That's fine, boys. Now take off their masks, but don't destroy them. They'll be useful evidence in court."

Charlie, the tall bartender, finally realized what had happened. "You set a trap for us," he wailed.

Whip grinned at him. "You're getting smarter by the minute. Maybe, by the time we're done with you, this beaver hat will fit you after all."

Rick directed all but six of the men to ride back into the open with the prisoners and wait for him. "We won't be long," he said.

Accompanied by Whip and the small detail, Rick went on to the saloon. Night had just fallen when they arrived, and the establishment was at its busiest. Rick and Whip pushed their way through the crowd at the bar, and the former signaled to the bartender in charge. "Tell George I want to see him," he said. "Right now."

"Who the hell are you?"

"Sheriff Miller of Sacramento Valley," Rick said, opening his coat and displaying his badge of office as the deputies quietly moved forward and formed a semicircular phalanx behind him and Whip.

The bartender's arrogance vanished, and he tugged at a bell rope behind him. The crowd grew quiet.

Big George appeared from a back room, his pistol in his belt, his lead-filled pipe clutched in one hand. "What's going on?" he demanded, then saw Rick before anyone could tell him. "Sheriff, what brings you here?"

"You do," Rick said. "George, you're under arrest for directing the efforts of a gang of thieves who have robbed a great many innocent travelers." He signaled to one of the deputies, who tried to hand the proprietor an arrest warrant that Ralph Hamilton had prepared.

The big man ignored the paper held under his nose. Slowly raising the hand that held the lead-filled metal pipe, he looked at Rick, then at Whip. "You can't prove I've had any part of this gang. I don't know what the hell you're talking about."

"You'll have your day in court to prove your innocence. In the meantime you have a private cell waiting for you in the brand-new jail. Think of it, George. You and your confederates will be the jail's first customers."

Big George contemplated the desirability of starting a riot by clubbing the sheriff over the head, but Whip Holt seemed to divine his intent, and a six-shooter appeared only inches from the side of the big man's head. "If you'll take the trouble to read the warrant, George," Whip said calmly, "you'll find it's legitimate. Besides, I urge you not to start something you can't finish. And don't think I'll feel sorry if I'm compelled to shoot you while you're resisting arrest. I'll have a good night's sleep, and so will a lot of other decent people."

Big George had to admit temporary defeat. "Keep the place going," he told the bartender. "And get hold of my lawyer."

"We'll send for him ourselves, George," Rick said as they led him away. "First thing tomorrow morning." He didn't mention that a long night's work lay ahead first.

Big George's hands were bound behind his back, a groom hurried off to the stable to fetch a horse for him, and deputies surrounded him as the party started off down the road. The evening was warm, and as they rode off, they could hear the sounds of laughter, music, and clinking glasses emanating from the saloon. Nothing, it seemed, could halt the festivities there.

After the group rode through the woods and emerged into the open again, the waiting bandits, guarded by their captors, were shocked to see that Big George had been taken into custody, too. They had been confident that, as he had told them so often in the past, he would come to their aid in the unlikely event that trouble developed. Now they could see for themselves that he was in no position to protect them.

Rick ordered the prisoners separated, assigning two guards to each and issuing strict instructions that the prisoners were not to be allowed to converse on the ride into Sacramento. The remaining deputies were given places at the head and sides of the column, and Rick brought up the rear, with Whip beside him.

"As soon as we reach town," the latter said, "I'm getting out of these fancy clothes. I'll have to take them home to show my wife, but she'll have to promise she'll never make me wear them."

Rick chuckled, then sobered. "I have a bone to pick with you," he said.

"Pick away."

"I was looking forward to a little excitement tonight. But you had the whole band of robbers pretty much under your thumb by the time the boys and I got there. And blamed if you didn't put a damper on Big George when he threatened to kick up his heels. You just can't imagine how much pleasure it would have given me—for Melissa's sake—to change the shape of his face."

Whip grinned complacently as he silently but carefully scrutinized his friend's face. As was his custom, he withheld comment.

"Do we hold to our original plan," Rick asked at last, "and tackle Charlie the bartender first?"

"I think he's vulnerable."

"Provided Melissa does her part."

"We owe our success tonight to her," Whip said. "Not a shot had to be fired, and the whole operation was as smooth as raindrops sliding off a piece of oiled buckskin."

"We're indebted to her, no two ways about that," Rick said. "We owe that woman a lot."

"See you remember it."

"What's that supposed to mean?" Rick became nettled.

Whip hummed under his breath but did not reply.

"I have a hankering to try and get Big George to talk, too," Rick said.

"Try it. You have little to lose. But he'll be a tougher nut to crack than Charlie."

"Sure. But maybe Melissa can bring it off."

"Make certain first you're not putting too great a strain on her," Whip said.

"Naturally."

"And don't expect miracles from her, Rick. She's already done enough for the cause of justice to wipe her own slate clean. Just be sure you tell her as much." Again the older man hummed under his breath.

Rick stared off into the night and did not speak again on the long ride back to Sacramento.

The prisoners were taken to the new jail, a two-story structure that stood directly behind the sheriff's headquarters. There the bandits were lodged in separate cells on the ground floor, with several deputies stationed in the corridor to prevent them from conversing with each other. And Rick personally conducted Big George to an isolated cell on the second floor.

By the time he came down to his office, Melissa was waiting for him with a platter of sandwiches and a pot of steaming coffee. "Whip has gone off to change," she said. "He'll be back soon."

"Officially," Rick said, his voice stiff, "I want to thank you on behalf of the state of California and the entire law enforcement body of the Sacramento Valley for your part in bringing a band of vicious criminals to justice. Speaking personally, I'm so grateful to you that I don't know how to put it into words."

Her only reply was a faint smile and a slight shrug.

He became even more embarrassed. "Whip says to be sure to tell you that the help you've given us more than wipes your own slate clean."

"Nothing can do that," she said calmly.

"That's where you're wrong, Melissa, but we'll have to talk about it some other time. Have a sandwich."

"I've already eaten supper," she said, but when he glared at her, she helped herself to a sandwich and went through the motions of nibbling at it.

That seemed to satisfy Rick. "You're still willing to go on with this operation?"

"Of course. I told you I would."

She was still a spitfire, he reflected, but she was no longer a rebel against society, and her contribution to the safety of the community was so great it could not be measured.

A short time later the bartender, Charlie, was escorted to the sheriff's office by two deputies, who stationed themselves outside the door, which they carefully closed behind them. The man stood uncertainly, a trifle defiantly, as he rubbed his wrists, from which his bonds had just been removed.

An unsmiling Sheriff Miller sat behind his desk,

writing a report in a log book, and he did not look up, letting the prisoner stand in uncomfortable silence.

There was only one other person in the room. A slender young deputy slouched in a corner chair, apparently sleeping under a broad-brimmed hat that was pulled low over his face.

"Sit down," Rick said, still not glancing at the prisoner.

Charlie lowered himself into a chair opposite the sheriff, not knowing what to expect.

"You realize, of course, that we caught you dead to rights," Rick said. "You were leading a gang that tried to commit a robbery, and that one act alone could get you ten to fifteen years in prison. But there were plenty of other robberies in the past. Add ten years to your sentence."

"You can't prove that I had any part in past robberies," Charlie said in a thick voice.

Rick ignored the comment. "On the other hand," he went on, "if you were willing to testify under oath that the real hand of the operation was Big George, I think I can promise you that the prosecutor would be sympathetic toward you. He well might ask the court for a sentence of no more than five years. There's a heap of difference between spending five years behind bars and rotting there for twenty years. So think about it."

"You want me to be a traitor to George," the bartender declared. "But you're basing your claim that I've taken part in previous robberies on guesswork."

"More than guesswork, Charlie." The "deputy" removed her hat, and red hair cascaded down Melissa's back. "I've already made out and signed a deposition about your past activities. And I'm prepared to take the witness stand."

The man stared at her, then slowly covered his face with his hands.

"As I was saying," Rick declared, "you might want to win leniency for yourself by telling the truth, that you were just working for Big George and that he took the lion's share of the money you obtained at gunpoint from a great many victims."

The bartender groaned.

"Maybe you'd like to think about it overnight," Rick suggested. "I can't give you more time than that because the prosecutor will go into court tomorrow morning to present his charges."

Charlie slowly removed his hands from his face and stared hard at Melissa. "I never thought you'd turn on us," he muttered.

Melissa met his gaze without flinching. "Get smart," she told him.

"Why are you doing this?" he asked in anguish.

She shrugged, and her faint smile was bitter. "I'll let you figure it out for yourself. What matters is that I'm determined to go ahead."

"Plead guilty to a reduced charge, and in five years you'll be a free man," Rick told him. "Try to fight us, and you'll be lucky if you don't hang. You'll have to make your own decision."

Charlie lowered his head. "What about the rest of the boys?"

"We're offering a break only to you," Rick said. "We'll talk to them if you balk. Otherwise, we won't."

"You're squeezing me hard, Sheriff," the bartender said, his anger flaring.

When Rick made no reply, the man turned back to Melissa. "Damn you, Lissa! You're giving me no choice!"

"George gave me no choice, either, when he forced me to go to work for him," she replied coldly.

Charlie slumped in his chair, despair in his eyes, defeat in his voice as he said, "Fix the papers, Sheriff. I'll sign whatever you want."

"Can you write?"

The bartender nodded, and Rick handed him a sheet of paper, dipped the quill pen in a jar of ink, and handed it to him. "Put the confession in your own words." He called in the two deputies stationed outside the door to act as witnesses.

There was no sound in the room but the intermittent scratching of the pen. When the document was completed, Rick read it carefully. "This will do just fine." The deputies signed it as witnesses.

"You've just saved yourself fifteen years in prison," Rick said. "Take him back to his cell."

Charlie was unable to look at Melissa again as he was led from the office.

"That was easy," Rick said.

"I suppose, but it wasn't very pleasant." Melissa spoke softly. "I had no grudge against Charlie. Like everybody else at the saloon, he did what he was told."

"Eventually," he said, "he'll realize we did him a big favor." He paused, looking at her. "Are you quite sure you want to go on with this? The next move will be much harder on you."

"Perhaps. But I've been looking forward to it, and I couldn't live with myself if I didn't go ahead."

He understood what she meant, and after nodding sympathetically, he sent another pair of deputies to fetch Big George.

Melissa donned the broad-brimmed hat, again concealing her hair beneath it, and slouched in the corner chair.

Big George displayed belligerence the moment he was conducted into the office. "You have no damn right to hold me here," he said. "If men who worked for me were robbers, I knew nothing about what they were doing. They're just trying to throw the blame onto me so they can get off with lighter sentences. I demand that you release me immediately!"

Rick eyed him coolly. "That's a neat story, George, but it won't hold up. You ought to know we wouldn't move against you unless we had proof."

"Like hell you do!" he growled.

"A confession," Rick said, "would save the time of

the prosecutor and the courts. The docket is crowded these days, so an admission of guilt would result in a quick sentencing."

"I have nothing to confess," the saloonkeeper said vehemently.

Rick sighed gently, then nodded to the "deputy" in the corner of the room.

"Are you quite certain of that, George?" Melissa asked as she removed the hat.

"Lissa!" He stared at her in astonishment, his face reddening, his features contorting.

"I'm prepared to testify that you directed the operations of the robbery gang," she said. "I'm also prepared to bring separate charges against you on the grounds that you forced me to become a prostitute and work for you."

Big George's booming laugh filled the small room. "You think the court will take the word of a whore against that of a respectable saloonkeeper?"

"I'll take my chances," Melissa said.

For a long moment he glowered at her. Then, suddenly, he reached into the top of a boot and drew out a short, double-edged knife, which the deputies had not found when they had disarmed him. Raising the blade high, he lunged at Melissa.

Her scream of terror brought the deputies stationed outside the door into the room, but before they could act, Rick Miller threw himself between Big George and his intended victim. With one hand he clutched the man's thick wrist before he could strike and with the other he delivered a short, sharp blow to the man's stomach. With a smash to the jaw, Rick sent him crashing to the floor. The deputies pounced on the man, disarming him and again tying his wrists behind his back. Rick continued to stand above him, looking down in icy fury as he massaged his knuckles.

Melissa was limp. "Thank you, Rick," she murmured.

He nodded, still looking at the fallen saloonkeeper. "I was hoping we could expedite your case, but now we won't bother," he said. "And I'm adding a new charge to all the others. Attempted murder."

Big George struggled to his feet, a trickle of blood dribbling down his chin from one corner of his mouth. He looked at Melissa, deep hatred in his eyes, and began to curse her.

Again Rick came between them. "For the sake of your health, George, I urge you to keep a civil tongue in your head when you speak to a lady."

"Lady?"

"You heard me."

"I know when I'm beat," Big George said. "It never crossed my mind that the sheriff would get sweet on one of my whores. That's what has done me in." The deputies surrounded him as they escorted him back to his cell.

It was very quiet in the office, and Rick did not look at Melissa. Instead, he walked to the window and gazed out into the night at the deserted street. "I reckon that wasn't too good an idea. If we had been able to pry a confession out of George, it would have saved you the embarrassment of having to testify about the life you've led. That was my aim, anyway."

"I see. I wasn't sure." Melissa was deeply touched at Rick's consideration.

"Instead," he said, "that big ox nearly killed you."

"The knife didn't even touch me. I've never seen anyone move as fast as you did," she said.

Rick's shrug was self-deprecating. "That was the least I could do after stupidly putting you in jeopardy in the first place."

Realizing he was blaming himself for what might have been a tragedy, she went to him and impulsively placed a hand on his arm. "Never mind, Rick," she said. "I suffered no harm, and we did get a confession from Charlie."

"Thanks for being generous," he said and turned to her. Their eyes met, and the unexpected current that passed between them jolted both of them.

Melissa had paid scant heed to Big George's words,

but he appeared to have sensed what she herself had not seen. If she knew little else in the world, she had come to understand men, and she knew it was true that Rick Miller had developed a personal interest in her. She could tell, too, that the knowledge was as jarring to him as it was to her.

How could any decent, self-respecting man want a woman with her background as anything other than a temporary bedmate? She quickly convinced herself that he couldn't. She guessed that he had enjoyed relations with no woman since his wife's tragic death, and it followed that he had the natural cravings of any normal, healthy male.

They had spent a great deal of time together lately, and knowing she was still physically attractive, she jumped to the only conclusion she could—that he wanted to sleep with her. Under no circumstances, she warned herself, should she attribute greater significance to his feelings. After all the time she had spent at Big George's place, she had grown weary of the lust she had seen kindled in men's eyes when they gazed at her. She couldn't blame the Texan for being like all the others, but she was saddened. Her future was blighted for the rest of her days.

Rick continued to look hard at her, and all at once he grinned. "We make a good team," he said, then turned away abruptly. "This has been a long day, and tomorrow will be even longer, what with Ralph persuading the court to rearrange the docket. Come along. I'll see you home."

They walked to the Hamilton house in silence, and at the door Melissa offered her hand. "You saved my life," she said, "and I won't forget it." She slipped inside quickly before he could speak.

Taking his time as he returned to the cot that he kept in a corner of his office, Rick tried to sort out his jumbled thoughts. His memories of Elisabeta were still fresh, and he was determined to keep his vow to find and punish her murderers. Until he fulfilled that obligation, he was not free. Assuming that he would succeed in his mission sooner or later, what then? Not since his wife's death had the question even crossed his mind.

It would be impossible for him to remain celibate for the rest of his life—and unnecessary. Certainly Elisabeta, had she known her fate, would have urged him to marry again.

What stunned him at this moment was the realization that, as Big George had said, he was sweet on Melissa Austin. Of course he wanted to sleep with her. That was something he had recognized in himself, but he had tried again and again to conquer the urge. She had suffered enough, and under no circumstances would he take unfair advantage of her.

With as much objectivity as he could muster, Rick tried to analyze his feelings. It surprised him to admit that he was not disturbed by the knowledge that she had gone to bed with scores of men. She had had no choice, and in his long experience as a law enforcement officer, he had learned that such brief relationships meant literally nothing to a prostitute.

Damnation! Melissa may have been a prostitute, but she wasn't one now. She had changed, and her wholehearted, unstinting cooperation with him and with Ralph Hamilton indicated that she was sincere in her efforts to rehabilitate herself. She was a wonderful young woman, as he well knew, willing to give generously and honestly wanting to please. Above all, she was vital, alive, eager to prove she could be a decent, useful member of society. He would be less of a man if he allowed her past to come between them.

Would the ghost of Elisabeta be even more of an obstacle? Rick had to be honest and admit he didn't know.

Dealing with facts as he was capable of seeing them, he did realize he was deeply concerned about Melissa's future. The court trials of Big George and his accomplices would bring her renewed notoriety, that much was certain. He was deeply obligated to Melissa and didn't see how, after the trials, he could allow her to go off alone to face an uncertain future in some remote part of the country. He owed it to her to offer her the sanctuary of marriage. But he didn't know whether his memories of Elisabeta would allow him to live with her and with himself.

Not until dawn broke did Rick drift off to sleep for a short time, his dilemma still unresolved.

XI

Gold fever had faded in the Sacramento Valley as more and more Californians realized the great agricultural potential of their land. John Sutter had been out of business for nearly a year now, having been ruined when his workers abandoned him for the gold fields and squatters overran his lands, and some of the original mines were already played out. But Sacramento had continued to grow rapidly, and it would not be long before it became the state capital.

The new three-room schoolhouse was the pride of Sacramento. It was solidly constructed of brick and oak. The principal was a one-time college professor from Pittsburgh, and the faculty was made up of qualified teachers from the East. The school operated on sound principles. Boys and girls in their teens arrived very early in the day, making it possible for them to be dismissed in time to help their parents on their farms, orchards, and vineyards. Younger children, bringing their lunch with them, did not arrive

323

until late morning and were dismissed in mid-afternoon.

So Sarah Rose Foster always went home in broad daylight, with two of her schoolmates walking a part of the way with her. The area was becoming calmer, and parents no longer worried quite as much as they had in previous years. The great Gold Rush had tapered off, with relatively few newcomers moving into the neighborhood. Conditions were not yet stable, to be sure, and only the main roads were regarded as safe. Disappointed prospectors, many of them hungry and consequently dangerous, still roamed through the hills.

But, as Sarah Rose knew, the improvement was steady. In the past few days her parents had been delighted when the owner of a large saloon in the area, a man named Big George, had been sentenced to life imprisonment on a number of charges, and five men in his employ had been given terms of ten years each. Mama and Papa had been disturbed because one man, a bartender called Charlie, had been given a minimum sentence of only five years.

Children obeyed the instructions of their parents to the letter. No one tarried on the way home, no one used shortcuts across the fields, and everyone walked only on the main road. Parents became very angry and upset when these orders were disobeyed. Sarah Rose dropped off her friends at their houses, then continued on her way, walking briskly and taking care to speak to no one other than family friends.

When she was less than a mile from her own house, she saw two men coming toward her, one very tall and the other very heavy. The little girl first took note of them on the heavily traveled road because they seemed to be swaggering. Then she saw that one was carrying a crystal punch bowl remarkably like one of her parents' favorite possessions, while the other held a matching pitcher, which her mother brought out only for important company.

The unwavering stares of the pair were unsettling,

but Sarah Rose had the good sense to pretend she didn't see them. She turned a bend in the road, just beyond Sheriff Miller's boarded, shuttered house. She recognized that these were the same men she had seen eating a meal in Mrs. Baker's kitchen and who she had seen in her own house the night she had hidden in the storage bin. They were Shorty and Slim, for whose capture, dead or alive, the authorities long had been offering a reward. Feeling uneasy, the child increased her pace.

The kitchen door was open, which was unusual, and Sarah Rose instinctively paused on the threshold and looked inside. Then her voice rose in a seemingly endless series of uncontrolled screams as she ran into the fields.

John Foster and his sons heard her terror-stricken cries and hurried to her side. Weeping and still screaming, the little girl was inarticulate and could only point in the direction of the house.

John was the first to reach the kitchen and, in a daze, looked at the dead, battered body of his wife.

Jane had fought hard for her life, and the kitchen was a shambles, with pots, pans, and utensils scattered everywhere. Thanks to her efforts, she had at least been spared the torments of rape before she had been bludgeoned to death.

Weeping hysterically, Sarah Rose clung to her father, who gazed in horror at the body of the woman he had loved, her face barely recognizable.

Young Scott stood with tears streaming down his face and needed no one to tell him to saddle his horse and ride at full tilt into Sacramento to notify Sheriff Miller.

Tracy, the younger brother, stood for a very long time looking at the remains of his mother, saying nothing, his face expressionless. In later years various friends of the family attributed his severe problems to the great shock he suffered on that occasion.

The funeral was held the following day, with everyone in the neighborhood crowding into the church.

Phyllis Gregg postponed her marriage to Ralph Hamilton for a month so she could take up temporary residence with the Fosters and help them. Melissa Austin, who had been talking of moving on now that the trials of Big George and his confederates had ended in resounding victories for the state, agreed to stay on to keep house for Ralph and the elderly, ailing Randy Gregg. Whip Holt had intended to leave the next day for Oregon but canceled his plans.

Melissa had not known Jane Foster, so rather than go to the funeral she stayed behind in Sacramento to look after Randy. When Ralph and Whip returned from the Fosters, followed a short time later by a coldly furious Rick Miller, she prepared a meal, then sat silently at the table with them.

"From Sarah Rose's description," Ralph said, "there can be no doubt that Shorty and Slim were responsible for this newest outrage."

"We're all agreed on that much," Whip said somberly.

"But we do nothing," Rick was too upset to eat. "We show up too late, time after time, as they commit one atrocity after another."

"There isn't much we can do," Ralph said, "except increase the reward. The state is contributing two hundred dollars, and private volunteers are giving double, but maybe we can raise the total reward to one thousand dollars. We can only hope that will bring results."

Rick shook his head and said in a tortured voice, "Before anyone can collect it, those demented bastards will kill again."

Melissa wished he wouldn't take the case of Shorty and Slim personally, but she knew why he felt as he did. He was the law enforcement officer primarily responsible for the apprehension of his wife's killers, and the murders they had committed since that time made him feel he was a failure.

"The reason they're so brazen," Whip said, "is because they seem to lead charmed lives. We're always too late to catch them."

"I'm turning over everything else to my first deputies," Rick said in a choked voice. "From now on I'm devoting *all* my efforts to finding Slim and Shorty."

Ralph was eating mechanically, paying no attention to the food on his plate. "The only trouble is that you don't know where to look for them."

"One time," Rick said, "the three of us spoke of baiting a trap for them."

"I've thought more about it," Whip replied, "but it just isn't practical or feasible. It's just too dangerous."

"I'm afraid you're right," Ralph said.

"Maybe I should assign a dozen deputies to patrol every main road in the Valley," Rick said. "Sooner or later they'll show up."

As they discussed various approaches to the problem, Melissa's mind worked furiously. Certainly she had triumphed over her own enemies: Jerome Hadley would be scarred for the rest of his life, and Big George would languish in prison until he died. She knew that Rick had developed an interest in her, but she refused to cripple him by becoming involved with him. Perhaps there was something she could do for him, however, before she went off by ship to the Eastern Seaboard and tried to find some place where she could settle inconspicuously.

"Am I allowed to join in this talk?" she asked, interrupting the conversation.

The men looked at her in surprise.

"You were talking about baiting a trap for Shorty and Slim," she said. "What did you mean?"

"Setting up a decoy, maybe," Rick replied, then dismissed the notion with a dispirited wave. "But the whole notion is too complicated. We'd have to find someone willing to act as the bait, and that would be too dangerous. I don't even know where we'd set the trap. There must be better ways of handling this problem."

"Until Mrs. Foster was killed," Melissa said, "I didn't even know you had a house in the immediate vicinity, Rick."

"It was my late wife's ranch," he replied. "After she died I sold the cattle, got rid of the ranch hands, and boarded up the house. I—couldn't tolerate living there anymore."

"That house," she said, "lies right in the heart of the area that the two killers seem to frequent more than any other. They go off here and there, but they always return to that part of the Valley.

He nodded somewhat impatiently.

"Your ranch house," Melissa said, "is in a perfect location to be used as the trap."

"She's right," Whip said.

Ralph agreed, but he didn't think the suggestion was practical. "A trap is useless without bait."

"I offer myself as the bait," Melissa said.

"You?" Rick was incredulous.

"Maybe you remember my telling you about the last evening I spent at Big George's saloon," she said. "Before I attacked Jerome Hadley with my knife, Shorty and Slim appeared, and they ogled me as no men—anywhere, ever—have looked at me. They were so intense that I—well, I felt sick. It wouldn't have surprised me if they had tried to drag me out of that bar, even though it was filled with people—and then had done the Lord knows what to me once they had me outside the place."

"I remember your story," Whip said.

"So do I," added Rick.

"I suggest," she said, "that I move into Rick's house. I have all my clothes from the saloon. I'll dress and make-up the way I did there. Can the house be seen from the road?"

"It stands just off the road," Rick said, realizing there was substance to her offer.

"Good," Melissa said. "I'll parade around the yard every day. I'll make certain I can be seen from the road. It won't take long for word to get around that the redhead from Big George's saloon has set up in business for herself."

"So there will be a stream of visitors to the house," Rick said sourly.

Melissa laughed. "You—and the men who relieve you on duty—can get rid of them easily enough."

Rick was forced to concede the point but did so grudgingly.

"I have no idea where Shorty and Slim do their drinking these days," she continued. "There are dozens of cheap bars in the area. But gossip gets around fast. At George's we picked up news from all over the Valley. So it shouldn't take too long for Shorty and Slim to find out I'm in that house. I know they'll want to see me again, so they'll come after me. The rest," she added, looking first at Rick, then at Whip and Ralph, "is up to you."

"I've got to hand it to you, Melissa," Whip said admiringly. "You've come up with a scheme that makes sense."

"No." Rick was blunt. "She's taking too great a risk."

"I'm willing," Melissa said.

"You'd be exposing yourself to vicious brutes," Ralph Hamilton said, remembering his reluctance to allow Phyllis to do what Melissa was now proposing.

"I've been dealing with vicious brutes for months now," Melissa said. "I know how to handle myself."

Ralph Hamilton pondered carefully. "It seems to me that the degree of risk depends on the extent of the precautions you take. Suppose, Rick, that you and Whip station yourselves at the house. Along with as many deputies as you believe you'll need to make certain Melissa is safe. Six men, twelve men, whatever number you choose."

"Slim and Shorty may be vicious brutes," Rick said, "but the reason we haven't caught them yet is because they're far from stupid. For the sake of argument, let's say Melissa's idea works. Up to a point. The killers hear she's in the house. They want her, so they go there. But they're not going to break down the door and force their way in. They'll not only want to assure themselves she's really there, but they will also want to make certain she's alone. If they catch sight of Whip or one of the deputies or me, they're sure to realize we've set a trap for them. So they'll take off, and they won't come near the house again."

"As we rode past the place on our way to the funeral this morning," Whip said thoughtfully, "I noticed that the woods on both sides of the house are crowding it, now that no hired hands are around to chop down the bushes. Those bushes have formed a wild tangle, and some of them are pretty near six feet high. What's more, they blend in with thick stands of trees behind them."

Rick challenged him. "What of it?"

"You know as well as I do," the mountain man replied calmly, "that the cover there is pretty near perfect. You and I—and as many of your deputies as you figure we'll need—can station ourselves in the woods. The weather is warm now, so living in the open is no hardship on anyone. We keep watch twenty-four hours a day, right around the clock, from outside the house, not inside it."

"And if men other than Shorty and Slim start coming around, I'd think it would be easy enough for you to discourage them," Melissa said.

Whip nodded. "Leave them to me. But if Shorty and Slim show up and look the place over, we'll be invisible."

"Anytime I see those two I'm opening fire," Rick said grimly.

"But not prematurely," Ralph told him. "You want to make absolutely sure that you have them cornered."

"I reckon you're right, but it won't be done at my ranch house," Rick replied. "I won't allow Melissa to take the chance of being killed."

"I don't think I'd be taking that great a risk," she said and looked to Whip for support.

"Unless we're missing some angles," he said, "I believe Melissa is right. And we can make sure we've arranged airtight security for her before we begin the operation."

"I'm still opposed to the whole scheme," Rick said.

His concern flattered Melissa, but she was excited by the opportunity to perform a service of lasting value before she left California. Honorable women could cook, sew, and keep house; some were the intellectual equals of the men they knew. But, she thought cynically, her only skills were those of attracting men. She might as well put her talents to good use.

"Come up with a better idea, Rick," Melissa said confidently. "If you can't, we'll go ahead with mine!"

Melissa continued to insist that her plan be utilized, and she was so firmly supported by Whip and Ralph that Rick Miller was forced to agree in spite of his objections. So the house was opened and aired.

The furniture and bric-a-brac were still in place, and the house looked precisely as it had when Elisabeta was still alive. Rick wandered alone from room to room and was badly shaken by the time he returned to the parlor. "Elisabeta," he said aloud, "for your sake—and for Melissa's—I pray to God we're doing the right thing. You died here, and I could never forgive myself if something happens to Melissa under this roof, too."

Details of deputies set up sentry watches in the woods on both sides of the house, maintaining a close watch every hour of the day and night. None ever came out into the open in the vicinity of the house itself. Instead, they entered and left from the far sides of the woods, a considerable distance from the road. So no passerby ever realized that armed men were lying in wait behind the heavy screen of bushes and trees.

Rick assigned himself to permanent duty in the woods, swearing he would not leave while Melissa was inside the house. Whip joined him, vowing to stay at his side. Each day they swam briefly in a small lake that could not be seen from the road, with deputies bringing them clean clothes as well as their meals. The weather was mild, but the ground was damp, and the arthritis in Whip's hip became pronounced, forcing him to walk with a limp.

"There's no need for you to stay around," Rick told him. "It may be a long time before Slim and Shorty show up here—if they ever come. You've neglected your family and your business for a long time, and I'm grateful for all you've done for folks in the Valley. But you ought to go home before your hip gets worse."

"I'm staying," Whip said, "until this matter is done." There was a note of finality in his voice.

Each day a scantily, outrageously clad Melissa, her face as heavily made-up as it had been when she had worked at Big George's saloon, wandered out into the open, then meandered through that portion of the yard on which the spreading bushes had not yet encroached. Noon and late afternoon were the hours she chose for these airings because the traffic on the road was heavier than it was at other times of day.

Passersby stared at her, but she pretended to be unaware of their interest, just as she was careful to give no sign that she knew there were armed men stationed in the woods for her protection. At no time did she encourage any passerby, and when a stranger sometimes followed her to the house, she went inside and locked the door behind her. Then Whip came out into the open from the woods and announced that his "daughter" wanted no company. Those who had assumed the young woman was a prostitute seeking clients quickly decided they had been mistaken and went on their way. No would-be swain lingered in the vicinity after Whip Holt gently but decisively urged him to take himself elsewhere.

It had been determined at the outset that the strain of waiting would be too great for Melissa if she lived a hermit's life, talking to no one. So Phyllis Gregg came to see her regularly, bringing her food for her meals, and staying for a chat.

The two women became increasingly friendly, and one day Phyllis gathered the courage to ask, "Don't you feel strange in those outlandish clothes?"

Melissa smiled and shook her head. "Dresses like this were my uniform at the saloon. I wore nothing else for so long that I don't even think about what I'm wearing. If I did, I suppose I'd feel a little silly. But they're not really as outlandish as you might suppose. Men are fascinated when they see a woman dressed as I am."

"Not all men, surely!"

The naive comment made Melissa laugh, and she felt years older than the inexperienced Phyllis. If there was anything Melissa had learned in her confused life, it was a knowledge of men, and she wanted to help this young woman who had led such a sheltered existence. "Every man likes it when his woman looks alluring. I'm convinced of it."

Phyllis remained dubious.

The interminable period of waiting for Slim and Shorty to appear was so boring that Melissa was delighted there was an opportunity to keep busy. "Come with me," she said, "and I'll show you what I mean."

They went into the bedroom that had been Elisabeta and Rick's, and Phyllis soon found herself clad in one of Melissa's flimsy, provocative dresses, with heavy makeup applied to her face. "I—I don't look at all like myself," she said uncertainly as she studied her reflection in a full-length mirror.

"Yes, you do," Melissa insisted. "An enhanced version. You're moving back into town from the Foster place in a few days. So take that dress with you, and I'll give you some cosmetics, too. Surprise Ralph, and see how he reacts when he sees you."

Although Melissa knew her advice was sound, she realized also that she envied Phyllis. It was plain that Ralph loved Phyllis for herself, not just for her body, and Melissa thought how wonderful it must be to know that one was wanted for one's mind and personality.

Phyllis agreed to take the dress and cosmetics, scrubbing her face, then changing back into her own modest attire before she left for home.

A few days after her return to the Hamilton house, where her father, Ralph, and young Isaiah had been keeping house for themselves, she changed into the costume after supper, then went down to the parlor, where all of them were sitting.

Randy Gregg stared at his daughter as he let fly with a stream of tobacco juice at a cuspidor, displaying his customary accuracy in spite of his physical infirmities. "You goin' to a fancy dress party?" he demanded.

Isaiah was reminded of the period he had spent working at Big George's saloon and giggled nervously. Ralph, for whom the display was intended, studied his future wife intently but made no comment.

The disappointed Phyllis hurried upstairs to change, cleaned her face, and then returned to the kitchen to wash the supper dishes. With her sleeves rolled up, she went to work furiously and was immersed in suds produced by the soft, yellow soap when Ralph quietly came into the kitchen.

She was afraid she might weep, so she averted her face. She knew he loved her, of course, but he still didn't think she was as attractive as Melissa Austin.

He came up behind her and put his arms around her. "You looked stunning in that new dress you were wearing," he said to her softly.

"Did you really think so?" she asked without turning.

"Yes. You're a beautiful woman—in all ways. And I see no reason to delay our wedding. We should make specific plans as soon as we can."

She hastily dried her hands and arms, then turned to embrace him. She was grateful to Melissa for her help and advice, and Phyllis made a silent vow that she would never disappoint Ralph as a woman or as a wife.

When Phyllis Gregg returned to Sacramento, Heather Taylor voluntarily took over the task of bringing Melissa food supplies every few days. Danny wanted to escort her, but Rick Miller refused to grant his permission. "You could spoil our whole plan if you show up with her, Danny," he said. "We don't know for sure how Shorty and Slim operate, and for all we know, they may be keeping a watch on the house right now. It might put them off if they see you and Heather are coming in and out."

Danny was forced to accept his decision, but knew he would never be able to forgive himself if anything happened to his wife. On the other hand, he realized everyone in the area was in jeopardy, and with Melissa courageously risking her life, he felt compelled to allow Heather to do her part.

If Heather knew that she, too, was taking chances, she did not admit it. "You don't know how much I admire you," she said to Melissa one day as she delivered some vegetables, meat, and fruit to her.

Melissa shrugged. "If I can help bring a pair of vicious murderers to justice, I'll feel I've paid my debt to society in full."

"You've already done that. You were wonderfully brave when you testified against Big George and his confederates."

"I did that for my own sake, to even the score with George," Melissa replied. "What I'm doing now is for everyone else in the Valley—provided the killers fall into the trap that Rick and Whip have set for them. I'm growing tired of waiting."

"Well," Heather said, "I just want you to know how much everyone in the neighborhood thinks of you."

"I can imagine," Melissa said dryly. "There has never yet been a trollop who has won the approval of ladies."

"That's nonsense and rubbish," Heather said. "Your

story came into the open at Big George's trial. You
lived the way you did because you had no choice. I
would have been forced to do the same thing if I had
been in your position. And every woman I know
around here feels the same way."

Melissa realized she was speaking the truth and
was shaken by that knowledge.

"I hope—and so do all of our neighbors—that you'll
decide to stay in these parts after the crisis ends. I
know at least a dozen women who would like to be
your friends."

"On condition that I never see their husbands, no
doubt."

"I haven't heard one person speak that way, Melissa. No one thinks of you as tainted."

That conversation lingered in Melissa's mind as the
days dragged on, and sometimes she felt her resolve, to
start life anew somewhere else, weakening. She could
not allow herself to think about Rick Miller, however.
She was willing to grant that he wanted to bed her,
but a former prostitute could not hope to compete
with the memories of his late, beloved wife. It was
absurd to dwell on the prospect of entering into a
permanent relationship with him.

What she could not admit, most of all, was that she
might have fallen in love with Rick. After what she
had experienced, she was convinced it was not possible
for her to love any man. She was drawn to Rick
because of his honesty and integrity as well as the
protective attitude he had taken toward her. So she
tried to tell herself she required no protection, that for
his sake as well as her own it was wrong to dream
about a future that could never materialize.

What made the problem more acute and distressing
was her isolation. She had seen no one but Phyllis
Gregg and subsequently Heather Taylor since moving
into the ranch house. She knew that Rick, Whip, and a
number of deputies were nearby in the woods on both
sides of the house, but she never caught sight of them,
never communicated with them in any way. She had

no way of occupying her time usefully, and being alone, she found it far too easy to imagine a life as Rick's wife.

Put him out of your mind and keep him out, she told herself repeatedly.

Shortly after noon one day a breathless, worried Heather appeared at the door. "Oh, Melissa, this is terrible," she said. "On my way here just now I saw Shorty and Slim down the road. I called to Rick from the bushes, but he wasn't there!"

Melissa felt as though ice water were flowing through her veins.

Heather continued excitedly. "Whip answered me. He said Shorty and Slim had been seen entering a house a few miles up the road, and Rick and his deputies went after them." She dropped her bundles on the kitchen table. "Whip told me he was sure Rick would find them or else be right back, and that I shouldn't stay more than a minute. And I'm under instructions to take the long way home. So I really can't stay."

"You have a husband and a baby," Melissa said urgently. "Go!"

Heather hesitated for no more than an instant. "God bless you," she said, and her eyes filled with tears as she fled.

This is it, Melissa thought, and she prayed that Rick would hurry back. But she refused to panic—Rick would not let her down. Instinctively, she checked her appearance in the front hall mirror, and she was annoyed with herself. For better or worse, she was wearing one of her more provocative dresses from her saloon days. Her breasts bulged above the low-cut flimsy satin, the slits at the sides of her skirt were absurdly high, and her heels were towering.

Opening the front door and leaving it ajar, she wandered out into the small front yard that faced the road. The thought occurred to her that she needed to look preoccupied, so she darted inside, picked up a small pair of shears in the kitchen, and returned to the yard. For want of anything else to make a pretense of being busy, she would cut some of the flowers that were blooming in profusion in the bed that stood adjacent to the house.

Her relief was enormous when she heard Whip Holt's voice come to her from the depth of the underbrush. "Steady, Melissa," he called softly. "Everything will be all right, so don't panic."

A lump in her throat made it too difficult for her to reply, so she smiled in the general direction of his seemingly disembodied voice.

"Rick will be back any second," he said. "Don't worry."

Out of the corner of an eye Melissa saw two burly men slowly sauntering up the road. They were moving into the trap, and she could only hope they did not destroy the bait before they were apprehended.

Her hands so cold and clammy they felt numb, Melissa pretended to be unaware of the pair as she looked intently at the flowers, then cut a blossom. It did not surprise her that her hands were shaking.

Shorty and Slim halted a short distance from the gate and observed her silently. Knowing she had to put on a show for their benefit, as she had done at Big George's saloon, she minced to another part of the flower bed, her hips undulating seductively. Lord Almighty, she thought, give me the strength to see this through to the end.

The men continued to watch her, neither of them moving or speaking, and Melissa continued to give no indication of any awareness of their proximity. She went on with the charade, her heart hammering so hard she could scarcely breathe. Finally, after cutting a dozen flowers, she clutched them in one hand and started back toward the front door.

There was no sound, no sign of life from the bushes at either edge of the woods.

As she stepped across the threshold, the pair near the gate sprang into action. Displaying remarkable speed and agility for men of their bulk, they bolted toward the house, pushing in before she could close the door.

There was no need for Melissa to pretend any longer. The lust and malice she saw in the eyes of the two men made her cringe, and she backed slowly into the parlor.

"Sweetheart," Shorty said, "this is our lucky day. You got no idea how often we wondered what had become of you."

"And here you are," his heavier companion declared, "runnin' a place of your own."

"You're in luck today," the taller of the men declared, grinning slyly, "because you got two customers at once."

"And we'll let you decide which you like better."

"Oh, she's goin' to be so crazy about the way we make love she won't be able to decide," Slim said. "And she ain't goin' to charge us one penny, either."

Where were Rick and Whip? A sense of panic engulfed Melissa, and she fought hard for enough self-control to remain coherent. She had to stall until her protectors arrived. "What makes you think I'm that kind of a woman?" she demanded.

The pair looked at each other, then laughed heartily. "Sweetheart," Shorty said, "we seen you at Big George's saloon."

"And you don't dress like ordinary women, neither," his companion added. "We know what you are!"

"We seen you slice the face of that gambler fellow somethin' awful with a knife. So if you know what's good for you, you'll drop that pair of shears you're a-holdin'."

She was frozen, unable to move.

"Drop them shears!" Shorty snarled, and she obeyed.

"You want to flip a coin to see which of us has her first?" Slim asked. His companion pretended to ponder.

Melissa knew she could not hold them off much longer. In a moment one of them was certain to take her, and she was powerless to resist them. Worse than that, they would injure her severely if she put up a fight.

Meanwhile, Whip Holt was slowly drawing closer to the house. Rick had not yet returned, but he realized he couldn't wait any longer, so he started forward out of the woods alone, his six-shooter in his hand. There had been a time when he would have been able to reach the house within seconds, before anyone could detect him, but his hip was so stiff, the ache in the joint so excruciatingly painful that all he could do was inch forward one small step at a time.

The snaillike motion attracted the attention of Shorty, who looked out the window and saw the older man limping painfully toward the house. Chuckling softly, Shorty went to the door and concealed himself behind it.

"I guess my partner wants me to be first," Slim said, leering at her. "Sweetheart, get rid of them fancy clothes before I tear them off'n you."

Whip stepped across the threshold.

At that instant the door slammed into his hip with all the brute force that Shorty could muster. In no way prepared for the sudden and painful attack, Whip lost his balance and sank to the floor just inside the doorway. Shorty leaped into view and kicked Whip's six-shooter from his hand, leaving him without firearms.

"Look here, Slim," Shorty called. "Our lady friend had herself a bodyguard."

Melissa saw Whip on the floor, the pain in his arthritic hip making it impossible for him to scramble to his feet, and her heart sank. Now he, too, was in mortal danger.

"Sweetheart," Slim said mockingly, "you should have knowed better than to hire an old man to look after you. Somebody of his age ain't much good."

"Grandpa," Shorty said as he drew his pistol, "start sayin' your prayers."

Whip Holt had faced death without fear more often

than he could recall. Yet at this moment, when he was in greater jeopardy than ever before, he was filled with self-disgust. He had tried to play a young man's game, but his age and his physical infirmity had betrayed him. Perhaps he truly deserved to die.

Shorty slowly raised his pistol, and there was a click as he cocked the weapon.

Desperate, Melissa impulsively threw the bunch of flowers she was still clutching into his face. The shot went wild.

A breathless Rick Miller leaped over the threshold, took in the situation at a glance, and instantly fired his own six-shooter. Never had there been a greater need for accuracy, and never had he responded better in a time of crisis. His bullet landed between Shorty's eyes, and he fell to the floor with a crash.

Slim was alone now, but he was far from defeated. Drawing a long knife from his belt, he swiftly grasped Melissa, holding her in front of him as a shield, then placed the blade no more than an inch or two from her throat. "I'm gettin' out of here," he said, "and the girl goes with me. Drop your gun, mister, or I'll cut her throat from ear to ear."

Rick needed time. "Are you willing to make a deal?"

"What kind of a deal? You already killed my partner," Slim said in an ugly voice.

No one noticed Whip Holt. One hand crept to the rawhide whip wound around his middle, and he drew it slowly, hoping the man holding Melissa as his prisoner would not notice. The excruciating hip pain made it impossible for him to stand before she would be killed, so he had to perform a near miracle from the floor, where he was still sprawled. Although he had created legends with his exploits in wielding a whip, he had never before been in such an awkward physical position, one which would make it necessary for him to shift his balance and adjust his aim. His skill was unique, but circumstances were requiring him to outdo himself.

All at once Rick became aware of what his friend intended to do. Every second was precious, so he had to keep Slim's attention occupied. "To hell with the girl," he said. "For all we care, take her with you. Our job is to recover at least part of the loot you've stolen in the past couple of years. Just tell me where we can find it, and we'll get out of here."

Melissa's eyes widened. She could not believe what she had just heard—"to hell with the girl"—but Rick had sounded completely sincere. Well, perhaps her fears had been right all along. What sensible man would want a permanent relationship with a whore?

"Now, ain't that somethin', Sheriff?" Slim's laugh was rough and taunting. "I bet you've searched the whole damn Valley for my shanty."

So the stolen goods were stored in a shanty, and Rick, continuing to stall, guessed accordingly. "All I know for sure," he said, "is that your hiding place isn't far from here. That's why you and your partner kept coming back to this area."

Slim made no reply, but the gleam in his eyes indicated that the guess was accurate.

Whip sucked in his breath, steadied himself as best he could, and took aim. The rawhide whip flashed through the air and miraculously curled around the blade without touching Melissa's skin. Applying all the force he was capable of exerting, Whip managed to jerk the knife out of the heavyset man's hand.

For an instant Slim was unarmed, and at that moment Rick acted, raising his pistol. Slim was still using Melissa as a shield, and Rick knew that if he missed, he might kill her. But he knew he had no choice. He aimed at Slim's head and squeezed the trigger.

Slim took a single step backward, releasing his grip on Melissa, and slid to the floor, dying instantly.

Melissa wavered, swaying back and forth, and it appeared that she might faint. Rick went to her instantly and folded her in his arms.

By the time Whip Holt managed to haul himself to his feet, she had revived sufficiently to slide her arms around Rick's neck and return the kiss he had given her.

Whip politely averted his gaze as he busied himself recoiling his rawhide whip around his middle.

"Melissa," Rick said, "you've taken enough risks, and the people of California are in your debt for all time.

"I've never been so frightened," she confessed. "I still can't quite believe I'm alive."

"You know I'd never let anything happen to you," he said, holding Melissa tenderly. "I wasn't at the house right away only because I thought I could catch these two swine farther up the road, and save you from having to face them. When I didn't find them, I came here so fast that I left my deputies in the dust. Anyway, it's all over now. You've just this minute retired from law enforcement work. And you need someone to take care of you and look after you before you get yourself into more trouble. So I appoint myself as your guardian."

She shook her head, unable to digest his obvious meaning. Thinking she was refusing him, he embraced her again. "You're marrying me," he said, "and I'll tolerate no argument."

"What will people say when they hear that the sheriff of the Valley has married a strumpet?"

"When the story of what you've done today has been told—and I intend to give the newspapers every last detail—folks will say I'm not good enough for you. And they'll be right."

"But I can't—"

"You're the most stubborn, cantankerous female who ever lived," he declared, interrupting her. "But for once you have no voice in the matter. I'm not going to spend the rest of my life worrying about what new mischief you've created for yourself. You're marrying me—and that's final!" He kissed her again, and the warmth of her response told him all he needed to know.

There was a sound at the door, and Whip turned to

see the deputies pour into the room, their guns drawn.

As the bodies of the two criminals were removed, Melissa turned to Whip and hugged him. "I'll never be able to thank you for what you did for me," she said.

"I don't want thanks," he growled. "All I want is to go home to Eulalia and our youngsters. Lordie, how I miss them!"

"You'll have to stay for our wedding," Rick said as they clasped hands and grinned at each other, both of them conscious of the superb teamwork that had been responsible for the victory they had achieved.

"How soon will that be?" Whip demanded.

Rick thought it wise to defer to Melissa. "Well," she said, her smile radiant, "I'll need to make a wedding dress for myself, and that will take a few days. And I—I'd like to be married in a double wedding with Phyllis and Ralph. It would be fitting, somehow."

Rick nodded enthusiastically, then sobered. "In the meantime, Whip, we can keep busy looking for the goods that Slim and Shorty stole. Finding out they hid their loot in a shanty somewhere in this area is a bonus, and we'd be stupid if we didn't take advantage of it."

Deputies methodically scoured the neighborhood, searching for the shanty that the too-confident Slim had mentioned moments before he died. Scott Foster and Isaiah Atkins asked for permission to join in the search, and Rick indulgently agreed. He and his subordinates were surprised when the two boys won the honor of locating the shack at the base of a cliff in a heavily wooded section far from any road.

The news was published at once in every newspaper in the Sacramento Valley, and citizens who had been burglarized were invited to inspect the huge mounds of property stored in the shanty. Two deputies were placed in charge, and a steady stream of people tramped through the woods to see the loot. Among them were many who had no legitimate claims, but they were slowly weeded out, and those whose losses were genuine were able to reclaim their property.

Large quantities of merchandise remained in the shanty, and on the eve of Rick Miller's wedding, he went there with Whip Holt to survey the loot. "I reckon we'll have to auction off all these goods and turn over the proceeds to the new county government that's just being formed," he said.

"I'm leaving right after the ceremonies tomorrow," Whip replied, "but here are a couple of things I'd like to buy. I want to take them to my children as presents."

Rick took a bone-handled knife with a double-edged blade from him and held it in the palm of his hand. "This has a first-rate balance."

"Toby has a talent for knife throwing, and this will help him. I've tried to teach him to handle a whip, but he's clumsy, so we'll concentrate on his knife throwing. In times like these, a man needs special skills to survive."

Rick nodded, then gently took the exquisite porcelain doll that Whip handed him.

"Cindy is a mite young to have this doll," Whip said, "but she'll appreciate it in a few more years."

"Take them as gifts from the people of the Sacramento Valley," Rick told him.

The older man tried to protest.

"If it weren't for you, Big George and his gang would still be preying on innocent citizens. If it weren't for you, Melissa and I would be dead, and Slim would be free to murder, rape, and steal. You haven't accepted a penny of pay in all the time you've been a special deputy, and this is the least we can do for you."

Whip hated to accept favors, but the gracious offer could not be refused.

"Are you taking something for your wife?"

"You bet! But I'll wait until I reach San Francisco to go shopping for her. Just thinking about getting home makes the ache in my hip feel better," Whip said as a smile of anticipation spread across his face.

A white wedding gown would have been a travesty, so Melissa made herself a dress of pale green silk. Rather than embarrass her, Phyllis chose peach-colored silk for her own wedding dress. All of Melissa's other belongings had been taken to the ranch house in the Valley the preceding evening, and she awakened early, then took her time bathing, dressing, brushing her hair, and applying a trace of cosmetics to her face.

The ceremony itself did not worry her. Whip, knowing she had no relatives, had offered to escort her to the altar, and she had agreed with great pleasure. "I may not be able to run very far or very fast," he had told her, "but you can bet that no ache in my joints will stop me from taking you down the aisle of that church."

Now, with only a short time remaining before leaving for the ceremony, Melissa was overwhelmed by a sense of panic. She sat in her room in the Hamilton house, where the reception would be held later, and gazed uneasily at her reflection in the mirror. Even the scents of turkeys roasting and hams baking in the kitchen below made her feel faintly ill.

Phyllis tapped at the door, then came into the room. "We'd best go downstairs," she said. "Pa and Whip will be coming for us in the rented carriages any minute."

"I can't," Melissa said and continued to sit on the stool in front of the table.

"You're not getting upset all over again by the way you had to live?" Phyllis asked.

Melissa finally exploded, the months of pent-up anguish, humiliation, and fear coming out into the open. "It's no good, Phyllis; it's just not going to work. A marriage has to be based on respect, and there's no way Rick Miller can respect me. Oh, I know he loves me—or he imagines he loves me—but what's going to happen after the first flush of romance wears off? What's going to happen after we've been sleeping together for a time?"

"I may not know as much as you about the desires of men," Phyllis said. "But it appears to me that you aren't attributing much depth to Rick Miller's feelings. He's a mature man, not a boy. He's been married, and he knows sorrow. Your background is no secret to him, but he's still eager to marry you. So I don't see what else you could ask of him." Phyllis looked out the window. "The carriages are here. Let's go. We don't want to keep the bridegrooms waiting too long at the church. You know how punctual Ralph is. He'll be having conniptions if we're late."

Melissa made no move. "There's something else that bothers me," she confessed. "You mentioned it just now. Rick was married before, and he loved his wife very, very much."

"Of course he did, and his grief for her was real. But he's old enough and wise enough to know that he isn't being unfaithful to her memory because he's fallen in love with you. I think you're torturing yourself needlessly."

"No. I agreed to live in the ranch house because it's the logical place and the only property Rick owns. But it was her house, Phyllis. Rick did take one hint I gave him and bought us a new brass bed. But it's still Elisabeta's house. She lived there—and she died there."

"Now it will be your house." Sympathizing with her, Phyllis tried to curb her own impatience.

"She was very beautiful—" Melissa began.

"So are you! Don't take my word for it. Look at yourself in the mirror."

"Oh, I'm pretty enough, but that's just the surface. She was kind, thoughtful, and sweet. I wouldn't know how to be sweet to anyone. I'm impulsive, I act without thinking. I'll try to put Rick first, but I'm scared to death I'll always be selfish. I don't see how he can help comparing me with Elisabeta—and find me lacking. Don't you see what I mean?"

"No, because Rick is sure to have weighed all that inside himself before he proposed to you."

"Our lives had just been in jeopardy, so the circumstances were dramatic. What frightens me is that I'll be trying to fill the shoes of Elisabeta Miller."

"Don't try. Just fill the shoes of Melissa Miller, and you'll do well. But you won't become Rick's wife unless you leave with me this very minute."

Melissa sighed and forced herself to stand. Both women made a final check in the mirror, then, arm in arm, descended the stairs to their waiting carriages, with Melissa doing her best to conceal her fears.

Whip, however, saw through her façade on the short ride to the church and patted her hand. "You're thinking how fortunate you are to be getting a husband like Rick," he said. "True enough. But he's just as fortunate. And don't you forget it."

"That's hard to believe," she murmured.

"If I was a generation younger—and didn't already have a wife I love—I'd fight him for you," he replied and gave her a broad smile.

Melissa was comforted, but the panic started again at the rear of the crowded church.

Lee and Cathy Blake had come from San Francisco and were sitting on the left side of the church, as were Danny and Heather Taylor, and John Foster and his children. Justices of the California Supreme Court, a senator, and two members of the United States House of Representatives were also sitting on the left side of the church, and a number of the deputies had chosen to sit on the bride's side of the aisle, too.

Phyllis, looking radiant, began the procession down the aisle on the arm of her father, and Randy, attired in a new suit, had heeded his daughter's plea and left his usual wad of chewing tobacco behind.

Melissa was solemn, her face pale, and her fingers clutched Whip's arm more firmly than she realized.

Ralph Hamilton and Rick Miller stood at either side of the altar, and the normally composed Ralph was making a valiant effort not to fidget. Rick was motionless, and when he caught sight of Melissa, he gazed only at her. Feeling his eyes boring into her, she promptly lost consciousness of everyone else in the crowded church. Instead of feeling comforted, however, her apprehensions increased.

Neither of the brides remembered much about the ceremony itself. Both responded to the clergyman at the appropriate places, speaking so softly that many in the congregation could not hear them. Ralph's responses were quiet, too, although his voice was firm. Only Rick spoke loudly and clearly, his whole manner indicating that here was a man who knew himself and knew what he wanted.

Melissa was jolted back to reality when Rick kissed her at the end of the ceremony. Then, by prearrangement, they led the way back up the center aisle of the church.

Everyone present was looking at Melissa, as she well knew. But she was surprised and heartened when she saw that most people were staring at her in admiration. She detected no smirks in the eyes of the men, no contempt or disgust in the faces of the women. They seemed to be accepting her for what she had become rather than for what she had been.

Whip refused to entertain the pleas of both bridal couples to remain in Sacramento long enough to eat some food and drink a glass of wine. Instead, he kissed Phyllis, gripped Melissa's shoulder hard as he kissed her, then limped off to his waiting stallion. Cathy and Lee Blake would also be departing shortly, traveling on the steamer that now made regular trips between Sacramento and San Francisco by way of the Sacramento River. The three friends had reserved their places on a ship leaving San Francisco for Oregon in two days' time, and they would allow nothing to prevent them from boarding that vessel. Whip had already sent word to Eulalia that the Blakes would be spending some time with them at their ranch, and he knew his wife would be delighted with the news.

The bridal party repaired to the Hamilton house, and Melissa's later memories of the reception there were somewhat confused. She and Phyllis were kissed by scores of people, and subsequently they stood at opposite sides of a huge wedding cake, which they cut simultaneously, then shared the first slices with their husbands.

Phyllis obviously was nervous, and Melissa thought it ironic that she herself should be even more jittery.

Randy Gregg sat in a rocking chair in the parlor, surrounded by a score of guests, whom he delighted with his tales of early frontier days in Texas. Isaiah Atkins beamed whenever he caught Melissa's eye. Scott and Sarah Rose Foster entered into the spirit of the occasion, too, and thoroughly enjoyed themselves. Only Tracy was silent and withdrawn, and those who knew him realized he was grieving for his late mother.

The wedding feast, prepared by the wives of a dozen deputies, filled the entire table and sideboard in the dining room. The guests helped themselves to roast turkey, baked ham, fish, and mounds of baked crabs from San Francisco. There was cold beef, too, as well as three kinds of potato salad, hot and cold vegetables, and a variety of fresh fruits, some of which had been grown in Danny and Heather Taylor's orchard. The young couple watched proudly as the guests enjoyed the fine produce.

Isaiah insisted on serving the bridal couples, heaping their plates high. Phyllis and Ralph, who were going off to San Francisco for a brief honeymoon, had good appetites, and Rick ate ravenously. But Melissa could only pick at her food. Soon she and Rick would be driving out to the ranch house, and her fears became greater.

It was late afternoon when the final toasts were offered, and the bridal couples escaped to their carriages in showers of flower petals. The throwing of uncooked rice was customary in some parts of the United States, but people who lived in a frontier state knew better than to waste precious food.

Melissa was silent as she sat close beside Rick, who handled the team of horses with his usual authority. He removed his hat, brushed flower petals from the crown and brim, then chuckled. "I never thought I'd enjoy my own wedding," he said, "but I did."

She wondered about the details of his first wedding but had the good sense not to ask.

"What about you?" he asked, placing his free arm around her shoulders.

Melissa sighed. "I'm glad it's done."

He knew what she meant and smiled steadily at her. What he failed to realize was her dread of the hours to come.

Traffic on the heavily traveled road was light at this time of day, and dusk was falling when they reached the house. "Wait here," Rick commanded, helping her down, then taking the horses and carriage to the stable at the rear.

Melissa stood obediently outside the front door, thinking that she knew this dwelling as well as she had known any house in which she had lived. After all, she had spent an eternity here, alone, when she had acted as the bait for Shorty and Slim.

Rick returned, unlocked and opened the door, then surprised his bride by picking her up and carrying her across the threshold. "I reckon I'm old-fashioned in some ways," he said. "Welcome home, Mrs. Miller."

"Thank you, Mr. Miller," she murmured, and when he put her down, she busied herself lighting several oil lamps.

Rick watched her, making no move. "You're on edge," he said at last.

"Maybe I am," she replied, "but I prefer not to talk about it, please."

"In some ways it isn't all that easy for me, either," he said. "This is a wonderful property, and the house was built to last for generations. I've fought my own battle inside myself, so I'm content to stay on here—if you agree."

"Of course," she said faintly.

"We'll soon know whether you want to stay or move. I guess I'm being selfish, but after spending almost my whole life in law enforcement, I'm ready to resign and take up life as a rancher. I have several able deputies who could take my place, and I want to live in peace. With you."

"I had no idea you planned to resign," she said.

"Do you approve?"

"Naturally. Whatever you want is what I want." She realized he was still standing, so she refrained from sitting, too.

"Thank you," Rick said. "But I won't force you to stay here. You have memories of this place, too, and if they're too much for you, I'll sell the property and buy another."

Melissa tried to frame her reply diplomatically.

"We won't worry about it," he said. "Some problems solve themselves." Giving her no chance to speak, he lifted her off her feet again and, kissing her, carried her toward the chamber in which she had slept and where, previously, he had slept with Elisabeta.

Melissa realized absently that Heather Taylor had filled the bedroom with flowers. She must have brought them early that morning when she had filled the larder with food.

It was just as well that the room was dark, Melissa told herself, and was annoyed when she discovered that her hands were trembling as she undressed. It was absurd to feel ill at ease, but she could use none of the tricks she had learned at the saloon, and she was neither deliberately seductive nor playful.

Rick had removed his clothes, too, and when he embraced her again, they moved to the bed. Aware of the tensions that made her rigid, he made love to her gently.

She marveled at his tenderness and gradually began

to relax. It was astonishing that this man, the scourge of criminals, could be so sensitive.

Little by little Rick became more insistent, and Melissa could not help responding to him. The artifices on which she had relied in her life at the saloon were gone, and her behavior was natural, as honest as the lovemaking of the man who had become her husband. Their mutual desire increased, and Melissa was startled to discover she wanted Rick as much as he wanted her. Only now was she learning she truly loved this man.

They became one, and their yearning reached a crescendo. Then together they achieved the climax of their love.

Afterward, they rested together, locked in an intimate embrace, and tears of joy dampened Melissa's face. Her gratitude to Rick was boundless, and she kissed him with a fervor unlike any feeling she had ever experienced. Then she astonished herself by announcing, "I'm starved!"

They donned robes and went together to the kitchen, where Melissa allowed Rick to light the wood fire in the stove. "Now," she said, "you'll sit, sir, while I make us a cup of coffee. How many slices of bread do you want with your cold beef?"

"Two, I reckon. But I can slice bread," he said.

"You'll do no such thing," she replied, a joyful lilt in her voice. "Rancher Miller—or Sheriff Miller—or whatever you want to be—you have your work. I have my responsibilities."

He watched her as she energetically cut the beef and the bread.

"I am the mistress in my own house!" Melissa exclaimed, and knew she spoke the truth.

Rick saw the happiness in her eyes and realized she had banished the ghosts of the past, both his and her own, for all time.

★ WAGONS WEST ★

A series of unforgettable books that trace the lives of a dauntless band of pioneering men, women, and children as they brave the hazards of an untamed land in their trek across America. This legendary caravan of people forge a new link in the wilderness. They are Americans from the North and the South, alongside immigrants, Blacks, and Indians, who wage fierce daily battles for survival on this uncompromising journey—each to their private destinies as they fulfill their greatest dreams.

22808	INDEPENDENCE!	$3.50
22784	NEBRASKA!	$3.50
23177	WYOMING!	$3.50
22568	OREGON!	$3.50
23168	TEXAS!	$3.50
23381	CALIFORNIA!	$3.50
23405	COLORADO!	$3.50
20174	NEVADA!	$3.50
20919	WASHINGTON!	$3.50
22952	MONTANA!	$3.95

**FROM THE PRODUCER OF WAGONS WEST
AND THE KENT FAMILY CHRONICLES—
A SWEEPING SAGA OF WAR AND HEROISM
AT THE BIRTH OF A NATION.**

THE WHITE INDIAN SERIES

Filled with the glory and adventure of the colonization of America, here is the thrilling saga of one of the new frontier's boldest heroes. He is Renno, born to white parents, raised by Seneca Indians, and destined to be a leader in both worlds. THE WHITE INDIAN SERIES chronicles Renno's adventures from the colonies to Canada, from the South to the turbulent West. Through Renno's struggles to tame a savage continent and through his encounters with the powerful men and passionate women on all sides of the early battles of America, we witness the events that shaped our future and forged our great heritage.

☐	22714	White Indian #1	$3.50
☐	22715	The Renegade #2	$3.50
☐	20579	War Chief #3	$3.25
☐	22717	The Sachem #4	$3.50
☐	20028	Renno #5	$3.25
☐	20559	Tomahawk #6	$3.50
☐	23022	War Cry #7	$3.50